REGEN

Regeneration: The Ability to Heal

CASSIE GREUTMAN

INDIES UNITED PUBLISHING HOUSE, LLC

INDIES UNITED PUBLISHING HOUSE, LLC

Chapter 1

Something tickled my face. I swatted at it. Or at least I tried. Had my arm even moved? There, again. *Whatever you are, go away.* I just want to… What did I want? Sleep.

Sleep sounded good. Was it night?

One eyelid complied when I told them both to open.

Dark, but not absolutely black. Early morning or late evening? Hard to tell in the rain. I flexed my fingers. They moved, stiffly. But the rest of me remained immobile. I shoved down the terror trying to flood up my chest. Why couldn't I move? What was going on? *Trish, what have you gotten yourself into this time?*

I gurgled out a sound, but it was hardly audible. No one was going to hear that unless they were right beside me. I blinked the one working eyelid. Water dribbled in and I groaned. A few blinks helped and I rolled my eye around, trying to get my bearings. Outside, that much was obvious. Mist, trees, and a dark sky. That was it. I crushed the panic again, my heart thundering in my ears. I couldn't get in a good breath.

How did I get here? And where is here? A voice. A man. A gun. I tried to yell again, with as much success as the first time.

After a moment my other eyelid started to cooperate. I blinked a few times, adjusting to both eyes working.

Definitely a forest of some kind. But maintained. Cut grass, trimmed bushes. Maybe a park?

Last night I had... I couldn't remember. I couldn't even remember what day it was. I swallowed, a knot catching in my throat and making me gag.

My hand clenched into a fist involuntarily. Good, that was good, focus on the positive. It had been evening, just getting dark. I was out here with... someone. And then...

Something tickled my face again. This time I could see what it was. A small bush, leaning over me. I shoved it away. Feeling returned to my arms and toes at the same time. I patted at my chest and sides to see if anything was wrong.

The rain had me too wet to tell if there was any bleeding. Everything hurt, but in a general kind of way.

I squinted up at the tree branches, shielding my face with a trembling hand and looking for some type of landmark.

The thick, nighttime gloom covered everything, making it difficult to see anything but trees. Lots of trees. I took a deep breath, trying to stop the quivering in my fingers by relaxing for a second. It didn't work. We'd gone out in the woods, and then... My body tried to bolt upright, but it didn't work. The guy had shot me!

A deeper investigation, with a little better idea where to look, and I found the hole in my dress. What if he was still out here? A whimper escaped, but I managed to keep it quiet. I had to get moving. I had to get out of here.

I planted my hands in the grass and pushed myself up into a semi-sitting position. Something popped and groaned behind me, and suddenly I was propped up by a huge tree root, dirt still crumbling and falling away from the wood.

A shriek ripped out of my throat, this one much stronger than the feeble yell I'd managed earlier. I tipped over, unable to catch myself. The root did it for me, setting me back up. I slapped at it. The tree didn't seem to care. It didn't move again. Trees weren't supposed to move.

I covered my face with my hands. "It's okay, Mom said weird stuff would start happening to me. It's okay, it's okay." I rocked forward, barely registering that the rest of my body was starting to function.

Shoot, too much noise. I looked over my shoulder, but the darkness blanketed everything.

Fumbling around I discovered that I had no pockets, which meant no cell phone. That was bad. Really bad. Now what? I rubbed the back of my neck, willing my body to start working, trying to come up with a plan. I couldn't think.

Should I try to get someone's attention? Stupid. I always rolled my eyes at people in the movies, internally telling them not to get themselves noticed, now I was thinking about doing it. Who would even be looking for me? Maybe Wade, but that was doubtful. My boyfriend knew I could take care of myself. Usually. I shoved my trembling hands into my armpits, which were bare.

I needed to get out of here. Needed to find somewhere better to figure out what to do. Somewhere the guy didn't know where to find me. A shiver tingled through me. I really wasn't dressed for this in… heels and a sequined dress?

What was wrong with me? I hated dresses.

Mushy leaves kicked over me hid half my body. I brushed them off with one hand. What was all over my dress? Mud? I took a better look. Blood.

Nearly hyperventilating, I patted at my body, looking for anything other than the bullet hole. Nothing.

Legs, start working!

My stomach growled and I nearly retched at the level of hunger that punched me in the gut. I bent over, hugging my stomach. I knew hungry, but this was extreme, even for me. I rolled over and pulled out a fistful of grass, pausing for just a second before stuffing it into my mouth. My crazy level of hunger was telling me I'd been doing some intense healing in the not so distant past. As in, bring me back from death's door levels of healing. Another shiver went through me. This one had nothing to do with the cold.

Still not able to move well, I drug myself into some bushes.

Whoever had shot me could come back. Or maybe they hadn't even left. I needed to get out of the open.

It took almost a minute, and a whole lot of lawn, but the calories from the grass finally kicked in enough for me to stagger to my feet.

I stumbled toward a smaller tree, pulled off some leaves and stuffed them into my mouth, nearly gagging as I tried to chew. They were dry and brittle, no doubt almost ready to fall, tasting like dirt. I forced as much of it down my throat as I could manage.

Squinting through the gloom didn't make any light bulbs ding. Why would I have come out here with someone? I hated nature. It reminded me of my mom. And at this time of night? Dan and Nina were going to be so mad. Hey, Dan and Nina, I was starting to remember stuff. My foster parents were going to be ticked. If the guy wasn't out here waiting to make sure I didn't make it back.

I swiped at tears trying to run down my face. This was not the time. Picking a random direction, I hobbled forward in my heels, sliding around a little on the wet leaves. I tripped on a stick and went down, the mud I landed in sending the chill on my skin down into my bones. The shivers started coming faster. I struggled up and kept moving, smearing mud down my fancy dress when I tried to clean my hands. Not leaving a trail for the killer to follow in this muck would be impossible.

At least I had an idea why I was here. Not here as in this spot, but here as in this situation. Mom had said strange things would start happening when I turned sixteen, but she hadn't mentioned me going all werewolf and showing up out in the middle of some forest with no memory of the last few hours. Okay, nix the werewolf, I still had my clothes on. Plus, I already knew what I was.

The popping noise was back. I turned sharply to look behind me, nearly toppling over in my heels. The tree root that had come out of the ground to prop me up was gone. Totally gone. "It's okay," I whispered to myself. "Probably normal. It's okay, weird stuff is supposed to start happening," then shuffled away faster, looking over my shoulder.

After about ten steps something tapped me on the shoulder. I whirled around, but no one was there. "Hello?" I squeaked out. No answer. The tap happened again. It was a branch. Like, just a normal tree branch. Or not normal, whatever. Once it knew it had my attention, it pointed back in the direction I'd come from.

I looked.

"You want me to go that way?"

The branch just swayed in the wind, like any regular old branch sticking out abnormally far from its trunk. That was probably a yes. But the real question was, what were the tree's intentions?

"Ah, no thanks," I said, staying on my original route. "It isn't safe back there. I'm trying to get away from someone." It tapped me on the shoulder again. I swatted it away. "What's with you? I don't want to go that way. Are you even real? Maybe I'm unconscious."

The tree branch wilted at my harsh tone. I almost felt bad. Almost. I stalked away faster but only made it a few steps before something grabbed me around the waist. I yelped and struggled, but the grip just got stronger. My feet left the ground and I went limp, making and discarding increasingly crazy plans in a split second. And then I was turned around and set back on my feet, the branch unwinding from around my body.

I rubbed my arms to hide the freaked out shivering. "Fine, have it your way," I muttered, and resumed my stalking, this time in the direction the tree had suggested. I nearly fell over three times because I was staring over my shoulder to make sure it didn't come at me again. The sky was getting darker, fast.

Apparently the tree was satisfied by my decision because it left me alone.

Mom had mentioned that nature loved the fae, but she hadn't ever brought this up. It was supposed to mean big gardens and stuff, not Narnia and living trees.

Suddenly a vine grabbed me, stopping a scream trying to rip from my mouth by covering it tightly. I struggled, but it just tightened until I couldn't move. The tears I'd been holding back flowed freely. *What do you want?*

No answer, of course.

A second later a shadow moved by. A person. A big person. My body went instantly limp, supported only by the vine. I stroked the vine a little, and it loosened. The thing had probably just saved my life. I was afraid to blink, afraid to lose sight of whoever it was, moving past me back toward where I'd woken up.

No one with good intentions would be out here on a night like tonight.

Slowly, like it was afraid I'd crumple to the ground, the vine loosened around me, letting me go. I patted it lightly in thanks, not wanting to say anything out loud that the shadow could hear.

I took a deep breath, almost afraid to blink. Had that thing been human? Which was better, yes, or no?

The heels had to go. If I needed to run, I wouldn't be able to. I pulled them off and gripped them tightly in one hand.

The farther I could get from this place the better, before that guy found out my body was gone. How long had it been since he'd shot me? At least an hour, judging from the darkness.

Stupid rain. It was getting worse. I wiped the excess water off my face for the fiftieth time. At least the rain would hide the tear tracks.

A rumbling sound pulled me from my thoughts. What was that? My heart clenched in my chest and I cowered into the closest tree. A rivulet of water flowed down the hill ahead. The only way I could tell the difference between it and the rain was the fact that it was a yucky brown. Gross water splashed on the already soaked hem of my dress.

The rumbling started again, this time even stronger, shaking the ground beneath my feet a little. No human could be causing that. It had better not be something crazy, like a dragon or whatever. I definitely wasn't equipped to handle that.

A small wave of muckiness crested the hill and rained down into my face. I spewed water out of my mouth and gagged, the gross mix trickling into my lungs. I got the coughing fit under control right before the rumbling started again, this time almost deafening in intensity. Oh crap. A huge wall of water surged over the hill, washing me from my feet. I slammed into a tree and bit back a scream as I felt a rib crack.

The water washed me off the tree and sent me head over heels down the embankment, shrieking like a banshee. I tumbled down the hill, my body crying in agony before going into a free fall off the last hill and plunging into a large mass of water.

Waking up after something like that is not pleasant.

Don't get me wrong, it's better than not waking up at all. I just wish that whatever part of me decides it needs to wake up before I'm finished healing would keep its opinion to itself.

At least my dress is getting clean. The thought floated through the fog in my brain. I shook my head, trying to get my bearings. Tough, considering I was underwater somewhere.

I clenched my fists and closed my eyes for a second.

Maybe this was a nightmare. Maybe it would all go away. I cracked open an eyelid.

Nope.

Don't breathe. It's okay. You're fine. Sure I was fine.

Sure. I was just under water, that's all. I shoved the thought away and tried to blow out some bubbles. Nothing happened. No air in my lungs. I thrashed around for a second, looking for the surface, freaked out. The water was too clouded. I couldn't tell which way was up.

Blinking seemed to help with the fogginess and I came around enough to dodge some debris flowing downstream faster than I was. Who needed Disney World? Just jump in a creek and dodge some logs here. Add in some injuries just for fun. I gave an experimental kick toward where I hoped the surface was but gasped in pain.

Apparently a broken leg wasn't finished healing.

I closed my eyes to wait, the current tugging on my clothes, sending my long hair tangling around my face. If the water wasn't flowing so quickly, this would almost be calming. Which would be really nice, because no matter how many times I kept telling myself not to freak out, I was almost past the point of trying not to.

No. Right now I just needed to get out of here. ASAP. I hadn't been very quiet while getting flung into the river, the shadow guy might have heard me. Ten seconds and the pain had faded to a manageable level. That would have to do, I needed out of here. Like, now. The bones could finish on my way up. I butterfly kicked my way to the surface. It took forever with no oxygen in my lungs to help buoy me upward. I popped up and pulled in a gulp of air. Big mistake. I hacked for a moment, spewing out all kinds of fluid, sunk under the surface, popped back up, and then took in that breath. Ahh, better. I spit the last of the foul tasting water out of my mouth. Note to self, next time try to get water out of lungs before filling them with air.

Treading water against the current should have made me tired, but it didn't. I was almost back to normal. Though not completely normal. A normal person would be dying of exhaustion right now. I squeezed my eyes shut in relief.

Another one of the blessings of being fae, along with the whole healing thing. Supposedly not all of us get the same gifts, but I didn't know for sure since I didn't have another of my kind to ask.

The rain had finally slowed to a drizzle. I squinted toward the bank of the river, the moon's reflection on the water giving me a little help in the light department. There had to be some civilization around here somewhere. I started kicking in the direction of the riverbank, the pain totally gone. Which bones had I broken this time? Hard to say.

I dodged random debris floating in the mess of a river, the stupid dress weighing me down. I'd lost my shoes somewhere in the fall.

Finally I made it to the bank, hauling myself onto the edge. Looking up was not encouraging. Steep. Really steep. I dropped my head in my hands. I would not cry. I was not a crier. Crying was not something I did. The sniffles were just from the water in my nose, that was it. I looked up the sheer mud wall again. The commercials about wild fires and yada, yada were all over this year. Guess they were right if the river was supposed to be that high. Just my luck.

I took an experimental breath through my nose and didn't choke. At least that was getting better. *Come on, Trisha. You can do this. Just pretend you're training with Mom.* Sure. Like this was anything the same.

Trying to climb the mud bank was like trying to scale a cliff covered in ice. It wasn't long before I had just as much mud on me as before I went through the rinse cycle on nature's washing machine. Further up, the base of the bank had eroded away, leaving an overhang up top. I turned left and crept along in the dark for a few feet before stopping. The lip only got worse in that direction. The right proved the same.

It was okay. I could do this. What good were my gifts if I couldn't climb some stupid little hill? Digging my hands into the freezing, sticky mire, I started up what had to be four feet of mud-covered dirt. The top layer was slick, but I could get a hold of the more solid layer under it. Maybe I wouldn't be doing this if I had to worry about six weeks in a cast, but since that wasn't a problem all I could think of was how tired I was of being out here in the rain. And the fact that there might be someone following me trying to kill me. But I didn't want to think about that part at the moment.

Smooth sailing until I reached the top. Here the lip was even more pronounced, hanging out over the bank. I was going to have to practically dangle to get over this. I latched on to a rock sticking out of the dirt tightly with my left hand, then reached over onto the ground with my right, flailing around as I tried to find something to grab onto. A pop and a groan sounded from above. I tried to jerk my hand back, but something rough was in the way. A tree root? Was it following me? Was that possible?

But I needed the help so I couldn't look a gift horse in the mouth, or whatever. I grabbed the new found hand-hold and heaved myself up over the embankment. Sure enough, a dirt-covered root stuck out of the ground, the dirt looking fresh.

"Thanks," I squeaked out, just in case the tree expected it. The root ignored me and burrowed back into the ground. I took off.

The slight drizzle faded and the stars were starting to peek out from dark clouds. Of course, right when I needed the rain to help get some of this ick off. At least it was hiding the blood all over my dress. I really should be concerned about that. I rubbed my hands in the damp grass, trying to scrape some of the mud off. Not much luck, but it would have to do.

A short walk and I literally stumbled onto a road. Now we were getting somewhere. A glance in both directions didn't give any revelations about which way I should try. Where were those friendly branch tour guides when you needed them? "Hey, trees. Got any opinions on which direction I should go now?" I whispered, then waited a moment.

Everything stayed quiet. What made the last one help me? I held up a hand and concentrated, squeezing my eyes closed. After a moment, I opened an eye a slit. Nothing happened. "Thanks a lot, stupid trees."

Without any help to figure out where I should go, I slouched right and started walking.

Would this night ever end?

Walking along in the dark is great for thinking. Once you find somewhere to walk where you don't have to worry about tripping every five seconds. Without shoes, I stayed on the very edge of the road, close enough to jump into the trees if I needed to hide, but off the bare ground full of sticks and rocks. The road rubbed at my feet, but they healed as I went. Thankfully it didn't hurt much.

Thinking was something my subconscious was telling me not to do. I didn't listen. I ran every conversation with my mom I could remember through my mind, trying to come up with an explanation for me being out here, for someone wanting to kill me. Nada.

Maybe it was random, but the odds of that didn't seem good.

After an unknown period of time trudging through the dark, something glowed in the distance. A light. Small, yes, but at least it was a light. I picked up my pace.

What was a light doing way out here, anyway? Campers?

Traffic? I squinted, trying to see if there was anything else ahead. Nope, just more trees. Nowhere near home with this many trees. "We're not in the D.C. suburbs anymore, Toto."

Water dripped off the branches above and onto my face. I scowled up. "Watch it, I'm wet enough." Apparently these trees weren't the thinking kind or they didn't like being told what to do because an even larger pattering of water splashed down my nose and dribbled into my left eye. I wiped my face on my arm, but it didn't help. I was soaked all the way through.

The light down the road burned brighter now that I was getting closer. I slowed to ask myself something that should have come up when I first saw the light. What was I getting myself into going there? Stopping in on people I didn't know, not wise, by all accounts. But I didn't have much of a choice. Even if I wanted to walk home, I didn't know how to get there. And what were the chances of these people wanting to kill me too, whoever they were. If the shadow man hadn't had a flashlight out when he was looking for me, he probably wouldn't have something that bright now, so it was a good bet it wasn't him.

Dan and Nina were going to be sooooo mad. My fosters were better than most, but they were still going to freak. I could call Wade. Maybe he could get me home and I could sneak in without them noticing. That's one of a boyfriend's duties, after all. But something about that felt wrong. Too bad I hadn't gotten the courage up to ask Amy for her number at the party last night, she'd have picked me up. Probably.

Wait, party, on Thursday. Halloween! That's why I was in the dress.

Now, if I could remember where I was, maybe I'd remember how to get back. But it didn't seem like that was going to happen so I upped the pace. At least I had started to remember other stuff. It'd be nice to get out of these wet clothes. My skin had finally warmed up to an acceptable level, but the clothes were chaffing. Plus I needed to eat.

Bad. Preferably not something lawn based.

When I got closer to the glow, I could make out lights flashing near a dump that was set back from the road. Maybe an old gas station. Definitely not a house like I'd expected. Compared to the stations Nina always went to in the suburbs, this place was below dump on the junk scale. I squared my shoulders. Back to that not much of a choice thing. Better a dumpy gas station than getting offed in the woods. Again.

The open sign blinked, sending waves of red along the wet pavement. My first piece of good luck since I woke up out in the trees. I wouldn't have to break into the place.

The door swung open easily, hardly squeaking on its hinges. I popped my head in, not sure I wanted to take that next step. Sure, if it was some serial killer holed up inside I'd probably heal. But I still didn't like the pain and it would be a disaster if anyone found out about the whole indestructible thing. I've seen Heroes, I knew what could happen.

"Hello?" I called out. When no one answered, my gaze began to wander. Food. All kinds of gas station food. Who knew that it could look like some major buffet? Chips, cookies, trail mix. Maybe they had one of those little hot dog racks. I couldn't smell it, but that didn't mean it wasn't there, considering that my senses were a little overwhelmed right now. It didn't matter. I'd even take that jerky off the rack up near the front.

I took a step inside and let the door shut behind me. "Hello?" I asked again. If no one showed in a second, they'd return to find their place cleaned out. I needed to eat. And eat a lot.

Scuffling started somewhere in the back. A baseball cap popped up from behind the rack of pork rinds. "Hi. Didn't see you pull up." The hat and voice belonged to a guy probably in his forties. I was still in the District of Columbia, right? Because this guy looked like something from a movie set way down South with the scruffy face, baseball cap, and matching vest. "What can I do for ya?" he asked.

Now that was a good question. Maybe I should have figured out a story before I'd walked into this place. I thought about going with "Oh, somehow I showed up in the middle of the forest, had a conversation with a tree and finally found a road, now I need to use your phone," but that didn't seem like a real plausible story.

The fact that I was wearing a dress, covered in muck, and reeking kind of gave away that there was interesting backstory.

"I don't really know," I said lamely, moving over so a shelf of junk food hid me from the window and the door. "Can I use your phone to call my parents?" Please say yes, please say yes. What would happen if he told me no and sent me back out into the rain? Whoever had tried to kill me would get a second chance.

"Sure, come on over." The guy, whose cracked nametag said Vince, moved past me and headed for the counter.

This was getting ridiculous enough I could almost believe I was having a nightmare. That would explain why I couldn't remember ending up in the woods. Nina was always telling me I shouldn't watch horror movies, that they'd give me bad dreams, but I never listened. That had to be it.

"Is the call long distance?" Vince's voice brought me back.

Probably, right? But I had no way of knowing since I didn't know where I was. And I didn't know anything about long distance anyway. I literally never used the home phone. "Yeah?" It came out kind of weak, but oh well. Having my cell phone would be really nice right now. Where was it?

Vince chewed on something for a second, staring me in the face. "Do you have a collect number?"

"Uh, no."

"Who's going to pay for the call then?"

"Ah…" no answer for that. "Can I use your cell?"

He stared at me for a second. "Don't have one."

My mind raced through all kinds of terrible scenarios, my favorite involved me being stuck here until I died of starvation, Vince standing over my emaciated body and eating pork rinds in front of me because I didn't have the cash to pay for them.

"I don't know. I guess I could just stay here til morning, then walk. Do you have somewhere I can sleep?"

Vince's eyes bulged. "Oh no, we can't have that. It's fifteen miles to the next station and they ain't open on Sunday. You wouldn't be out of here til Monday."

Sunday? This guy was obviously on something. It was Thursday. Oh well, it worked. He jerked an old phone from the wall and shoved it in my direction, cord trailing behind.

"Thank you," I said, nearly ripping the phone out of his hand before he could change his mind. Would that shadow in the woods be willing to come out in public? Not that this was very public, but still. I didn't want to find out. Punching in the familiar number of Nina's cell, I looked out the door, straining to see anything in night. Nothing.

Hopefully Nina answered. I didn't want to take the chance of getting Dan by calling the home phone. Nina was definitely going to be the more understanding in this situation.

The phone barely had a chance to ring before someone picked up. "Hello?" The winded voice on the other end was hardly recognizable. Whoever it was needed to take a breath.

"Nina?" I asked. Surely I hadn't dialed the wrong number. But Nina always sounded perfectly in control. Ol' Vince wouldn't be happy about two long distance calls if I had misdialed.

"Trisha? Trish? Is that you? Where are you, honey?"

Good question. I probably should have found out before I dialed. "Yeah, it's me. Give me a second." I turned to Vince. "Where are we exactly?"

Instead of bulging, this time Vince's eyes narrowed. I liked the bulging better. Much less strange looking. "Not far from the entrance to Prince William Forest Park."

"Prince William Forest Park, I guess," I said into the phone, keeping my eyes on Vince.

"In Virginia?" I had to hand it to Nina, though her voice did rise a little, she was keeping herself nicely under control. Hopefully that continued, even after they made it out here to get me. Wait, Virginia? "Just a second, honey." Her voice faded. No doubt she was conferring with Dan. I'd always hated it before when she'd called me honey, but for some reason it didn't sound quite as bad right now.

"Dan says we can be to the park in thirty minutes. We were already out this way showing your picture around. What happened?"

Heat blossomed in my chest, the first warmth I'd really felt since I'd woke up in the woods. They cared. For real.

Sure, Nina had always said they did, but words were cheap. My mom had said she cared and look how that ended up.

"Just tell them where you are. You can get your lecture later," Vince whispered loudly. "Joplin Road. You're spending my money."

"Who was that?" Nina asked. Apparently Vince hadn't whispered quieter than her mom ears could hear.

"I can't talk about it right now, Nina, as soon as you get here, I promise. I'm at…" I squinted at Vince's name tag. "Vince's Fill Up on Joplin Road."

Another few seconds of conferring. "It showed up on my phone, we can find that."

"Okay, see you soon." Vince was making hang-up motions. Man this guy was serious about long distance.

"No, wait! Can't you just stay on the line? Do you have a number we can call you at?"

I paused, the thought of hanging up and losing my weak link to home and reality making my stomach roll. But there was Vince, looking even more grumpy. "No, can't. See you soon. Please hurry."

Chapter 2

Exactly twenty-eight minutes after the phone call, Dan's black Mercedes pulled into Vince's.

A small figure flung itself from the passenger seat and hurtled toward the station's door. Nina was only an inch taller than me, and probably wouldn't be for long. I'd never been so happy to see her short frame since… well, ever.

"Thanks Vince, for everything," I called toward the back where he was stocking shelves. Surprisingly, I meant it. He had been good to me, even breaking out a can of Pringles and a bottle of water after I'd gotten off the phone. It must have been the way I was devouring the shelves with my eyes that gave him the idea I might be hungry. He lifted a hand, then went back to stacking Hershey bars. Strange man, but I liked him now that he'd given me food.

I barely made it out the door before Nina grabbed me, crushing me to her and ignoring the partially dried mud. I hissed. Apparently my ribs hadn't fully healed after that tumble. Or the gunshot. Whichever. That woman had a lot of strength for her size.

"Honey, I was so worried! What happened?" Nina asked, moving her grip to my shoulders and leaning back to stare straight into my face.

"I don't want to talk about it," I muttered. Mostly because I still had no idea what had happened. And I really wanted to get out of here. Now. "Can we just go?"

Dan leaned over the passenger seat toward the rolled down window, his face the proverbial storm. "Did that boy do this to you?" By the tone of Dan's voice, someone was about to get it. Hopefully that someone wasn't me.

He hadn't, of course he hadn't. The only boy Dan could be talking about was my boyfriend, Wade, and he would never do this. A flash of a memory popped up. I'd left after a huge argument with the fosters about Wade, leaving with him to head to that stupid Halloween party I didn't really want to go to. Now this was embarrassing. If he didn't have anything to do with this, where was he?

"No, no. It was all me."

Some birthday this had turned out to be. I'd just wanted to spend time with Wade and away from home. Sure, our relationship had started out as just a way to bug the fosters, but it had become something more. Was spending time with my boyfriend really too much to ask for a sixteenth birthday?

Another memory popped into focus, hazy like my mind had filled with too much water. Wade teasing me until I left the party with him. The memory continued with us stepping out on the trail, then far into the trees. This was getting weird, hadn't we walked far enough? Especially in these stupid shoes. I told him I might get tired even though I probably wouldn't. It takes a lot more than a hike to make me tired. His face changed and he leaned in toward me, said something about being sorry and pulled a gun… A gun. My spine went ramrod straight. Wade had been the one to shoot me!

"Trisha, I want an explanation." Dan's voice dragged me back. My palms were sweaty and my stomach rolling again. I looked beyond the car. Wade could still be out there, trying to find my body. Or worse, figured out my body was gone.

"Uh, what?" I asked, still slightly dazed by the memory that had just hit me like a truck. The fosters hadn't seemed to have noticed that I was about to have a melt-down. Or they were just letting it go.

"I want to know what happened," Dan said. Uh oh. That tone was not good.

"Later, Dan, first let's get her home and out of these clothes."

"Yeah, can we get out of here, please?"

Dan sighed from the driver's seat. "Fine. But that's just delaying this conversation. We will be having it. Hop in. Let's go get something to eat, you have to be hungry."

I slid into the back seat, wincing at the streak of mud I left across the leather. I hated screwing up like this. The kids at school liked to tell me that Dan and Nina only took me in for the government money that came along with housing a foster kid. I figured that couldn't be true or they would have sent me back. Maybe asked for an easier kid. No amount of money would have been worth dealing with me those first few months. Things were more settled now, but I still wasn't sure of their motives.

Mom had warned me a long time ago about people, humans that knew about us and wanted proof. They'd do whatever it took to find it. And even if that wasn't the case with the Inzas, I could still end up back in a group home for bad behavior. I wouldn't blame them after this. But I would do anything in my power to keep that from happening. This was the best home I'd been in so far.

A flash of movement outside the car caught my attention, sending my pulse skyrocketing. But it was only Vince, come to watch us leave. He wasn't as creepy as I'd first thought and he'd given me food, making him a friend for life. "Dan, can I have a ten?" I asked.

He looked at me like I was crazy. I nodded toward Vince. "Ah," he muttered, grabbed his wallet and pulled out a twenty. "I'll give it to him." He got out of the car and walked toward the station. They man-talked for a minute and then Dan came back and got in the driver's seat.

I lifted a hand and waved goodbye to Vince. He did the same, then headed back into the store. He was probably just lonely, out here away from everyone. No wonder he was worried about the long distance call. It wasn't like he had a line of customers. Probably just tourists and rangers.

Nina jumped into the front seat and started talking to Dan,

sticking her hand in the back to pat my knee, like she was trying to reassure herself that I was okay. I would have felt bad if it had been my fault that she'd been worried. But it wasn't my fault, not really. It had been Wade. Why? I didn't buy some weirdo reason, and we'd been getting along really well. Like, seriously well. Like I might have even gone to prom just so I could show him off well. My heart thundered for a second and I pushed the thought away. Later, when I was alone. Dan picked up his phone as he flipped on his turn signal and coasted onto the road.

"Nina, please let Lester know we found her. Just send him a message. He can call everyone else." Dan handed his cell to Nina.

Lester. The social worker. Why had they called him? This wasn't the first time I'd run off for a couple hours. I tuned out Nina's voice and strained to bring back the piece of memory that had gone through my mind. It wasn't cooperating. That wasn't totally a bad thing. My mind must have known I didn't really want to deal with it right now. But seriously, Wade? And a gun? What had happened? I started to hyperventilate again, doing my best to shove down the fear.

I buried my face in my knees. Now was not the time to go over this, not with Dan and Nina right here.

We drove in sweet silence for a while, but by the way Dan kept looking at me in the rear view mirror, his expression full of concern and a hint of something else. Every mile we put between us and the gas station, a vise holding my guts loosened just a little.

Dan would keep me safe, even if Wade did show up. Tears leaked onto my ruined dress, but I kept the sobs inaudible. I hadn't even considered he would ever do something like this. How many times did he have the opportunity? Why had it happened now?

"How did you get all the way out here?" Dan's later wasn't very much later. "Do we need to call the police, Trisha? Did Wade do anything to you?"

Here is where I should have been honest, but nice as they were, they were still fosters. When I first heard that Dan worked in government, I almost panicked and ran. The only reason I could figure them taking me in when they obviously didn't need the money was that they had heard something, maybe from one of the other kids at the home. Maybe someone had seen me heal. Luckily I still had some scars from back before I healed so quickly. Maybe that threw them off.

No, I wasn't getting them involved. If Wade had done something, I was going to figure it out on my own. No way I was going to leave him to do it to anyone else, to someone who wouldn't pop back from almost dead. Or dead even. How far gone had I been? I shivered, but blamed it on still being chilled. The heat blasting out of the vents wasn't nearly enough.

"I was alone," I twisted the truth, my gut churning at the deception. As fae, I couldn't lie, not like I had a strong conscience or anything, but none of us could. I couldn't lie, but finding ways around the truth came naturally after growing up in the home. Problem was, I was growing a conscience about it since the Inzas took me in and seemed to actually care what went on in my life.

"Then what happened?" Nina asked as she stared into my soul, her brown eyes sad.

"Some people I thought were my friends weren't." True. I'd thought Wade was a friend, a great friend. The first real friend I'd had, other than my mom. My real mom. Sure, I'd been close with some of the other kids at the home, but they were in and out. Every time I got close to one, they were moved on. Wade had seemed to understand me, even without knowing all the fae stuff. Somehow he'd always known what I was thinking.

Dan looked back at me, his blue eyes harder than Nina's. "It didn't have anything to do with us fighting about Wade before you disappeared, did it?"

I rubbed my arms with my hands, trying to get some of the warmth back. "No, nothing to do with that." Memory flashed. I screamed something at Dan and ran from the house, slamming the door behind me. I winced. Was that how I always sounded?

So we'd fought, I'd called Wade, he showed up acting like my knight in shining armor and offered to take me away to that party I'd been back and forth about going to.

Then he shot me and left me for dead. I patted for a wound

again, now that I didn't have to worry about being shot from behind. Nothing. I fought back a wave of nausea. Some prince he'd turned out to be.

The real question was why? Wasn't there supposed to be motive or something? We were getting along great. I'd thought things were getting serious. It had been over a year since we'd met. That was serious in teenager time. I rubbed at my eyes. No way was I going to cry again. That idiot was going to be sorry. Who did that to a person they were supposed to care about? I probed at my chest and found the bullet hole in my dress. Thankfully the mud had covered that along with the blood.

The conversation was still going on in the front seat, but I wasn't listening anymore. Dan didn't sound very happy though.

Nina squeezed Dan's arm and it seemed to calm him.

Good thing she was here.

I settled into the heated seat and closed my eyes. Healing always exhausted me and I'd done more of it in the last few hours than I'd done these last few months combined. Maybe last few years. The darkness outside didn't help me with the exhaustion. I cracked an eye open and looked at the clock on the dashboard. 1:26 a.m. No wonder Vince's was empty.

"How long was I gone?" I asked, keeping my eyes closed.

It went quiet up front. I cracked an eye open, enough to see Nina, who looked like she might cry.

"Since we passed midnight, it's Sunday, Trish," Dan answered. "You were gone two full days."

I sat up. Two days? No way! How close to dead had Wade left me? I caught my teeth grinding and had to tell my mouth to stop, letting myself go limp again. Healing didn't normally take that long. My memory was still hazy.

Had I spent that whole time lying out in the woods? What if a bear had found me? There were bears in the woods, right? Or a hiker. I might have ended up on an autopsy table. Or worse, in the ground. I clenched my teeth again. Now was not the time. I wasn't going to figure anything out right now. I just needed to relax, calm down. I was with Dan and Nina now. They would keep me safe. I settled back into the warmth of the seat, literally telling my muscles to relax. Everything was going to be okay now.

The adults in the front went back to their conversation.

The heat started to make me sleepy, even through the hunger pains. I half listened to the voices up front, just in case something they said would jog a memory, but it was getting more and more difficult to stay awake. The trees drifted by outside in the dark, nearly mesmerizing. My mind fought hard, trying to figure out what had happened, but my body won and I drifted off into sleep.

I HAVE ONLY hazy memories of getting myself from the car to my room, where I fell into bed without even a shower. I slept late into Sunday, waking up glad that it wasn't a school day. Not that Nina would have made me go, but the school thought I was enough of a troublemaker as it was. No need to miss any more days.

I groaned as I tried to pull myself out of bed, body still exhausted. I could put off being tired for an indefinite period of time, up until I slowed down. Then it hit me like a freight train. Dirt broke off of my hair and plunked down from my shoulder to the floor.

Renewed groans burst forth when I caught a glimpse of myself in the mirror. I didn't normally care what I looked like, but this was enough to make even me cringe. My normally light brown hair was almost grey from mud. Nina had tried to get me to shower last night, but I wouldn't listen, too tired to even think about it. The pajamas I wore were clean, but that was it. I looked like an Aborigine going hunting. Wait a second. I leaned in closer to the mirror. Was that... yes, a zit. Ew, my first one ever. Regenerating skin didn't get zits. Unless it had dirt over it all night, apparently.

Grabbing my towel, I rushed for the bathroom. The water never seemed to take so long to get warm before. I stripped and jumped in while it was still cool, not learning any patience, even after all I'd been through the last few days.

Finally it started to get hot. Ahh, wonderful warm water. I cranked the hot handle on even more. I was never going to take hot water for granted again.

After nearly turning myself into a prune, I hopped out and towel-dried, making a quick check for new scars. A small puckered scab on my chest. I touched it, no pain. I pushed.

Still nothing. Fully healed. The scab would fall off and I probably wouldn't even have a scar. I turned around and looked at my back in the mirror. Nothing. No exit wound. Was the bullet still in there? Not that it mattered, but it was kind of icky to think of a hunk of metal stuck in my body.

Hopefully it had worked its way out. It was just going to have to stay there if it was still inside me. No good way of getting it out, and I couldn't exactly ask for help.

I grabbed my dirty pajamas off the floor. I owed Nina at least that, and headed back to my room.

I shut the door behind me, locking it before heading to the closet for some clean clothes. Nina always kept everything perfect. I tossed my once clean pjs at the hamper and missed. Normally I'd leave them there, but not today. I picked them up and stuffed them into the hamper on top of my other junk. Strange that there were still clothes in there. Nina always did laundry on Saturday. I couldn't imagine her not going about her routine, even if I was missing. In fact, I hadn't heard anything from downstairs. Had they gone to church without me?

Suddenly desperate, hoping they were worried enough about me to stay home and yet telling myself I was being stupid, I threw on the closest pieces of clothing and ran for the stairs.

"Is everything okay?"

I grabbed my chest, heart nearly popping out. Dan. He had stuck his head around the wall that separated the living room from the kitchen.

"Yes, sorry," I mumbled. They were here. I should have known they would be. Even if I didn't understand why, they cared.

"Okay." He didn't look convinced, but he didn't push it. "Hungry? Nina has breakfast almost ready."

As if on cue, my stomach let out an embarrassing squeal. Dan lifted a dark eyebrow and smiled. Sure, it was a strained smile, but at least it was a smile. "Let's get that taken care of."

I followed him into the kitchen, the smell of everything bagels and melted Velveeta cheese hitting me like someone had tossed a brick. Poor Nina. The entire refrigerator was going to be emptied over the next few days if I had my way.

"You're up," Nina said, smiling brightly. Hers was less forced than Dan's, but still not her normal smile. She flipped the bacon in the skillet and then turned back toward me. "This will be ready in one minute."

One minute? My stomach gurgled out a protest.

Dan chuckled. "I don't know if she can wait that long, babe, maybe you should just give it to her now."

"The bacon isn't crispy."

"That's okay," I interjected. "I don't mind it being a little under done." This was weird. No yelling? No questions? Now I was worried.

Nina shrugged, used her spatula to fish out two pieces of bacon and plopped them straight onto the golden mountain of cheese and bagel. She put the perfectly toasted top on and slid the plate to me. I grabbed the plate and the food filled my mouth in a flash.

The sandwich was nearly gone before I looked up. Dan was staring at me while Nina finished another sandwich, thankfully back pointed toward me. She was always so perfect, so polite. If she saw me eating like that she'd probably have a heart attack. She turned to us and slid the sandwich to Dan.

"Gone already?" she asked after a glance at my plate. I nodded, not able to speak with my mouth full.

Dan shook his head, chuckling at me, then bowed his head to pray before he ate. That was something I'd always appreciated about them, they believed in something but didn't try to make me. The state wouldn't let them force me to go to church, but there were other ways to get me to listen if they'd wanted to.

Another two sandwiches with eggs, cheese, and bacon on them disappeared. By the last one, I was slowing down enough to actually taste. These things were awesome, nothing like what I had grown up eating. Mom only had a hotel microwave to work with most of the time, which meant lots of mac and cheese. I still don't eat mac and cheese unless I'm really, really desperate.

"Thank you," I mumbled around my last bite. It was still awful quiet in here, about the whole me going missing thing.

My stomach flipped, suddenly heavy with the anxiety added to all the food.

"You're welcome," Nina said. "I'm just so glad you're here for me to do this for."

"And thanks for coming to get me last night." I meant it too. I don't know if I had ever really thanked them before, other than the basics, but right now it was heartfelt.

"Are you ready to talk about what happened? It's best to get the police involved early," Dan said, his food completely chewed and swallowed of course. "Lester is coming over later. I'm not trying to push you, Trisha, I just want to get this handled."

There it was. They'd just been waiting. Of course they had all morning to relax and think about what they were going to say. I'd just gotten up. I should have come up with a plan before putting a foot on the stairs, but I'd needed to know they were here.

Nina put her hand on Dan's shoulder. "It's his way of protecting you," she explained for him.

"I appreciate the thought, but I don't need to be protected."

Nina slid another sandwich in front of me. I fiddled with it for a second, fighting the urge to devour it. I wasn't the one who needed protection. Wade was. The next time I saw him, I was going to… something. Wasn't sure about that part yet. I pushed the last sandwich away, my body at odds with my stomach, muscles screaming for fuel but stomach feeling like I was out to sea right now. I needed to get this Wade thing handled. I needed to know if he cared that he'd killed me, if there was a reason.

"Are you okay, honey?" Nina asked. I tore my gaze away from the table and glanced her way. She looked honestly concerned.

"I think I'll go lay down for a while." I shoved my chair away from the table, keeping my eyes pointed toward the floor so I didn't have to see Dan and Nina's worried expressions.

"Are you feeling okay?" Dan asked. I nodded but headed for the stairs. "Maybe we should have taken her to the ER. Just to make sure nothing's wrong," I heard Dan say to Nina behind me.

"No, I just need to rest a bit," I said, halfway up the staircase.

Nina followed me to the base of the stairs. "We'll be right here if you need anything. If you don't feel good, we really should have you checked out. How long were you in the woods?"

I shrugged and climbed the stairs faster. I made it to my room, but I could hear the two of them talking downstairs. I shut the door and moved straight for the window, sliding it up and slipping out in one well-practiced move.

They weren't going to like it if they found out, but I had to go see if Wade was still around. I wasn't going to let what happened to me happen to anyone else. I dropped to the ground outside the house, my left ankle sending up a little twinge at the distance down but instantly healing.

Practically tiptoeing, I grabbed my bike off the front porch and pushed it toward the road. The sight of Dan's Mercedes in the drive made me pause. Was this really how I wanted to handle the situation? They had been there as soon as I'd called for help last night. And they would find out that I'd snuck away again. Dan was going to be so mad. I so wanted to go back to the house, to pull up a chair in the kitchen and down two more sandwiches while trying to explain what had really happened Thursday.

But I couldn't. I couldn't get them involved in this. For them to know what had happened, they would have to know what I was. I definitely wasn't ready for that. While I was starting to love the Inzas, I didn't trust them yet. Look where almost trusting Wade had gotten me. And it wasn't just trusting that they weren't going to turn me over to some government program. There was another kind of trust involved, the kind that meant I could believe that they wouldn't look at me like I was some kind of freak if they knew. I definitely wasn't even close to there yet.

Sure, I might be a freak, but I didn't want them thinking that.

Just in case Nina decided to check on me and found me missing, I took a hard left at the first intersection, then a right at the next. My legs felt like butter for the first few pedals, then set into a rhythm. The calories were starting to kick in. Every time I heard an engine I'd duck into some bushes or behind a neighbor's vehicle. I was going to be in so much trouble. Couldn't think like that. I had to find Wade.

The ride to Wade's wasn't far. He had his own apartment about a mile from the Inza's place, something extra that Dan hadn't liked about him. Plus the fact that he was out of school already. He'd never mentioned his parents and with my own parental guidance problems, I'd never asked.

Looking back, that might have been kinda dumb. But I'd met him in the library for Pete's sake. I was just there to get out of the house. Who knew what he was doing there. Now that I thought about it, that was a little fishy. He wasn't really the library type. Had he known something? He'd never even hinted about anything fae. But maybe that was why he'd killed me, he was part of one of those groups and had figured it out.

Getting close, I pulled into a small alley and coasted to a stop. I leaned my bike against the building and peeked around the corner. No one in sight. The walk from where I'd stashed my bike to the parking area for his apartment should have only taken about two minutes, but I was in stealth mode. Another good thing about the fae blood, we were a sneaky people.

I made it around the last corner and stopped. His junky pickup wasn't sitting there. He was always home on Sunday afternoons. It was the one day he didn't have anything scheduled and there was no way to get him to go out, or so he'd always said. I guess killing his girlfriend might have changed his mind. I waited there, hidden around the corner until dark, nearly bored out of my mind. He didn't show.

Disappointed and yet somehow relieved, I went back for my bike and rode to the Inzas' in the dark. Once there, I stowed my bike and headed for the front door. Might as well get it over with.

"She's back," Nina, apparently on the phone. "How long? Okay."

I walked her way.

"That was Dan," Nina said. "He's five minutes out. Have a seat. We're going to wait for him."

I did as she asked, sinking deep into the black leather couch in the living room. This was going to get ugly. And I couldn't even explain to them where I'd been. Right now I was wishing my ability was time travel instead of healing. I'd fast forward a few days. Nina moved over and sat down in the matching chair across from me. We waited in silence. I couldn't look her in the face, so I stared at a picture of the three of us sitting on the end table. It was taken the day I'd moved in and I had a terribly fake smile on. The Inzas looked tired but excited. Look where that had gotten them.

It was a long five minutes before I heard the car in the drive. The engine shut down and a door slammed. Dan came stalking around the hallway and stopped a few feet from me, looking totally un-Dan like, completely disheveled. "Where have you been?"

"Out," I mumbled lamely, not able to come up with anything better even with all the time I'd spent staring at Wade's apartment.

"I got that part," Dan said. "What were you doing?"

"Trisha," Nina said, her voice teary. "Why do you keep doing this to us? We were so worried."

Okay, that was unfair. But it wasn't like I was going to tell her I was stalking the guy that killed me before I popped back to life. They were very understanding for fosters, but I didn't think even they would be cool with that.

"There was something I had to do," I said.

"I think we deserve a better explanation than that," Dan said. "We were giving you time before we asked about this week, letting you rest a little before we got into it, but this is getting ridiculous."

"Does this have anything to do with that?" Nina asked. "You being gone last week?"

How could I answer that without lying? I couldn't, so I didn't try. I stared at the floor, making sure not to let Nina make eye contact. If she kept tearing up, this wasn't going to go well for me.

Dan raked a hand through his hair, completing his disheveled bum look. "Trisha Penchant, don't treat my wife like this." His voice sounded almost angry. This was the closest I'd heard him to upset with me, and I'd deserved it a time or two. Or more. I turned toward him, ready to let him have it with both barrels, just to hide the fact that I didn't like it that he was upset. Nina's expression stopped me. I just kept quiet. What could I say?

"Go to your room," Dan finally said. "We'll talk about this later, after we've all had time to calm down. And you had better be there when I come up to get you."

I couldn't meet their eyes as I slunk past them and headed upstairs. They waited until they heard my door close, then went at it. Lots of firsts this week. This was the first time I'd heard them argue with any heat. I sat down on my bed with the purple comforter that I hated and leaned up against the purple wall I hated at least as much. Why couldn't I have one normal relationship? It was this stupid curse of being fae. I dropped my forehead to my knees and cried.

Chapter 3

Buzz. Buzz. I cracked open an eye. What was that?

Whatever it was, I was going to kill it, no questions asked. I rolled over and looked at the clock. Seven a.m. On… today was Monday, right? Shoot, school! I popped up in bed and made a wild grab for my phone to shut off the alarm. It wasn't on the bed stand. It took a moment to register, but I hadn't had it with me on Thursday because I hadn't wanted Nina or Dan calling me while I was out with Wade. I'd left it here. Somewhere.

I followed the charger under the bed and pulled out my phone. It was just a cheap slide phone, but none of the other families I'd stayed with had let me have a phone at all, so I was happy. I crawled out from under the bed and turned off the alarm. The screen lit up. The only notification was one new text message. Not surprising considering the only person I ever talked to was Wade. waiting on you. when will you be here. His normal no caps texting. Right before I met him to go to that stupid party.

That little… wait until I found him. I crushed down the pain trying to bubble up. I still hadn't decided what to do after that. One problem at a time.

A quick shower and I headed downstairs. The smell of pancakes met me halfway to the kitchen. My stomach rumbled, announcing it wanted at least five pancakes. After not eating most of yesterday, it deserved seven.

"Good morning," Nina said from her usual spot in front of the stove.

That was it? No freak out? "Morning," I answered, moving in from the hallway.

"Good morning, Trisha." I pinched my lips together in a super-human effort to smother a groan. That voice. Lester. No reason to ask why he was here. That didn't help the slight feeling of betrayal.

I ignored him.

Dan glanced up from his plate, leaning back in his chair. "Have an explanation for last night? Or for the days before that?"

There it was. Straight into it because Lester was here. And I still hadn't come up with an answer. "No." I caught myself picking at my t-shirt and forced my hand to stop. Lester would be watching for signs like that.

"Trisha, why don't you have a seat?" Lester said in his silky, keep the situation calm, voice. I hated that voice.

"I'm good, thanks." I concentrated on not looking at him and kept my eyes on Dan. Dan wasn't happy with me right now, obviously, but at least I knew he cared.

"If you leave again without permission, there will be consequences. As it is, you're grounded," Dan said. "I get that there is something going on that you feel like you need to handle, but we need to know where you are. Understand?"

I dropped my gaze. "Yes." Being grounded would not help finding Wade. But I couldn't really protest.

"Good." He nodded toward Lester. "Your social worker is pretty unhappy with us." Dan was never one to hold anything back. Something I admired, most of the time. Wasn't really a fan at the moment.

"Now, now, I never said I was unhappy with you. I just mentioned that if Trisha is miserable enough here that she continues to leave, maybe it's time we find another home for her."

I sucked in a breath. "What? That's not true! I like it here."

They couldn't take me away from here. This was home now. After a year with the Inzas there was no way I could adjust to another family. I'd never made it this long anywhere else. Never long enough to get attached, for sure. Not that I was attached. I totally wasn't attached. In no way was I attached. Crap.

"What are we supposed to think, Trish?" Nina asked, flipping a pancake in the skillet on the stove.

There really wasn't an answer for that. I still needed to find out what had happened to Wade, I would just have to be a little more careful about how I did it. "I'll do better." I had to be careful how I worded it so I didn't get stuck not being able to do any sneaking. That no lying thing was a pain.

Dan didn't look very convinced. He lifted an eyebrow. "Good." He turned to Lester. "Good enough for you?"

"Yes, unless it happens again. We can't have wards of the State running around wild. Maybe it's time to think about sending her to a therapist."

"A therapist?" Nina asked, turning from her pancakes. "What good would that do?"

"It would allow her to get some of her feelings out, maybe make her feel like she didn't have to run. It could be very beneficial."

I turned pleading eyes on Dan. A therapist could not be good. I might say something that would give me away, even if I was being careful. And if I just went in there and didn't say anything, they might think something was even more wrong than it was.

"I think we should skip on that for now," Dan said, seeing my face. He was looking out for me. Even after I'd been a jerk. Again. He lifted an eyebrow. "But we will keep it open as an option. She says she isn't going anywhere and I believe her." He cocked his head a little, staring straight into my eyes. I took that as I'd better not break his trust. I nodded and he gave me a small smile. "All ready for school? I'll drop you off today, if you want."

I looked from him to Nina and back. I'd been hoping they would let me take the day off, giving me the chance to watch Wade's place. Nina lifted an eyebrow and I deflated. Not a good idea to argue in front of Lester.

"Thanks for the offer, but I'll ride my bike to school. Gives me time to think." Plus time to swing by Wade's. And, ha, how was he going to argue with me wanting to think?

"Okay. I want you straight home today."

I nodded, not making eye contact.

"I called the school and handled things. You shouldn't be getting any questions about missing last week," Dan said.

"I talked with your principal as well," Lester interjected.

I slid into my chair at the table feeling a little queasy. Dan was taking care of me even when he knew I wasn't being honest with him. Was this what family was supposed to feel like? Then why did I feel both loved and crappy at the same time?

Lester stood and picked up his briefcase. "I'd best be going." He sent me a pointed stare. "I have quite a mess to try to untangle, what with last week happening." His face went stern. "I hope you know all the trouble I'm going through to try and keep you with the Inzas. The higher-ups are beginning to think they are incompetent foster parents."

Incompetent? I glanced toward Nina. Her back was to me, shoulders stiff enough I knew she was mad. But she didn't say anything.

"Thank you," I said, not knowing what else to say.

He nodded and Dan got up to show him out. I breathed out a sigh of relief when I heard the door close after him.

Dan came back and sat in his chair at the table.

No one seemed to know what to say after all that, so breakfast was eaten in relative silence. I finished my pancakes, pushed my chair back from the table and stood. "Thanks for breakfast."

"You're welcome," Nina answered. "Supper at six-thirty."

"Okay, thanks." I felt like there was more I should be saying, but I didn't know what so I headed for the door, grabbing my backpack and jacket on the way.

For once I was leaving early. Wade's apartment was about ten biking minutes out of the way to school. I pedaled hard. The Inzas knew I'd left a little early, so if I got detention for being late to school they would know something was up. And they were going to be watching. It was kind of surprising that Dan wasn't following me in the car right now. I checked behind me again, just to make sure.

No beat up white Chevy at Wade's apartment building.

Where was he? I didn't have time to hang around right now, but I'd be back after school. Ugh, school. I started pedaling again, trying to ignore where I was going. And all the stories said fae were cruel, what about the public school system?

Didn't that count as torture? Why couldn't I have been home-schooled. Probably because Nina knew me too well.

Fifteen minutes and I was pulling up on the school grounds. I locked my bike to the closest bike stand and headed for the front door. I barely made it inside when I heard a voice.

"There you are!" Rissa, a girl I saw in class sometimes but didn't know at all, was power walking in my direction. I looked around to see who she was talking to, but there wasn't anyone else close. She came at me with arms wide open like I was about to get a hug. I wiggled around to avoid it. She didn't seem to notice, just kept talking. "We all heard about you going missing Thursday night and were terribly worried."

Oh great. If this girl knew, everyone knew. I looked behind her to the kids milling around. No one I really talked to. But then, I didn't really know anyone here, I never let myself. I'd talked with Amy for like ten minutes at the party, but I didn't see her here with half the rest of the school. They all looked terribly worried. Not. "No need to worry anymore, I'm fine." I gave her a fake smile and pushed past her toward my first class room. I was not going to get detention. That would mean no checking up on Wade's apartment on the way home.

Passing my locker, I made it to Mrs. Hemp's lit. class just in time to slide into my seat before the bell rang. It must not have been the first ring, because she closed the door before it was done echoing.

She got started enthusiastically, like always, and I drifted off into my thoughts. It wasn't long before the bell rang again and I was through the first class of my day.

"Trisha, I'd like to talk with you," Mrs. Hemp said as I tried to slip past her. I sighed and nodded. Had she noticed I wasn't paying attention today? What other reason could she have to talk with me? Not about missing Friday, hopefully. Dan had said he'd handled that.

After the other kids drifted slowly out, their curiosity practically seeping from their skin, Mrs. Hemp shut the door behind them.

"Are you okay?" Having just gotten myself prepared for some type of lecture, her kind tone knocked me off guard. "I heard about you being gone over the weekend and was worried. Your parents even let some of us from the school join in the search."

"Fosters," I said, out of habit. They had failed to mention that little fact to me. "I'm fine, thanks. Is that it?"

Her face full of concern, Mrs. Hemp nodded. "If you ever need anything, just ask."

How about some help tracking down a murderer? Or attempted murderer, or whatever? No? Okay then, she couldn't help me. I shook my head and waited a second. When she didn't add anything, I slipped out the door.

I went to my locker to switch out books. Something caught my attention out of the corner of my eye, but by the time I looked over, there was nothing but other students. Whatever. Just still jumpy after being followed around in the woods. Wade wouldn't come here looking for me.

I still hadn't figured out why he'd done it in the first place. But even if that had been him in the woods and he'd found out my body was gone, he wouldn't come to school. I tightened my hands around my notebook. Yeah, keep telling yourself that, Penchant.

"Hey, Trisha!" A bright voice called, pulling me gladly from my not so happy thoughts. Gladly until I saw it was one of the popular girls.

"Hey, Heather." I kept it short and sweet. Hopefully she'd just keep walking.

"You okay?" she asked after a second. "You look kind of freaked out. And no one knows what happened last week, so we're all worried."

So people kept saying. I forced a smile. "All good here." She probably just wanted to know where I'd been so she had the scoop.

She didn't look like she believed me. "Okay. Well, if you need to talk, find me."

I nodded and she smiled, then walked away. It was going to be a long day.

Two classes later and it was finally time for lunch. Lunch and I had a love/hate relationship. Not for the obvious reason that I didn't have anyone to sit with, but because I loved to eat. There's the love, and the hate part. Eating was awesome, but even with this many kids people were bound to notice if I consumed as much as I'd like to. So I usually ended up leaving still hungry. Better than calling attention to myself.

Standing in line was the strangest experience of my life. Other teens smiled and waved. The lunch lady grinned at me and gave me an extra helping of chili. Apparently I should have gone missing a year ago, assuming I was going to learn to like this attention.

I went to go sit at my normal table, but it took me forever as people all tried to tell me hi. I nodded at the first few, then ignored the rest. I dropped my tray on the empty table and settled in, barely getting that first bite down before the feeling of being watched hit me again.

A quick look around the cafeteria told me nothing looked out of place. I probably looked pretty stupid with a spoonful of chili halfway to my mouth. I shoved it in and started to chew, but it turned my stomach. There really was a first time for everything. Me not wanting to eat was definitely a first.

"Trish!" Okay, hearing my name was getting old. Real old.

I looked over and forced a smile, until I saw that it was Amy. Then the smile became a little bit more real.

She jogged over and literally slid across the bench to sit across from me. "Hey! It's so good to see for myself that you're okay! I was really worried after you didn't show up Friday morning."

Well now, here was someone that might remember more about what happened than I did. "I'm all good. The party went pretty late, huh?"

"Late enough that I had a hard time making it to first period." Amy laughed. "But you left early. How was Wade's surprise?"

Ha. Quite a surprise. "Interesting," I said, deflecting.

The bell rang first warning. I hadn't hardly touched my food, but I didn't really feel like eating anyway.

"Oh, gotta go. Maybe you can tell me about it some other time?" Amy smiled, then took off without waiting for an answer.

"Not likely," I muttered.

I took another couple bites just out of principle, but the rest of my lunch ended up in the trash.

The rest of the day pretty much followed the precedent the morning had set. I watched the time slowly tick by until I held my breath while the last minute disappeared on the clock. The final bell rang and I was off like a shot.

People I barely knew called greetings to me as I ran down the hallway and out the front door to my bike. Were they always this nice and I just hadn't noticed? Surely if they hated me as much as I'd thought they would have been glad I went missing.

The eerie feeling that someone was watching me hadn't showed up since the lunch room. I hoped it stayed that way.

I pedaled hard to get to Wade's apartment as fast as possible. I needed enough time to check things out and get back before Nina started to worry. I really didn't need Dan driving around looking for me again. If Wade's truck still wasn't there, I was breaking in. I screeched to a halt in the alley, propped my bike against a wall and snuck around to check the parking lot. His truck still wasn't here. Had he ran after that night in the forest?

Time for me to find out. I crept toward the door that led to the stairway to his apartment, until I felt it. I looked around wildly, not seeing anything out of place. It had been bad enough at school, surrounded by people, but here it was enough to make the fear from Sunday morning thrum through my veins, making me want to puke.

"Miss Penchant?"

The small voice behind me nearly scared me out of my jeans. I whirled around to face the owner of the voice and came eye to top of bald head with a small older guy. I looked down into his watery greenish eyes almost hidden by a bulbous nose.

I crossed my arms in front of my chest, sure my heart beating this hard had to be visible. Should I admit that was my name? Who was this guy? "What's it to you?"

"Please drop the attitude, Miss Penchant. I'm here to offer you a job."

My face hardened into that expression that Nina called the block, arms tightening even more. "I didn't apply for any jobs."

"No, but you are certainly qualified. Willingly or not, you will be coming with me and hearing what we have to offer." He tilted his head, the sun reflecting off the giant bald patch on top.

"Oh really," I snarled. "Is it you that's been following me all day? And just how are you going to drag me off in the middle of an apartment complex with no one noticing?"

The dwarf sighed, loosening his red tie with one hand. "I was hoping it wouldn't come to this. If you insist on continuing to be rude, we will have no choice but to do this the hard way."

I raised an eyebrow in challenge, tensing up a little. No way this pipsqueak was making me go anywhere. Wade was a big guy and he'd had a hard time getting me down. Wade.

Coincidence that this guy found me outside Wade's apartment? I didn't think so. Curiosity was definitely one of my weaknesses, but I wasn't ready to die twice in one week. Though, this could be my only chance to go after Wade. And what would it hurt to just see what the guy had to offer? If he tried to take me into a building or whatever, I could reevaluate.

With an absolutely serene expression, the dwarf lifted his wrist to his mouth. "Snatch is go," he said, hopefully talking into something. If not, he was even more nuts than I'd first thought.

What were the chances this was connected to last week and ending up in the woods? Almost no doubt. "No, wait. I'll go with you."

"As you wish." The dwarf moved his wrist back up to his mouth. "Cancel the last order, subject has agreed to come of her own volition." He put his arm down and looked at me, not blinking. "Please follow me."

He took off around the building, moving fast for the length of his legs.

I ran after him. I caught up when he paused at a brick wall in a secluded alley. As soon as we locked eyes, he stepped into the wall. Literally. The wall bowed around him and he disappeared.

Great. So much for being in a public place. I had a feeling he wasn't just going to leave me alone if I didn't follow. What happened if he tracked me down and confronted me in front of Dan or Nina? Not going to happen. Better to just get this over with right now. Plus the guy was starting to tick me off. Did he really have to be so rude?

I closed my eyes and jumped through the wall. It felt really weird, like the time I fell in quicksand at Yellowstone, before mom dropped me at the home. It held me out for a second more, then snapped me forward and spit me out, nearly sending me sprawling across the floor.

The dwarf was waiting for me on the other side, back lit by cool blue lights floating along chiseled stone walls.

"Stay close," he said and bustled away.

"Where are we?" I asked, shuffling along in the sandy footing.

"Now is not the time for questions. Let me get the pleasantries out of the way, even if you don't seem to be a pleasant person." The dwarf spun around and faced me, then went into a deep bow. "I am Mr. Cumat."

A giggle tried to escape. How did he take himself seriously? I held it in and gave him a polite smile. "Nice to meet you." I dropped the smile. "Now where are we?" I'd been asking that question too much lately.

Mr. Cumat snorted at me, no doubt considering how rude I was being. "We are in one of the tunnels." He turned and continued down the tunnel, apparently expecting me to follow.

"What tunnels?" I asked, staying only a couple steps behind him. "You can't just say one of the tunnels and expect me to know what that means."

As we moved farther in, the walls changed from stone to some building material that was such a bright white it was nearly blinding. The walls themselves seemed to be the source of the only light in the hallway, now that we were past the entrance and the little floating lights were gone. I'd definitely never seen anything like this before. The floor changed from the sandy footing of a cave to white tiles.

The dwarf sighed and pinched the top of his nose as he walked. "The tunnels that lead from Faerie to the human world. Do you know nothing?"

I was going to ignore the last part of that. And he'd just walked me through a wall, so I didn't need to pretend I didn't know about the fae. "You mean I could take this tunnel from my world to Faerie?" Doors started showing up along the walls. Lots of doors. I inched toward the middle of the tunnel.

"Not your world, the human world. You forget where you're from."

Oh no he didn't. "I'm not forgetting where I'm from, that little ball in the sky called Earth, that's where I'm from."

"That is where you were born, but not where you are from."

I crossed my arms and stopped walking, heat starting up my neck. "You aren't taking me to Faerie, are you? This isn't going to work if you think you're going to get me to take one more step toward that place." Faerie was chock full of liars, deceivers, and all other kinds of low lives that I really didn't want to be around. Plus, there was all kinds of weird stuff there that would probably find a way to kill me. At least according to my mom.

"You will not be taken to Faerie right now, if you cooperate. And why do you seem to think that would be a bad thing? It is the place of your ancestors." I glared down at him and he threw up his hands. "It's useless to argue about this now. Shall we continue?"

"Not until you give me a better idea of why I'm here. I'm not going any farther until I know. Did Wade send you?"

The dwarf muttered something to himself. He looked like he was about to speak when a voice from down the hallway interrupted him.

"Hey Cumat, you need any help? Starren said to..."

Was that... no way I could be so lucky. I spun around to get a better look. Sure enough. He must have come out of one of the doors we'd passed.

"Trish!" Wade blinked several times. "I thought…" he trailed off.

I lunged at him without thinking, taking a swing at his face. He dodged and grabbed my wrists, tight but not enough to hurt. I struggled for a second, every possible way I could kill him going through my mind. But first I needed to get free.

"Thought I was dead? Do a better job next time," I snapped. I stopped struggling, trying to get him to relax his hold. I assessed for a moment, and noticed a couple of weird things. Wade was wearing some funky clothes. Like really funky. And he looked like a couple of the blows I tried to land had hit, an almost sick expression on his face.

I took a step toward him holding back a growl. This was going to hurt, but it was worth it. I jumped up and planted both feet in his chest, pushing as I pulled back against his grip. We fell and I scratched at him, clawing and kicking. He wasn't going to get a second chance at killing me.

"Trish, stop!" Wade yelled. "I don't want to hurt you!"

I wiggled my elbow free and slammed him in the gut, getting a satisfying oopmph' as all the air left his lungs "Coulda fooled me!"

"No need to get violent, Miss Penchant," Cumat called. "I'll have to call security." He looked at Wade, then back to me, tangled on the floor and glaring. "You two know each other?"

"Yes," we said in unison. I sneered at Wade, just to let him know that I didn't appreciate us being on the same page.

"And you don't get along?"

"No!" we chorused again.

"He tried to kill me," I spat out. Security or no security, I was not letting him get the drop on me again. Not now that I knew what he wanted, even if I didn't know why.

"I didn't try, I did!" Wade yelled back. "How are you here?"

His admission was like a punch in the gut, making me pause. I'd never told him how I felt about him, but still, we'd been dating for almost a year. Didn't he care at all? He could just throw that out there and have the gall to seem freaked out that I was still breathing?

He let go of me and we both scrambled to our feet, staring each other down. Wade had some very gratifying scratches down his face. Served him right.

"What do I know, I'm just a retrieval specialist. They never tell me anything," Cumat's voice hardly registered over the roaring in my ears. Did he not care that Wade had just admitted to murdering me? "Of course, if they know each other they wouldn't get along, the girl is terribly rude."

"I'm here to make sure you don't do it to anyone else," I spat out and launched myself in his direction. I got a good swing in before he grabbed my wrists and jerked me around, gripping me in a bear hug.

I kicked back and caught him in the knee. "Security!" the dwarf yelled in the background.

"I got this, Cumat," Wade panted out.

I slammed my head back and got him in the throat. I'd been aiming for his nose, but the throat worked fine. He gasped and then shook me until I was dizzy.

"Trish, stop. We need to talk."

Really? Seriously? "You should have tried that before you shot me!" I bit down on his forearm and he yelled. Then he crushed me to his body so hard my chest couldn't expand enough to get a breath. I batted at his arm, trying to pull it away enough to get some air, but he was just too strong. I couldn't do anything.

He must have felt the fight go out of me. His grip loosened a little "Truce? You won't attack me?"

If I agreed to that my stupid fae ancestry would never let me go back on my word. But I liked being able to breathe. "Not for... an... hour," I gasped out.

His arms went to his sides and I stumbled away from him, moving to the wall and propping myself up. He bent over and put his hands on his knees, watching me. That look meant he knew I would be keeping track of that hour.

"All done, Miss Penchant?" Cumat asked primly.

"Not by a long shot." That came out much stronger than my last attempt at a sentence.

"Well, that is unfortunate considering you've been assigned as partners. You are going to have to learn to work together," Cumat broke in, putting himself in danger from both sides.

"I had no idea this job opportunity you mentioned included people like him, people who off other people in their spare time," I shot out, getting angrier as the words poured free. "I won't work for a place like that. Plus you haven't even gotten to why this is so important for me, anyway."

"Is that what you think?" Wade yelled back, straightening up and moving close to tower over me. I squared my shoulders and pulled myself to my full height. Which was nothing compared to his. He was probably trying to figure out how to finish me off. "After a year together, all the things we said to each other, that I wanted to kill you?"

"What else am I supposed to think?" Heads popped out of doorways down the hall. Our screaming was starting to draw atten-tion. I didn't care. Let everyone know what kind of guy they worked with.

"Now, now, let's try to keep this from escalating into-" Both our glares turned to Mr. Cumat.

Wade's shoulders slumped. "I didn't want to hurt you," his confession came out almost as a whisper.

"Well I'm pretty sure that shooting someone in the chest will do that." He actually looked sad. More sad than I'd ever seen him. But he was either a murderer or crazy, and I wasn't sure which was worse.

"Miss Penchant, I'm sure you would understand the position Wade was in if it was explained to you. It was all part of the job."

"All part of the job?" Did that make it better or worse? Had the whole relationship been part of the job? "Oh, well then, I guess it's fine if the job told you to do it. No way you could stick up for your girlfriend or anything, that would just be too archaic." Part of the job? What kind of work was this, that expected you to kill people you were supposed to care about? I seriously was not getting involved with these people. Before I knew it, they'd be asking me to kill Dan. Or worse, Nina.

"I wouldn't have done it if you hadn't been fae." He was back to yelling. This was a whole new side of him. I'd never seen him angry. Everything I knew about him was probably wrong. "You were supposed to go to Faerie if something like that happened, just like everyone else."

Okay, now I was really confused. So confused I couldn't even be angry for a minute. He didn't just say fae, did he? Because he really wasn't supposed to know about that. "What? What's a fae?"

He gave me a look that said he totally knew I was bluffing.

"When one of the fae dies on Earth, they are sent back to Faerie. In extreme cases we use it to get criminals back, or in your case sent home for evaluation. We weren't sure how you would react to a summons, or even if you knew that you are fae, so it was decided this was the best method to return you to Faerie," Mr. Cumat interrupted. "And that is all you can know for now. Shall we continue and meet your new team leader?"

"You were going to force me to go to Faerie? No way. I'm not working for you loons." I planted my feet and made sure my expression was sending out my feelings about this place loud and clear. I should be plotting my revenge against Wade, not trying to help him. Even if he was just trying to send me to Faerie, which I was having a hard time believing, he had risked my life without even thinking about it.

"Miss Penchant, I do believe that working here will bring you great satisfaction. Those who work hard are always well rewarded."

"You expect me to go around killing people and just trusting you that they pop up in Faerie, totally fine? Seriously?" Wade at least should have known I wouldn't go for this. But then, he had looked surprised to see me. Maybe he didn't know the dwarf was bringing me in. I gave him another glare. "There is nothing you could possibly give me that would make me want to work for you."

"Really?" Oh, now the little dwarf was looking so smug. If only I could wipe that expression off his face. He was making me mad enough that his next words took a moment to register. When they did, it was like waking up in the woods all over again. "Nothing can compel you to work with us? Not even your freedom?"

Chapter 4

"What? Why would you even say that?" Now the people down the hall were really going to get a show. I didn't care; I was mad.

"Ms. Penchant, no need to get upset. Your happy home here on Earth will be your reward for helping us with a particularly hard case. If you should choose not to join us for this case, you give up your freedom. Are we clear?"

I glowered at him for a moment, contemplating all the different ways I could use to make him talk, to give me a better explanation for what was going on here. Wade cleared his throat behind Cumat and shook his head. He knew me well. I sent daggers streaming out of my eyes in his direction, but they seemed to glance off. He didn't even look offended. After the shock of seeing me alive had faded, he went back to his normal cool, reserved self. Fine, two could play that game.

"Give up my freedom how?"

"Whose child are you?" Cumat asked, sounding exasperated. "Didn't they teach you anything about protocol?"

I crossed my arms in front of my chest and deepened my glare. No doubt my mom had been on the run for a reason. It wasn't like people did that for fun. Which meant there was no way I was telling him who my mom was.

Cumat sighed. "I suppose that if they didn't take the time to teach you manners, I should not expect you to know anything else. All fae children born in the human world are supposed to return to Faerie when they come of age, to be trained in the ways of the fae. Living on Earth without being trained is strictly forbidden. If you have been living here without permission, you have been violating the law and you will be imprisoned if you refuse to work for us. You are not on any of our lists, therefore we assume you were not returned?"

It sounded like a question, but he already knew the answer. Was that why Mom had always kept us on the run, never living in one place longer than a month? Was she trying to keep me away from these people? She'd never had anything good to say about Faerie. A cold feeling, strangely like fear, started in the pit of my stomach. I kept my face impassive.

"Do you even know who your parents are?"

"No." Truth. Mom had never said anything about who my father was, and I really didn't know that much about her either. Especially now that it had been so long since she had left me and it was hard to tell if my memories were accurate or just things I'd made up as a kid to make me feel better.

"That explains so much," Cumat muttered. "If you refuse to help with this job, you will be taken to Faerie for training. If you do agree to help us, the Council has decided to allow an exception to the rule."

Wow, they must be desperate. From some of the things Mom had said, it had become pretty obvious that fae were sticklers for rules. Somehow I got the feeling I wasn't going to like what they asked me to do. It had to be bad or they wouldn't have to blackmail someone into doing it. But the choices were to stay with Dan and Nina, something I'd figured out wasn't so bad, or get dragged off in handcuffs to some other world. Did they even have handcuffs? Probably not, they'd probably use some kind of magic.

"Fine," I said. "I'm listening. But what could I possibly do to help you?"

"It isn't me you need to listen to, dear girl, as I said before, I'm only the retrieval specialist. Let me take you to your new team leader, as I was attempting to do earlier. Before you attack anyone else while you are my responsibility." The dwarf bustled off down the hallway.

Wade motioned for me to walk ahead of him, but I shook my head. No way that guy was going to be at my back. Now that he knew I wasn't so easy to kill, I wasn't taking any chances, even if the dwarf had said they needed me.

With a roll of his green eyes, Wade went off ahead of me. What I wouldn't give for a weapon right now. He'd already proved I couldn't do a thing against him without one. He was a brave man, looking the other direction. I wanted to ask him what his ability was, what Faerie was like, a million fae-related questions, but all of that would require talking to him.

And then there were the more personal questions, like if he'd felt any regret at all when he pulled the trigger. Had everything we'd had been fake. I wasn't following this dwarf because of the job, I was just giving myself time to think about how to get to Wade. After I took care of that problem, I'd figure out what to do about the taken away from the fosters problem. I hadn't really thought about what I would do with Wade when I found him, but now a solution had presented itself. If something happened to him he would just appear in Faerie. Hopefully that meant he couldn't come back, but I still hadn't murdered him. Murdered him all the way, at least.

Each door up the white hallway slammed shut as we got close. It was like we were walking down one of those funhouse hallways, the end never getting any closer, doors stretching on forever. I never got a good look at anyone in any of the rooms. It was like they didn't want me to see them. The absolute pristine white of the hallway started to make my eyes hurt. Cumat led us past several more doors before choosing one that looked exactly like the rest. He pulled it open and bowed at the waist. "After you."

Wade waited a second, like he thought I would go in first, then snorted and stepped through the doorway when I planted my feet. After he was all the way through I followed slowly.

"Where is this guy?" I asked, halfway into the room. "I need to get back home before Nina calls out the cavalry again." And she would too. I'd lose my happy home if it happened again, whether I helped these people or not.

"I am the one you need to speak with," a smooth voice answered from the other side of the room. It belonged to a girl who, at first glance, looked about my age. After a moment though, I found it harder to guess how old she was. Something about her whispered she'd been around a while. Fae, so hard to tell. She could be a hundred just as easily as the twenty or so she looked like.

The room was nearly bare and even more blindingly white than the hallway, if possible. The girl was wearing white too, making her blend in. Some Jedi robe outfit. Awesome boots that made me so jealous peeked out under this side of the desk she was behind. All the white made the girl's jet black hair stand out like ink on one of Nina's bleached sheets. Something about her made me really uncomfortable. Maybe the fact that she was probably the one that had ordered me snatched.

She glanced up from her paperwork, her face showing her utter disdain for the entire situation. "My name is Starren." She nodded and to two chairs, exactly like the one she was sitting in. "Sit."

I stepped forward and slid into the chair, half expecting it to grab me. With Wade being my only example of fae character so far, I was beginning to understand Mom's paranoia. Easy to say I wasn't a fan. But I would behave, follow along with their little games for now. Until I figured out if what Cumat had said was true or not.

"Mr. Cumat, you are dismissed," Starren said. "Job well done." Ah, so maybe the rudeness was reserved just for me.

The dwarf bowed to the girl behind the desk. "Thank you, milady."

Milady? Was she some kind of royalty or was that normal? *Mom, why don't I know any of this stuff? You taught me all kinds of things about the fae, but nothing relevant!* At least relevant as far as I could tell. I waited while the dwarf left. Starren didn't say anything until the door clicked behind him. "A great retriever but a terrible gossip. That's why when he complains that we don't tell him anything, he's telling the truth."

"What do you guys want from me?" I asked, not even trying to find a polite way to get it out there. The sooner we got done in here, the sooner I could get out and the better chance I had of not being sent back to the group home because Dan thought I was being an idiot.

Starren raised an eyebrow. She turned to Wade. "Are you sure she's fae? She's too direct." True. I got that from the humans in my life. Fae were all tricks and games. Like Wade. Which reminded me how mad I was at him right now.

I turned a heated look toward Wade who had taken the seat beside me. He raised his hands as if to say no contest, he knew what I was thinking. "I don't really consider myself one of your kind," I said.

"Your services will only be forced for one job," Starren ignored my comment. "After it is complete, you will be able to choose if you wish to continue working for us or to be left alone in peace. One retrieval and you will be free."

"And clarify why I would trust you? You sure changed your mind quick, one week having me murdered and the next asking me to help you go after someone else." I really wanted to avoid getting caught up with these guys if at all possible. They were bad news, always. I had a feeling that was why Mom left Faerie in the first place.

Starren winced. "About that. Most fae's powers don't manifest until the day after their eighteenth birthday. According to your paperwork with the homes you've been at, you aren't there yet. You were supposed to be transported to Faerie where you could be properly trained. No one intended for you to die. How long have you been regenerating? Because you were unregistered, we don't know who your parents are and therefore don't have a good guess at your abilities. Do you have any other talents?"

"Wouldn't you like to know." Me too, actually. I wasn't supposed to start healing until eighteen? I'd started years ago.

"Trish, cut the crap," Wade mumbled. "Not here."

I ignored him, keeping my gaze on Starren. She seemed totally unfazed by my lack of cooperation.

"We suspected as much." Starren said. "We weren't even sure that you were fae. One of our trackers noticed something odd when he was doing a sweep and discovered you. Wade was sent to investigate. Once we knew that you were indeed fae, he was forced to act."

Forced? I sent him a glare to tell him I didn't believe it for a second.

"After our superiors heard of your ability, they decided to bring you in on this job. We are prepared to make you a deal. You obviously did not go back to Faerie. The Court frowns on this," Starren said. "In normal circumstances we would be taking you there now, with or without your consent."

So, she was a backstabber like Wade. Good to know. And this situation could become a whole lot more serious than I'd thought. Also good to know.

"If you help us complete this job, you will be left here where you wish to be. Otherwise you will be collected for training."

Collected? I held back a shiver. She said it so calmly, like it was an everyday thing. Maybe it was for her. My interest in bumping Wade off today was slowly waning as I figured out how bad a mess I was in. They would really just drag me off? What was I thinking, of course they would. And I'd just walked into their lair. This was so not good. I wiped my palms on my jeans, then snapped my arms up to my chest to keep it from happening again. Wade didn't need to know how I was feeling.

"As I said before, once this job is finished, you will be able to choose if you wish to continue working with us or not. I can guarantee you that the rewards for continuing to help with the Council's work are extremely beneficial. We are hoping this will be the first of many times you assist, that you may become part of the team eventually."

Okay, this was a little freaky. Why did they need me so bad that they would offer a deal like this? Something felt off. "So tell me about it. The job. I don't want to sign on without knowing what it is." I didn't want to sign on at all, but if it was something simple and they would leave me alone afterward, it would be worth it. If it was legit.

"Does it matter? Do you wish to be dragged to Faerie and placed in training?"

Good point. I eyed Wade in a sideways stare. I could probably get away from these thugs, but I would have to run for the rest of my life. That could potentially be a very long time. And there would be absolutely no chance of seeing Dan and Nina again. Unless it was at their funerals when the fae took it out on them that I had escaped.

But back to that whole why me thing. Didn't they have a whole civilization to choose from? Why would they ask me, someone they didn't know? Might as well find out. "Why do you even want me?"

"Your healing ability speaks for itself. It is an uncommon gift. And you know humans, which could be very helpful. The fae have studied them since the beginning of time and yet they still surprise us. You grew up among them. Also, the job may require someone that can blend in, and won't be easily recognized by another fae. If you agree to give the job at least some good consideration, I will give you the basics."

I crossed my arms tighter and slouched back in my chair, which was really uncomfortable. What did they do to these things to make a person want to sit straight? I ignored the ache and held my ground. Distrust the fae or not, it looked like I wasn't going to be given many options. "Fine. I agree." That needed clarifying. "To consider it."

"You must also agree to not speak of what I'm about to tell you to anyone other than those of us on this team. Including Cumat."

"That means no humans either, Trish," Wade added.

One of Starren's perfect eyebrows rose. "I should think that would go without saying."

"She grew up with them. She doesn't know any better."

Well that was vaguely insulting. This I had to think about for a second. It wasn't as quick a decision for fae, agreeing to something, because we can't change our minds whether the circumstances change or not. It had something to do with the no lying thing, but no one had ever really explained it to me. But who was I going to tell anyway? Somehow I didn't think Dan or Nina would take the news well. They knew I was kind of a brat, they didn't need to know I was a freak too. "Fine."

Starren touched something on her desk and a bright color photo of an extremely dreamy guy showed up against the far wall. Dark hair, dark eyes. All fae were good looking, at least the human type ones, according to my mom.

Somehow that seemed to have skipped me. I believed her though, now that I'd met a few. Even after what he'd done to me, I couldn't stop my gaze from wandering toward Wade. As soon as I noticed, I snapped my attention back to the picture.

"As hard as we try to keep Faerie and Earth separated, once in a while a new breach is formed that allows fae to travel to Earth without going through the proper channels." She stuck a thumb over her shoulder, pointing to the picture. "This is Jaden Martan. He found one of them."

Another tap on the desk and the picture changed. In this one Jaden no longer looked nearly as good. His face was haggard, eyes dark with exhaustion. I felt a pang of... something for him. Empathy maybe. That was probably how I had looked Saturday when the fosters showed up to save me from Vince and the Land of No Food but Junk Food.

"Why did he do it?"

Starren stopped talking at my question. I ripped my gaze from the picture and looked at Wade, who had a disgusted look on his still handsome face.

"Who did what?" Starren asked.

"Why did this guy disobey the rules and cross over when he had to know the consequences?"

Starren's face went stormy. "It's not for you to ask questions, just to do as you're told. This is the job you were assigned to, if you'd like the reward promised, you will listen and then accomplish the task." She took a breath. "He's a wanted criminal. Considered very dangerous. Several guards were severely injured during his escape."

"What was he in for?" So curiosity killed the cat. I'd just heal. Plus I was making Wade mad. Bonus.

"I was never told." Her face got that grumpy look again, and I wasn't sure if it was directed at me or the Council. She continued talking, but I just cocked my head and stared harder at the picture. What was his story? The fae were mostly a no rules society; except when it came down to revealing themselves to the humans. And listening to the Council if they told you to do something. Sure, if you broke one of the rules, you were pretty much dead, but there weren't a lot of them. What had he done to get himself locked up?

Everyone had a reason for the things they did, especially the major things like crossing between worlds when the stakes were so high. Maybe that was it. Maybe he thought on Earth he would have an advantage over humans, if he was as dangerous as Starren said he was. And she must believe it or she wouldn't be able to say it.

"You can act like a human, so you will be used to draw him away from any other humans. While capturing Jaden is high priority, nothing is ever more important than keeping the fae a secret. Then, after you have drawn him somewhere we will have access, you will keep his attention as Wade moves in."

Obviously the conversation had continued on without me. This slightly troubling bit drew me back in. "You're going to use me as bait?"

"What job did you expect? You can regenerate, you're the perfect candidate."

Was this how I came across to everyone? All snarky like this Starren? Maybe I needed to drop a little of the attitude after all.

"Well, yeah, but that doesn't mean I want to get messed up in the first place. It still hurts. Don't you have someone that regenerates and is trained to do this stuff?"

A look passed between Starren and Wade. "Regenerating is a rare gift. And the high fae prefer Faerie to Earth. We don't have anyone that could pass as a human. Looks, yes, mannerisms and speech, no. The few that are available, he already knows. You he won't even notice, he has no way of knowing you're fae."

I looked back at the pictures. He didn't look dangerous.

But I'd thought that about Wade too. "What are his powers?"

Starren just stared at me.

I looked at her and then to Wade, then back. "All fae have some type of power, right? What is his?"

"Not all of us have powers, Trish," Wade answered. Ugh, did he have to call me Trish? He didn't have that right anymore.

"Don't you know anything about Faerie?" Starren asked.

She didn't seem upset, just resigned.

But I did know quite a bit about Faerie. My mom had told me stories of the place like they were bedtime stories; only these weren't the happily ever after kind. Faerie was a rough place, where everyone cared only for themselves. The Council had final authority over everything, but basically left everyone to figure things out on their own. Survival of the fittest and all that. No, it was definitely not somewhere I wanted to go. Ever.

"Powers aren't supposed to manifest until eighteen. We have a week to catch him before we need to worry about that. We assume your records are wrong," Wade said, like he was reading my mind. "Do you know when your real birthday is?"

I had been healing since I was eight. Ten years early.

What did that mean?

I ignored Wade's question. If he thought we were going to be friends now, he was dead wrong. Not only had he tried to kill me, he had also only wanted to date me because of his job. He was toast where I was concerned. I was still bumping him off and sending him to Faerie if the chance came up.

"So he has no powers, but he's dangerous and was able to injure guards in Faerie and escape. Nice. What happens to him if we do catch him?" That was the part I wasn't sure about. Doubt wiggled through the pit of my stomach. Did I really want to be a bounty hunter? The actual job sounded kind of crazy, but nothing I needed to worry about physically. It was the whole getting involved with the fae thing that was giving me pause. What had the guy really done? It didn't matter in the end. If it was him or me, I was definitely picking me.

"He will be returned to the facility where he was being held in

Faerie, where he can be contained until the Council decides what to do with him. Are you ready to leave for California? His last known address is there. His home is being watched, but so far nothing. We will be searching any areas where our tracker can feel unregistered fae activity until we find the right one."

California? As in, on the other side of the country, California? "How am I supposed to miss school without my teachers noticing? What about Dan and Nina?"

"What about them?" Starren asked. "They are your foster parents, correct?"

Wade nodded at her and I glared his way for answering a question aimed at me.

"Yes. They wouldn't take kindly to me disappearing again." And I would worry them to death. But I didn't need to say that part out loud.

"Who said anything about disappearing? You will ask for a new foster home and one will be provided. One that is more, shall we say, open to the job description."

Nina's sad face filled my head and my stomach clenched. It would be so easy to get a new home after Lester's visit this morning, but as much as I complained to myself about them both, they had been nothing but kind. No, when it came down to it, they were the closest thing I had to family since Mom had left me. But I wasn't going to let these fae know that. Somehow I got the feeling they'd use that knowledge against me if they thought they needed leverage. I wanted badly to dislike my fosters, for their own safety, but they made that pretty difficult.

"How are you going to get me to California? I don't have any way of getting on a plane without my fosters."

"We have ways of traveling more quickly than humans," Starren said haughtily.

Portals. They had to have portals of some kind. Mom had mentioned them before. "If you find a way that the school doesn't complain I'm gone and give me an excuse for being home late every day, I'll help during school hours. If this doesn't work out I need a place I can go back to and I've got Dan and Nina trained." So that wasn't completely true, but it must have been true enough or my fae blood wouldn't have let me say it. I carefully kept all the emotion off my face. So far Starren hadn't been too happy when I tried to think for myself and so much hinged on this. If they were going to try to force me away from Dan and Nina, I wasn't really left with many options.

"You aren't giving the orders here," Starren gritted out between clenched teeth. So she had a temper. Good to know.

"Starren, be careful." Wade said. He jerked his head toward the corner and headed that way. Starren followed. "We're supposed to bring her in on this, no matter what." Obviously they didn't understand the fact that my regenerating also helped my body function better in every way, his voice was almost as loud as if he was talking straight to me. "Don't get her mad. She'll walk. Trust me, I know her. No matter what the incentive, her temper will get the best of her." So that's what he thought of me. Good. I thought a lot worse of him. "The Council won't be happy if we lose her."

Starren closed her eyes and a breath hissed out between clenched teeth. Apparently my personality grated on her. I got that a lot.

They came back over together, Starren hiding her emotions very well. Stereotypical fae. At least I had broken all the molds growing up with humans.

"Time is of the essence with this case. We can't allow a criminal to roam free here. We agree to your terms. Can you start tonight? Tell your parents you will be at a sleepover, or some such human nonsense. It will be close enough to the truth that you should be able to get it out."

Wade snorted. I glared.

"What?" Starren asked.

"Trisha? At a sleepover? She doesn't have any friends."

I glared even harder. So what if it was the truth, did he have to be such a jerk about it? I could be a jerk back and remind him that he was supposed to be my only friend. I sighed. That meant I was back to having no friends at all. Amy had been nice at the party, but I didn't think us hanging out for an hour made us friends.

Starren rubbed her eyelids. "I should have known. First light in the morning then. Surely you can find an excuse to leave for school early."

I nodded. Maybe this would be a good time to make some friends. At least friendly enough to be able to tell Dan and Nina I was heading to the movies or some such nonsense, hit the movie theater for five minutes and then come here. It was enough of the truth that I could get away with it, and they might lift the grounding if they thought I was being social. Now just to figure out how to make friends. On top of not being in school. I sighed again. Things were always so complicated.

"You may go. Prepare whatever you need before you come back in the morning. Seven-thirty sharp." She went back to looking at stuff on her desk. My blood started a slow boil. Did she really think she was so much better than me that she could just dismiss me like that? I was going to have to work with two jerks. At first she'd seemed okay, but I should have known better. My mouth opened by itself, about to hurl an insult, but I caught it. If I had to work with them, I needed to keep things as civil as possible. Just until we caught this guy. Then I was home free and could say anything I wanted and there was nothing they could do about it. I stood and stalked to the door.

Wade held it open for me on my way out, then followed me through the doorway and closed it behind us. I refused to look at him. Cumat was waiting for me on the other side.

"Ready to be escorted out?" he asked. No doubt they'd had him wait for me because they didn't want me getting curious about what was behind any of the other doors. They didn't need to worry about that. I'd met enough backstabbing, rude, obnoxious… and everything else fae to last me a lifetime.

I nodded at Cumat, not really wanting to talk. He didn't have the same problem. He chitchatted about everything and nothing as we walked up the hallway, but I wasn't listening. No matter what, I could not show these fae how I felt about Dan and Nina. That thought kept cycling through my mind, chased by worry. And I couldn't let them take me away. And I couldn't get killed by this criminal, or let Dan and Nina find out I was skipping school. Wonderful. Plus, I still wanted to do something to Wade. I just needed to figure out what.

Maybe stabbing him or whatever wasn't really a good idea anymore since he was supposed to be watching my back on this job.

We finally arrived at the entrance. "We'll see you tomorrow, right here," Cumat said cheerfully, like I was coming over for tea, not to hunt some runaway fae guy that I hardly knew anything about.

"Him or me" that was going to be my new mantra. And he was a criminal, which meant he had done something. At least that was what I was going to go with. Maybe I'd get a better idea of what in the morning.

The sun was just about where I'd left it. I hadn't been in there long. I looked back at the wall I'd just walked through. Nothing. I put a hand out and pushed, but was just met with rough, cool brick. I walked to my bike slowly, trying to sort things out internally. If I did what the fae wanted, they wouldn't be looking for another way to put pressure on me, so they wouldn't go after Dan and Nina. And hopefully they wouldn't be able to find a way around the leave me alone part. The fae were just as tricky as all the human legends said, at least from what my mom had told me. I was just going to have to be great bait tomorrow. My bike was right where I left it. I jumped on, flipped up the kickstand and started for home.

Once there, I coasted into the driveway, hopped off my bike then quietly tipped it up against the house before heading in the front door.

"Hi, honey," Nina called from her usual spot in the kitchen when the door slammed behind me. She must have been waiting. "How was school?"

"Fine," I answered, half-way up the stairs.

"I'm baking cookies." How had I not smelled that when I walked in? Too distracted. I needed to get that under control or I might end up dead for real. Mom would have whacked me upside of the head if she were here. "They should be done in about ten minutes, if you want to come do your homework down here."

Bribery. It was going to work today. I was starved. I turned around right there on the stairs and headed for the kitchen. I acted like nothing was wrong, threw my book bag on the table and leaned up on the green and black swirled marble counter.

"What kind?" I asked. I probably could have been more polite, but now I couldn't get the smell out of my mind.

Peanut butter.

"Peanut butter chocolate chip. But they aren't ready yet."

I waited until Nina turned to put a tray in the oven and swiped a large hunk of dough from the bowl. She would yell at me if she saw me do it, always worrying about salmonella poisoning or something. How was I supposed to explain to her that I didn't have to worry about that? She started to turn back and I popped the whole wad into my mouth.

"How was school today? Did anyone bother you about missing Friday?"

I shook my head, trying to swallow the dough without choking, the amazing peanut butter/chocolate taste filling my mouth.

Nina raised an eyebrow, then went back to putting dough on a cookie sheet like nothing had happened. I watched her in silence. When had she become so important to me? It wasn't so long ago that I would have jumped at the deal Starren had offered today. A foster home that wasn't really a foster home. That could have been awesome. I could do my own thing, not worry about keeping my secret. But somehow, this was so much more awesome. I dropped my head on the counter. Why was life so confusing?

"You okay?" Nina asked over her shoulder. I left my head on the welcoming coolness of the counter and did a strange nod thing. She turned back to start putting ingredients away. I lifted my head, waiting for an opening. There. I swooped in for another chunk of dough.

"Have you thought about what you'd like to do for your birthday?"

I almost choked on my wad of dough. "What?" I got out around a fit of coughing.

"We didn't do anything last week, with everything that

happened. I'd really like to have some type of party. Maybe we could invite your school friends?"

"Ah, no. But thanks." I was never going to want to celebrate my birthday again. I mean really, what could top my sixteenth? Lying dead out in the woods somewhere. Or mostly dead. Whatever. I still hadn't sorted that out.

She leaned over and put the next cookie tray in the oven, brushed off her hands and leaned on the counter. "You sure? It isn't every day you turn sixteen."

"Yeah, I'm sure."

Nina raised an eyebrow and stared me down for a moment. I almost cracked.

"This isn't about your mom, is it?"

"No," I answered. I hadn't even thought of that.

"Okay, it's up to you, honey." She turned around and checked on the first tray of cookies she'd put in the oven.

"Nina?" I asked tentatively after a moment. She might not be my real mom, and she certainly wasn't an awesome fae like my mom was, but she tried. Hard.

"Yes?" she answered, sounding distracted.

So many things raced through my mind. I couldn't get all mushy on her, she would know something was up. But what if we weren't able to catch this guy? What if the fae did drag me away? After last week, Nina and Dan would believe the worst. Believe that I just didn't want to be with them. I had to see this through. "Never mind."

Nina chitchatted while the cookies finished in the oven. I made a show out of trying to get my homework done while I waited, then polished off six cookies before Nina made me stop, telling me I'd ruin my supper. As if that was possible.

The rest of the night was spent in beautiful routine.

Normally it drove me nuts, but today, with the chance of it all going up in flames tomorrow, it felt nice. Dan got home, kissed Nina and then asked about my day. He seemed to study my answers closer than usual, but didn't have any comments. After spaghetti, he asked if I needed help with my homework like he did every night, and like every night I told him no, only this time I said it nicer. He really was a good guy, I just had daddy issues.

I did my homework, spending extra time on each problem. Whatever way Starren came up with to get me out of school, I didn't want to ruin it by doing sloppy work. My mind kept wandering. How were things going back at headquarters? Hokey, I know, but I didn't know what else to call the place. The fae distribution center? I brushed my teeth and changed into my pajamas in a daze.

"Goodnight," I yelled down the stairs to Dan and Nina.

Dan came to the base of the stairs. "Going to bed already? It's only nine."

I nodded. Best get as much rest as I could. If I could.

"Are you feeling okay?"

"Sure," I answered. I guess almost sarcasm wasn't considered lying, because I definitely was not feeling okay right now. "Tired."

"Okay then, see you in the morning."

I gave him a little wave and headed for my bedroom. I shut the door behind me, went over and collapsed on the bed. No, I seriously wasn't feeling okay right now. No matter how hard I tried to convince myself it was because of the danger, I knew in my heart it was because there was a chance I was going to be taken from the first family I'd ever been a part of.

Chapter 5

Breakfast the next day was quiet. Dan and Nina didn't have much to say and, with my guilty conscience, I couldn't think of a thing. As soon as I could get away without starting Dan's suspicious mind turning, I said my goodbyes and headed out. I took my book bag, checking to make sure the front pocket was still zipped. Not sure what one packed to go on a quest, I'd thrown in some cash and my phone charger.

Cumat was waiting for me outside the fake wall. "Good morning, Miss Trisha." First time I'd ever been called that. He took off and I followed him inside, the feeling of passing through the portal not quite as weird this time.

"What excuse did Starren give the school so they won't check with Nina about me skipping?" I asked as I followed Cumat down the long white hall. We were probably headed for the same door we went through yesterday, but since I hadn't counted and all the doors looked the same I couldn't tell for sure.

Without answering, Cumat flung one of the doors open, bowed and gestured for me to go ahead of him. I stepped in and then nearly jumped back out of the room.

"Trisha Penchant, meet your doppelganger," Wade's voice came from somewhere over by the far wall. I'd missed seeing him until he spoke up, so busy staring into my own face that I had no idea who else was in the room. I really needed to work on that. The whole tunnel vision thing.

I waved my hand in front of the other me's face. She was even dressed like me. This was so awesome. I was never going to school again. Creepy thought though, how had they known what I was wearing today?

Wade pushed off the back wall where he had been leaning and sauntered toward us.

"I will tell Ms. Starren you are here," Cumat said. He left and shut the door.

"She isn't perfect. She might not answer questions correctly and won't talk much, but she should get you through the day without anyone knowing you're gone. They'll just think it's one of your space cadet days." He lifted an eyebrow and gave me that grin, the one I used to not be able to resist. Used to. The grin slipped off and he got a puppy dog look on his face, one that I'd never seen before. "Trisha, I..."

I growled at him but didn't have a chance to say anything before the door swung open again. Starren marched in, followed closely by an almost running Cumat.

"Are you two quite ready yet?" she asked.

"Yep," Wade answered, going back to not talking to me now that other people were here.

"I'm not, how'd you get another me?"

Starren barely glanced at me. "Someone else's gift. I told him I wanted another you, here she is. Her clothes have switched three times today, know anything about that?"

I felt my face flush red. I'd been trying to find a good questing outfit, then figured out the temperature in California might be warmer than here and changed again. I was done asking questions now.

"Cumat," Starren said, nodding toward me number two, "take... that to Trisha's school. Make sure it gets inside, but don't be seen."

Cumat muttered something grumpy under his breath. "What?" Starren asked sharply.

"Nothing. Nothing at all. Come along, doppel." He waited until the second me was through the door, then slammed it behind them. It had to be hard for the poor guy, a dwarf working for the fae. Lots of species lived in Faerie, not just the fae, and they didn't usually get along. He probably had a pretty interesting story. At some point long ago in history he would have been considered fae too, but the classes had been split by a previous Council and now dwarves were of the lower class. Assuming that some of Mom's bedtime stories were more than stories.

"So are we just supposed to wander up and down the streets of California looking for this guy? How do you even know that's where he is?" I asked once the door was solidly closed.

Wade snorted. "No." He nodded toward the far wall. There was a slight kid sitting there, his blond hair almost covering his eyes, big framed glasses sitting on his nose. Between me number two and Wade, I hadn't even noticed him. His features were much more petite than Wade's, not as masculine. Until now, Wade was the only male fae I'd ever met, so this was interesting. This kid may not have looked like I would have expected, but he was still really cute.

"That's where Cray comes in." He must have seen the blank look on my face. "He can sense fae energy. Anything out of the ordinary passed by an area in the last three days and he'll know. He's been out in Cali the last two days already, getting a lead for us. Now it's our turn to come in and protect him, just in case Jaden has caught on."

I watched the kid for a second. Okay, maybe not kid, he had to be older than me to have his powers if he went by normal fae rules and didn't cheat like I had somehow. What was his story? What made him so sad and quiet? Maybe his girlfriend had killed him. Just the thought made me send a glare at Wade. He shrugged, looking mystified. Like he didn't know what I was miffed about.

"Ready?" Starren asked the kid in the back in a surprisingly gentle tone. Sure, she'd started out like that with me at first too. It would be interesting to see how she treated him by the end of the day.

The kid, Cray, nodded. Starren walked over and grabbed a backpack off her glass desk, then charged for the door. Did she rush everywhere she went?

Wade took off right behind her, then me after him. I heard Cray's footsteps following me. Starren turned left out of the door, heading deeper down the long hallway. If we just kept going, how long would it take us to reach Faerie? I squinted, trying to see a change, to guess how long the passage was, but it just stretched on and on.

Starren stopped three doors down from her office. I made it into the room just in time to see her open another door, step through and disappear. Poof, just like that, she was gone. Wade didn't even pause, then he was gone too. I waffled for a moment. Mistrust of Starren and Wade aside, this would have been really interesting. But as it was, a little intimidating. I glanced toward Cray, who just looked at me like I was crazy.

I took a deep breath and jumped through the portal after Wade, hoping against hope there wasn't a padded cell on the other side. The others didn't know it was them I was unsure of, not the portal or destination. Out of the four of us, I had the least to worry about going into dangerous situations. I couldn't hold them up and look like a wimp. I got the impression Starren didn't care much for weakness and it would be really bad if she changed her mind and decided to just snatch me. I got the feeling there was another reason they wanted me, other than just Jaden wouldn't know my face and I had a handy gift. Which just made this an even more wonderful experience.

Instead of bright sun like I expected, jumping to Cali and all, here there was just a light glow all around us. Was it still sunrise here? How far behind us were they time-wise? I got my sight back, adjusting to the dimness after the bright white of the hallway. Great. Another woods. As if I needed a reminder to watch Wade. Things looked familiar, the kind of trees anyway. I'd been here before, a long time ago with my mom. Yosemite, or somewhere close. And here I thought we would get to go shopping after we were done taking this guy down.

Something crashed into my back. I jumped forward and twisted around in one move. Oh. Maybe I should have stepped away from the portal. "You okay, Cray?" His big glasses were askew on his face, his eyes wide behind the lenses. He pushed his glasses up on his nose and nodded.

Were glasses normal for fae? I had perfect vision, but was that because of the regenerating thing?

"I brought us in a mile from where you suggested, Cray," Starren said. "I didn't want to drop right in on him in case he knows we're coming. There haven't been any signs to indicate something else fae could be in the area, so it should be him. Can you feel anything?"

He closed his eyes for a moment, then they flew open and he nodded.

"Lead the way," Starren said.

Cray looked nervous for a second, then moved forward.

I followed the team, not really paying attention to Wade or Starren as I studied Cray. Being able to sense fae energy would really come in handy, especially when you wanted to avoid fae in general. Not that I didn't like the regenerating thing, but that would probably have been more helpful for me. I'd have never gotten involved with Wade in the first place. Never hung out with him, never started to lo-… nope. Not going there.

The amount of light was growing. We really must have hit here just at sunrise. Trudging through the woods, small sticks and plants breaking underfoot, the smell of the trees. It all brought back memories of the last time I went hiking. I glanced at Wade to see if he was thinking the same thing, but he wouldn't look at me. That either meant he was, or he was so focused on the job ahead he hadn't noticed. A thought made my evil side happy. We could trudge around in these woods all they wanted. Blisters. I was immune. How about these city fae?

A mile on city streets should only take a person fifteen minutes. Out here where we had to dodge around rocks and massive trees, it was a good half hour before Cray stopped us, looking down into a dished valley.

"The energy is coming from that hill," Cray said. It was the first time I'd heard him speak. His voice was surprisingly deep.

"Trisha," Starren said.

"Yeah, yeah, I know. Go be bait."

"Be careful," Wade said. Strange coming from the guy that had killed me last week. And I still wasn't sure they weren't trying to kill me now. Something seemed off about this whole situation. I ignored him, took a breath and started down the slight grade.

It leveled off after a couple minutes and soon after the trees thinned. Before they were gone I paused, staring at a strange hill in the middle of the forest floor. "I feel you, Atreyu. I hope this doesn't turn out to be a giant turtle, I don't want to get snotted on," I muttered. I'd probably watched too many movies at the children's home. Something about the two worlds in that one made me think about Faerie, thereby reminding me of my mom. I'd watched The Neverending Story a bejillion times. I glanced back at the trees, hoping to see Starren. For once, I wanted her to tell me what to do. They were gone.

"They're probably just trying to get me killed," I snarled quietly. If I didn't know that the fae couldn't lie, I'd be running the other way right now. It was get this job done or get dragged to some world I didn't know anything about, with people I didn't know. I'd had enough of that growing up, thank you very much.

A step. Another. Something sniffed. I froze.

I didn't move for a few seconds, then almost laughed at myself. A sniff? Really? Was that Jaden's new, unknown power, a super sniffer? I laughed at myself quietly until the sound came again, louder and longer.

Okay, no way that was Jaden. A bear? That would not be cool. I'd heal while it did the damage, but how long until it decided to let me be? Ouch. I backed a few steps away slowly.

The earth began to shudder, nearly knocking me to the ground. The little hill shook, dirt rained down as something stood up from underneath it, knocking the soil from its body. My fingernails bit into my hands. Maybe a bear wouldn't have been so bad. This thing was massive, its stony looking head nearly as tall as the trees.

Without warning, whatever it was moved over to a small stand of trees and ripped one out by the roots. It paused to get its bearings, more dirt raining down off its greyish skin.

"Oh crap," I whispered as its gaze finally found me. It hefted the tree up like a club and took a step in my direction, covering the distance between us in that one stride. The club came down hard, right at me. I jumped to the side and it missed. The impact of the club on the ground still knocked me off my feet, dirt and small stones raining down on me. A fist sized rock slammed into my arm.

I tried to catch my breath, flat out on my back, the wind knocked out of me and my arm screaming in pain. That's going to leave a mark, the nearly hysterical thought ran through my mind. At least for a few minutes. I looked over to assess the damage. Shoot. My sleeve was shredded and my clothes, unfortunately, would not regenerate like the rest of me. Nina was going to have a fit when she saw this. I scooted back a little but had to bite my lip to keep from yelling as my hip and side shrieked. I'd landed on a rock and hadn't noticed while I was trying to catch my breath.

A rumbling started. The thing was trying to talk. It had massive moss green eyes with big crooked teeth hanging out of its mouth. The rest of its body looked fairly human, other than the size. It rumbled something again, then coughed.

Troll or ogre? What was the difference?

I rolled over to stand and a crunch sounded from my pocket. Shoot again. My phone. I pulled it out. The screen was shattered. Great. No time to worry about it right now. I stuffed it back in and moved into a crouch.

The troll took a step toward me, ground shaking under its massive foot. So this was why California had so many earthquakes. So much for the fault theory.

"I'm gonna rip your head off your body," the troll finally got out. I could barely hear the words, his voice was so deep.

I wished I hadn't been able to understand because for the first time since I'd started regenerating, I felt a thread of panic. How did that work? Even I probably couldn't recover from that.

"Starren, Wade, where are you?" I muttered under my breath.

The troll swung again, this time making contact and sending me flying. I crashed into a tree and rolled to the ground. A groan slipped out of my mouth, my body frantically trying to deal with the damage. The troll shuffled my way. I stood and limped toward the trees, panting, fast as my battered body could move.

Two gunshots sounded and then there was Wade. A confusing amount of happiness went through me. It was just because he was saving my life. And he was just saving my life because the team needed me. He didn't come forward, just raised his gun again.

The troll didn't even notice the shots. The bullets must not have penetrated. Didn't fae have anything better to use than a human weapon? Suddenly there was Starren, standing between me and the troll, some type of bright sword in her hand. Where had that come from? She swiped a couple figures in the air.

The troll lumbered to a stop, confusion on its massive face. "What you want, Fae? Leave my supper alone."

Not just something to be crushed then. Dinner. So much better. That hysterical feeling was back, full force.

"This isn't supper. She's fae too. You know the rules."

A massive hand went up and scratched the tuft of hair on the things head. "She no look fae. Clothes human."

Starren relaxed a little, letting the tip of her sword sink toward the ground. "Yes, she does have some style issues, but she is one hundred percent fae, I promise you. And you know I can't lie."

A nod started slowly. "I believe you. But I'm still hungry. And we aren't in Faerie, so no rules."

Starren tensed back up, the sword slipping into a defensive position. "Take another step and lose a finger," Starren snapped. "And after that a hand. We'll see how far you get before you're lying on the ground in pieces."

A low growl came out of the troll's mouth. It stared at Starren hard for a moment, then turned and started away. It vanished between trees on the other side of the clearing, its footsteps still shaking the ground for a good couple minutes before they started to fade.

"Now what?" I asked Starren.

She slid her sword into a sheath on her back and it disappeared. I blinked, but it was still gone.

"Now we hope that wasn't what Cray was sensing and that Jaden is actually around here somewhere."

Seriously? She was just going to go on with the mission? "We can't just leave it here," I said.

"What?" she asked, like I wasn't making any sense at all.

"We can't just leave it here. What if some poor hiker comes along and gets eaten?"

"The things of Faerie have a way of not being seen if they choose. If a hiker gets eaten, everyone will think it was a bear, or some other Earth creature."

"What? How can you say that so calmly?"

Starren looked genuinely confused. "They're just humans, why do you care?"

"Is that what you two think?" I turned and asked Wade and Cray. They were barely out of the trees, I had just caught sight of them out of the corner of my eye. "Where were you anyway?"

"You don't want to make a troll uncomfortable. Once Starren got his attention I knew she would get him talked out of eating you, so I moved back into the trees. Too bad for him she didn't let him have you, that would be the last lunch he ever needed. You'd just keep coming back." Wade started laughing at his idiotic joke.

"You really don't care if people get killed?"

Wade calmed down a little. "You've lived here too long, Trish. You need to make a trip to Faerie, then you'll understand. These people are not your kind."

"So what?" I exploded. "They're still people!" I had so much on my plate right now that I shouldn't be worrying about a troll, but for some reason I just couldn't let it go. What if the hiker that got killed had a kid waiting at home for them? What if they had a kid with them when it happened? For that matter, what if it was a kid? It was that great power, great responsibility junk. "Whatever. I'm not leaving until that troll is sent back where it belongs. How did it get here anyway?"

Wade crossed his arms and glared at me. But he must have seen the expression on my face, because he sighed and loosened up after a second. "There must be a cave or pool around here that has a hole between worlds," Wade said. "If we put enough pressure on the troll, he'll go back on his own and we can report the hole. Then we've taken care of the problem and the Court will thank us for finding the hole."

"What about Jaden? The more time he spends here, the greater likelihood he's getting into trouble. He could be much more dangerous than that troll if he isn't taken care of," Starren said. "And we don't have much time before he gets his powers."

"He could be more dangerous. Or not. We don't know." I crossed my arms. "I'm not asking about this. It needs done."

"She's stubborn, Star. No use arguing when she gets like this," Wade said.

"Maybe we don't need her as bad as the Council thought," Starren said, her eyes going into slits. "Cray, let's go. You can find the kid, I'll drag him back, with or without these two."

Cray looked uncomfortable. He looked to me like he was asking for help.

"He thinks we should take out the troll," I said for him.

"Cray?" Starren asked.

He nodded.

"This is ridiculous, I can't find Jaden without you, Cray. I don't have any idea where to start looking. Let's go."

Cray shook his head and moved over to stand by me.

Starren's eyes narrowed into slits. "Are you sure about this?"

He nodded again.

"Wanna explain it to me?" He shook his head.

Starren closed her eyes. "Fine. Be it on your heads if Jaden gets away and the Council holds us accountable." She stared hard at each of us until we nodded in turn. "Then let's go hunt a troll."

Chapter 6

I'd survived my first battle. Not too impressive considering I was able to survive being shot point blank, but still, it was something. The other two probably wouldn't even consider that a battle, but I was going to. It was life threatening, after all. I bet Cray would agree with me.

"Can you feel where he went, Cray?" Starren asked. Cray nodded and headed off north… or was it west?

It didn't matter. We followed him in silence. I took a deep breath as we walked. Mom had hauled me all over the U.S., but no other place we'd visited had smelled as good as this one. Just being here again brought back memories, picnics and sleeping in our car until a ranger caught us and kicked us out of the park after dark. Good times. At least it had felt that way to a nine-year-old. I'm glad now that I hadn't known then that Mom and I would only be together another month, before she dropped me at the kids' home.

Wade stopped ahead of me, nearly sending me straight into his back.

"What are you doing?" I growled.

He put a finger to his lips and moved to the side so I could see. A gorgeous waterfall sparkled down the rock face ahead of us, marred only by the ugly appearance of my troll. And… another troll? Two more trolls? Wait, not one, not two, but four trolls? One had almost gotten the best of me, now there were four?

"What now?" Wade asked.

"We should call this in, wait until the Council can get more people here," Cray said.

"Can't." Starren drew her sword. "They might move on before the Council sends anyone. Plus we have a job to do. The sooner we get this over with, the sooner we can get back to it. And we don't want any hikers showing up while we're waiting."

"So? I thought you didn't care about humans?" She gave me a withering look, but I wasn't being mouthy this time. I just actually wanted to know.

Her expression eased as she realized I was being serious. "One troll and the humans would think it was a bear. This many and we are in for major problems and major cover-ups. Easier to handle it before things escalate."

"The portal here must be huge, for trolls to find it. They aren't the brightest of creatures," Wade said.

Starren nodded. "We take down one of them and the rest will run. They aren't social creatures, so they won't know how to fight as a group. They will run to where they feel safe, which will be home, leading us to the portal."

Somehow that didn't sound like a plan to me. Attack one, take it down, make the rest run and then chase after them? But who was I to say anything? It was better than me being bait.

"You and you," Starren said, pointing to Cray, then me. "Follow us down and let them think we are evenly matched, but don't get involved. I don't want to have to rescue you again."

Rescue me again? Well wasn't that rude. She was the one that had put me in the situation in the first place! I opened my mouth to let her have it, but noticed Cray watching me. I snapped my mouth closed and stared back. He looked down, avoiding further eye contact.

"What about weapons?" I asked. Surely that was a reasonable question.

Without answering, Wade walked away from me, scanning the ground. He kicked a couple small sticks before finding one that must have suited him. He couldn't be serious. Never mind, he was doing something with it. He closed his eyes and concentrated. The wood slowly re-formed itself into a sword. Probably not too strong, but it looked good. And pointy. Pointy was good.

"Thanks," I managed when he handed it to me. I looked at Cray again, mostly to avoid looking at Wade, and noticed that he'd made himself one too.

"Can all fae do that?" I asked Cray.

He nodded. "A little bit."

Okay, that was new. Mom had taught me all about the history of the fae, had even started weapon training and made me as close to a black belt in hand to hand as a nine- year-old could get, but she said I wasn't ready when it came to the powers. It had always sounded to me like she had planned to teach me some day, but then she'd disappeared. I'd never been able to figure out what had changed, no matter how long I'd spent thinking about it.

"Set?" Starren asked.

"Yep," Wade answered. They went shoulder to shoulder and stepped out of the tree line. Clearly this wasn't their first battle together.

Cray and I looked at each other, then mimicked them, walking so close we bumped into each other every few steps.

Trolls really were very dumb. Sure, I'd seen plenty of movies, read plenty of books that showed how stupid they were, but humans got most things wrong about the worlds they couldn't see. Like the fact that trolls turned instantly to stone in sunlight. I figured the intelligence level, or lack of, I guess, had been exaggerated. Apparently not. We were super close by the time my troll noticed us. The only reason I could tell our troll apart from the others was that its skin was slightly pink on top of the grey, like it had been in the sun too long.

The whole sun turning them to stone thing was a myth, but they did burn, really, really easily. I would have felt bad for the poor guy if he hadn't been planning on eating me thirty minutes ago. He must have been back long enough to forget the whole incident, none of them looked too worried. I wiped my sword hand down my shredded jeans before gripping the hilt again. Things were about to get interesting. As if they hadn't been before.

Starren marched forward until she was close enough to yell. "On the authority of the Council, I command you all to leave the human realm and return to Faerie."

"She can't do that, can she?" one of the smaller ones asked, the words slurred as it continued to pick at its broken yellow teeth with a tree limb while it talked.

"Course not," one of the bigger ones answered. "She's little."

Our troll slunk away from Starren. "Little, but she's mean. She wouldn't let me eat that one today," he pointed a finger at me. At least it passed for a finger, it was about as big around as an electric pole.

Another one, this one very small, popped out from behind the waterfall. "Can we eat them? Please?" Great. Five. Any more that we hadn't counted hidden in there?

"Yes, go, eat," the next-to-biggest said. Its voice was a little higher. Female?

"Yay!" The small one jumped down from a ledge, shaking the ground under me. My body jerked, but I stayed on my feet. I looked over to see if Starren had noticed. Nope.

Starren and Wade moved into battle poses, swords up.

"I think this is where we get out of the way," Cray whispered, tugging on what was left of my sleeve.

Yes, this was the point Starren had wanted us to get out of the way, but I would heal and the two of them wouldn't. At least not as fast, or from as bad of injuries. Plus, Starren didn't know that Mom had done some training with me before she left. Sure, that was seven years ago and I was pretty young, but being fae had to count for something. I wasn't going to leave Starren. The trolls could have Wade.

Cray left when I didn't budge. Whether it was the troll he was scared of or Starren was anyone's guess.

The adult trolls watched as the youngest started our way. None of them seemed concerned.

"Do we have to kill the baby?" Cray called from his new position at the tree line.

Wade snorted.

"He has a point," Starren said. "We go after one of the adults, we scare them. We kill their little plaything here and they'll be mad. No killing blows."

"Seriously?" Wade complained. "Finally a real fight and no killing. I've been waiting on this for months, been stuck in a city trying to…" he trailed off, studiously ignoring me. "Never mind."

He'd better say never mind. If we didn't need him to help get rid of these trolls, I'd poke this sharp stick he'd made me straight through his body. Stuck in the city courting me, that's what he'd been about to say.

"Lover's quarrel later, troll right now," Starren interrupted.

The baby was getting close, no fear whatsoever on its face. Wait. Did their faces show emotion? It reached down, grabbed a rock and hurled it toward Starren. She jumped lightly out of the way, the rock not even coming close. It flew past her and hit a tree, exploding a hole right through it. Ok, scary. Even the kid could throw that hard? No wonder we'd stopped all the way back here.

"New plan. Trisha, keep it distracted while Wade and I hit an adult," Starren said over her shoulder.

Great plan. The troll threw another rock at Starren. For some reason it liked her.

"Hey you, ugly. Over here." I waved my arms. When that didn't seem to work, I put my hand to my mouth and let out a piercing whistle.

All the trolls clapped their hands over their ears. "Don't like that," the little one whined.

I did it again.

"Stop," one of the big ones roared.

"Keep it up, Trish," Wade called as he bounded forward.

Starren went around the other side and the fight began.

Putting all the force of my extra good lungs into it, I whistled again. Something whistled back. I noticed that the sound was coming from a rock headed my way with barely enough time to duck. The young one was not happy. It charged me, hardly giving me time to get my hand to my mouth to whistle again.

Huge, angry voices came from the direction of the waterfall. Starren and Wade were having no problem hacking at the trolls, who didn't seem to notice as they started my way.

"I think maybe it worked too well," Cray said from behind me. I'd almost forgotten he was here.

"I think you're right. Run."

Cray took off one way and I took off in the other. No use them chasing us both when it was me they wanted to pull to pieces.

"Rip its arms off so it can't squeal like that," one of the voices growled behind me. How would my regenerating body handle that? I sucked in an extra breath, pushing forward even faster. Probably just heal over the stump, but I surely didn't want to find out.

"Head for the lake!" Starren's voice.

I changed directions toward an opening in the trees.

Hopefully that was the lake.

Right, left, left, right. I dodged around trees, branches smacking me in the face and leaving welts for a few seconds before they healed. An object whizzed past my head. I didn't take the time to figure out what it was. My heart nearly pounding out of my chest, I burst out of the tree line. A half- sob of relief leaked out. There, the lake, after twenty feet of plants and ten feet of small stones.

Adrenaline pumped. I could do this. I charged forward, made a flying leap into the water and swam toward the middle like mad, my warm weather clothing weighing me down.

Angry roars and yells echoed out over the lake. I swam out until I needed to rest, treading water to conserve a little energy. With the healing back at the clearing, I was starting to get hungry. I could hear the trolls arguing. They were deciding if I was worth getting wet over. If this wasn't so depressing I would laugh.

"You're the strongest," one of the smaller ones sniveled at the biggest. "Water won't make you sick, no, not water. You'll just be clean. And smell bad."

"Go," the big one commanded. It pushed the smaller one into the lake, sending a wave of water my way. I coughed as it got in my mouth.

"You," the big one pointed at another brute, "other side. Make sure it don't go that way."

The one ordered to not let me escape on the other side lumbered off. The sniveling one tried to climb up on shore, but was met by glares from the other two. It slowly started wading my way, the water not even to its knees. How deep was this lake? I was a goner if it could touch all the way out here. *Starren, Wade, where are you?*

Chapter 7

Think, think, think! The troll was getting closer. No panicking, just thinking. Ding. Idea. Thanks to Wade. I blew the air out of my lungs and slipped under the surface. I paddled a few feet away and sank down to the bottom, murky water hiding the once bright orange of my t-shirt.

Yuck. But the weeds down here would be great camo.

Yelling started above the water. Being underwater when someone yelled above the surface always sounded weird. Multiply that by ten when it's a group of trolls. A minute later a huge head plunged under the surface, big eyes searching for me. I scrambled away, unable to tear my gaze from the huge creature. It only made it a second before going back up. Soon it was joined by another set of eyes. Closer, closer. I tried to sink deeper, dredging the bottom to cloud the water even more.

It didn't work. The plants around me started going crazy, moving against the current. I headed toward a patch of some type of underwater weed, and it wrapped around me. I jerked back and it let me go. Um, that was a little weird. But I wasn't going to argue. I moved back in closer and the leaves of the plants slipped around me, blanketing me in the greenery. This could work. Maybe. Hopefully. Apparently my lungs could convert the little amount of oxygen in the water into something useable, but I wasn't going to take the time to think about that right now.

I knew the instant the troll caught sight of me. Its eyes widened and it gurgled like it was trying to shout under water. I stabbed upward with the wooden sword I miraculously still had in my hand and got it in the eye. It jerked back, and I nearly floated away in relief. But then the water turned red, hiding me better but making my stomach turn. I about lost the breakfast Nina had made for me. The plants worked together, pulling me backward as I freaked out. I'd never physically hurt anything before. I was still on my back, so I dug my feet into the mire at the bottom of the lake and did a strange crawl/float thing away from the troll as fast as I could.

The hollering and pounding got louder up top. A massive leg knocked into me, sending me twirling through the water. Two more sets of feet pushed by, dredging up junk from the bottom of the lake and making it impossible to see a thing.

Something grabbed me by the back of my shirt. I swung at it, the weight of the water slowing me enough that I didn't get a very good blow in. Whatever it was dragged me toward the surface struggling as hard as I could, then pulled me out onto the rocky beach.

I shoved away, trying not to let the air get into my lungs too quickly.

"Trisha? Trisha, can you hear me?"

I coughed out the water in my lungs. Wade. The sense of relief flooding me felt strange considering who had caused it. I slumped over, barely able to stay upright even while seated. He must have pulled me out. He pounded on my back. "Are you okay?"

"Yes," it came out a little too forcefully considering he had just risked his life to drag me out of the lake. I hacked a couple more times. "My cells still regenerate under water."

Wade looked nearly sick with relief. "All that blood. We thought…" he trailed off.

I held up my little sword and gave it a wave. "Wasn't mine."

"Glad you're okay. Let's go make sure they make it through the portal," Starren's voice came from somewhere behind Wade and she was off.

Too wrung out to brush him off, I let him prop me up against a log.

"I'll be right back." He gave me another concerned look and took off after her. I needed a moment to catch my breath. They seriously owed me at least that. How could Wade send so many emotions through me at the same time? Anger still, of course, but he had come into the lake after me, knowing full well how easily I heal and he didn't.

That was a Wade I didn't know. The Wade I'd thought I'd known only truly cared about himself. The Wade I'd found out he actually was had killed me. Now I was just confused. I'd love to believe he had a copy of him like I had at school for me right now, but he'd pretty much admitted what he'd done back at the Hall with Cumat.

Another cough forced its way out, removing what I hoped was the last of the water. I groaned and attempted to push myself to my feet. Someone grabbed me under the arm and helped me up. Cray.

"Thanks-"

"What were you thinking?" Cray yelled in my face, his getting red. I recoiled a bit. This wasn't the same calm kid I'd spent the day with, was it? "You better never do that again, we're a team. No solo."

I raised my hands, trying to cool him down. "Hey, I regenerate, and, as far as I know, you don't." He didn't answer. "I just didn't want you to get hurt."

"Well, don't do it again." He turned and followed Wade and Starren, back stiff with anger. What was his problem? I'd probably saved his life. This was so backward with Cray mad at me and Starren telling me she was glad I was okay.

I took off after him, even my regenerating body crying as I pushed it like I'd never pushed it before. How were the normal fae handling all this without stopping? Hurry. I needed to hurry. As little help as I was able to give, they might need it. I ran through a bit of brush following the creek and was back at the waterfall.

Hah. I could have saved myself the worry. One of the trolls lay on the ground, not moving. The rest were crowding each other through the waterfall, each of them trying to get ahead of the others.

Wade stood on top of the dead troll looking like some hero in a story. Starren was whacking at the trolls with the blunt of her blade, forcing them to move even quicker. I didn't see Cray.

I walked over to the massive dead troll and kicked its giant, dirty foot, almost taller than my head. "What do we do with this?"

"We'll get a squad in to take care of it," Wade answered from his perch. "Can't just leave it here, strange things happen when wildlife eat anything from Faerie."

I shivered at the thought. Once for the strange things that could happen, then again at the thought of something eating this dirty giant.

"They'll be half an hour," Starren said, sliding down the rocks leading up to the waterfall cave. She stood and knocked some of the dust off herself. "Settle yourself in. Some of us will have to watch the body. Where's Cray?"

"I don't know," Wade said.

"He helped me up and took off after you two, I haven't seen him since," I said.

"I'm here," his voice came from behind one of the larger trees. "I thought I felt something strange, but it's gone."

"Strange how?" Starren was right on him.

"I'm not sure." Cray was back to his normal, quiet self. "Just strange, like we're being followed."

"So can you feel humans too?" I asked.

"Yes," Cray answered. "If I know what I'm looking for. It's a little more work. There are a lot more of them around."

"So you aren't just following the feeling of fae magic in a non-fae world, you can track specific beings?"

Cray pushed his glasses up on his face, his eyes flicking from Starren to me, and back. "Sometimes. But I need to actually know them. I don't know Jaden, so I can't just track him like that."

Great. That pretty much cut out running if things went south. I sat down on the ground and leaned up against a rock, needing a second to recover from the last fifteen minutes.

"Cray and I are going to start trying to sniff Jaden out again. You two stay here and guard the body until the clean-up crew arrives. I stepped into Faerie and had a message sent." She grabbed Cray and took off before I had a chance to argue. She couldn't just tell me to stay here. And I wanted to hear more about Faerie, even if I didn't want to go there.

Had she really just stepped in and out of it while in the cave?

Just about to push to my feet and follow her, Wade's voice stopped me. "I wouldn't."

"What?" I knew what.

"Don't ruin your chances, Trish. Don't make her mad."

Ugh. I'd been pretty open with him back when we were dating, he knew me too well. Especially frustrating now, when I didn't know if anything he'd told me about himself had been true or not. Obviously his feelings hadn't been or he wouldn't have killed me. Or tried to kill me. Whatever, I was getting all mixed up.

Time crawled by, not helped by the fact that I couldn't check it on my phone. How was I going to explain that one to Nina? That along with the ripped clothing could make for an interesting night.

Wade passed the time by going through the dead troll's pockets. The pockets were huge. The first thing he discovered was some string the size of a large rope. He tugged and tugged, pulling more and more out until a shiny rock popped out, tied to the end. I sat there, pretending I wasn't paying attention, but really, how often did a person get to see the contents of a troll's pockets?

Next came out some more shiny stones like the first. They flashed in the sunlight. Wade must have seen the look on my face.

"From the shores of the Crystal Lake, in Faerie. It's beautiful there. He must have had a rock in his pocket and this is the sand left over."

I didn't answer him verbally, but when he held them out I took them. Unlike most stones or crystals, these were slightly warm. Whether they were that way naturally, that way from Wade's hand or still held the warmth from the troll, I didn't know.

"Can I have them?" It took quite a bit of effort to get the words out of my mouth, considering who I was asking, but something about the inner light of these things was mesmerizing.

"No. We aren't allowed to keep anything from there. Don't want any humans finding it on us. The cleanup crew will take care of everything." He took them from me and tossed them on the ground before sticking his arm back into the pocket. So gross, who knew what things that monster had put in there.

While Wade stuck his head into the opening almost the size of a tent, I scooted over and scooped up a couple of the stones. They were in my pocket in a flash. Good thing I'd had a lot of practice pilfering stuff. If these were just the leftovers from a rock the troll had thought was shiny, I could only guess at how big it had been.

Wade threw more random junk out of the pockets, but I stopped paying attention. The stones cooled as I played with them in my pocket. Strange.

A sound in the woods made me flinch. I jumped up and turned that way, lifting my wooden sword. I saw Wade out of the corner of my eye pull his not so fake sword and face that direction, subtly shifting his weight so his body moved between me and the woods. Nice thought, but that didn't even begin to erase the last week. He had a lot to make up for.

Cumat's head popped out of the tree line. "Is this the correct place?" I knew the exact moment he noticed the troll. His nose wrinkled and he sniffed loudly. "Obviously it is. What are we supposed to do with that?" He sighed. "Watch it for another moment. I'm going to have to ask for more help." He disappeared back into the trees. I could hear him talking to himself until the sound of cracking branches faded away. Poor guy, with his shiny shoes and pressed pants, he was definitely out of his element.

I kicked at a tuft of grass and pretended to ignore Wade.

When he acted all sweet, the way he only was to me, it reminded me of before. A couple times today he'd tried to take care of me. It had to be because I was part of the team. Had to be. Or he had some other reason, something worse. Whether it was that or not, I was going to tell myself it was. No room for that mess right now, I had plenty of others to deal with.

It took ten minutes for Cumat to show up again. This time he had a crew. My jaw nearly dropped. More fae in one place than I'd ever seen, not counting all the ones that had stuck their head out to watch me yell at everyone yesterday at headquarters. And all sizes and looks too. One guy might as well be a troll himself, he was so huge. At least he was dressed better, actually like a person except for the crazy colors of his clothes. Two more men followed them out of the woods, no doubt fae also, but nothing stood out about them.

"What happened?" Cumat asked Wade. "At least you had the decency to drop it in a forest, not in the middle of a city this time. I'm always having to clean up your messes," he muttered to himself without waiting for an answer. He walked around the troll, inspecting everything. "He's big enough that we will need to do a full sweep." He looked up into the giant's face, nearly tipping over backward because of the height difference. "Can you drag it to the portal, Jack?"

"Yes," the giant said, his voice making me feel a little better. At least he didn't sound like a troll. Didn't really look like one either, once I got over his size. "Shouldn't be a problem at all. One time I took care of two trolls bigger than this at the same time, and it was a rush job too."

"Good, good." Cumat looked at Wade. "Where is the portal? Starren mentioned it when she called for a clean-up team."

Wade nodded toward the waterfall. "Behind there."

"Did you hear that Jack? Get to it so our other friends here can do their job too."

The giant nodded, reached down and grabbed the troll by its ankles. He leaned back, the muscles cording in his forearms, his face going red. He let out a loud grunt, gave an extra tug and the troll moved, leaving a slight groove in the ground.

"You got this then?" Wade asked.

Cumat turned to look disapprovingly at Wade. "Of course I've got this. Don't you think I know how to do my job?" He turned back to yelling directions to the giant without waiting for an answer.

Wade shrugged, then started for the tree line. "Guess they don't need us 'til Cray comes up with something else to track. Might as well get you back."

"What happens if a hiker comes along and sees that giant?" I asked.

"It would have to be a special human to see any of those guys without them wanting to show themselves. Haven't you ever used that skill? That's something all fae share."

My mind flashed back to Waterton Heights, me sitting under a tree, alone, feeling invisible. "Not intentionally." But maybe I had been invisible. I was going to have to figure out how to do that, but I sure wasn't going to let Wade be the one that helped me learn. Now that I was thinking about it, Mom may have said something about it in our lessons. I could probably figure it out by myself. Or ask Cray. He seemed like an okay guy. Being invisible was definitely something that could come in handy, something I needed to learn ASAP. Maybe I'd be able to sneak out of math class.

Wade was walking in the opposite direction I thought we'd come from. Maybe I was wrong; I wasn't very good in the woods, that was certain. I paused. No, we had come at the waterfall straight on. Wade was taking us to the left of it.

"Where are we going?"

"Back."

He was so annoying. "I got that part."

"We have to get to a static portal. The one we came through is gone."

"So that portal can drop us anywhere, but we have to go to another portal to get back?"

"That's right," Wade answered.

"How far is the closest one?"

"Five more miles."

"Five miles?" I groaned. Hungry had become an understatement. With the healing, swimming and walking, I was burning a ton of calories. Besides, walking was so boring. Especially when it meant I had to spend time with him. We covered some ground in silence.

He must not have had anything to say and I didn't want to be the one to start a conversation.

He stayed silent and stealthy as the miles slowly trickled by. I swung my wooden sword at everything within reach. I watched Wade out of the corner of my eye. Why did he have to be such a hunk, even by fae standards? And why had he come into the lake after me? Grr, I needed to think about something else.

There was only a ten minute span where I was semi-content whacking at foliage. Eventually the boredom outweighed the fact that I was still ticked at Wade. "Why don't I have one of those swords like Starren's?" I asked. "Shouldn't I have something to protect myself with?" Plus they looked really cool.

Wade snorted. "You don't have one because you'd probably kill me." Okay, maybe there was some truth in that. "And swords like that aren't so easy to come by. Starren had to travel down into the HighCrest Mines and get the ore herself because no one else wanted to go in after it. That sword is one of a kind."

"What's so bad about the HighCrest Mines?"

"Ogres." He glanced back and must have seen the blank expression on my face. "Ogres are similar to trolls, only with the intelligence of a high fae. The High Crest Mines were taken over by them years ago."

And Starren had gone in there just to get metal for a sword? It was not a good sign that the Council thought it necessary to send someone like her after Jaden. What exactly had he done to get himself locked up in the first place? And why did they really want me to help her? I was having a hard time believing she really needed my help, especially after today. Not that the answers to those questions mattered much. I couldn't let anything stop me. If I didn't help, I'd be the one they were hauling away.

I squashed a small sense of guilt about the fact that I was trading some guy's freedom for my own. He was a criminal. And it wasn't like I was helping kill this Jaden guy, just bring him in. They wouldn't do anything to him unless he gave them a reason to; Starren had said so. They would get their guy, I would be off their radar, and everything would be good for all involved. Except Jaden of course.

This trip was taking forever. Poor Cumat, in his fancy clothes. Hopefully Jack the Giant would give him a ride. Ha. Jack the Giant. I hadn't caught that til just now. Kind of ironic. All this walking was definitely giving me too much time to think. What was with those plants back in the lake? I glanced at Wade, wanting to ask him but afraid to give something away. What that something was, I had no idea.

But this wasn't the first time nature had helped me. That tree, when I was trying to get out of the creek last week had helped me too. I watched Wade out of the corner of my eye. Thoughts of the tree reminded me yet again of what Wade had done to me. Or tried to do, whatever. Yep, too much time for thinking, for sure. Wade finally pulled us to a stop quite a while later.

"So," Wade said, then stopped. "About the children's home you lived in…"

I eyed him sideways.

He winced. "Never mind."

Okay, what was that? I would have pushed him, but it wasn't something I wanted to talk about. And he didn't do well with being pushed anyway.

We'd had so many good times. I would never have believed anyone if they'd told me he'd someday hurt me, betray me. I'd loved him, and I thought he'd loved me.

We kept on in silence, my mind whirling even more. "Here it is." Wade finally said, sweeping an armful of ivy off the face of a large rock. A door shape glowed in the stone. He gestured for me to go ahead of him.

"Huh-uh. I'm not going first." Maybe they hadn't found a way to kill me, but if they had a cage I wouldn't be able to do anything about it. If they caught Jaden without my help, they could say I didn't hold up my end of the bargain and haul me back to Faerie. I wouldn't put it past Wade, obviously.

Wade rolled his eyes and stepped through. Well this was great. Now he was over there waiting for me. Maybe I shouldn't have had him go first. Now what? If Starren and Cray'd had any luck and they no longer needed me, the three of them could be waiting to jump me. Okay, two of them, I couldn't see Cray jumping anyone. Oh well, I was going to have to risk it. Maybe a cage on the other side, but it was that or be stuck in California, with no way home and only the small amount of cash I'd thought to bring. I stepped through after him.

I popped out in a small office similar to Starren's. The only difference was that this one was bare. Wade was just walking out the only other door. So nice of him to wait and see if I followed him through the portal or not. I took off after him into the long hallway.

He stopped but didn't turn to look at me. "It could be a while before Cray locks on to the next target. See you tomorrow. Good-night, Trish."

I ignored him, pushing past him and charging down the hallway. All I could concentrate on was getting to my bike. I needed to see Nina, just to know she was okay. I wouldn't put it past the fae to snatch her on some lame charge, just to get me to try harder or some other stupid excuse and the more I thought about it the more worried I got. The hallway was empty, none of the heads sticking out of the doorways right now.

Going about normal life the rest of the day was going to be awkward after spending the morning fighting trolls. Not sure how to explain about my phone, I decided to just not bring it up.

Nina was working in the flowerbeds when I got home.

After leaning against the house in relief for a second, I scooted forward, trying to sneak past her. No such luck.

"Trisha, the school called."

Crap.

"Apparently one of your teachers was worried about you today." Nina straightened and wiped a gloved hand across her face. "Mrs. Hemp? She said you were acting strangely. Is everything okay?"

I bit my lip in relief. The doppelganger was working, at least the school still thought I was there. "Sure, everything is fine." It was fine now, at least.

Nina looked me over good, an eyebrow arching perfectly by

itself. I looked down. Shoot. I'd forgotten about the state of my clothes. "You're sure nothing is wrong?" she asked.

"Wrong? Oh no, nothing is wrong at all," I said, big cheesy grin on my face, blood drips all over my clothes. Hopefully it looked like paint from over there. My fae blood must believe in sarcasm to let me get that half-truth out.

"If you need to talk, I'm here. And if someone is bothering you, we will get it handled." I didn't answer and after a second of staring straight at me, she went back to pulling the last of the dead branches out of the flowerbed. Whew. She was going to ignore the fact that I had skin showing in all kinds of places the clothes I was wearing weren't designed to show. Oh well, weren't holey jeans the "it" thing right now?

"What was your bike doing outside of Wade's apartment all day? Is he giving you rides to school?" And wham, she got me by surprise. Were they spying on me? How did they know my bike was there?

"No, he isn't. There must be a ton of bikes in this city that look like mine." Nina's look told me she didn't appreciate my little side step. "Really, Nina, I'm fine." I could have told her that we broke up, but I didn't want to talk about it right now. I turned and headed for the house.

"Trish, wait." She pulled her gloves off.

I stopped but kept my back to her, keeping her barely in sight out of the corner of my eye.

"You know you can trust us, right? With anything? You are our daughter."

Could she just say that? Just feel that way for real? I didn't know how she could. Plus, she was probably thinking my secret was a school bully or some other teenage problem. How was I supposed to explain this? But at least she was trying. I might like it here, a lot, but that didn't mean I could completely trust her. I knew better than to trust anyone. And I was starting to trust her too much. I needed to nip that in the bud. So while every part of me screamed to go over and give her a hug, I didn't listen. "Thanks. May I go now?"

She sighed, the sound so sad it made me want to break down

and try to make her feel better. But no. That was probably what she was trying to get me to do. "Sure. Just be ready for supper on time."

That wouldn't be an issue. I was starving again. But the whole bike thing, that was an issue. I was going to have to be more careful about where I parked it. And about who was watching me on my way to school.

Chapter 8

The next morning I got to headquarters early enough to wave goodbye to the other me. She stared at me blankly before waving back, then heading out. Man, I was going to look even more stupid than I actually was until we found Jaden. I'd spent the whole night going over homework that somehow had been waiting for me on Starren's desk. I didn't ask. Other Me probably dropped it here. The homework had taken a lot more effort last night since I hadn't been in class that day, even if I didn't usually pay much attention.

The rest of the team was waiting for me when I got back to Starren's office, carefully counting doors so I didn't walk in on some other fae doing some other fae thing that I probably didn't want to know about.

"Cray has another hit," Starren didn't even take time to say hello. "Let's head out."

I followed them to the portal. Starren stayed focused and ignored everything. Wade totally ignored me. What was wrong with him? Polite yesterday and now this today? That guy had issues. At least Cray had the decency to smile at me. I returned it. We stepped through the portal together and instead of ending up in the forest, this time we were spit out in a dark, dirty alley of some city.

A strange sense of déjà vu swept through me, of not knowing where I was, making it hard to breathe for a second. It was okay, this was a city, not a forest. And people flowed by in both directions. I wasn't alone. But I still needed to know where we'd ended up. "What city is this?" I asked.

"San Francisco," Cray answered after waiting a second to see if either of the other two would.

San Francisco. See, not that bad. It was a cool city. I glanced at the others to see if they had noticed my near panic attack. Starren hadn't, or was acting like she hadn't. Wade was watching me. I sneered in his direction. The whole panic attack thing was his fault. I caught myself getting upset and nipped it in the bud. When he saw my look change his face went impassive.

Jerk. But it didn't matter. No way he could ruin this for me. I hadn't been to San Francisco in a while, and it was a neat place. Maybe we could hit Chinatown after checking out Cray's lead. They had the best restaurants.

Cray closed his eyes for a second. "About a mile from here."

"Ugh, why do these trips always involve so much walking?" I asked. "Can't the portal get us any closer?"

"We can't pop in too close, we don't know his ability. If he has anything like Cray does, he'll feel the portal being used and he'll be gone before we have a chance to lock onto him," Starren answered.

That made sense, but it didn't make me feel much better about the walking. "I still don't get how you don't know what his ability is."

"It hadn't manifested yet when he escaped."

Starren glanced back at me and kept walking. I jumped forward to keep up with her. "Part of the reason he's considered so dangerous is that he's a direct descendant of a previous royal couple and has not had his eighteenth birthday yet, so his powers are unde-termined. The fact that he escaped without them is disconcerting, once he has his power we don't know what he'll do."

"When is his birthday?" I asked, stepping over a trolley line. Glad I noticed it before I fell flat on my face.

"November ninth on a human calendar," Starren answered.

"You mean we have less than a week to catch him before he becomes a super-villain?" I squeaked.

Starren's forehead crinkled in the first sign of confusion I'd ever seen from her.

"A bad guy with powers," Wade interrupted. "She made me watch a lot of superhero movies."

I stuck my tongue out at him. A man walking toward us gave me a funny look. I gave him a glare and went back to the conversation. "Is there any way to know what powers he might get once he turns eighteen?"

"No accurate way," Wade said. "We can do some guessing, considering his family line. But if we get it wrong, things won't go well for us, preparing for one ability and he actually has another."

"So, being descended from the royal couple, he's a prince or something?" And we were hunting him down like an animal?

"No, he is a descendant of a previous royal family," Starren said, like that should make things obvious.

"We aren't humans. Our leaders aren't chosen by who's next in line," Wade explained. "His grandparents led the fairy court for a hundred years, then were exiled."

"What did they do?"

Wade shrugged.

Did they not know anything, or was that his way of avoiding the question? "Why are you worried about him having his powers when he isn't eighteen yet?"

"The birthday we were given for you was false, who is to say his was recorded correctly?" Starren answered.

"And the fact that sometimes the royal line comes into their powers early," Wade added.

Wait, what? What did that say about me? They didn't know that I'd had my power a lot longer than they thought.

I'd always healed quicker than other kids, but the first time I specifically remember regenerating was when I was eight and fell skiing. It was one of the few times my mom had let us slow down enough to do something fun. My bone had been sticking out of my leg. Mom must have known about the healing, she pushed it back into place, held me while I screamed for a couple minutes and voilà, all better.

She had made me promise not to tell anyone unless they saw me heal. Under the no lying rule, I couldn't break that promise even if I'd wanted to. Not long after the skiing incident, she'd dropped me off at a kids' home, first of many. She'd said she'd be back, but it had never happened, leading me to believe she was dead. Not that I wanted her to be, but she better not be on a beach somewhere. At first I'd thought she'd left me because of the new power thing, but as I got older it didn't seem to make as much sense. Then I just stopped thinking about it.

"Speaking of families, Trisha, what is yours like?" My head whipped over to face Starren. Her tone was far too casual. And she'd never cared about any life details before. This was weird.

"Your fae family, not the humans," Wade added, just as casual.

"I don't know," I answered, keeping it short. Where had that come from? It wasn't like they were just trying to find something to talk about. They let it go though, and didn't keep asking. So weird.

We walked and walked, me deep in thought, the others just naturally quiet. Eventually the air started to smell like salt. "We must be getting close to the bay," I said.

"It does smell like water," Starren said. "What do you know about this bay?"

"It's big. People swim it. I don't know, what is there to know about some water?"

Starren rolled her eyes. "Is there somewhere nearby that would attract fae?"

I shrugged. "I don't know. What attracts fae?"

"You're fae," Cray said.

"Yes, but I'm not sure what you mean. I find Orlando Bloom attractive, does that make him a fae magnet?"

Starren sighed and pinched the bridge of her nose. "Should I ask who that is?" Wade shook his head. "Fine. Fae are attracted to anywhere that has energy, good or bad." Starren said. "Non-humanoid fae are attracted to the bad energy in this world while we are basically immune."

I glanced at Wade. He was being awful quiet. "Alcatraz," I said. That had to be it.

"What's an Alcatraz?" Cray asked.

"It's an island. It used to be a prison. They put the worst criminals in the U.S. there."

Cray pushed up his glasses and stared at me blankly. "What's the U.S.?"

"The United States you idiot," Wade broke in.

Wow. Grumpy. It wasn't Cray's fault he'd been pulled from some other world and didn't know the geography here. Poor guy just blinked behind his big glasses, looking even more confused.

"How do we get to this island? Sounds like a good place to start. Take us the direct way, Cray can find him from where we end up."

Like I just automatically knew how to find Alcatraz because I lived in this world. "Follow the slope down. All these hills lead to the bay eventually."

"This way then," Wade said and took off downhill.

"Watch out for the trolleys," I called after him.

"Yeah, yeah," Wade said, moving like there was a fire behind him. Good. He must want to get done with this deal as much as I did. The sooner we got done, the sooner we wouldn't have to see each other anymore.

"What's a trolley?" Cray asked.

I sighed and took off after Wade. Starren stayed behind with Cray and said something, but I couldn't make it out over the traffic.

This early on a weekday, the roads were pretty empty. We'd left home at 7:30, which meant it was probably only 5:00 am now. The ferries wouldn't be running yet. No reason to bring that up until we got down there and Cray made sure that was the direction he was getting a signal from.

It took us ten minutes to get to where the signs started pointing us toward the wharf. At least now we knew which direction to head in for sure. I'd been here once, a long time ago, the same trip Mom and I had gone through Yosemite. Too long ago to remember much.

We walked down the pier together, passing the occasional jogger who didn't even look our way. The sound of barking started when we got close.

"What's that?" Cray asked, his eyes wide under his glasses.

"Sea lions." I couldn't keep the smile from taking over my face. I pointed down at the pier where twenty or so sea lions were floating on whatever perches they could find down on the water.

"Lions?" Starren frowned. "Those are supposed to be big cats, not some kind of water animal. Or was I misinformed?"

"Nope, you're right. I never really got that either." We stopped talking for a moment to let a biker pass. "I think there are a lot of them this time of year. Sounds like it anyway. They're really cute. You should see them when they're little."

"Why?" Starren asked.

"Because they're cute and squeaky and stuff."

"And you think I would be interested in a cute Earth animal because?" She looked genuinely confused. I groaned inside. Apparently Wade wasn't the only fae incapable of feelings. Were all of us like this? "Once this chase is over I plan to never leave Faerie again. I wouldn't be here if Jaden Martan had not escaped. You can keep your not cat lions."

We made it to the pier without any more conversation, but it was closed. "The ferry doesn't leave until nine and even then we might not get on. The sign says they sell out in advance most of the time," Wade said, coming back from the ticket booth.

"It's off season," I answered. "We should be able to get on."

"That would mean wasting four hours," Starren growled. "Find us another way out there."

"We could swim," I offered. "I don't know any other way. But it's going to be really, really cold." We all looked at Cray. I'd be fine, and I'd hazard a bet that Starren and Wade would be too. But Cray?

"No. Let's take one of those." Wade nodded toward some small boats tied to the dock.

"There are all these people around, how are we supposed to do that?" I asked.

Wade lifted an eyebrow. "They can't see the three of us. None of the humans can unless we want them to. Why aren't you staying hidden?"

Well, duh. I forgot all about asking Cray to teach me that last night. I hadn't even seen him once I got back to headquarters. "Show me how," I said to Starren.

She lifted an eyebrow.

"I'm serious, no one has ever shown me how."

"It isn't something someone has to show you, Trish," Wade said, his tone gentle. "You just have to concentrate. There are several gifts all fae have and this is one of them. It's been sitting there waiting for you to use it since you turned eighteen. Whenever that was."

Great. Concentrate. I wasn't the best at doing that. I closed my eyes like Cray always did when he was looking for a target and concentrated like Wade said. Nothing.

Starren snorted. "She's too human. We'll hide her in the bottom of the boat." She headed down to the docks, walking toward a small rowboat no one was paying attention to.

Wade looked at me and shrugged, then headed after her.

Cray wouldn't look at me at all.

I closed my eyes and tried again, focusing with all my might. After a moment, I cracked one eye open. Nothing looked different. I waved at a businessman in a suit. He looked at me strangely but waved back. Shoot.

Obviously this was going to be something I had to work on. I took off down the dock after the others. There were quite a few people here already. Why did fishermen have to get up so early? Starren and Cray were in the boat by the time I caught up. Wade was waiting for me on the dock. He put out a hand to help me on board. I slapped it away.

Muttering something under his breath, Wade got on after me. Once we were situated, he held a hand out over the padlock chaining us to the dock. It flashed and fell off.

"You row, Trisha," Starren said, unchaining two oars from the floor.

"Why me?"

"Because it will look pretty strange to see a princess sitting in a boat as it floats against the current out into the bay," Starren answered. Today I must be more work than I was worth. She was sounding even grumpier than normal. But she did have a point. I grabbed the oars and dipped them into the water.

"Plus, if you get any blisters on those delicate hands they'll take care of themselves," Wade said, clearly enjoying this.

Ugh, they both had good points. But it was quite a ways out there. Sure, my muscles would fix themselves and not be sore, but did I really have to row the whole way? The thought had barely pinged through my mind when a head broke water beside us.

Starren and Wade instantly pulled their swords, which really wasn't something I was comfortable with in this small of a space.

"It's just a sea lion, calm down."

Starren eyed the creature doubtfully as it slipped onto its back and splashed water toward us.

"I think it likes you," Cray said.

"Me?" I asked, my voice a little higher than normal. I was not an animal person.

"Yes, you. Ask it to help us," Wade said.

"What?"

"Ask it to help us," he said again, this time slower like that would help me understand. I just stared at him. "Animals here sometimes listen to fae. All nature here. We can even manipulate it on a small level, like the sword I made you. Ask the creature to help us."

Feeling ridiculous, I leaned out of the boat and stretched a hand toward the animal. It swam over and bumped my hand with its nose like my hand was a ball and it was some trained aquarium sea lion, not a wild animal.

"Would you mind pushing us to that island out there?" I asked, pointing at Alcatraz. It looked that way, then dove under water. I glared at the others, half expecting them to burst into laughter at the way they'd made me look ridiculous. "Was that some kind of joke?"

"No. But apparently the boys were incorrect to believe it liked you," Starren said. "Row. We need to get further from the docks in case the boat's owner comes looking for it."

I growled under my breath but started rowing. Within seven or eight minutes it was getting harder to make out details back on shore.

"What are you feeling, Cray?" Starren asked.

"This is right. I don't know how far it is, but we are going in the right direction."

Another ten minutes of rowing and people on the shore were getting tiny. There was a small splash from behind the boat, then three laughing sea lion heads popped out of the water together. I stopped rowing. "What's up, guys?"

The smallest one, which I got the strangest feeling was the first one that came to visit, splashed me. "Hey! That's cold!"

"We can't be taking water on like that." Cray's fingers went white from gripping the sides of the boat.

"It's not going to hurt anything. Why are they here Trish?" Wade said.

How was I supposed to know? It wasn't like they were talking back with me. "Are you boys going to help us out?"

The two bigger sea lions put their heads against the back of the boat and started pushing, propelling us forward at a much faster speed than I'd even gotten close to. We weren't pointed straight at the island, but they could get us that much closer at least.

"Give me one of the oars," Wade said. He snatched one out of my hand and muscled past me, then Cray, on his way to the back.

"Don't hurt them, they're helping." I grabbed his wrist, determined he wasn't going to hurt anyone or anything again, at least not while I was around.

"I'm not going to hurt them." He looked at me like he thought I was crazy, twisted his wrist free and finished his short trip to the back of the boat. He stuck the oar into the water and used it as a rudder, putting us on a direct heading for the island. I turned into the cool spray of the water off the bow, sure I was blushing hot red. Of course I would assume the worst from him, he'd shown me his true self. Or was it his true self before, when we were dating? Nah, that was just an act, right?

Poor Cray was shivering over on his section of the bench.

Whether from fear or the cold water, I couldn't tell. The regenerating also helped my cells stay a good temperature. It had to be freezing out here, but it just felt cool to me.

This could be it. If we found Jaden today, I would be done with these guys and officially be allowed to stay on Earth. Was this why Mom had been running? To keep me away from the fae? She'd been open about everything else but that. The island rushed toward us with all the sea lion power in the back. I rested my arms on the wood and my chin on my arms and watched it get bigger and bigger.

The island looked gloomy today. A thick fog hung over the whole place. Hopefully that wasn't a sign.

"That's close enough, call off your pets," Starren said.

I inched toward the back of the boat, having an interesting time staying on my feet while we moved at a good clip. How had Wade done it? If he could, I could. As long as I didn't go pitching off the side.

"Thanks guys, that's close enough." I had to yell over the wind. It was picking up more and more as we moved farther from shore. The sea lions instantly stopped, sending the boat lurching. Wade reached out a hand and steadied me. I glared at him. He threw his empty hand in the air as if to say he was hands off.

Three heads popped up out of the water. "Thanks again. We really appreciate it."

"Ask them to stick around. We might need a ride back," Starren said.

"Do you think you could stay here? Just for a little while until we're ready to go back?" They looked at each other, then my lion nodded. He splashed me and then they all disappeared under water.

I wiped the moisture off my face with my hand. "Thanks a lot," I yelled after him. "I wasn't wet enough already." I turned back to the island, foreboding welling up inside me as we drifted toward the rock face. "Now what?"

"Time to row," Starren said.

"I got it." Wade moved to the middle of the boat and grabbed the other oar.

The island looked even worse than gloomy now that we were closer. It looked downright cursed. Tendrils of fog floated toward us, twisting and contorting into strange figures. This was so different than when Mom and I had come to visit in July years ago. Then there were huge amounts of people, the sun was out, everyone was on vacation. Today there was no one in sight. The sun hadn't come up enough to burn off the fog yet, that had to be why there was so much of it. I hoped. No matter what the reason for the strange weather, Alcatraz looked like it could still be in business.

Wade paddled close and let the boat bump the dock, the sound echoing across the water and making me cringe. Cray grabbed hold until Wade jumped out and pulled the boat close, using the chain in the front to tie it to the dock.

Something felt wrong when I stepped off the boat. The mist swirling up and around us was unnatural. This was more than just fog. I looked at the others to see if they were feeling it too. Cray was for sure, poor guy looked nearly sick. But then, he could feel all this much stronger than the rest of us could, so it was probably about overwhelming him right now.

"You'll have to lead, Cray," Starren said, her tone the most gentle I had ever heard it. She was picking up on something bad being here too. It was still bugging me that I didn't know what Jaden had done to be imprisoned in the first place. Had he killed someone? Or a lot of someones?

Cray started up the concrete steps slowly. The only sounds making it through the heavy fog blanket were the slight scuffs of his boots on stairs. Wade and Starren pulled their swords and followed him. The cheery colors of the fall flowers mocked us as we wound our way to the top. One of the signs said it was a fourth of a mile. It felt so much longer in the damp, half dark.

Finally Cray stopped. "We're on top of it," he whispered.

"Trisha?" Starren asked.

"He's down in the cells maybe?" It came out as a question, but she must have taken it as gospel, because she headed straight for the door that somehow had no fog blocking it and was in plain view. That seemed like a bad plan. And of course Jaden couldn't be standing up on top, he had to be down in the dark, scary area. Hopefully fog was his power. That I could deal with.

Wade touched me on the shoulder. "Watch for security cameras. They won't see us, but they will see you."

Another thing to worry about, other than the fact that we were chasing some guy with unknown powers down into a scary rock fortress. I pushed against the door. Locked.

"Move aside," Starren pushed me out of the way and put her hand on the door. A flash and the door popped open.

Wow, nice. Beat picking a lock with tools. She pushed the door open. Another handy trick I was going to have to learn. Was that another ability all fae had? If it was, then what was her ability anyway? That probably would be a good thing for me to know.

My fae eyes adjusted to the dark fairly quickly after stepping inside. Dark. Dark was good. No, dark was bad. Okay, both. Good because of the cameras, bad because it could lead to our deaths. I shivered as we passed cell after cell. What must it have been like to live here? The cells were tiny, not even as big as my bathroom I'd bet. If low fae fed on bad energy, this was definitely a feast. We came to a stairwell. Starren didn't pause, just headed down.

"The stairs are damp, be careful," Cray said.

"But still, much better than a fae prison," Wade said.

Not something I ever wanted to see. If the fae I'd met so far were any indication of general faeness, I was better off with the humans. At least when they stabbed you in the back it wasn't literal.

"We're getting close Starren, be careful," Cray said.

Starren slowed a little, but otherwise didn't acknowledge Cray. I moved in closer to Wade, not liking it but liking the thought of losing a limb even less. Starren stopped us.

"Okay, Trisha, go ahead."

"Me?" I squeaked, craning my neck and trying to see around her.

She glared at me for a second. "Isn't that why you're here?"

Well, yeah, but still. "Just tell him you are here on the authority of the Council and king and he needs to go with you without a fight. It works on all high fae. Or, it should."

It should? Great. Just wonderful. My heart thundered in my chest. If nothing else, the trolls had taught me to be more cautious. "Don't I at least get a sword or something?"

"Oh, one sec." Wade reached into his pocket. The hilt of a sword came out, the blade wrapped in some type of cloth following as he tugged. "I got this for you last night."

What in the world? I needed pockets like that. "How did you do that?"

"It was a lot of work on such short notice but I-"

"Not how did you get the sword, how did you fit it in there?"

"Oh." He sounded disappointed. "My pocket has a small portal. I can reach in and grab anything I left in Faerie near the opening." He pulled off the material and shoved it back in his pocket, then held the sword out to me. It gleamed in the dim light, made of the same type of crystal I'd stolen from the dead troll. "I saw how much you liked the stones the troll had, so I got you one made out of the same stuff. I hope it's okay."

It was more than okay. This was something the old Wade would do. The Wade I'd loved. *You will not cry, you will not cry.* Not here. "It's beautiful." He held it out to me by the blade. I grabbed the hilt and swung it around, leaving little streaks of light through the dark.

Wade grinned at me. "I hope you like it."

Like it? I more than liked it. And it was so sweet that he had remembered me wanting to keep the stones. I gave him a small smile. "It's amazing."

"If you two are done staring into each other's eyes, we have business to attend to," Starren interrupted the moment, bringing me back to reality. *This Wade is not my Wade, not my Wade,* I chanted internally. Getting distracted down here was dumb anyway.

I pushed past Starren without a word, letting the light gleam off the sword in front of me. Better to see, not so good with trying not to be a target. But I was just supposed to talk with him. It was going to be okay. Supposedly he hadn't turned eighteen yet, he shouldn't have his power, we were fine. Just needed to find him, get him out of here and then live happily ever after, never to be bothered by the fae again. Even the good-looking male variety.

One step forward. Two. I didn't hear anything behind me.

I looked back at Starren. She shooed me forward.

The sword was light in my hand, the crystal weighing practically nothing. Much better than the wooden swords Mom and I used when she played with me, growing up. Now my body automatically went into one of the stances she'd taught me as a game. Had everything we'd done together been more than a game, just like this? What about our trip across California? Had it meant something more? We'd been to Yosemite, been here, and now I was at both places again. That didn't seem like a coincidence.

Focus. I needed to focus. Those thoughts could wait for later. I had three people behind me that needed me to do my job. I inched forward another step.

"Who's there?" a windy voice asked me from somewhere ahead. Wait. That was a female voice. Cray had better not gotten this wrong again. I looked back at Starren. She shrugged.

I didn't answer, moving forward slowly. No decapitation, no removal of limbs and I would be fine. No problem, I would be fine.

"I said, who's there?" The voice was much louder this time, and sounded angrier too.

"I'm here on behalf of the Faerie Council. They, along with the king, request you to give yourself up for questioning." Hopefully that's what Starren had wanted me to say, something about this voice gave me the creeps. It felt worse than even the trolls.

"Your king and Council have no authority here," she whispered, her voice bending around the room and coming at me from all sides. Definitely getting less and less friendly.

"Please show yourself so we can talk this through." Amazing. My voice sounded completely in control. I was going to be good at this by the time we caught Jaden, if things continued the way they had so far. And I still had all my limbs.

A strange scratching noise drifted up from the hall in front of me. A fresh batch of fog floated in front of the sound. Lift my sword or not? What if she, whatever she was, was doing what I'd asked? Then it would just come across as an act of aggression. So many things public school hadn't taught me.

About six and a half feet from the floor, the fog drifted away in a small circle, revealing a pale corpse-like face, long black hair surrounding the white, white skin and golden eyes that burned.

"Don't you love it down here?" The voice was going sing-songy. I found myself enjoying the cool dark. Why would I want to go back upstairs into the heat and light? "Why would you want to leave?" the voice drifted past me. She was right. Someone else could find Jaden, why should it be me doing all the work? Just so I could stay with boring humans.

"Trisha." Who was that? "Trisha, stop." I looked out of the corner of my eye and saw Cray creeping toward me. "It's controlling you. Don't let it."

I looked past him to Starren and Wade. Starren looked nearly dead, and Wade not much better. What was she whispering to them? I could hardly bring myself to care.

Why should I care about anything they wanted? They didn't really care about me. The only one that cared about me was… who? I couldn't remember. Someone I was staying with.

"Trisha, snap out of it," Cray's voice was getting desperate. He grabbed my shoulder and shook me.

"Bother Wade and Starren." I shrugged him off.

"No." He turned toward my new friend. "Let them go."

She laughed. "Why?"

"We're here for a reason. Let them go. You don't want to get on the wrong side of the Council."

She laughed again. The creatures face was vaguely human, but its teeth sure weren't. I stared at the thing for a full thirty seconds after it closed its mouth. "Whatever you say."

Suddenly the fog in my mind lifted, taking the air out of my lungs with it. I coughed and then sucked in new air. The others. Were they okay? Cray backed away, hopefully to check on Starren and Wade. I counted to five, taking deep breaths in through my nose, forcing the urge to vomit down.

"What questions do you have for me, little fae?"

"Um," I looked back at Starren. She still looked nearly asleep. A lot of help this team leader was. Apparently quick healing helped with whatever had been done to us. "Do you know where Jaden Martan is?"

The creature raised itself higher on its tail. "Why should I care where this thing is? Is it human or fae?"

"Fae."

"Then leave it be. Whatever the Council wants, ignore it. They have become far too controlling. We are supposed to be a free people."

That was it? Seriously? "Okay, thank you." I backed away slowly, afraid this thing would change its mind. Then something occurred to me. "You aren't eating any people here, are you?"

An angry mutter of some kind came from behind me.

Starren had told me to handle it, she was just going to have to deal with how I did.

The creature snorted. "No, unless you include basking in the energy left behind here." She was fae. She had to be telling the truth.

"No, that doesn't count. Thanks again."

The thing laughed louder this time, a hissing, choking sound, showing long sharp spikes where teeth were supposed to be. "So polite. Refreshing from a high fae. You're welcome, child. Return if you have any other questions. I will answer them best I can." She nodded toward Starren and Wade. "Just don't bring those with you. I don't answer to the Council here." The fog rippled in across her face. I could hear the scratching again, this time moving away. A breath of relief left me. No human eating, no me eating, this was turning out much better than I'd thought it would a few moments ago.

Something conked me on the back of the head. I swung around and looked up into Starren's angry face. "Hey! What was that for?"

"You let her leave."

"Yeah, so? It doesn't seem like she's causing any problems here.

The park service would have closed down the island if something was happening to people."

"She's here without the authority of the Council. We need to take her in." Oh sure, willing to leave a troll in the forest but not to leave this thing here. Did we always have to be on opposite sides? If she wasn't hurting anyone, why force her to go back to Faerie? Innocent until proven guilty and all that.

Wade looked at Starren, then looked at me. I set my jaw and crossed my arms. He should know by now that I was not going to budge on this.

"It's not what we are assigned to do, Starren," Wade said. "We'll report it when we get back. For now we just need to get Cray working again."

Starren groaned. "You know what this could have done for me? A nest of trolls one day, a hyran the next?"

"Yeah, yeah, we all know about your ego. You'll be fine. Let's just get out of here."

Starren whacked him with the side of her sword and put it back in her sheath.

"What exactly is a hyran?"

"That," Wade said, vaguely gesturing in the direction the thing had slithered away.

"Very helpful," I muttered.

"Do you two always have to fight?" Cray asked. "Can't we just get out of here?" I squinted his way. His white face stood out in the dark since the fog had faded. I couldn't say I blamed him, being the only one who knew what was going on had to have been terrifying. Why hadn't he been under the hyran's spell? And he was right. It was probably better not to linger.

"Wade, do you have a sheath for me?"

"Just a sec." He rummaged around in his pocket for a moment and pulled out a beautiful rainbow scaled sheath, which looked about the perfect size for my sword. "I didn't have the sword in the sheath in my pocket, just in case I needed to grab for it quick." He handed the sheath to me. "That thing is made out of mermaid scales. Humans won't be able to see your sword while it's put away. It even has a cloth to wrap over the hilt."

"Thank you," I said quietly. I threw the strap over my shoulder and slid the sword in. Why would he do this for me? Another thoughtful gesture. Nothing made sense any more. Wait, mermaids?

"Let's get Cray back. It will probably be tomorrow before he finds us another target as it is," Starren said.

I followed them up the dark halls of Alcatraz, the sound of scales escorting from behind us causing me to re-draw my new sword, just in case. Things were much brighter by the time we reached the outside world.

When we got back to the boat, Wade held it while the rest of us jumped in. The sea lions were nowhere in sight. I sighed when Starren looked at me, automatically knowing what that meant. Time to get rowing.

"So, anyone want to explain to me what that was?" I asked after the island was a little ways behind us.

"A hyran," Wade said. "They feed off the energy left by pain, emotional or physical. They love places that have both."

"But they can't cause the pain themselves, or the energy is ruined," Cray added.

"So that thing wasn't really any danger to us?"

Cray blinked at me like I was crazy. "Just because she couldn't feed off of it doesn't mean she won't create it. If she thought we were a threat, we would all be dead right now. There is no stopping a hyran."

Starren lifted an eyebrow. "Don't be so sure." The rest of us looked at each other, but she didn't elaborate.

"How's come whatever she was doing to us didn't work on you, Cray?"

"My ability prevented it from affecting me." He shuddered. "I've never had to use that part of it until today."

So that thing could have slaughtered us if it had wanted to. I wasn't going to think about that, even if Starren seemed to think she could have gotten us out of it. She'd been under that thing's sway just as much as Wade and I had been. No one had much to say after that.

Wade let me row halfway, then took the oars from me without asking or giving me a chance to complain. Starren was already watching us enough, I wasn't going to give her any more ammo. Wade didn't need to act all chivalrous now. He rowed until the people on shore were starting to turn into clear shapes instead of distant blobs, then handed the oars off to me silently.

Within fifteen minutes we were bumping into the dock. I grabbed the chain and hopped out. Wade jumped out behind me and hovered. "I got this," I said, shoving him out of the way. Just as I bent over, a splash hit me in the face. "Hey!" A head popped out of the water and laughed, before diving under the surface again.

"Thanks a lot for your help getting back," I said. "Traitor." I turned around to lock the boat to the dock and noticed an older guy staring at me. Just me. Of course, he probably couldn't see the others. I really needed to get the hang of that invisible thing.

"Hey, that's my missing boat," the guy finally said. Oops.

Time for me to get out of here. I started walking toward shore.

"What were you doing with it?" he called after me.

"Um, sorry about that. I just needed to borrow it," I turned to him when I spoke, but backpedaled the whole time, putting as much distance between us as possible.

The guy didn't seem to be buying it. "You stupid kids and your pranks. We're all tired of it here. You better sit and wait kid, I'm calling the police." He whipped out his cell phone and started dialing.

"Trish, run," Wade whispered loudly.

I took off, running up the dock, practically bouncing off everything in my way. I had the small advantage of not getting tired, but several other men from the dock joined the first guy, all of them trying to grab me as I ran past.

Dodging another man, I barely caught sight of Cray tripping one of my pursuers. I almost laughed, then thought better of it. *Go Cray,* I cheered silently. Starren ran ahead of me, waited until I got past and knocked a trashcan into another guy. Only three left. I laid on another burst of speed and a few blocks later started to lose them. And Cray too, but he could catch up.

"Whew, that could have been bad," I said after the last pursuer had been left behind and the team was gathered around.

Starren sent me a withering look. "Wade," Starren said. "You'll be spending the rest of the day teaching her anything a normal fae would know. Like how not to be seen, so we don't go through all that again."

"I'm not working with Wade." Starren had a point, but that didn't mean I had to learn from Wade. "Cray can teach me."

Cray had just caught up. His eyes widened at my statement.

"He can't. He's going to be busy finding us our next target. It'll have to be me," Wade said.

Did I dare ask Starren? Could it be any worse than being forced to spend time with Wade? Maybe if I appealed to that ego Wade had mentioned. "You would be a great teacher, Starren. Could you give me some pointers?"

"No." She turned and walked away. Okay then, who did that leave?

Cray looked at me for a second, then hurried after Starren, whispering to her. I took off after him, not wanting to be left behind with Wade. Things were awkward between us again, now that I wasn't quite as sure that I could hate his guts.

"Are we headed for a portal?" I asked.

No one answered. I guess that meant duh. We walked several blocks before heading down an alley. Starren didn't even look around before stepping into a wall. She didn't really need to, no one could see her. I checked behind us before jumping through after Cray. Home again. My watch read eleven. Strange with the time change.

"Cumat," Starren called.

"Yes, ma'am." The dwarf was already there.

"Take Trisha somewhere and teach her how to be fae, starting with invisibility. Cray, you're with me. We need to find Jaden." She headed for her desk, totally dismissing us. Something Cray had said to her must have changed her mind about who was going to teach me.

Cumat sighed, crooked a finger at me and headed for the hallway without even questioning Starren. I followed him two doors down and into a room similar in size and décor to Starren's. Were all the rooms the same here? Except for the empty portal room. After closing the door behind me, Cumat walked forward and sat down on the other side of the large desk. He gestured for me to sit across from him.

"What do you already know?"

I shrugged.

"I don't understand this human body expression, Miss Penchant, does this mean you don't know anything?"

"Well…" I broke eye contact and looked at the floor. Close enough. "Yes."

Cumat threw up his hands. "Whoever heard of a fae that didn't know how to use her powers? Fine then, first we are to start with remaining out of human sight." Like I hadn't been in the room when Starren gave the order. "All it takes is concentration."

That's what they'd told me back in San Francisco, but it hadn't worked. "You sure there aren't any magic words or whatever?"

The poor dwarf sighed and pinched the bridge of his thick nose between his thumb and forefinger. "No. No words. Just thoughts."

I tried to do what he'd said and concentrated. Really, really concentrated. Harder than I'd ever done in my life. "How's that? How do I know if it worked?"

"You'll look strange, even to yourself. Try again, just one part of your body at a time."

We worked like this forever, me struggling, him giving me tips. I finally went from trying my whole body, to my upper body, to my arm and finally my hand. My eyes closed, I begged my hand to listen so I could leave this stupid place. It was starting to feel like a jail. When I opened my eyes I wasn't expecting anything to change, but my hand had a strange pearl cast to it. My gaze flew to Cumat. He was blinking hard, like he didn't believe what he was seeing. He probably wasn't, after hours of failure.

"That's it," his tone was cheerful. "You've got it. Keep working on just your hand until it happens naturally, then move on to the rest of your body. Don't forget to make your hand visible again. You might get some unwanted attention if a human sees you without it."

I nearly squealed in delight, then remembered where I was and held it in. I was doing it, for real, like a real fae. I'd always known I was fae, but until this moment hadn't really known what that meant. The regenerating thing happened on its own, I didn't control it. Here was something tangible about being fae that only happened when I told it to.

"Continue working on just this tonight and you should be able to disappear completely by tomorrow. Fae will still be able to see you, it's only humans this works on, they are so dull. But they can still hear you for now, so be careful. It should be late enough for you to go home. Tomorrow you can show me your progress. If you've done well enough, we will start on something else."

"What? What something else?"

Cumat looked ruffled at my question. "I will talk to Ms. Starren and see what she prefers."

I rolled my eyes at his back as he walked toward the door. Didn't he feel like an idiot catering to her?

No one was around to tell me goodbye when I got into the hall-way. Cumat walked me to the brick wall and gave me a small bow before leaving me standing there. I guessed that meant I was dismissed. Time to go home and eat a massive amount of food. All this concentrating had worked up an appetite.

Chapter 9

The next morning I pulled up to headquarters early, just like Cumat had told me. Wade was the one waiting on me today. My heart gave a little thump, seeing him leaning against the wall waiting on me. I whacked the offending organ and put a scowl on my face.

"Starren had something for Cumat to do," he explained as soon as I stopped my bike.

"Okay." I could be civil. I really could. At least I could try. "Ready to go in?"

"Actually, Cray hasn't found us anything that isn't registered with the Council yet, so we have nothing to track. Starren wants you to go to school, make sure your doppelganger is doing an okay job as you."

Well wasn't that nice of her. Not. "I can't stay here and work with Cumat? He's teaching me stuff."

"Nope. What Starren says, goes. Cumat is running errands."

I jumped on my bike and shoved off without answering.

"Trish, come on, at least talk to me," Wade yelled after me. I didn't give him the satisfaction of looking back. It was so confusing to be around him right now. I could really use this day off even though I just wanted to get this whole thing over with. What were we now? Obviously not boyfriend and girlfriend. Not even friends. Teammates, I guess, but somehow that didn't seem to cover it. I groaned and pedaled faster, trying to get my mind off the whole mess. It didn't really work.

What happened if Cray found something while I was at school? Served them right if they needed me later and couldn't get me out of math class. Hopefully Starren had locked the other me up in some closet. It wouldn't do to run into myself at school. This was probably my fault though, refusing to work with Wade. Starren might have let me spend the day at headquarters learning more fae tricks if I'd had a teacher. He could be teaching me something useful right now, instead of me heading to school where I'd be trying to memorize the periodic table. How was that helpful again?

It was strange riding to school. It had only been two days, but it was almost another life. Thursday, right? Now my days were getting mixed up. I should know though. Nina had been all misty eyed this morning over the fact that it had been a week since I went missing.

Once I made it to school, it was surreal. I had always known I didn't belong here, that I should be off in some woods somewhere with the rest of the fae, but just didn't know what the fae world was like. Now I did. A little bit anyway.

Mrs. Hemp watched me as I walked past her to my desk, intently enough to give me the creeps. What had the other me done to attract this much attention? I settled in to listen to the story of Odysseus, which made me wonder, how many other legends were true? Most people didn't believe fae existed, yet here I was, sitting in the middle of them. Maybe Odysseus was fae. Or the sirens were under fae. So many possibilities.

When the bell rang, I shot out of class at top speed, not giving Mrs. Hemp the chance to call my name. I stumbled through my next two classes, hardly even there.

At lunch I grabbed a tray and started through the line.

Yum, tacos today. I loaded my plate with two soft shells and two hard, then slathered on the sour cream. A little extra never hurt. I turned to look around the room, actually thinking about where I should sit for the first time since I came to this school. I sighed. Making friends would create a great excuse for me to be gone at night, but I had no idea where to start. I'd never cared before. Plus whatever progress I made today would probably be destroyed by my look alike tomorrow. And really, tomorrow was all I needed if everything went well. Cray would figure out where Jaden was tonight, we'd go get him in the morning. After tomorrow, I'd be free. Hopefully. If we could break our losing streak.

I started for my regular table against the wall in back, the perfect place for me. I could see everything going on but still stay under the radar.

"Trisha, wait up."

I turned, trying not to let my face show any emotion. So far the only time someone had wanted to talk to me here it hadn't turned out so good for me. I saw who it was. Never mind, I had to take that back. It was Rissa. She'd asked about me earlier this week. And now she was talking to me again. Twice in one week? The world really was going crazy.

"Um, hi," I said brilliantly. What a great come back.

"Want to sit with Amy and me for lunch today?"

Sit with her and Amy? Okay, yes, it was possible for me to die. I was going to fall over dead from shock. That was something any other girl in this cafeteria would just about kill for. Problem was, it wasn't such a good idea for me.

When I'd been thinking about the need to make friends, the two most sought after girls in school hadn't even crossed my mind as possibles. Especially since I'd spent my time here doing my best to be ignored. Sure, they'd been nice, but to ask me to sit at their table? A whole different story.

But saying no would be a major insult, resulting in attention I didn't need right now. "Sure?"

"Great!" She linked her arm through mine and tugged me toward the diva table. We got there and she dropped her tray in her normal spot. "I got her to come," she stated the obvious to the other girl at the table.

"Great, glad to have you, Trisha." Amy smiled.

I studied her for a moment while the two of them chatted, trying to figure out why I was here. Same dyed hair, black underneath, blond on top, check. Designer jeans, holes pre-ripped, check. Same intense green eyes, check. Why was she staring? Had she asked me something?

"Sure," I said, looking down at my plate and hoping with all my might that she hadn't just asked if those jeans made her look fat.

"Great," she smiled again. This wasn't so bad. I could do this. If she stopped saying great. Great was getting annoying. "Meet us out front after school."

Meet them out front? Meet them out front for what? Obviously I'd missed something important. Amy stood. "Sorry, we were just finishing up and I've got to get to the gym. See you after school."

"See ya," I said. She didn't seem to notice, she was gone, Rissa following right after her.

I just sat at the diva table for a full minute, no longer interested in my tacos. What just happened? And what had I agreed to do after school? I came-to enough to pay attention to the lunchroom. Kids were pretending not to notice me sitting at the diva table by myself, but I caught the quick glances and whispers. Suddenly the thought of eating those tacos made me sick.

The walk to the trash can by the door to the hallway felt like it was farther away than the portal had been back in the woods. I ignored everyone I passed, something I'd gotten really good at doing. After dumping the contents of my tray into the trash, I slid into the hallway.

Now what? I'd rushed out of class and got to lunch early, so now with me skipping the food I had way too much time, at least forty-five minutes.

Almost without thought, I wandered toward the gym. There was a small window in the swinging doors, mostly there so a person didn't slam someone going the opposite direction. I snuck up to it and peeped through the three-inch square.

There was Amy, playing some one-on-one basketball with a girl I didn't know. When she'd said she was heading for the gym, I'd automatically filled in the blank with cheerleader. Basketball player? Never crossed my mind.

"Who are you watching?" a voice asked from behind. I jerked back from the window and turned that way.

"Starren? What are you doing here? Did you find something?"

She walked forward and nudged me out of the way and looked through the glass. "No. Wade asked me to check up on you."

"Wade? What does he want?"

"You first. Which one of the girls are you watching?"

How much did I want to know why Wade had asked her to spy on me? Quite a bit. "Number eighteen. Something weird happened at lunch. None of your business, just high school stuff."

"Until we find Jaden, everything that happens in your life is my business. Is it something I need to know about?"

"No. I answered your question, now you answer mine. Why did Wade ask you to come out here?"

"I wasn't supposed to let you see me, but I'm tired of all this nonsense. He still cares about you. Either forgive him or kick him in the teeth, either way I don't care, just get it handled. We don't need all this crap going on; it's distracting both of you. Someone will get hurt."

I snorted. "Oh yeah, he shows his feelings really well. Here honey, let's see if this pistol works."

Starren glared. I tapped my toes in my shoe, trying desperately to not let her see that she was intimidating me. "I don't care how much either of your feelings get hurt, but no one is getting physically hurt while on my team. We need to get this worked out."

"Like it's that easy. He betrayed me."

A kid walked by me toward a row of lockers. He was staring at me like I was crazy.

"What?" I asked him, my voice echoing a little in the hallway as I let out a little steam.

"Nothing," he mumbled as he scooted past us.

"What's his problem?" I asked Starren. "I'd think he'd be staring at you, not me. You're the one that would be new to school, plus the fact there's something about you that's... not human." I noticed the glint to her skin. The glint I'd learned to see when I was working with Cumat. "Wait. I'm talking to myself again, aren't I. Oh great. Now the whole school is going to think I'm crazy as well as just plain strange."

Starren's face hardened. "Why do you care so much about what these humans think? Why do you even come to this horrible place? You can't be learning anything useful here."

I waited until another kid walked by. "What's so different about us that we shouldn't care about them?" I was arguing just to argue now. I didn't even know the names of ninety percent of the kids I went to school with. The only humans I specifically cared for were Dan and Nina, and my children's home family. Sure, I didn't hear from any of them very often, but they were still family.

"If I hadn't seen what you can do, I wouldn't believe you are fae. Be back to the Hall by seven a.m. tomorrow." She turned and started to leave, then paused. "He went to Faerie, you know. Waited two days at the holding cells. He started getting upset about an hour into it and was devastated by that second day. Thought he'd killed you for real."

"That's his own fault," I muttered. "He never should have hurt me in the first place."

"You might find he had his reasons, if you took the time to talk with him."

"Do you really think I'm going to just forgive him?"

"No. I just want this resolved. I can't have two members of my team that aren't willing to look out for each other." She turned and left, dodging students who didn't even know she was there.

What she'd told me didn't make a difference. There wasn't a good enough reason to make Wade shoot me and hope for the best. None. The waves of kids going by intensified. Starren and I must have been talking longer than I'd thought. I started slowly up the hallway toward my next class, lost in thought. Wade had been sick waiting for me? He'd gone to Faerie to be there when I arrived, to walk me through things? That wasn't how I'd been picturing the whole murder thing since I'd woken up. I went through the rest of my classes in a daze, probably no better than my doppelganger.

Finally the last bell rang. I practically ran to my locker, threw my books in and headed for the front door, not sure whether to hope Amy and Rissa were waiting for me or not. Sure, I could just not show up, but what if they confronted the other me about it tomorrow while I was gone? That could be not good in so many different ways.

The sun was shining as I pushed through the main entrance/exit. It took my eyes a second to adjust. There they were, standing out by the road, waiting.

"Ready?" Amy asked me when I got within hearing distance.

"Sure?" I said, not liking the question on the end.

"Are you going to play in that?"

Play? Play what? "Yes?"

"Okay then, let's head out. Did you drive or do you want a ride?"

I pointed at the bike rack. "I rode."

"Nice," Rissa smiled. "I didn't know you were green."

Not green, just didn't have my license yet. I'd missed my appointment to try for my driving permit - that was supposed to happen last Friday. Instead I'd spent the day lying in the woods getting rained on. What a great trade. Not that I was going to tell her that.

"You can ride with us. My dad set up a great court, he's hoping I get a basketball scholarship." Amy said. "Have you played much?"

Basketball? I'd agreed to backyard basketball? "Nope, I can honestly say almost never." Much to Dan's disappointment. He'd set us up a hoop before I'd even arrived. We had literally never used it.

I was terrible at sports. Not that I'd tried much. Most sports required a team of some kind, and I wasn't a team player. How had this happened? I needed to learn to pay better attention when people were talking to me.

Yep, and here Amy was talking again. "I can get someone to take care of your bike for you," before I could stop her she yelled, "Hey, Kevin, you bring your truck today?"

A big guy in a football jacket turned our way. "Yeah. Need it for something?"

Amy nodded toward me. "Can you haul Trish's bike to my house? I'll figure out how to get it home from there later."

"You don't have to do that," I interrupted. "I can catch a bus back here and pick it up later."

"No way." Amy led me toward the bike rack. "Which one is yours?"

"The one on the end." At least it was a pretty nice bike.

Dan had gotten it for me soon after I moved in, to go on rides with him and Nina. That didn't really work out since I avoided them at all costs for a while, and then they just gave up. But I used it a ton on my own.

The big guy jogged off and was back in a minute, pulling up in a huge pickup, definitely not green, and pretty impractical for the city life. Guys. I unlocked my bike and wheeled it over. He jumped out of the cab, took the bike from me and hoisted it into the bed of the truck in one smooth move.

"Thanks," I said.

"You're welcome." He grinned at me, then stuck his hand out. "Kevin. You new?"

"Not exactly."

"New to us," Amy saved me.

"Cool. See you in a few." He hopped in his truck and revved the engine, nearly deafening me, then peeled out and headed up the road in a cloud of smoke. Hopefully my bike would survive. I wasn't looking forward to telling Dan about my phone and sure didn't want to add my bike to the casualty list.

"Let's go. Addison is going to beat us there," Rissa said.

Amy and Rissa walked ahead of me, talking about Kevin and his driving, then moving on to the girl's basketball team. I walked along behind them, feeling out of place, but glad to be here at the same time. To think I'd been trying to find a way to skip out. This was the type of thing people were supposed to do together, not trying to stay alive while taking swings at monsters.

The girls walked up to a blue two-door Mitsubishi convertible and opened the doors in tandem. I slid into the back seat on Rissa's side. They both hopped in and put on their seatbelts, which surprised me. I did the same.

We drove for a bit before Rissa looked at me in the rearview mirror. "So, tell us about you, Trisha. I've seen you around, but you never talk to anybody."

Panic, panic. "I just moved here last year. Haven't really had a chance to get to know anyone yet. You know how crazy it is settling in at a new school." All truth.

"Yeah, that can be hard," Amy said. "Rissa wouldn't know, but I've moved."

They stared at me in the mirror like they were expecting me to continue, but I didn't have anything else to say. What else was I supposed to tell her? I didn't do this often enough to know.

"How many other girls are meeting us to play basketball?"

"Just one," Amy said. "You're our fourth for two on two. Thanks for coming to play."

Rissa took a turn down a familiar street. It wasn't my street, but it was one nearby. No way one of these rich girls lived this close to me.

After weaving around parked cars for a couple blocks, Rissa swung into the drive of a small tan house with dark brown shutters. It was only a one story. Amy swung her door open, Rissa just popped over hers. I scooted to Amy's side and slid out. My bike was sitting in the grass by the drive.

Apparently Kevin had been here and left already. Another girl I'd seen in the gym this morning was warming up at the hoop hanging off the garage. Rissa waltzed over toward her.

I couldn't believe I was here. It was so strange seeing the cool girls right in front of me in their natural habitat instead of at school. And I'd actually been invited. I'd never cared before but, somehow, today it felt different. The urge to fit in welled up and nearly overwhelmed me, scaring me with its sudden grip on my emotions. I'd never fit anywhere before, with any humans, but I'd had an excuse, knowing I wasn't one of them. Now I wasn't fitting very well with my own kind either. I needed to choose who my own kind were. And right now, between Starren being so controlling, Wade being a murderer, and the Council ordering Wade's hits, the humans seemed like a better fit for me. Which meant I actually needed to start trying, to stop pretending that I was going to be part of the fae someday.

I still had to work with Starren and Wade to get that chance at a normal life, but I was also going to do real human stuff, like play basketball. "Can I use your phone? Mine got smashed yesterday."

"Sure." Amy pulled a new iPhone out of her pocket. So not fair. "How did you smash your phone?"

I'm sure I looked like an idiot, but no immediate answer came to mind. "Ah, I fell on it?"

"Okay, well glad you didn't get hurt. Just sit mine with my gym bag when you're done and come on over." She walked toward the other girls and tossed her bag on the ground out of ball range.

I dialed the Inza's number. No answer. Shoot, it was Wednesday. Dan was still at work and Nina had a meeting at church. And shoot again. I'd totally forgotten I was grounded. But this could work. The beep for the answering machine sounded. "Nina, it's Trisha. Just calling to tell you I went to play basketball with some friends. I know technically I'm grounded, but you really wanted me to make friends and I'm trying. I should be home before you are, but if not, don't worry. Bye." I hit the end button. Hopefully Nina and Dan were just so glad I was out with friends that they wouldn't say anything.

After sitting the phone carefully on the bag, I headed toward the basketball hoop.

"Trisha, this is Addison," Amy said, nodding toward an African-American girl in a red and blue school colors t-shirt.

"Hey." She was smiling at me and it actually looked real. Girls my age did not smile at me. What was going on? Maybe I should be legitly worried.

"Hey," I answered, giving her my best smile back.

"Amy," a woman called from the porch. I looked that way. She looked a lot like Amy, just without the black/blond hair. "Are you girls coming in to eat?"

"Any of you hungry?" Amy asked us. I waited until Addison said yes, then I nodded. "Coming," Amy called back to her mom.

I followed the girls in. They were talking about some new store at the mall I'd never heard of. When I'd first moved in, Nina had tried to take me to the mall for weeks. She finally gave up about two months into my stay. But who wanted to go shopping with their mom, foster or otherwise? Maybe I'd go if these girls asked me. Maybe.

The entranceway of the house was filled with pictures. So many family pictures. Nina had started a collection of us, but it was only a year old, not seventeen or eighteen like this one. Amy, her mom, a guy I guessed to be her dad, and a kinda cute guy a couple years older than us filled the entire hallway.

"Amy's older brother, Steven. Hot, isn't he," Addison whispered to me.

"Oh yeah," I answered, even though compared to Wade he wasn't that great. Wade, with his dark blond hair and those green eyes… No. Not going there. But I could do this, talk about guys and stuff. I could be one of them.

We piled into the kitchen. Amy introduced me to her mom, Francine. She had a vegetable tray, Oreos and milk sitting out on the counter. We all went straight for the food.

I looked around at the other girls laughing and talking as they dunked their Oreos. So this was what life was supposed to be like. This was what Nina was always trying to do for me with the snacks and telling me to invite kids over from school. Maybe I should have let her do it for me. Maybe I'd have my own group like this if I had. But then, maybe this was going to be my group now.

Snacks all consumed, we headed back outside.

"So, teams," Rissa said once we were back at the court. "I say Amy and Trisha, since Amy is the best one here and no offense Trish, but we don't know how you play."

"No offense taken," I answered. They were about to find out just how bad I was. I'd always been clumsy, but it had gotten worse over the last year. So much for gracefulness being in the fae DNA.

"Great. Addison, that leaves you and me."

"Let's get it on," Addison said. She laughed and swiped at the ball Amy had scooped up from the ground.

"Okay then, you against me, Trisha," Rissa said. "Rock, paper, scissors for which team gets the ball first."

The words weren't even out of her mouth before she started, leaving me scrambling to catch up. I picked scissors, my default choice. It beat Rissa's paper. She shrugged. "I had you pegged as a rock girl." She tossed me the ball.

Amy patted me on the back. "Now that's what I'm talking about. You and I are going to get along just fine. Take it out behind the tape."

I looked to the ground at the court that had been taped on the cement and headed out of bounds. Addison was instantly all over Amy, and Rissa came straight for me. Now how was I supposed to get the ball to Amy? After a moment, Amy broke free of Addison and shot across the homemade court. I threw the ball hard. It bounced off the cement straight into her hands and she drove toward the basket for a layup.

"Oh yeah, look at that," Amy crowed.

Rissa turned to me and looked me over, then grabbed the ball off the ground and tossed it to Addison, who went behind the line. I moved toward Rissa, staying just far enough away to make her feel like I wasn't a threat, but close enough to stop her from getting any easy points. Amy stuck to Addison like glue.

It took a moment, but Addison found an opening and tossed the ball toward Rissa. I jumped forward, hit the ball before it got to her hands, knocking it toward Amy who barely had time to turn and catch it, going in for two more points.

"Why aren't you on the basketball team?" Addison asked.

"I don't play much," I said, not sure how to answer.

When had I become so coordinated? Something had changed since the last time I'd tried a sport, more than two years ago, before Dan and Nina. Some fae puberty thing?

"Well, you should," Amy said.

We went back to playing. We played hard for twenty minutes or so, Amy and I creaming the other two until Rissa and I both went up for a rebound at the same time. She slammed into me, knocking me back against the corner of the garage and to the ground. My arm screamed in pain as it brushed across the cement, peeling off layers of skin.

"Trisha, are you okay?" She moved in close, looking me over. "I am so sorry. I didn't mean to, seriously."

Amy dropped to her knees beside me. "What hurts?"

I hid my arm behind my back. Heal, heal quick. It was going to heal either way; it just needed to do it quickly before the girls saw it happening. I could lose everything I'd caught sight of today. "Nothing too bad, I'm fine."

"Let me see."

"Nah, it's okay, let's just get back to the game."

Amy looked at me quizzically. "Okay, if you say so." She turned and went after the ball, which had flown out into the yard with my not so graceful landing. And this was why I didn't have friends. Stupid, stupid. I needed to be more careful.

We went back to playing, but with far less intensity. I played carefully and it wasn't long before Addison and Rissa were catching up. How long did I need to play before they didn't know that I was leaving because of the fall? I went another fifteen minutes before calling them to a halt.

"I better head home guys," I said after Rissa made a crazy three point shot.

"Really?" Addison actually sounded disappointed.

Probably because they wouldn't be able to play two on two anymore, but still, it sent the warm fuzzies through me.

"No one answered when I called, I left a message, but you all know how that goes."

"Sure do," Rissa said. "Who can we get a hold of to take her bike home?" she asked the other two.

"Actually, I don't live too far from here. I can ride."

"Oh yeah? What street do you live on?" Amy asked.

That wasn't really something I wanted them all to know, but how did I get out of answering? "Truit."

"Nice. Close enough you can come play again. You should think about joining the team at school, you played great today."

"Thanks," I answered then headed for my bike, trying to get

away before they asked anything else. I wiped at my nose with my shoulder. I wasn't going to cry. Nope. Wasn't happening. I'd only spent one afternoon with them. I'd be fine without them. It wasn't worth someone finding out about me. The Council wouldn't go for that and I'd end up changing my permanent address to Faerie.

"Sure you're okay after that fall?" Amy called after me. "I don't want you getting half-way back and something starts to hurt. Especially since you don't have a phone."

"I'm fine, thanks. And tell your mom thanks for the snack, it was great." I hopped on my bike and took off, not caring which direction, just needing to get away. I pedaled hard for a few blocks, then slowed to catch the street names. Not far from home at all, maybe fifteen minutes. I'd drag it out as long as I could. Maybe by then I'd be able to get these emotions under control. And hopefully the tears would be dry.

Chapter 10

Friday morning. At this time last week, I was dead in the woods. Time went by so fast. It didn't help that I'd been out of it for two of those days, but still. I learned more about fae in the last week than in all the years of Mom teaching me.

Not so much book type knowledge, but real life knowledge. Only so much came across when being explained, instead of experienced.

I left for headquarters super early for two reasons. One, Nina was being all emotional. She was the only reason I remembered the whole being dead a week ago thing. Two, I wanted to get there in time to tell Starren to not send Other Me to school. It would be better to take the risk of the school calling Nina about me not showing than it would be for Amy, Rissa, or Addison to try to talk with O-Me at school. That thing didn't seem too smart and it had no idea what had happened yesterday.

Actually, I didn't know how that worked, now that I thought about it. Did they make a new Me every time they needed one with all the memories intact, or did they just send the old one out? Either way, it just didn't seem like a good idea. I'd gotten home last night before Dan and Nina and deleted the message I'd left for them.

What they didn't know wasn't going to hurt them. Especially Nina, who'd be so excited about me having friends.

I biked to the entrance and stopped just outside. Cumat wasn't here to greet me like normal, so I pushed my bike tire against the wall in just the right spot. It disappeared. I shoved off with my feet and coasted through the portal on my bike. I slid to a stop, barely through.

Plopping my bike down, I half jogged up the hallway. Today was the day. I could feel it. We were going to find Jaden.

I met Cumat part way up the hall. He was probably on his way to get me. He nodded a good morning but was uncharacteristically quiet, just spinning around and leading me to Starren's door.

The others were already there. I could hear them fighting with the door still closed. Something about a mom. My mom? I looked over at Cumat, but he didn't pause. Shoot. If he hadn't been here I would have stopped and listened.

When Cumat shoved the door open, Starren snapped her mouth closed.

She didn't say anything, just brushed by me and headed for the portal room.

Wade shrugged when I sent him a look, and we followed.

My mom was coming up an awful lot. Did they know who my mom was? If so, they knew more than I did.

We followed Starren at a good clip. Starren moved into the room, stopped us outside of the portal door and grabbed Cray, who had been waiting inside. "Where in Chicago? We have three portals to choose from."

Chicago? What happened to California? No one seemed to be in the mood for questions, so I kept my mouth shut.

"Near water. Something to do with wood?"

Starren thought for a moment, then nodded. She grabbed the doorknob and flung the door open, then stepped through without a backward glance.

The rest of us jumped through after her. We arrived in the early morning sometime. What was the time difference anyway? Mom and I had skipped this place on our tour. She had never said why, just didn't want to go there. I remembered because I had wanted to come to see the aquarium but she had said we couldn't.

"Lead," Starren said. Cray looked down at the asphalt and headed out.

I kept about ten percent of my attention on him, the rest I used to check out the city. We were in a nice section, for sure. What section, I had no idea. The shops were amazing, crazy styles that I'd never seen before decorating the windows.

There was a record shop, a shop selling painted china. I stopped at a clock shop and looked inside for a moment. The clocks all ticking in tandem was nearly hypnotizing. I looked at one of the clocks closer, a grandfather clock, wood shining a beautiful dark color.

Nine o'clock here. Ten at home. Mrs. Hemp definitely knew I was a no show for class by now. If she'd called Nina about me acting strange, what was she going to do when I disappeared for the second time in a week? Poor Nina. She was going to think I was lost in the state forest again.

"Hey, guys, wait up," I called after the others who were leaving me behind. "Can I use one of your cell phones?"

The group looked at me.

After a moment Wade took pity on me. "None of us have cell phones, Trish. We don't have anyone here to call."

True. Now I felt stupid. "Well, can we find a pay phone? I need to come up with a reason that makes sense for me not being at school and call Nina."

"We don't have time for that," Starren snapped. What was wrong with her today? She was so uptight.

"I don't have a choice. Dan will throw a fit."

"You think I care about what these fake parents do? You think I care about their feelings? You're crazy," she practically snarled.

"Hey, take it easy," I said, blowing a breath out of my nose, fighting the urge to yell back. Obviously something was wrong today, she was being weird. "No, I don't think that. But he works for the government here. Trust me, you don't want my face plastered all over everything." Okay, so the news that I was missing again probably wouldn't make it this far unless I was gone for at least a week, but it was a good excuse. "You need my help with Jaden. Just wait two minutes."

She got in my face, her eyes slightly crazy as she leaned in. "You think we can't do this without you? What did we do until we met you this week? Sit around and wait to be rescued?"

"She's right, Starren," Wade said.

"We probably shouldn't be doing this even with her help," Cray said nervously, pushing up his glasses. "I would prefer waiting to hear back from the Council, but if you aren't willing to do that, we don't stand a chance without Trisha."

Starren snarled under her breath, her face contorting into something scary.

Wait a second, why were they so worried?

"Tomorrow is his recorded birthday. We have to find him today," Cray whispered to me.

Oh crap. How had I not thought of that? We did seriously need to find him. But first I needed to call Nina.

I ignored Starren and walked away. There had to be a pay phone around here somewhere. I knew they were getting rare, but we were in a very public area. It took a couple blocks, but I found one next to a bus stop. I reached for the phone and paused, hand in midair. Did I really want to do this? Which was worse, calling Nina and making her and Dan mad, or letting them worry? I stood by the payphone and chewed my lip.

"If you're going to do it, just do it," Starren said.

They would be mad either way, maybe less mad if I warned them. I dropped in some loose change and dialed. Good thing I'd thought to bring money, couldn't depend on these fae for everything. The phone rang and rang. I let out a quiet breath of relief. A message would do.

Then, of course, Nina picked up.

"Hello?"

"Um, hi Nina," was all I could think to say at first. I'd been going over the message I was going to leave in my head. "I'm going to be home a little late."

"I'm glad you called. Are you going to a friend's house?" She laughed. "Where are you calling from? The caller ID says Chicago. Obviously something is weird. Unless you're traveling?" She laughed again, cracking herself up.

Oh, crap. I hadn't thought about caller ID. What did I say to that? What a stupid idea. Had I actually called because they needed me to, or because I wanted to hear Nina's voice? "Gotta go," it came out rough, the week catching up with me. I wanted to let everything that had happened pour out to her right then and there, but I couldn't. For one, fae or not, she'd probably kill Wade. "Talk to you later."

"Wait, Trisha, where are you? What's going on?" Her voice faded as I reached forward and put the phone on the hook. I wasn't going to feel bad. Nope, not bad at all. Okay, maybe a little. But I'd done the right thing in calling her. I couldn't help it if she worried more.

"Ready yet?" Starren impatience radiated from her stiff body.

"Yep, let's go."

Cray led us forward. We followed him, twisting up and down the streets for more than an hour. Every once in a while he would pause, close his eyes and focus, then we would be off again. Slowly the city changed from skyscrapers and fancy shops to office buildings, from office buildings to nice homes and from nice homes to not so nice homes. It was a good thing Cumat had taught me how to go invisible. Somewhere along the way we had all done it automatically.

The houses were starting to look a little unkempt as we moved further from the actual city. Weeds were growing in tiny fenced yards, bars showing up on windows.

Eventually we got to a small house, better kept than the ones around it. The flowerbeds out front had some nice plants. I didn't know what they were, but they were nice. The paint on the house was a faded blue that had probably once been pretty, and the picket fence around the property was missing some boards.

"This is it," Cray said quietly. "If it's him, he's in there."

Starren pulled her sword. "You stay here, Cray. Wade, Trisha, come on." She let herself through the fence gate and moved toward the front door.

This really was it. Somehow I knew it was. No weird fae power or anything, just a feeling. Hopefully the Fae Distribution Center had Jaden's birthday right. A flutter went through my chest but I clamped it down. I glanced in both directions at the houses around us. How were we going to protect these people if he had some type of dangerous power? Starren and Wade wouldn't care unless it exposed the fae, so I was on my own if it came down to that.

With a motion of her hand, Starren sent Wade around back. She took off for the front, apparently expecting me to follow her. I did. What choice did I have? I wasn't coming this far and having her say I didn't fulfill my side of the bargain, even if we didn't know what this guy could do. Starren was in a bad enough mood right now to have me taken back to Faerie and locked up until I was fifty. Only let out on good behavior, which wasn't likely to happen.

Starren paused to listen at the front door. Then, apparently satisfied, she reached forward and tried the handle. Locked. She held her hand over it and the lock clicked.

I drew my sword, the slight rasp of metal on scale making me bite my lip. Starren glared at me for a second, then motioned me forward. The fae shield, yay, what an exciting role. No seriously, it was actually a little more exciting than I would like.

I moved around her, sword held out in front of me. Somewhere inside a TV was on. Pots and pans banged around in the back of the house. The same vanilla air freshener Nina liked at home was in the air. This seemed like such a normal place, not some evil den. I slid a few more steps forward and looked around a corner. There was a little girl, probably seven or eight watching some Disney channel show. Seriously, a little girl? What was she doing here? I leaned around to get a better look and her gaze flew from the TV in my direction, like she could feel me. I jerked back around the corner before remembering that unless she was fae, she wouldn't be able to see me. How could I know if she was human or not? Was there something that gave it away?

Someone shoved me from behind and I swung around, sword in front of me. I nearly sliced Wade right open.

Stupid, stupid. Lots of training one on one with Mom didn't seem to be helping me much right now.

"Nothing that way," Wade mouthed to Starren and me. He walked around me and headed straight into the living room, toward the girl watching some guy play guitar on TV. I should probably be embarrassed that I didn't know what show that was, it was on Disney channel. Weren't teens supposed to watch that stuff? Whoever he was, he was super cute, but acting like a little kid. Wade was definitely more my type. The more manly type. I glanced in his direction. He didn't notice.

The kid looked around again, almost like she knew something was up. Her gaze went right through Wade though, like she wasn't seeing us.

Something slammed me from the side. I twisted as I fell, barely catching sight of a blur. I crashed into the fake wood floor, the little girl shrieking above me, screaming something about it happening again as she ran toward the back of the house. I caught a better look at what had hit me. A guy, probably a year older than me, dark hair and fae good looks. It was the same guy Starren had showed me a picture of last week. Jaden. We'd found him. He lunged at Starren. She had her sword up instantly, making him change his mind. He took off for the front door.

"Stop him," Starren yelled.

I scrambled up off the floor and tore out of the house after everyone else. Wade was turning a corner by the time I was through the small gate and out into the street, Starren only a step behind him. I jumped sideways, nearly getting plowed by some gangster vehicle. I opened my mouth to scream at the driver, then realized he couldn't see me.

Cray stopped where the other two had turned and waved me after them. I took off following.

It was a good thing we were in a housing section of town and not some high traffic area, the way those three were tearing across streets and jumping over and around anything in their way. I watched people's expressions as I passed, wind blowing back their hair, their confused faces nearly making me laugh even while we were chasing a criminal.

Poor people probably thought they were going crazy, hearing us run by but not seeing anything. I slowly gained on the three fae ahead of me, leaving Cray behind. They were in great shape, but not nearly as good a shape as me.

Even I was starting to get tired after dodging around fifteen more people and racing up five more blocks. I was catching up though. Then Jaden disappeared around a corner. At least I assumed it was Jaden. This wasn't exactly how I had expected confronting him would go down. Soon after, I lost sight of Starren and Wade as they popped around the same corner. I pushed myself to catch up, afraid that they would make another turn before I got there. Oh nope, there they were, looking furious.

"Where were you two? We could use some help here," Wade said, nearly snarling.

Maybe super speed was Jaden's power. Somehow he'd managed to get away from all four of us.

"Cray," Starren called. A pedestrian looked in the direction her voice had come from, his eyes going huge when there wasn't anyone there. Starren didn't seem to care. "Stop and feel. Where is he?"

The random guy jogged off, looking behind him. A pretty funny sight considering he was dressed like a punk with tattoos all down his arms. Not as tough as he'd thought.

I looked toward Cray. He was leaned over, sweat beading down his face. His eyes were closed and he was concentrating intently. "That way," he panted out, flapping his hand. "Two blocks."

Starren and Wade took off at a run.

"You can keep a lock on those two, right?" I asked Cray. He nodded. "Good. We're going to cut around and see if we can get ahead of him." We jogged after them, keeping them in sight for a few minutes, then cut through a dirty alley, pausing on the other side.

"See them?" I asked.

Cray didn't answer.

"Cray?" I looked over. His face was white and he was staring off behind me. I turned to look. Jaden was standing there, beckoning us forward with a crooked finger. He looked even better in life than in the pictures Starren had shown us. Dark hair wavy, even though it was a little disheveled. Where had he been living since his escape? At the house with his family? He had that warm California skin, all nice and tan. Maybe they had been there, before they had come to Chicago. I shook my head, rearranging my thoughts. This guy was a killer.

I took a step back, Cray moving to keep behind me. What did he want, to get us out of hearing range and bump us off? I pointed at myself in question, my face no doubt letting him know I thought he was crazy.

He nodded and tried waving us over. What was with this guy? Didn't he know we were chasing him? Well, of course he did, or he wouldn't know to ask us to come over. My first reaction was a no way. But, if he wanted us dead, we'd be dead by now, right? That's what everyone always said on TV. And it seemed to fit here, if the fae were so scared of him.

"Should we?" I asked Cray. Surprisingly he heard me. I could barely hear myself the way my voice cracked. He shook his head no. Hard.

But Jaden looked so earnest and he hadn't made one move in our direction. Plus, he'd been at the house with what I assumed was his little sister, with both of them and their dark looks, so maybe he didn't want a fight around here.

This could be my chance. There was no way the Council could say I hadn't held up my end of the bargain if I caught him single-handed. I'd just go over there, pretend I was going to listen to him or whatever, then knock him on the head. Good plan. I took a deep breath. "You stay here then," I told Cray. "I'll heal, you won't." I started forward.

"Trisha, there have to be things you wouldn't heal from either," Cray hissed after me.

I just kept walking. I heard a huge sigh behind me, then footsteps. Stupid of me to allow him to put himself in danger, but I sure didn't mind the company.

I stopped a few feet from Jaden and waited.

"Can we talk?" he asked, his tone calm, his voice a deep rich sound. I shivered a little. He could talk all he wanted. Nope, no, bad idea.

"Why should I talk with you? I'm calling Wade and Starren." I had to make it look good until I could get close enough to lay him out. Bet if Wade knew about this right now he'd wish he had a phone.

"No, please, wait," Jaden said. Something in his tone made me pause. He looked at the people on the sidewalk minding their own business and backed up into the alley, waiting to see if we'd follow. I moved after him slowly. Cray stuck to me like glue.

"Are you going to kill us?" Cray asked after we were out of human earshot. Wow, he was getting brave. Except for the octave his voice was in.

"Why did you break out of Faerie?" I asked.

"I ran from Faerie because my family is in danger. That's why I need you two."

His family? They had forgotten to mention he had a family. But of course he did. Even I did, now. So, that really was his little sister. Funny how that part had been left out in that little presentation before I'd said yes to the job.

"And how do you know your family is in danger? Did the Council just come and warn you or what?"

"The Council is who they're in danger from. They want to use them to get me to do what they want."

"And what's that?"

He moved in closer, looking over his shoulder again. "I'm going to trust you with this, but only because I've seen you." He leaned in, making the height gap between us a little smaller, his dark eyes mesmerizing. What was this guy's ability? Because I was starting to feel all gooey inside.

Hopefully he didn't have some kind of hypno skill like the hyran.

"I can read people. Their heart and their intentions. And I'm going to be completely honest with you since I believe you are going to help me." He blinked and I blinked back. "I can see bits of the future."

Whoa, okay, that brought me back. He could see the future? That was his terrible power that he was going to use for evil? Either he was keeping part of the truth from us, the Council had guessed incorrectly about his power, or something was really, really wrong. And he already had his power?

"If you can see the future, why were you in the house when we got there? I'd have thought you would have been long gone," Cray asked.

"I can only see pieces, never very much at a time and I can't choose what I see." His gaze swung from Cray to me. "I knew I had to meet you. I saw your heart and I hoped you would help me."

Okay, this was a little awkward. I was supposed to be catching him, not having him 'see my heart.' Whatever that meant. My fingers started tapping on my thigh, itching to reach for my sword. "How?"

"My family," Jaden said, his voice going rough. "I finally found my way back to them and they can't even see me. I'm some kind of… ghost. To other fae, I'm completely normal, but to humans, I'm not even there. How am I supposed to protect them?" His voice trailed off but the intensity on his face only grew. He couldn't be lying, he was fae. I wasn't going to trust him, no way, but he was telling the truth about his family. The rest I didn't know about. I didn't know enough about Faerie.

"Cray?" I asked. Surely he would have a better idea if this was possible or not.

Cray had his head cocked, staring at Jaden. "I don't know. I don't know of any other fae that has come back to Earth after being terminated here."

"Terminated?" Jaden asked. "Really? That's what you call it?" His voice was getting higher. "That's definitely not what I'd call it."

"Wait." I threw a hand up. "Don't get all excited." That had to be the first time it was me saying that to someone instead of the other way around. Wait a second, terminated? Like Wade had done to me? I was starting to get the feeling I'd somehow ended up on the wrong side of all this. "Tell me, right now, that you don't have any bad intentions. That you didn't commit some terrible crime to get locked up in the first place."

"Bad intentions? Like what?" His handsome face really did look confused. "As for what I did to get locked up, nothing. They just wanted me because they know who my father is."

I ignored his question. That feeling about being on the wrong side? It was getting worse. Much worse. Who was his father? That was a discussion for another time. "What do you want me to do?"

My mind's eye flew to the little girl watching TV. She was so cute, but had a strange sense of sadness for a kid that age. No bouncing around, not glued to the TV, just kind of watching. She reminded me of me after my mom dropped me off at Waterton Heights. A kid that age wouldn't understand why her brother wasn't around, if they really were siblings like I got the strong impression they were. She wouldn't understand unless she'd had other things happen in her past that helped a kid understand stuff they shouldn't.

He stared into my eyes, intensity crackling under the surface of his gaze. "Talk to them for me. Warn them."

"Why can we see you but your family can't? Aren't they fae?"

"My mother is actually my step mother. She's the only mom I've ever known, but she doesn't have a drop of fae blood in her. My two little sisters are half, and they can feel when I'm around, but they still can't see me. Jaime at least knows I'm there. I think Lucy feels it, but she won't admit something is going on."

This was kind of a toss-up for me. Trust the complete stranger, who was an escaped convict, or trust the guy who'd tried to kill me and the girl he'd gotten me to work for. No good choices here, but I was getting used to that. Ah, why couldn't I just be fae and fully believe the end justified the means. I just wanted to stay on Earth in peace. I needed this guy.

What chance did Cray and I have of holding him here until Starren and Wade started wondering where Cray was? Not a good one, considering how the guy was on high alert. And Cray and I alone had no chance in a fair fight. This guy was built. "If we help you first, will you go back with us willingly? Let me turn you over to Starren? I've got stake in this too."

Jaden's face grew dark. He thought about it for a moment. "I agree. You have my word."

I looked to Cray. He was studying Jaden. After a moment, he said "He is fae. He can't lie. He'll have to turn himself over."

Jaden heaved a huge breath. "We just need to head to my house and warn them. I think my mom will believe you. Enough has happened since Dad died for her to know there's something going on. We have to do it right now. Things are getting worse, and I won't be able to protect them alone anymore."

"Protect them from who?"

"The Council."

"Trisha?" Wade's voice, from down the alley.

Jaden stiffened. "Meet me at my house. Please." He didn't wait for an answer, just took off in the opposite direction Wade's voice had come from.

I looked at Cray. He shrugged. Now what? Did I really want to risk losing my home with Dan and Nina? Maybe we should just grab him, and then I could warn his family. But if he could see the future, he might know I was going to try something and then I would lose my chance of getting him to turn himself in. Not worth the risk. I could tell Starren, but she wasn't exactly one for compassion of any kind. What could go wrong talking to some human lady? It would only take a couple minutes, and then Jaden would have to come with me. It was worth a try.

"We lost him," Wade panted out when he was closer. "No idea where he went."

Starren was right behind him. Somehow I had to get Starren to split us up again. No way I was going to be able to explain to her why I wanted to go back to Jaden's house without telling her what was going on.

"Starren, when do you think we'll be heading home for the night?" Maybe I could get them to jump through the portal, then spilt. She'd think I was just dumb and missed it.

"We won't be going back tonight." Starren was still on high alert. She didn't even look at me while she answered. "Not when we're this close. He could be anywhere by morning."

"I can't do that, just not show up at home. Nina and Dan will freak out. They'll call my caseworker and I'll be in so much hot water. Besides, he could be anywhere by now, not just by morning. Why does the Council think he's going to be so dangerous?" Might as well plant seeds of doubt. They had already sprouted in my mind. Not that it mattered to me in the long run, if he was innocent or not. At least that was what I was going to tell myself. I was staying on Earth, no matter what.

"I'm not asking," Starren said. "Have a good time finding your way home on your own. Might take a little while without a portal."

"Fine. But if it gets after nine at home, I'm calling Nina again." That part was true. I seriously didn't want them on my case. What good would all of this be if they sent me away because I was a bad kid?

Starren rolled her eyes. Good thing she couldn't read minds. At least I hoped she couldn't.

"Cray, do you feel him?" Starren asked.

Crap. That could be bad. Shoulda thought of that.

Cray looked at me, eyes wide. I gave him a slight shake of my head.

He pretended to concentrate for a minute, or at least I hoped he was pretending. He better not give me up. "Maybe this way?" he made it more of a question than a statement. Good thinking. He wasn't lying.

"Lead the way, just don't get too close," Starren said.

Cray walked past her, hopefully leading us on a wild goose chase until I could figure out a way to get Starren to let me go somewhere on my own. Not like I could pretend to sprain my ankle. Wait. Food.

I waited a block so I didn't annoy her right away again. "Starren, I have to eat soon."

Starren growled something under her breath. "Are you a small child? You've been acting like one all day. I think you can wait a bit to get something to eat."

"We still don't know why the Council is after him," I said. Even though I'd do what I had to, that wasn't sitting well with me. So far all I'd seen is that he wanted to be with his family. I definitely couldn't fault him for that. Maybe if I planted some doubt it would help him in the long run. " And I can't help it. My metabolism runs too fast."

"She probably is incredibly hungry, Star," Wade said. "It's the regenerating fae's weakness. I did some research after I'd found out Trish was still here."

Great. So now he probably knew different ways to kill me. Oh well, we were almost done. After today, once I'd led them to Jaden, I'd be finished with the fae and I'd never have to see this guy again. Any of them. A pang hit me. Did I really not want to see any of them again? Wade was watching me out of the corner of his eye. I didn't smile, but I didn't glare either. He had just stood up to Starren for me, which was back to something a boyfriend would do. So confusing.

"Fine. Get something to eat. Try to find us after. Cray, Wade." She took off again, body rigid.

Whew boy, good thing I was bringing Jaden back with me, otherwise I'd be afraid to show my face. Handing him over would make up for whatever else I had to do in the next few hours. Hopefully.

That or she'd run her sword through me, just to make herself feel better. Oh well, it definitely wouldn't feel good, but I'd get over it.

The others were gone quickly. I moseyed off for a minute or so to make sure they were gone, then headed for Jaden's house at a good clip. My stomach rumbled as I trotted along, showing that I'd been telling the truth when I'd told her I was hungry. Not hard. I was always hungry.

It took me a lot longer than it should have, but I found the place. I let myself into the house quietly. Just relay his message, grab him and go. No reason to get involved. The murmur of voices came from the back room. I headed that way, pausing to catch a look at pictures every few feet. Most of them were of Jaden with the little girl that had been watching TV earlier and a girl who looked like she was between the two of them in age. They looked so happy. A real family. How was any of this fair? Some of us didn't start out with a family in the first place, some of us were torn away from them.

The house was neat and somewhat sparse. It didn't look like the family had much money, or maybe hadn't lived here long. Which made sense, with everyone thinking they were somewhere in California. There wasn't much, but everything was well taken care of. Someone ahead of me laughed.

The noise was coming from the kitchen. I peeked around the hallway corner. The two girls from the picture were there, with a woman about Nina's age who looked nothing like Jaden. The kids must have gotten the dark looks from their dad. She was sitting at the table, paying bills. There was Jaden, standing behind the little girl as she colored. The teen leaned against the counter, working on a piece of pizza. My stomach growled. I clapped a hand over it, trying to distract myself. Luckily no one seemed to hear it.

The little girl cocked her head my way for a second, then went back to coloring. The lady and the other girl just kept talking. Something about school. Jaden made his way over, headed for the back door and gestured for me to follow.

I stepped around the corner wall and waited until the voices were loud enough I didn't think they'd hear the door and slipped out with Jaden. Hopefully he wasn't about to jump me, I'd ditched my backup. We stepped out into a neat little back yard, the sparse grass clipped, a couple balls on the ground.

"How do you want to do this?" I asked.

"Get my mom alone. First we have to get her to believe you."

"Got any great ideas for doing that?"

"Yes, just get her out here. Before your friends come back."

He had a point. We definitely were on a schedule here. And the sooner this mess was done the better. Cray could only stall so long before Starren wanted to come back and check the house. I took a big breath. This should be interesting. I dropped the cover Cumat had taught me to make and made my way to the back door. I rapped on it twice. The noise inside the house stopped.

"I'll get it," I heard a woman say. The same voice that had been talking to the girls in the kitchen. She was at the door a few seconds later.

"What can I do for you?" she asked from behind the screen door.

"Mrs. Martan?" So much for sounding sure of myself. That didn't come out as confident as I would have liked. "Would you mind coming outside for a moment? I need to talk with you."

"Her name is Rebecca," Jaden whispered to me. I don't know why he was whispering, obviously she couldn't hear him or I wouldn't be here.

Rebecca looked past me, like she was checking to make sure no one was hiding out here. With the neighborhood they lived in, I didn't blame her.

"What are you doing in my back yard?" she asked.

Here's where things would get a little harder to explain. I took a second, trying to come up with something that wouldn't get the door slammed in my face. Maybe I should have made Jaden be a little more forthcoming before knocking.

"Who is it, Mommy?" a little voice asked.

"Jaime," Jaden said.

"Just someone who wants to talk. Go finish your picture." Little footsteps headed back toward the kitchen. Rebecca pushed the screen door. It squealed all the way open.

"What's this about?" Rebecca asked.

"Jaden."

She sucked in a breath, took the first couple steps down and let the door bang shut behind her. "Do you know something about his death?"

"Ask her if she knew dad's secret," Jaden said.

Great. Start with a secret about the dead husband when I was talking to her about her dead son. Wonderful plan. "Do you know of any secrets your husband was keeping? Not from you, of course, but from everyone else?"

Rebecca's face went ashen, like she was bleeding out somewhere. She had better not faint. I was bad enough at dealing with my own emotions, let alone someone else's.

"What are you talking about?"

Okay, so I'd hit a nerve. I'd never been one for tact. "Did your husband tell you where he was really from?"

Her face went smooth as marble. "Milwaukee." Oh she knew all right, she just didn't want to be the one to say it out loud.

"Just tell her," Jaden hissed.

"Well, apparently my parents were from Milwaukee' too. Anyway, I'm here with Jaden. He wants to talk with you."

Rebecca's face went from fake calm to anger. "Jaden's dead. Supposedly a freak accident, a transformer fell from a pole. I don't know what you expect to get from me, but I'm not giving it." She turned to go back into the house. I jumped forward and grabbed her arm, surprising us both. I wasn't normally big on physical contact.

"Wait, please. Just one moment."

She paused, keeping her stiff back toward us.

"Jaden is with me. When we die here, we get sent back to… Milwaukee. We can make it back to Earth in spirit, but not body. Like a ghost, I guess. Kind of." I wasn't really clear on this either. "Anyway, he came all this way to talk to you."

Rebecca spun to face me, making me jump back. She pushed her way into the yard and closed both the screen door and real door behind her. "You had better not be lying to me."

"Wow," Jaden said from behind. "You are really good at this."

I glanced over my shoulder his way. "Shut up. You told me you'd answer the questions."

"What?" Rebecca asked from behind.

"Not you!" I said. Man, this was getting too complicated.

"Like I said," Jaden crossed his arms in front of his chest. "Really, so good at this."

"Hush. Now what do you want me to tell her?" I asked him.

"Nothing until she knows it's me. Ask her what will convince her."

I turned to Rebecca. "How can we prove to you that it's him?"

She thought for a second. "Ask him about Lucy's birth."

"I don't have to ask him," I said. "He can hear you, you just can't hear him."

I waited until Jaden told me his answer, then passed it on. "His dad didn't trust hospitals so you had her at home. He also didn't trust anyone else to watch Jaden, so he made him stay. It was torture listening to you scream. Thankfully his father, Thomas, had loosened up a bit before Jaime got here."

"Jaden?" Rebecca whispered. Her eyes filled with tears.

Aw man, this was getting way too sappy for me. I looked over at Jaden. His face was sad, his hand lifted like he wanted to touch her face. Okay, this was so not good for my resolve to take Jaden in and give him to Starren. A person should be able to be with their family, period.

How could anyone do this to a person, fae or not? I reached forward and touched his arm. He jumped like I'd hit him with 1000 volts.

"Please tell her they aren't safe here," he said. "We need to move them."

"Mrs. Martan, Jaden believes you are in danger here. He'd like you to move."

"Move soon," Jaden interrupted.

"A.S.A.P." I added.

"Where?" Rebecca started to look scared instead of mad and incredulous. Progress, I guess. "Where can we go that they won't find us? We just moved here from California, after both Thomas and Jaden… so close, I was worried and wanted to get away. Why do they want us anyway? Who is doing this to our family?"

"We don't know why they're after you exactly." Not a lie, Jaden had a good idea, just no proof. None that he'd provided anyway. "They took Jaden out because of his fae power. They take all of us back to Faerie for training if we grow up here. Once killed here on Earth, we can only return as a spirit." Or that was as close to truth as I could figure out anyway.

Rebecca looked at me skeptically. "If they take all of you, then why are you perfectly visible?"

"It didn't work for me." I didn't go into detail. Jaden might not be able to lie, but his mom was human enough and humans were expert liars. Sure, I was trying to help them, but that hadn't stopped people from stabbing me in the back before. She didn't need to know about my ability. "Do you have somewhere you can go? Someone you can live with where you won't be found?"

"No, no one."

The gate around the side squeaked. I pulled my sword and whirled in that direction. Jaden jumped between his mom and the sound. Not sure what he thought he could do, but I wasn't sure about anything that had happened today.

Cray's head popped around the wall. "Is it safe?" he whispered loudly.

"Cray?" Obviously, but I was surprised, so give me a break. "How did you get away from Starren?"

"Do you trust this guy?" Jaden asked, like he hadn't met him in the alley earlier. I guess it was a little different now that we were on his home turf. "I know he's the one that's been tracking me. I've seen him in my visions."

"I just want to help," Cray said.

"Who are you talking to now?" Rebecca asked.

What? Oh, Cray was invisible to her too. Great. Rebecca was looking seriously confused. I didn't blame her. I was getting there too. I reached up and pinched the bridge of my nose, trying for some clarity.

"I was listening," Cray said, ignoring Rebecca and focusing on me. He spoke so quietly I could barely hear him, there was no way Rebecca could without the enhanced hearing my regenerating gave me. "There is a place, Trisha, a place where they would be safe." Cray nervously pushed his glasses up his nose, continuing to act like Rebecca wasn't even here. No doubt he just didn't know how to deal with her right now. How much interaction had he had with humans? Probably not much, if any. "There are certain spots on Earth where Faerie and your world touch. Fae can't use their powers there. It is supposed to be a sanctuary, a no fighting zone for the fae. But I don't know how that works for humans."

I looked Cray straight in the eye. He held my gaze for a second, then dropped his. How did I know for sure that Starren hadn't sent him after us by himself? That he hadn't taken my job as bait? "Tell me again that you just want to help," I said.

Cray glanced up at my face and then went back to staring at the ground. "I can't say I only want to help. I'm going against everything I've been taught here. Part of me is telling the rest of me I'm doing the wrong thing. But I can tell you that I want this family to be together and I don't want the Council catching them. That's the best I can do."

It was just going to have to be enough. What had happened in Cray's past that would make him go against the Council and help a family? I'd probably never know. We wouldn't ever see each other again after today. Hopefully.

"Where is this Sanctuary?"

"What sanctuary?" Rebecca asked. I held up a hand. One crazy conversation at a time.

"In a place they call Mexico. As close as I can figure out."

"Mexico?" I said.

"What about Mexico?" Rebecca asked. Okay, this was getting way too confusing.

"They don't have passports," Jaden interjected. "Besides, they wouldn't have any way of taking care of themselves down there, Mom doesn't even speak Spanish."

"What are passports?" Cray asked.

"Crossing into Mexico without passports isn't that hard. They just wouldn't be able to come back very easily, and they don't want to do that anyway. Get them on their way and they will be somewhere safe soon enough." And I'd have Jaden turned in. This whole mess would be over with.

"No way you're sending my family to Mexico. Do you have any idea how much trouble they could get in?" Jaden said. "Have you been down there? Some of those places are crazy. Not to mention lack of medical facilities. And that's a problem because-"

"But think of the trouble if they stay," I stopped him. "We just need to get them out of here."

"Is there another place, Cray?" Jaden asked, frowning in my direction. "Mexico won't work, Jaime needs-"

"What?" Rebecca asked, interrupting Jaden and not knowing it. Poor lady, this whole conversation had to be terribly confusing, even worse than it was for me.

"Cray, I need you to drop the charm and come over here." He looked at me like I was crazy. "Really, Rebecca isn't going to do anything, and it will help this conversation a lot."

Cray sighed and let the charm go. I saw a little shiver of air, like a fire before you can see the flames. Rebecca took a step back toward the house and let out a little squeak.

"Rebecca, this is Cray. Cray, Rebecca. He's trying to help us."

Rebecca squinted at him a second and then glanced around. "How many more of you are here right now?"

"None. It's just Cray, Jaden, and me at the moment. Cray found a place in Mexico where you would be safe, but Jaden would rather keep you out of Mexico." I turned to Cray. "Know of anywhere else?"

"Hurry it up," Jaden said, moving over by the gate. "Your friends are persistent. I wouldn't be surprised if they show up here any time. We need a plan."

Cray closed his eyes for a minute. "There is another place. It's called The Fort of Wayne, Indiana. You know it?"

"Does it have dialysis?" Jaden asked. "It has to have a dialysis center."

"What's that?" Cray asked.

"What's what?" Rebecca asked. She sounded like she was starting to get frustrated.

"Dialysis is where they take the blood out of your body, clean it and put it back in," I told Cray.

His face tightened in horror. "Take out your blood?"

"How did we get from talking about Fort Wayne to dialysis?" Rebecca asked.

"Jaden says make sure where we take you has it because..."

"Jaime," he interrupted.

"Because Jaime needs it," I said. The kid? I thought dialysis was for old people. I felt a slight pang of guilt. She'd been through so much for a kid her age.

"Jaden?" Rebecca whispered. Ah no, she was starting to tear up, like she was just now believing that he was here. What did I do with this?

"Does she have carinin?" Cray asked. "This Jaime?"

"Carinin? What's that?" Rebecca sniffed and used a thumb to swipe away a tear.

Cray scrunched his face up like he was thinking. He gave up. "I'm not sure what you humans call it. It can happen when fae and human have children. One of the reasons we aren't supposed to intermarry. It is a disease that affects the blood."

"That might be it," Rebecca said. "Doctors here didn't really seem to know what it was." Her face lit up. "Is there a cure?"

Cray looked like a deer in the headlights all of the sudden. He probably didn't want to disappoint her. Not when she'd been crying a second ago. "Not that I know of."

Rebecca sighed and her shoulders slumped, but she didn't look surprised. "I didn't really expect you to have a good answer. It doesn't sound like the fae have to worry about doctors very often."

Okay, maybe she knew more about us than I did.

Obviously I knew I didn't ever need a doctor, but I hadn't really thought about other fae and their medical needs.

"So Dad did talk about Faerie with her, more than just mentioning it," Jaden said.

"When can you leave for the Fort? The sooner we get them out of here, the better," Cray said.

"True. Something bad will happen soon. They're coming," Jaden said.

Oh great. Now not only did I have my own paranoia to worry about, but his too. How did I know if he was having a gut feeling or his ability was telling him something? How was it even working, he wasn't supposed to be old enough yet. Like me. So that meant he was a descendant of the Faerie Court too? "Did you see what's going to happen?"

"No, sometimes I don't see anything, I just get a feeling. Supposedly I should be able to control choosing what I want to see and forcing it eventually, but I don't know how yet."

Rebecca pinched the top of her nose. "We have to wait until tomorrow afternoon. Jaime is scheduled for her dialysis in the morning and she can't go without. I don't know where we could find a dialysis center on the way, plus they probably wouldn't take a walk in. It's too much paperwork. She has to have it every other day or she gets sick, very sick."

"There's something we can do that will buy you a little time. We'll give you one night to get packed up. I'd stay to help but we need to get back to Starren and Wade, they are going to start wondering what happened to us," I said.

"Are they the ones after Jaden?" Rebecca asked. "I heard you mention a Starren earlier."

"Yes, and you don't want to meet them, trust me. Especially in the mood Starren is in right now. Just get together what you need, get it in the car. You can leave whenever you're ready. Tonight Cray can lead Starren on a merry chase."

"You mean you're just going to send them away?" Cray asked. "Not even help them get to Sanctuary? The Council isn't going to be happy about them leaving, they will send someone after them. Someone worse than Starren. If they're intending to use them to manipulate Jaden, this could be very bad for them."

Shoot. When he said it like that it made me feel super cold hearted. Like it was me breaking apart the family, not the Council. I was supposed to talk to the mom and Jaden would turn himself over to me. That was what I'd signed up for. I pointed at Jaden and then pointed over toward the fence. He nodded and headed that way. I followed, not bothering to answer Cray, who looked nearly panicked at being left alone with a human.

"So, my side is done, now it's your turn," I said.

"You really want me to turn myself in while my family is running for their lives?" he asked, his face turning slightly red. "I understand if you don't want to help, fine, but you want me to just let them go on their own?"

"That was the plan, yes. Plus, Starren and Wade are after you. You give yourself up, your family is automatically safer. They could probably just stay here."

"No!" Jaden practically yelled, making Cray look our way, concern obvious on his face. "I'm telling you, the Council is after all of us. Something has changed. I don't know what changed or why, it has something to do with my dad, but I won't let them get my mom or the girls."

"Really? You don't know how this works?" I tried to keep my voice down so his mom couldn't hear me threatening him. "You made a promise. You're fae, you can't get out of it." Sadly I'd found the truth in that when I was five and told mom I wouldn't take any of the cookies off the counter. She left the room and the cookies taunted me until I tried. But no matter what I did, I couldn't get one into my mouth. A stupid part of being fae.

"I do know how it works. And I know that the one the promise was made to can release the one who made the promise." I glanced toward Cray to see if he'd noticed how loud Jaden was getting. He had. "Please, Trisha." And then the loud was gone and sad was back. I liked mad better. Much better. So much easier to deal with. "You have to know something is going on here."

Okay, yes, I could see his point. So far there had been no red flags about Jaden. He truly seemed like an okay guy.

Would a real criminal risk his freedom and safety to move his family if they weren't in danger? Probably not. Even if he wasn't a criminal, he wouldn't have come back knowing he wouldn't be able to interact with his family unless he truly believed they were in danger. I sighed. I was about to get myself into all kinds of hot water.

"So what do you want from me?" I thought I already knew the answer, but just in case…

"Get my family to Fort Wayne; get them settled in. Then I'll let you turn me over to Starren."

I sighed again. This was not going to be fun explaining to Nina and Dan where I was. Maybe I should just stay out here overnight. Nah, that would probably be even worse. But what if I couldn't get away in the morning? Wait, what was I thinking? I could turn invisible for Pete's sake. Sneaking out of the house would not be a problem.

"Please, Trish," Jaden asked. "I want you along in case something comes up that I need help dealing with. Or, more likely, if I need to talk to mom."

"Fine. But I'm holding you to the whole turn yourself in thing next time. I have my own reasons for doing all this."

"I'm sure you do," Jaden said, his voice going soft. He stuck out a hand. "Thank you."

I reached forward slowly and shook his hand. It was warm and slightly calloused, sending a tingle down my arm.

I pulled my hand back quickly. "And you owe me one. I'm not doing this for you, I'm doing it for your little sister."

"Fine, as long as you're doing it. Now you actually have to release me."

Okay, that was a little awkward. "How do I do that?" He gave me a little smile, the first one I'd really seen.

"Just say out loud that you release me from my promise to be turned over to Starren tonight."

"Jaden, I release you from your promise in exchange for a new one. That once your family is safe in Indiana, you will allow me to turn you over."

He lost the smile and got very serious. "As soon as my family is safe. I promise."

I nodded, not really knowing where to go from there. Thankfully Cray saved me from any further awkwardness.

"Trisha?" Cray called from the other side of the yard. I moved his direction. "We should help them with their stuff as much as we can. I can keep watch for Wade and Starren. They are far away right now, but I'll let you know." It was a good thing this tracking didn't work both ways. Wade and Starren wouldn't be able to find us until we wanted them to. Or they came back to the house, which would be bad. Very bad.

"He just knows where they are like that?" Rebecca asked, looking at me. I nodded. She shook her head. "Thanks for the offer to help but we don't have much. Nothing we can't leave behind other than the pictures. After losing Jaden and Thomas, stuff doesn't seem as important anymore."

She sounded so sad. I shook it off. Ignore it, ignore it.

Just get the job done. I was already helping way more than I should be. "Okay then, the plan is we come tomorrow afternoon, everyone loads up in your car and we head to Indiana, how's that? How long of a drive is it?" Dan and Nina were going to freak. Hopefully they would forgive me. No time to worry about it now. I'd figure it out later.

Cray shrugged. "I don't understand human travel."

"Mom?" a little voice asked from behind the screen door.

I hadn't even heard her open the inside door. Some protector I was.

"Yes, Jaime?" Rebecca asked, turning to the door.

"Who are those people?"

"Just some friends. What do you need?"

"He was here again, mom, I could feel him. I think he might still be here now. Do you think we should try talking to him?"

"I'll be in to talk in a moment, honey, just step back inside." Rebecca sighed. She waited until the door clicked closed. "She's been telling me for the past week that Jaden was here. I didn't believe her. I guess that if we make it to Fort Wayne I'll have some explaining to do. I'll tell Lucy what's going on. She'll want to know why we're moving, but it would probably be better to hold off for Jaime. Is Jaden still here?"

"Yes."

She held her hand in the air. "Goodnight, honey, I love you."

He reached his hand up and pressed his palm against hers. She obviously couldn't feel it. He looked down and dropped his hand to his side, his face stony, like he was trying not to show how much this was affecting him. I knew what it'd do to me if that was my mom. Didn't matter it was his step-mom, just like it didn't matter anymore that Nina was my foster mom. They were just moms. I'd be ready to kill someone if they had done to me what they'd done to Jaden.

Rebecca turned and headed for the house. "See you both tomorrow."

"Cray and I better find Wade and Starren," I told Jaden. "See you tomorrow." He nodded and followed his mom into the house, strolling right through the wall. Yuck. He really was a ghost here. "Lead the way," I said to Cray.

We walked quite a while in silence. I lost track of the blocks after seventeen. How had I gotten myself into this mess? This was what happened when I let myself care about stuff. I shouldn't care about Dan and Nina. Shouldn't, but did. How was I going to explain being gone all day today?

And how was I going to get away tomorrow if I went back today? I could always use the invisible thing, but would Dan let me come back, or would that push him over the edge? I growled under my breath. I was getting tired, something that didn't happen often, and it was making me cranky. "Are Starren and Wade at least headed in this direction?" I asked Cray.

He nodded. "Getting close."

"The least amount of talking with them, the better," I said. "Starren will be hard to fool."

Cray nodded again, but didn't say anything.

"How did you get away from them, anyway?"

"I said I saw something and when they ran off I slipped away."

Ha. I wouldn't have thought he had it in him.

The area was getting livelier as we finally reached the tourist section of town. Neon lights blinked everywhere. People were laughing and hanging off each other having a good time. I guess I'd be having a good time too if I was here under different circumstances. I weaved through them, hardly having to think about keeping myself invisible. A couple passed us, the guy carrying a bunch of packages for the girl, who laughed at something he said. Would that happen for me someday? I'd thought I'd found it once before. Thought I would have it for life. That hadn't turned out so well.

Another block and I caught sight of Wade headed our way, Starren not far behind him. He stood out from the crowd, partly because of his height and good looks, but mostly because he looked pretty angry.

I nudged Cray. "Ready? Here they come."

His eyes got wide, but he nodded. Poor guy. Today had been a lot for him, for both of us.

"Where have you been?" Starren asked, pushing ahead of Wade.

"Nice to see you too, Starren." Okay, a very typical movie response, but what can I say, I was nervous. And it was a non-answer, which got me out of telling her where we'd actually been.

"Where is he? We've been looking for him, and you, for over an hour." Oh yeah, she was mad. Even more mad than when I'd insisted on making that phone call.

"I don't feel him right now, Starren," Cray said.

"What? Try harder. We can't lose him after getting so close!"

"Are you getting too tired?" I asked. Maybe I could save him from getting chewed out. Somehow I felt responsible for getting him into this. "You know he can't sense things when he's tired Starren. That's why you let us go home at night."

"He is new to his power." Wade said. My hero. Ha. "We can't push too hard or he could lose it for a while." He turned to me. "It's possible to push your ability too far and shut it down." I had to keep an evil smile off my face. Wade was helping us and didn't even know it. Just what he deserved.

"Ah!" Starren slammed a palm against the nearest building, sending that slapping noise ricocheting. A lady walking by swung farther away from us, looking right through our little group.

"Don't get the cops sent after us," I whispered. We were invisible, but that probably made the whole situation worse. If they somehow found us I'd hate to have to try to explain how that had happened to some officer. No way we'd be making it back to help Jaden's family if we got caught.

"Let them come. I could use a fight right now. We almost had him. I can't believe you idiots let him get away."

"You know we can't do that, Star." Wade's tone was very soothing. I hadn't heard him use that tone of voice since he'd been trying to calm me down about the Inza's not letting me go to his place as much as I'd wanted. "We can't get the humans involved. The Council would not be happy if we took out a bunch of the local law enforcement. Let's go home for the night, get Cray up in the morning, and try again. He could be miles away right now, in a car, for all we know. We wouldn't be able to catch up anyway. If we do it that way, we can use the portal and get the drop on him."

"Fine. We will use the portal to our advantage tomorrow." She swung toward Cray. "Now that you know his aura, will you be able to pick him out even among the presence of other fae?"

Cray looked at me, then nodded reluctantly.

"If you haven't found his location by morning, you will be coming back with us and combing these streets until we find him."

"What about me?" I asked, slightly insulted.

She waved a hand at me like I didn't matter and took off walking. Cray and I looked at each other, then followed.

"Don't make her mad at you, Trish," Wade said from behind me. "She's pretty far up on the chain. If you really want to stay with the Inza's like you told us, I suggest you listen to her, otherwise you might find yourself waking up in some place you don't know again. Only this time it won't be in a forest close to home." He passed me and caught up with Starren, not even sparing me a glance.

Grr, someday... something. I didn't even know what. Was he trying to look out for me, or was something else going on? How was I supposed to know? It wasn't like he'd been very forthcoming with me so far.

No one had anything to say the rest of the short trip down into an alley. Starren walked straight into a wall, disappearing. How did they remember where all these random portals were? I'd go around crashing into walls forever before I accidentally hit the right one.

I stepped through after Cray, keeping my eyes closed for a second after the portal sensation faded.

"Back here by seven a.m.," Starren told me, then took off.

Wade clapped Cray on the shoulder. "Come on. You need to get some rest." Cray glanced in my direction.

I lifted an eyebrow. He nodded. Tomorrow. Tomorrow we were going to help Jaden's family, and then I was going to turn the guy in. Dan and Nina would be safe, and I would be able to stay with them. I was going to do it, no matter what my conscience was trying to tell me. I had to.

Chapter 11

I pedaled hard. I was running way early, but it didn't matter. All the better to keep an eye on Cray, make sure he didn't chicken out. Starren had quite a hold over him. The portal let me through on my own again.

This morning I had left the house before Dan or Nina had noticed I was awake, slipping out the door, invisible to human eyes. We hadn't fought the night before. They were past being mad. Now all Nina showed me was the pain that I wouldn't trust her with where I was sneaking off to. But I couldn't. The tiny part of me that kept whispering I should tell them what was going on was easily squashed. What if they didn't believe me? Or worse, what if they did, and thought I was a freak? Better to keep things the way they were.

Cumat looked up from where he stood part way down the hall, mop in hand. "Miss Trisha. Good morning."

"Good morning," I said, even though it wasn't. I started down the hall toward Starren's door.

"No use," Cumat said, stopping me in my tracks. "They left over an hour ago. Miss Starren gets impatient and they had no way of contacting you."

My vision rolled, making me dizzy. They'd left without me? No! What about Jaden's family? What about our deal? This was not good. So not good. I took a deep breath. Cumat didn't need to see how upset this was getting me. "Can I follow them through the portal? I'll just find them when I get there."

Cumat dipped his mop into a gold bucket, pulled it out infuriatingly slow and went back at the floor. "I'm afraid not. Miss Starren sets those portals, without her here, who knows where you might end up. Somewhere horrible no doubt."

I bumped my forehead with the knuckles of my closed fist. Think. Think. Come on, I had to get there somehow. "What are the chances the portal will take me to Chicago?"

Cumat looked up, irritation plain on his face. "Weren't you listening? Zero. The portal must be set."

"And you don't know how to do that?"

He went back to his work. "No."

Great. Now what? A plane would be the quickest way, but that would take at least six hours, if I could even figure out how to get on one. But they were behind here in time. I glanced at my watch. Five a.m. there. And Jaime had dialysis. This could work. I just had to convince Dan and Nina to get me on a plane. They'd probably be glad to get rid of me by now, after everything I'd put them through recently. Yeah, keep telling myself that. I tore out of the hallway, barely feeling the portal on my way back outside. I grabbed my bike and started running, jumping on at full speed.

I thought I'd been moving fast on the way to the Hall, but that was nothing compared to the speed I was flying along at now. Dodging through early morning traffic, I made it home a good ten minutes faster than it had taken me to get to the Hall. I tore up the drive and dropped my bike, then crashed through the front door and headed for the kitchen.

"Trisha, is that you?" Dan's voice, from the kitchen. "Is everything okay? I didn't hear her leave, did you?" The last part was meant just for Nina, but I overheard.

I rounded the corner into the kitchen. They were both there, doing dishes together. Dan finished rinsing a plate from breakfast and sat it on the rack. I took a breath, then took the plunge. "Dan, this is going to sound crazy, but I need a ride to Chicago. Right now."

Dan raised an eyebrow and grabbed a dish towel. "Chicago? What's in Chicago?"

"Family," I said, not really lying. They were the only other fae I knew, so other than Dan and Nina, they were the closest thing to family I had.

Dan paused and looked at Nina. "We thought you didn't have any family. That you were left at the children's home without any information as to who you belonged to."

"I was. But that doesn't mean I don't remember anything. I just got in contact with some of them and I need to go."

"What family do you have there? Does this have something to do with why you keep disappearing?" Dan went back to drying dishes. He was so calm. Infuriatingly calm.

"Ummm," too specific, how did I get around this one? "A little distant, but still family. They're expecting me."

"You didn't answer my other question," Dan said, reaching for another dish. "Is this why you've been disappearing?"

Well that was an easy answer. "Yes. They want me to come visit."

"Then why didn't they send you a ticket?" Nina asked.

"I didn't know if you'd let me go." And planes weren't their normal mode of travel, but I didn't need to mention that. "And, honestly, they don't have a lot of cash to spare." I could probably slip onto a plane invisible, but I didn't have the time to spare getting to the airport and trying to figure out flights and stuff. And also, this way Dan and Nina knew where I was for the day, and maybe they wouldn't kick me out. Hopefully.

"I'm not sure I'm going to like this family of yours, if they are getting you to do stupid things like skip school," Dan said.

"But at least now we know why she was gone," Nina whispered. Sometimes I loved being fae. Super hearing was definitely a perk. "It didn't have anything to do with us."

Wait, they thought I was disappearing because I didn't want to be around them? It was totally the opposite. Sigh. I should have figured that one out a week ago.

"I know, and I'm sorry, but I just need to do this. For closure. I'll pay you back for the ticket."

A look that I didn't understand passed between Dan and Nina. Was that a good look, or a bad look? "Can you give us a couple minutes?" Dan asked.

That had to be a good sign. They hadn't outright said no. "Sure." I headed for the stairs. Time to work on Plan B in case they said no. Of course to work on Plan B, there had to be a Plan B. I sat on the bottom step and tried to listen to the conversation going on in the kitchen.

No luck, mostly mumbling. And they never left the water running that long, Nina had to being trying to cover up their voices. I leaned forward on the step, like that could help me hear better. No such luck. Their tones intensified, then lowered again. How long had this talk taken already? Plenty long enough. My knee jiggled and I pushed down on it with my hands, trying to channel the nervous energy. This had to work. I couldn't even begin to come up with a Plan B. The invisible thing, but that was a super longshot.

Whatever was going on down there was serious. This was taking forever. I knew it was kind of a big decision, at first glance. But not really, I'd pay them back for the ticket.

"Trisha," Dan called.

I shot up off the step and bolted for the kitchen. He didn't say anything, just kept working on the dishes. Why wasn't he saying anything?

"Here," I said after a moment of silence.

"Okay," Dan said. Really? Just like that? "I can't go right now, I can't get away from work. You and Nina should have a great time once you get things settled. Maybe the two of you could spend an extra day going to a play or something."

"What?" It just came out. Nina could not come. That could be bad on so many levels. "Nina's coming?"

Dan finished drying his hands and threw his towel down on the counter. "We can't let you run off to Chicago by yourself, especially if we don't know this family of yours. You've never asked us for anything like this before, so I assume it's important, that's the only reason I'm going along with it in the first place. Nina is always talking about going to Chicago to visit her sister but things haven't really worked out." He smiled in her direction. "I guess that just changed."

Nina walked over and gave me a half squeeze. "This will be so much fun, Trish. Summer would have been nicer but this is fine. My sister is stationed just north of Chicago, once we're done with your family, I'll finally get to introduce you to mine." Her smile was so big it almost made my heart crumble.

That was so not going to happen. As soon as I hit Chicago, I was getting the Martans out of there. Nina had brought up my Aunt Wren many times, but I hadn't met her yet. No doubt Nina was thinking this would be some kind of family bonding thing. Shoot.

"I have to go alone."

"Not going to happen, Trisha. We are glad to show you how much we love you by doing this, but you aren't doing it alone."

My shoulders slumped and I rested my forehead in the palm of my hand. Now what? I absolutely had to go. I was just going to have to try to keep Nina in the dark when I got her there. And keep her from calling her sister. "Fine."

"When would you like to leave?" Nina asked. "My weekends are pretty free."

"Actually, I need to go now. Everyone is together this weekend. If I want to meet everyone I need to leave ASAP." That was true. If I didn't leave now there was a chance they would all be dead.

Dan and Nina gave each other the look again.

"It is Saturday," Nina said. She looked at Dan with a hint of pleading.

Dan turned and leaned his hip against the counter, crossing his arms and staring me down. I did my best to keep my face all innocent. Not easy when I was as guilty as sin at the moment.

"Fine," he finally said. "I'll see about tickets, you two pack." Grabbing his briefcase off the floor by the counter, Dan shooed me toward the stairs and pulled his laptop out.

There wasn't much I needed to pack, just a couple changes of clothes. I grabbed my phone charger and just about threw it in the bag. Habit. Not like I had anything to plug it in to right now.

My bag zipped easily, not much in it. I'd always been a light traveler, something my days on the road with my mom had taught me. I dragged the bag off my purple comforter and headed for my bedroom door.

Nina was all ready to go. I could see her over the railing, pulling her suitcase out of her room. She looked so happy, like the two of us were going on a fun trip together. No doubt she thought I was having some parentage crisis or something, not that we were going to help a family move before they all got killed. And she thought she was going to get to see her sister.

A pang hit me, square in the gut. What was I getting her into? But I didn't have a choice. It was this or betray Jaden and his family. I didn't have time to argue with Dan and try to go by myself. Not like I was ever going to be able to change his mind anyway. In a way, I was doing this for our family. I couldn't just turn Jaden in without helping his family, but I had to turn him in so I could stay here. And if he were to tell on me if the others captured him without my help, I had no doubt whose family Starren would be after next.

"Plane leaves in two hours and thirty six minutes. We better get a move on it," Dan yelled up the stairs.

Nina said something to him quietly. I strained to hear. "I know, but thank you. I feel like this could be the breakthrough we've been waiting for. A chance to show her how much we care."

Breakthrough? She had no idea. "Stay in public areas," Dan answered.

"It's not like her family is going to murder us, Dan. Do you think she'll try to stay with them?" Try to stay with my fae family? Not likely. So opposite of the truth. I was doing all this to stay with my human family. Family? That was a weird thought. I peeked over the railing at my foster parents for a second. Yeah, definitely family.

"They won't be able to murder you for sure if you stick in public areas. Make them meet you." He reached forward and rubbed her arms. I ducked back behind the stairs even more, afraid one of them would glance up and see me. "And I don't think she'll want to stay with them. Even with all the problems we've had, I get the feeling she likes it here."

"I'm surprised you didn't want to get their names from her and do a little digging before you let us go."

"I thought about it. But I want her to be able to trust us with anything. I think this is a great step in the right direction. And you'll have Wren to help you if you need her. We both know what she's capable of. If you don't like the family, you won't have to be around them long."

I almost snorted, catching myself just in time. She was going to be spending a lot of time with them, cooped up in a mini-van if everything went well.

"If she meets her family and they aren't what she's expecting, maybe it will put a stop to all this sneaking around. Best-case scenario they don't even show up. It's worth a try. If we don't get it handled, she's going to get taken away from us. Or worse, leave and not come back. Get it out of her system, get her home. We can all relax then."

"I hope you're right," Nina murmured.

"I usually am."

I took that as my cue and jerked on my bag, letting it clump down the stairs after me. Dan was hugging Nina when I made it to the lower level. They were so grossly cute.

"All ready?" Dan asked.

I nodded.

"Good. Load up. I'll drop you off on the way to work."

I headed for the garage, threw my bag in the trunk and waited for Nina to do the same. She wiggled hers in next to mine and stepped back, giving me room to shut the trunk. "Thanks, Nina."

She reached around and gave me a half hug. "Of course, Trish. I hope you'll explain a little better what's up while we're on the way."

Yeah, I'd figure something out. I could be mostly honest, just not with the why someone was after Jaden thing. I pulled free just as

Dan walked out. He locked the house behind him. We all piled into our respective seats and we were off.

Traffic was pretty good for a Saturday morning. We moved along quickly, soon signs for Dulles International Airport were flashing by.

"Here, Honey," Dan said, passing Nina a couple papers. "I printed off your tickets."

I stuck my head up between the two front seats, straining against my seatbelt. "How long is the flight?"

Nina flipped the paper over in her hand and squinted at it for a second. "Two hours and seventeen minutes."

"Two hours?" What time was it now? I leaned to see around Dan's shoulder. Eight forty five. "When does the flight leave?"

"Ten fifteen," Dan answered.

Ten fifteen, plus two and a half hours, twelve forty five? What if Jaime was done with dialysis and we weren't there yet? I took a breath. An hour time difference. That would help. We would be to their house by one or so. It was going to be okay, it'd be fine.

"Trisha, are you okay?" Nina asked.

"Yep," I said. She didn't look convinced but let it go.

Dan threaded through traffic and miraculously found a spot to coast to a stop near the entrance to our airline. He put the car in park and hopped out to help Nina with her bag.

By the time I got around the car, Dan had both our bags sitting on the curb. He gave Nina a hug and a quick peck, then turned and pulled me into a hug. I didn't wiggle like usual. "You get this business handled, then just have fun with Nina, okay? You're going to love your Aunt Wren."

I hugged him back and pulled away. He wouldn't be so happy if he knew the truth. I was putting his wife in danger. Maybe if I told him, he'd be able to figure something out, maybe he could keep the fae from taking me. Maybe he would ship me off to some government facility for aliens.

"Wow, I wish I was going with you, ladies. Have a great trip."

No. Not worth the risk. What if they found out what I was and decided I was a freak? Or accepted me anyway and then the

Council found a way to get to me? Either way was so not cool. I could handle this myself. "Thanks," I said.

"You know we will." Nina's grin was huge. "Don't mess the house up too much while we're gone."

"Wouldn't dream of it."

Nina stood on tiptoe and gave Dan a quick kiss on the cheek, grabbed her bag and headed for the sliding doors.

Dan and I looked at each other and shrugged, then I took off after her, afraid to lose her in all the airport craziness.

Nina was already most of the way to the check in line before I caught up. Her smile was big, like we were going on vacation, not to a crazy get away attempt. Well, as far as she knew, we were. She was probably thinking we would spend an hour with my bio family, then head off to enjoy the amazing shopping with her sister. Guilt chewed at me.

Hopefully she liked road trips. Someday I was going to have to pay them back for the return tickets that wouldn't be used.

At the counter, Nina provided the paper tickets Dan had printed for us, her license and my school id. The attendant behind the counter didn't look too excited about her job.

"Would you like to check your bags?" the attendant asked.

"No, we're in a bit of a hurry, we don't want to have to wait for them in Chicago," Nina said. "We'll just do carry on."

"Please place them in the luggage rack and make sure they'll fit," the attendant monotoned. "Next."

First step done, now security. Nina kept up a running commentary about things we could do in Chicago while we took off our jackets and shoes and threw them on the belt. She paused her speech to answer a text. "Wren says she's pretty free this week! She's going to meet us in Chicago tomorrow morning, and then we can catch an evening flight home. This is going to be awesome."

"Uh huh," I managed to get out. My palms started to sweat as we slowly moved forward. I nearly fainted from relief when they didn't have the newest type of scanner like I'd seen in the movies. Just a metal detector. I'd never tried getting through one of the new ones before. I didn't even know if it would be a problem. It never had been on field trips into the city. It just made me nervous. How different was fae physiology from humans? We lived longer and had magic, but other than that we were basically the same, right? So far no one had noticed anything at any doctor's visits.

They couldn't see magic on a machine. Could they?

We found our gate and sat to wait the twenty minutes until boarding time. A little surprising that Nina hadn't been freaking out in security about the plane leaving without us. Normally she made us get everywhere way early.

"So, what are we doing? What time do you think we'll be done today? Do you have a meeting set up? I've been trying to find places for us to visit. The zoo of course, what else would you like to see?" She tapped away on her phone for a second. "Wren wants to go to the aquarium with us, so we'll wait for her on that."

"I'm not sure how long it's going to take. Better just not plan anything yet." Nina's face dropped and I wanted to slap myself for disappointing her again. But it was kinder to do it now than to wait until we were loading in the car to head to Indiana.

A strange feeling came over me, like something wasn't right. Like someone was watching me. I looked around, but no one seemed to be paying any attention to either of us.

Weird. We waited for the boarding call, her playing on her phone, probably texting Dan and Wren both, me keeping an eye on the crowd. Talk about teenager/adult role reversal.

Finally they called boarding for our flight. I waited impatiently for the announcer to get to our row.

"Zone Two, you may now board. If you have Zone Two on your ticket, please board."

Nina elbowed me. "That's us, we're in row seven." As if I hadn't been sitting here staring at my ticket for the last fifteen minutes. But I shouldn't complain, she was taking this trip for me.

After letting the attendant scan our tickets, we filed down the long, cold, collapsible tunnel into the plane.

"Here we are." Nina stopped at our row and threw her bag up, then reached back and took mine from me, smashing it in beside hers. She gestured for me to squeeze in to the seating section first. I moved in and plopped down in the window seat. I watched them load suitcases into the hold below, waiting to get this trip started. What time was it in Chicago now? Had Jaime started dialysis yet? "What time is it?" I asked Nina.

She looked down at her phone. "10:10. Looks like we'll be leaving right on time."

10:10. 9:10 in Chicago. Rebecca and Jaime were probably just getting started. This was going to work. It had to work.

A voice came over the speakers and the flight attendants went out in the aisles for some kind of safety demonstration. Everyone else on the plane seemed to ignore it, but I watched carefully. This was my first time flying, I needed to know this stuff.

About halfway through the speech I felt a prickle on my skin. Nothing bad, just nothing I'd really felt before. I looked around but nothing seemed out of place. Probably just the excitement of flying.

The stewardess finished her talk and moved out of the line of sight. A minute after a voice that introduced himself as the pilot came over the speaker. Clear skies ahead, hoping to land on time. Perfect.

I leaned against the glass, staring at the ground as we slowly backed away from the gate. Pressure built in my ears.

Nina patted me on the shoulder. "So exciting!"

Not exactly the word I would use, but we could go with that. We moved out onto the tarmac. Two other planes were ahead of us in line. My fingers curled around the arm of my seat involuntarily as the first one thundered by. The other plane ahead of us moved out onto the runway, then sped away. Our turn. The plane started out slow, a great lumbering beast, but picked up speed fast. My stomach clenched.

It was only a second later that there was a slight jolt and we were in the air. I gripped the arm of my seat tighter, eyes glued to the shrinking ground. And that was it. We were flying.

"You okay, honey?" Nina asked.

"Yeah," I answered. "Never been on a plane before." Probably because my mom had never had any ID.

Nina's smile covered her face. "Really? I haven't gotten to do many first experiences with you. That's neat. Hopefully we have a lot more of those this weekend."

It was kind of neat. That Nina would do this for me was amazing. Like something a real mom would do. I studied her for a second while she looked past me and out the window.

I'd been pretty lucky to land a home with her and Dan. Plenty of other home experiences had taught me the difference.

I followed her lead and looked back out the window. Cars were barely visible below. How high were we? Would I heal if we plunged to the ground from this height? Probably, but Nina sure wouldn't.

"Can you tell me yet? What the plan is for Chicago?" Nina asked.

I kept my gaze out the plane window, my stomach leaping every time we hit a slight bump. So stupid, with all had I been through. Trolls, the hyran, and now I was scared of something so normal as flying. Pathetic. I consciously loosened my grip on the armrest, my fingers aching for a second. "I don't really want to talk about it here." Truth. But I also didn't want to talk about it anywhere else. Not that I was going to get away with that.

Nina glanced around the plane. "I guess this isn't too private. But you're going to have to get into better detail once we get off this thing, or I'm sitting us down until we can get a flight back and we're going straight home."

Fair enough. I nodded. Nina laid her seat back and leaned into it. "Nap time."

I tipped my chair back too. Nina's eyes were closed already, but every time I shut mine I got that same uneasy feeling of being watched. I let her sleep and kept an eye on the other passengers.

Nina didn't even wake up when the attendant stopped by with drinks and snacks. I told her what Nina would want and then ate mine. The snack worked for a few minutes, but then I was eying hers. I was able to control myself for thirty minutes or so, then I gave up and ate hers too.

A tedious hour later and the fasten seatbelt light dinged on. No wonder no one else seemed all that excited about flying, this was boring. I sighed. But the light meant we were about there, right?

Sitting here, my mind on little Jaime was torture. How could anyone even think about putting a kid that age in danger?

"Flight attendants, prepare for landing," the pilot's voice said over the speakers. I reached over and nudged Nina. "We're almost there." She stretched and yawned. "Did I sleep?"

"Only the entire trip," I fake grumbled.

She grinned. "Good, I needed that. What time is it?"

"Here? 12:45." We were cutting it close, but it would be fine. Cray would keep Starren and Wade away and the family had stayed safe without my help this long. Everything was going to be fine.

"I can't believe I slept that long. But it has been a crazy couple of weeks." In other words she hadn't been sleeping because she'd been spending her nights worrying about me. Ugh, why had I started caring about stuff? It made life so much more work.

The plane sank through the clouds toward the ground.

The city formed beneath me, buildings stretching up into the smoggy sky. It looked a lot different from up here, the buildings not as tall, the streets much cleaner. Which I wasn't supposed to know. The ground rushed up, then we were hovering over it for just a second before a slight jolt.

"Landing," Nina said. "Glad that's over, flying is so boring."

I raised an eyebrow. Maybe for me, but she'd slept the whole time.

"What?"

"Nothing."

The plane coasted nearly to a stop, then lurched forward toward a gate. Once we stopped for good, the attendant made the last of the announcements and seat belts started clicking off up and down the rows.

I wiggled past Nina and stood up in the aisle. Man, that felt good after sitting for so long. At least it felt like a long time. I didn't sit much, other than school. I reached to grab my bag and that same feeling of warning swept through me. Something was definitely wrong. I looked around the plane. No one was even glancing our way. The man in the seat ahead of us was going after his own bag, the lady with the kid across from us was looking frazzled, trying to collect all their junk. What was going on?

"Don't you think?" Nina was asking.

"What?"

"That it's time to get something to eat? I'm starved."

"Yep, you know me, always ready to eat," I answered, not really paying attention to her yet. Something had to be going on. Still, no one stood out to me.

Nina laughed while she stood, putting an arm around my shoulders. "Sure do, I bet you're even hungrier than I am, even if you did eat my in flight snack. Whatever it was, I didn't even see it."

"Can we get it to go? The food I mean?" Because no matter how much I tried to convince myself otherwise, something was going on. I'd never really felt like this before. The creepy feeling. Another squint around the plane didn't change the fact that everything looked normal.

"Sure. But what's the hurry?" Nina grabbed her bag from the upper bin.

"Just want to get this done." We waited together for a minute until the line ahead of us finally started to thin.

It started up again, the feeling, causing the walls of the plane to close in around me, trapping us. I took a breath, trying to fill my lungs to the max, but my chest was so tight. What was going on? What was causing this? Something was definitely not right, but I had no idea what.

"You okay?" Nina asked, her voice somewhat distant.

"Yeah," I answered. "Just hungrier than I thought."

Hopefully that was it. Because if not, things were about to get interesting.

Chapter 12

One train and two buses later we were only a couple blocks from Jaden's house. I'd told Nina that I already had a meeting set up, and that it was at a place she wouldn't have to worry about anything happening to us. I just didn't tell her it was their house. We'd grabbed some food at the airport, but I was starting to get hungry again already. One annoying thing about the regenerating, when I got nervous I burned a huge amount of calories, like my body was just waiting to heal.

Nina had started looking suspicious when we left the shopping district and moved into a more residential area. I stopped us in front of the Martan's home.

"This doesn't look like a restaurant or other public place," Nina said, crossing her arms.

"I know, I'm sorry," I answered.

Nina eyes widened. This was probably the first time I'd ever told her sorry sincerely.

"Before we go in, there's something else I need to tell you."

Nina tipped her head and raised an eyebrow.

"This is a family, just not my family," the words tripped out of my mouth. *Forgive me, please*, I begged silently. "One of my friends, his family is in trouble. I'm helping them get out of the city."

Nina closed off, her face going blank. "Don't you think you maybe could have mentioned this earlier? Dan might have been able to fix things. What's going on? How are we going to help?"

"You wouldn't understand."

"Try me."

I didn't even know where to start. Trusting was definitely not one of my strong points. Trust Nina to want what was best for me, sure, trust her not to freak out and call some government agency? Not happening.

"There are some people threatening them. We just have to get them somewhere safe."

"How did this job fall to you? And why haven't they called the police?"

"It's complicated."

"I think I can probably handle it," Nina said. She stared straight at me, arms still crossed tightly across her chest. She wasn't even a real mom and she still had the mom look down, how did that happen? "We are going somewhere to discuss this before we get into something that I don't understand."

The front door flung open and banged into the wall inside, Jaime popping her head out. "We've been waiting for you," she yelled in our direction. Her little pigtails flopped to the side as she tilted her head, clamping her mouth shut and staring at Nina.

Nina looked at me. "Who's this?"

I shrugged.

"How many kids are involved? What kind of danger are they in?"

Man she asked a lot of questions. "I'll answer all your questions in a few minutes." I turned on my begging face.

"Please? We're already here, they already know we're here, it's too late." Nina huffed at that, but followed me through the gate over to the front door.

"Hello," Nina said once we were closer to the kid. "I'm Nina. And you are?"

"I'm Jaime. I'm not allowed to let strangers in the house, so only Trisha can come in. Mom said we were waiting for her."

"Who's here?" Rebecca's voice, from inside.

"It's me," I called in past Jaime.

Rebecca showed up behind Jaime and opened the storm door. "About time. Where's Cray?" Her gaze flicked over to Nina. "And who's this?"

Nina held her hand out to Rebecca. "Hi. I'm Trish's mom, Nina." Trish's mom, without the foster. I liked that.

Surprising she'd admit it right now, when she probably wasn't very happy with me, but I still liked it.

"Oh, so you're one of them too?" Rebecca asked. She didn't look very happy about another fae being involved.

Shoot. "Foster mom," I clarified, giving Rebecca a look. She must have caught on, her expression definitely changed. I looked over at Nina. Her face had changed too, gone all mask like. I'd hurt her feelings, no doubt about it, right after she'd claimed me. My conscience squirmed, but I hadn't had a choice. I was saying that a lot lately.

"About time you got here is right," Jaden said from behind his mom.

I crossed my eyes at him but didn't answer. Nina had been exposed to enough in the last five minutes, she didn't need me talking to an invisible guy.

"We got the van packed," Jaden continued. "Without any help from you."

"Not much help from you either, I bet," I answered before I could stop myself, then instantly felt bad. Not like he didn't want to help.

"What?" Nina asked.

"Never mind," I answered. "So you're totally ready to go?" I asked Rebecca.

Rebecca looked at me weird for a second, like she knew I'd been talking to Jaden. But she must have caught on to the fact that Nina was in the dark about all this because she didn't ask. "Yes, we're ready. I found Jaime a dialysis center, already made her an appointment for Monday. We should be settled in by then."

"Be where?" Nina asked.

There it was again, that creepy feeling. What was with that? It was starting to annoy me. I glanced over at Jaden, but he didn't seem to notice anything. "Glad you're set. I think we should get out of here. Something doesn't feel right."

"What about Cray?" Jaden asked.

"He'll be fine. He just won't be able to go with us. Maybe he can distract Starren."

"I'll go check on the house one more time," Jaden said. "Make sure they got everything important."

"Who's Starren?" Nina asked, looking a little concerned. Probably for my sanity since what I'd just said to the empty air didn't follow the conversation we'd been having with Rebecca.

"Hopefully you'll never have to find out," I muttered. It almost made me feel bad. Starren had tried to take care of me while I was on her team. But I wasn't under any illusions about what would happen if she found out I was helping Jaden's family.

"Will someone please explain to me what is going on here?" Nina asked.

"Trish, get them in the car, now!" Jaden's voice, from inside the house.

"Load up, everyone to the car, now," I said, not waiting to find out what had Jaden so upset.

Rebecca instantly picked up on the urgency. "Here," she shoved Jaime toward me. "Buckle her in, I'll get Lucy."

I grabbed Jaime's hand. "Come on." I told both her and Nina.

"Not until you tell me what you've gotten us into," Nina said, planting her arms across her chest. Great. There went the arms again. When she got like this there was no changing her mind.

"We don't have the time right now, Nina. I promise, I'll explain later." Explain yes, everything, probably not. I half dragged Jaime to the side of the house, opened the mini-van door and tossed her inside. It looked like the back was full of stuff. It was going to be a long ride to Indiana. Six people in a seven person mini-van, not too bad except for the boxes. "Get in the back, get your seat belt on." Jaime looked at me like I was about to murder her or something, eyes all wide.

Silly kid, I was trying to help.

Nina stepped in close and popped her head in the open van door. "Everything is going to be okay, sweetie. Just buckle up, okay?"

Jaime nodded and reached for her belt.

"Thanks," I said. Credit where credit was due and all that. "Would you stay with her while I check with everyone else?"

Nina nodded. "But we aren't getting in this van until I have some answers."

Ugh, adults. I dumped my suitcase beside the van and took off for the house. Not that I knew Jaden well or anything, but he didn't seem like the panic without reason type. Lucy was busting out of the front door when I made it there.

"Thanks," she said, sticking her face in mine.

"For what?"

"Forcing us to move again. Mom had talked about it before, but now we're actually doing it and she won't tell us why. It's too big of a coincidence that it happens the night after we meet you. What did you say to her?"

Rebecca opened the glass door. "Not now, Luce, just load up." Lucy grumbled something and headed toward the van. Rebecca waited until she was out of hearing distance. "Is Jaden in the van?"

"No. Go ahead, I'll go in and grab him." I pushed past her and went inside. The house didn't look that different, even with the stuff all packed up. It had been mostly bare when I was here yesterday, but it felt different now. Void of life. All the family pictures gone from the walls, the keys not hanging on the key rack by the front door. All the non-personal items were still here, all the décor. Rebecca knew how to pack.

Something told me this hadn't been the first time she'd been on the run. No wonder she'd taken everything so calmly yesterday. She probably knew more about the fae than I did, if Jaden's dad had told her much.

"Jaden, you in here?" I called.

"The living room."

I walked in. He was standing by the couch, staring at the floor.

"What's up? Why are we in a hurry?"

"Something bad is going to happen, soon. It hit me, really strong a minute ago."

I shivered. He was feeling exactly what I'd been feeling all day. Not good. "Then why are we standing around? Let's get out of here." I grabbed his hand and jerked, trying to pull him out the door. He didn't budge.

"Wait. It's Jaime's panda. I can't pick it up. Can you grab it?"

I looked to where he was pointing, a small teddy bear that had apparently fallen off the side of the couch. "We're going to be in a world of hurt if she doesn't have it when it's time for bed." I reached down to grab it just as the sound of the back door creaking open hit my ears. I froze.

Jaden grabbed my wrist and put a finger to his lips. I nodded, reached down and picked up the bear and we started toward the front door, practically on tiptoe. If he got himself killed over this stupid bear, I was going to be so mad. I still needed him so I could stay with Dan and Nina.

We reached the front door just as a guy who looked a few years older than me stepped around the corner from the kitchen. He was the most gorgeous guy I had ever seen, and that was saying something after Wade. I stopped, not feeling like I had a choice. My eyes met his, such a beautiful light blue they were almost white. He held out a hand toward me. Involuntarily my hand started to go up. Someone gripped my wrist and jerked me out the front door, nearly knocking me down. No, I wanted to go back. I needed to see him again.

"Let me go!"

"No, we're leaving." Jaden dragged me toward the van at a run, much like I had pulled Jaime out there a few minutes ago. How was he a ghost and still so strong?

"Who was that?"

"I don't know and we aren't sticking around to find out, let's go."

We rounded the corner, me still pulling back from Jaden, feeling like I was waking up from something. The feeling I'd had at the airport was back, of being watched. Surely I would have noticed that hunk if he'd been around. Me and everyone else, unless he'd been invisible to humans. The sliding door on the van was already open. I grabbed my bag in one hand and Nina's, which was propped up next to mine, in the other, tossed them in and jumped through after Jaden, slamming the door. "We need to get out of here!"

The sliding door on the other side of the van was open and Nina was standing there talking to Jaime.

"Nina, please, get in! There's someone in the house, we need to go." I was shouting now, but she didn't understand the urgency of the situation. How could she when I hadn't told her what was going on? Her eyes got wide and she slammed the sliding door, jumped in the front seat and slammed that door for good measure.

"Is… everyone here?" Rebecca asked.

"Yes," I yelled. "Go!"

She looked in the mirror, slammed the van into reverse and hit the gas.

The guy was just coming out of the front door as we shot out onto the street. I craned my neck to watch him as Rebecca threw the van into drive and peeled out. Something about him made me want to stop her, to get out and go back and find out everything about him. He raised his hand and the van jerked to the right, causing Jaime to hit her head on the window and Rebecca to pull the wheel to the left, over correcting and sending the van screeching into the left lane.

A car in the other lane slammed on its horn, swerving to miss us. Rebecca jerked the wheel and we were back in our lane.

What was that? Had he done that to us?

Nina turned from the front to glare at me in the middle set of seats. "Who was that?"

Jaime was crying softly in the back seat. I turned around and gave her the rescued teddy bear, trying to avoid the question. Nope, not going to work if the look on Nina's face was any indication.

Rebecca glanced at me in the rear view mirror, clearly hoping for some type of explanation also. I looked at Jaden who had moved to the back seat, but he was too busy worrying about Jaime.

"I don't know."

"Does someone want to let me in on what just happened?" Nina asked, sending death looks around the van. "If no one is talking, I'm calling the police. I don't know why I shouldn't anyway." She waved her cell around in the air as if to prove she was ready to call at any time.

Rebecca caught my eye in the rearview mirror. I shrugged. I had no idea what to tell her. "My husband, well, he was mixed up in some things," Rebecca said. "We're trying to move on, that's all."

"What kind of things? And how did you get in the middle of this?" Nina asked me.

Good question. No good answer.

"Can you blame her for wanting to help people?" Rebecca asked.

"No, but that doesn't make me any less curious about how we ended up out here."

"Trish?" Jaime said from the back seat.

"Yeah?"

"Thanks for saving Dudley. Was that man bad?"

"You're welcome."

"Whoever that guy was, he was hot," Lucy said.

The moms in the front looked at each other and stopped talking. Whew. The assist was going to Jaime here. No one wanted to fight in front of the kid.

"Can we at least talk about where we're going?" Nina asked.

"Fort Wayne."

"Fort Wayne? Indiana?"

"Yep."

"What's there?"

"A new home," I said, twitching my head toward Jaime, using her as the excuse to not have to explain things further.

"How big of a reach do these people have? And how many are there? I think we need to get Dan involved."

"No!" Rebecca and I said at the same time. She didn't even know who Dan was, but she probably didn't want anyone else involved at all. Not when she had Jaden to worry about.

"We should be fine now," Rebecca added.

Nina gave me a look that screamed we were going to have quite the conversation later. I was going to have to avoid her when we stopped for gas. She leaned toward me and I took that as an order to do the same. I unclipped my seat belt and moved closer, our foreheads nearly bumping.

"I'm all for helping people, Trisha, you know that, but what are we doing here?" she whispered. I glanced at Rebecca, hoping she couldn't hear us. She was staring straight out at the road. "If these people are in trouble we are just going to make it worse. They need to get law enforcement involved."

And now to convince her without lying or telling too much of the truth. "Stuff happened and they don't trust the cops. We are free and clear from here on out. We just need to help Rebecca with the girls. You can take turns driving. Nothing else is going to happen, we left the bad stuff behind. It's like a five hour drive, with potty breaks, what could go wrong?"

She raised an eyebrow, definitely not looking convinced. But she didn't look ready to yell at Rebecca to pull over and let us out anymore either.

"Serious, Nina, it's smooth sailing from here to Fort Wayne. And then we can catch a plane back to Chicago from there. Or rent a car. Please?"

She grunted and sat back in her seat, staring out the front window. I sighed and moved back, putting my seatbelt on just in case I was wrong about the whole safe now thing. I'd heal, but I didn't want anyone in this van knowing that.

"It looks like we can take 30, which will run us south, or 80, which goes east and then down. I checked this morning, but I didn't know if there was a reason to choose one over the other. Does it matter?" Rebecca asked after some time driving in silence. I really hoped she hadn't been able to hear my conversation with Nina, but I didn't know how she could have missed it.

"I've heard 80 is a nice drive," Nina answered when no one else did. "It's a toll road, so we can make good time." She was still shooting me death glares, but at least she was trying to be polite to Rebecca.

I had no idea about this route stuff though. My fae job was just to be bait. Cray was the one who could tell us which route to avoid.

"Don't let them take 80," Jaden said from the back seat.

"Why?"

"Do you always talk to yourself?" Lucy asked. "Or are you pretending my brother is here? Mom told me about how you say you can see Jaden. I don't believe you."

I shot a glance at the moms, but they were talking about driving and hadn't heard Lucy. Try to make friends, or ignore? Obvious. I was never any good at making friends. "Is there something along 80 we need to miss?"

"I just have a feeling," Jaden answered.

I stared at him hard for a moment, trying to get him to give me more than that. It didn't work. He just sat there with a blank expression covering his face. Where was he getting these feelings from? Was his power coming in stronger?

Lucy huffed and sat back.

"80 it is then," Rebecca said from up front.

"Fix it," Jaden said, face no longer blank. Now he was looking worried.

"I think we should take 30."

"Okay, any specific reason why?" Rebecca asked.

"We're trying to avoid places we have to slow down," Nina said. "30 would take us through a lot of small towns, places it would be easier to get stopped." Somehow she'd gotten a map while I was snarking with Lucy. Rebecca must have had it. That was one prepared woman. And how did Nina know how to plan like that?

I jerked my head toward the back and widened my eyes at Rebecca. "Oh, a little voice in my head just thinks we should take 30."

"Oh!" Rebecca looked to the back seat, straining like that would help her see her son. "Okay, 30 here we come."

Nina shrugged, turned the page in her book of maps and bent over it. She was adjusting fast. Maybe it wouldn't be such a bad thing for her to be along. Especially with a new player in the game. Who was that guy? And what did he want? Had the Council gotten tired of Starren failing and sent someone else? How much did he know about me? The Martans? It didn't matter now. We were on our way. Fae Sanctuary, here we come.

I settled back and tried to get my body to relax. Might as well. Today might be the day I sat the most in my entire life.

Chapter 13

We didn't make it an hour before Jaime was complaining she had to pee. I'd been impressed how she was sitting there, riding so well until she brought that up. Nina had been sending me looks and asking Rebecca gently probing questions, which Rebecca avoided amazingly well. Rebecca pulled in at a gas station and sent Lucy inside with Jaime. I got out of the van to stretch and try to keep an eye on things.

Nina hopped right out too, headed over to an empty area and pulled out her cell. Uh oh. Big trouble now, if the man ended up mad. I squinted against the sun to watch as she held it to her ear without saying anything. A minute later she said a few words, then hit the end button. Safe. Until Dan got his voicemail anyway.

"Trish, can I ask you something?" Rebecca said from over by the pump. I moved her way. This was probably something she didn't want overheard. She shivered, reminding me that it was cold out, even if I didn't really feel it. "So Thomas, my husband, he's somewhere back in… Milwaukee? Why hasn't he tried to come back?"

Well here was a great chance to show someone I knew nothing about my homeland. But then, I was getting good at faking my way through things. "I don't think it's that easy or everyone would be doing it. I'd have to ask Jaden, though, to know for sure. And we appear in a specific place when we go back, so they might have been waiting for him…"

Rebecca went white at the implication and I got slightly nauseous about the fact that I'd just destroyed a flicker of hope that I'd accidentally given her. But it was true. He was probably dead. Fae weren't very forgiving, and disobeying one of the Council's few laws was the ultimate slap in the face.

"Where is Jaden right now?" Rebecca asked. "Is he doing okay?"

"He followed the girls inside. He's a pretty protective big brother, isn't he?"

"You have no idea. The only times he's ever been in trouble, it was over those two sisters of his. He loves them." She turned back to the pump and hung up the handle.

The gas station door chimed open and the girls came out, followed by their guardian angel. Made me kinda wish I had a brother, one that would have been with me at Waterton Heights. Or maybe if I'd had one, Mom would never have left us in the first place. She wouldn't have had to worry about me as much.

The girls got back and piled in, Jaime in the back again in her little booster seat and Lucy with me in the middle. Jaden slid in back with Jaime. His long legs nearly took up the whole area back there.

Rebecca stuck her head in. "I'm going to hit the bathroom too, real quick." She passed me the keys. "You can start it if you want, keep it warm in here. I'll be right back." She headed toward the station, Nina meeting her part way there and they went in together. She must have given up trying to get a hold of Dan.

"Jaime, switch me seats," Lucy said. "I want to lay down."

"No, it feels safe back here."

"Come on, I'll give you some of the Runts I just bought."

Jaime thought about that for a second. "Okay."

They wiggled around each other. Lucy dropped the booster seat in the middle chair and plopped across the back seat, throwing her legs into Jaden's chest. He let out a whoof of air and coughed. That was interesting. Must have just been a gut reaction because his mom hadn't been able to touch him the night before. Or could he feel things, just people couldn't feel him? So many questions. But answers led to caring, and I wasn't going to risk that.

"Um, you can't spread out like that," I said after waiting a moment to see if she noticed that she was sitting on her brother. She hadn't, and I was totally being weirded out.

"Why not?" Lucy asked.

What a jerk. Did she really have to use that tone? I was just trying to help. I opened my mouth to let her have it.

"Don't get her mad, please. She doesn't calm down easily. And I can't really feel her there anyway, it's just kind of disconcerting."

He thought it was disconcerting? He wasn't the one in the next row of seats, squinting to figure out where one body ended and the next started. But that did answer my question.

"Okay, if that's the way you want it. You're kind of creeping him out, though."

"Trish, a little nicer, please," Jaden said from his seat.

"Oh, here we go," Lucy said, slumping down in the seat, a defiant look covering her face. "Quit with the Jaden is here crap. Mom might be falling for that, but I'm not."

"What?"

"I heard you talking in the back yard last night. Just because you know some stuff about him doesn't mean you're talking with him. Maybe you met him online or something, I don't know."

"Lucy, don't say that!" Jaime said. "He's here, I can feel him. I've been telling you that." She turned her accusing gaze on me. "Why didn't you tell me you can see him?"

"Jaime, we talked about this before." Lucy reached out and picked up Jaime's small hand in hers. "He's gone. I'm here for you, but you need to let Jaden go. I miss him too."

I watched Jaden, the muscles twitching in his jaw. "What?" he asked roughly when he noticed.

"Nothing," I said.

Lucy gave me a look that said I was either an idiot or some type of con artist. I couldn't really blame her. If I didn't know about the fae then I'd feel the same way. It didn't look like Rebecca had explained as much to her as she'd said she would. That or Lucy was in denial.

The front car doors opened at the same time and the moms slipped into their seats. "All set?" Rebecca asked as she buckled her seat belt. She sounded kind of funny. Crap. I shouldn't have left her and Nina alone. Had Nina said something to her? More importantly, had Rebecca told Nina something I wasn't ready for her to know?

"Yes," Lucy answered quietly.

I looked out the window, pretending not to notice that she looked like she was about to cry. Whatever problems she had, she obviously loved Jaden if she got this upset when he was brought up. I was going to have to try not to talk to him in front of her. Losing family hurt like nothing else, and she didn't even have the hope that one day he'd show up with some explanation why he'd left like I did when it came to my mom.

I handed Rebecca the keys. "We didn't need them."

"Trish, over there," Jaden hissed.

I looked to where he was pointing. The guy from the house, standing along the road a hundred or so feet away, no car, no motorcycle, nothing. How had he kept up with us? Or found us, or whatever? "Rebecca." I pointed.

"What is he doing here?" She cranked the key. The van turned over but didn't start. She tried again and still nothing.

I looked back toward the guy just in time to see Starren come flying out of a portal, sword drawn and ready. I ducked behind the headrest of the seat in front of me. *Please don't see me, please, please, please,* I begged internally. All of this was for nothing if she saw me in this van. If she knew I was helping the Martans. Actually, if she even thought.

She stepped out of the way and instantly Wade was at her side, his sword also at the ready.

"Oh that's great," I heard Jaden mutter in the back.

"No kidding," I answered, ducking even lower. She wasn't looking this way, but that didn't make me feel much better about her being here. "Rebecca, we really need to get out of here." I looked back at Jaden, trying not to panic. Nina was here. Nina was here and so was Starren. Starren could not know I cared about my foster parents, period. We needed to get out of here, now.

Rebecca cranked the engine again, right at the same time Starren and Wade caught sight of the other guy. They did not look happy. He straightened and glared at them, even more unhappy than they were. Who was this guy? Hadn't he been the one that called for them? Starren yelled something that I couldn't make out over my racing heart, the sound of Rebecca turning the key, and being inside the vehicle.

The yelling stopped and Starren launched herself at the guy. She was caught in mid-air by a ball of light and blasted backward. Wade dodged to the side and ran straight at him.

"Try it now!" I shouted at Rebecca.

She turned the key again and the beautiful sound of the engine catching was the only thing I cared about for a second.

"Get us out of here!"

I grabbed onto the seat as Rebecca tore out of the drive. It was barely a second before we were on the road, then right off the exit ramp back onto the highway.

I twisted around in my seat to watch behind us. He was gone and Wade and Starren were arguing wildly, arms waving all over in the air. How had they found us? Was Cray okay?

"Who is that?" Nina asked. "Do you guys know him? Is he part of the problem? I thought you said it was going to be smooth sailing." That last part was directed at me. And it wasn't happy.

'How did he find us?' Of course they only wanted to know about the hot guy. They couldn't have seen Starren and Wade. No one but Jaden and I could have. We exchanged glances, but he didn't have any great explanation.

Rebecca looked at me. "Trish? Do you know who that was?"

"Me?" How could she expect me to know what was going on? I hadn't gotten involved until yesterday, and now I was starting to wish I hadn't. The family would have been fine, right? The fae were after Jaden, not his sisters. Jaden. That's probably why Rebecca was asking me what was going on.

He'd said back at the house he didn't know who the guy was. "No idea." I didn't even know how Starren and Wade had found us. Unless Cray'd switched sides again. I wanted to believe that Starren wouldn't hurt him to try to force him to help, but I knew that wasn't the case. I shivered, trying not to think about what it would take to make Cray talk. Probably not much. What if he'd never been on our side in the first place, and this had all been some plot? Ah, too many things to consider.

"What do we do about him?" Rebecca asked.

"Any chance he knows where we're headed?" Nina asked.

"I really doubt it. I don't know how he could. We didn't even know until last night," Rebecca answered. "But then, he did find us here." She sighed. "Let's just get on the road, the sooner we get to Fort Wayne, the better."

"And you'll be safe there?"

"Yes, they will," I answered. Hopefully. If Cray hadn't tricked us, somehow found a way to twist the truth enough that his fae blood didn't think it was a lie. "He probably just followed us. We'll lose him."

"Then we just go, as fast as we can. No unnecessary stops for now, until we lose him. There are so many highways around here, if he doesn't know where we're going, he can't get ahead of us, only follow."

"Makes sense," I said. Keep the van calm, that's what we needed to do right now. I shrugged toward Jaden and he seemed to understand that I was trying not to make Lucy upset. He shrugged back. Apparently he hadn't had any sudden revelations about the guy's identity either.

The next couple hours in the car were subdued. Nina texted like mad, no doubt talking to Dan about what was going on and letting Wren know that we'd no longer be meeting her. That was what I felt the worst about. Nina had been so excited that I was going to meet her sister. That was probably at least half of the reason she'd agreed to go on this trip in the first place. But I was doing this for us, even if she didn't know it. Once I turned Jaden in, things could go back to normal. To better than normal, now that I knew for sure that Dan and Nina really wanted me.

After a bit, the state line sign flashed by and the city signs started saying Columbia City. Hopefully that was on the way.

Nina opened her map again and laid it across her lap, bending over it to get a better look. Jaime snorted in her sleep, making me smile. Lucy was listening to music in the back seat. Thankfully she wasn't sprawling across Jaden anymore. As much as she'd protested that he wasn't there, she sure hadn't moved to take up the whole seat since I'd told her he was.

Jaden was resting against the seat, eyes closed. Did ghosts sleep? He wasn't really a ghost. He wasn't dead. But he was dead, here. Never mind. This was too confusing.

Slowly the traffic disappeared until we only saw the occasional car. It was actually pretty nice without a bunch of vehicles clogging up the road. Rebecca drove a lot faster than I expected.

Suddenly Jaden bolted upright in the back seat. "You hear that?"

"Huh?" I asked. Everyone else might have been able to doze off, but my mind was still going over everything that had happened today, trying to figure out what the whys and hows, trying not to panic on the hows. So far, no luck. On either front.

"Do you hear something?" Jaden asked slower, like I was an idiot.

"No, what?"

"What, what?" Nina asked. I probably sounded crazy to her, considering the girls were sleeping and the women hadn't said anything.

Jaden sat up in the back and twisted around to look out the window. "Motorcycles, a lot of them."

I turned toward the back to watch with him as a group of motorcycles took shape in the distance behind us. They were moving fast. Really fast. Within a few minutes, they'd caught up with us.

"Those guys must be crazy," Rebecca said, looking in the rearview mirror. "It's way too cold to be out on a bike."

Nina nodded in agreement, but no one said anything.

The lead biker pulled up beside us and grinned through the window at me. His face was strangely lumpy. He gunned his bike for a second and moved up beside Rebecca, wiggling his eyebrows at her.

"What do these guys want?" Nina asked.

Two bikes peeled around us on the right, bouncing around on the berm, and got ahead of us, forcing Rebecca to slow down or plow them over.

"Goblins," Jaden said from the back. "They guarded the prison back in Faerie. I'm guessing I'm what they want."

After hearing that, when I stared at them they looked a little different. Kind of like someone under water, their faces not quite right. It had to be a glamour of some kind, making them look human.

Two more raced up from behind and we were boxed in. Soon the original five were joined by six more, all revving their engines and grinning.

"Girls, get down," Rebecca called, her voice terse as she tried not to hit any of the bikes. Still half asleep, Jaime looked nervous enough to make me want to punch a couple of those goblins in the face. Thankfully she didn't really know what was going on. Lucy on the other hand, had jerked awake and was now blinking at a million blinks a second, like she was trying not to pass out. I almost felt sorry for her. Almost. The girls didn't listen to Rebecca's order to get down. Didn't listen, or didn't hear.

"Lucy, keep Jaime down," I said, appealing to whatever big sister instincts she had. I unstrapped Jaime and shoved her in the back. Lucy gripped Jaime's hand and jerked her into the seat beside her, buckling her in faster than I could blink and pulling her down as far as she could while still wearing their seatbelts.

One of the goblins revved his engine and swooped in our direction. Rebecca swerved so he didn't hit us, face going white.

"I'm calling 911," Nina said. She took out her cell and started dialing. I didn't stop her. Either the troopers would scare them off, or they would at least be a distraction.

Nina talked to the dispatcher for a moment, then hung up. "The closest trooper is at least twenty minutes out. She wanted me to stay on the line, but I'll call back if something changes."

Great.

Everyone in the van was quiet as Rebecca fought against the bikers, doing her best not to hit one.

Then one hit us.

Sparks shot off his Harley as he bounced off the van. Rebecca jerked the wheel to the right, trying to get away, while the girls in the back screamed.

Another did the same thing, farther back, then another. Soon we had bikes bumping us from all directions. Except the right side.

"They're trying to drive us off the road," Jaden whispered.

"Does everyone have their seatbelt on?" Rebecca asked without taking her eyes off the road.

"Yes," I answered.

"Right!" Nina shouted, barely giving Rebecca a chance to jerk the wheel.

This was not working. We were not going to last until the trooper got here. Time for some Fast and the Furious. "Ram them," I yelled from the back.

"What?"

"Ram them, it isn't going to kill them, just send them to Milwaukee. Do it!"

"What is that supposed to mean?" Nina asked. We ignored her.

The van accelerated in answer, hurtling down the lonely stretch of highway. One of the bikers ahead of us didn't gun his bike enough in answer to our burst of speed. Rebecca tapped him with the van bumper and he went tumbling backward out of sight. The other goblins all started howling, the sound eerie over the straining minivan engine. A strong burning smell filled the air. I didn't know anything about engines, but that seemed like a bad sign.

En masse, the rest of the bikes started bouncing up against us, driving the van off the road. Dirt and pebbles flew up behind us as Rebecca kept the accelerator floored. Two more bikes took tumbles, putting our odds down to eight, none of which stopped to check on their fallen comrades.

Didn't they care? Poor Jaime started crying behind me. I reached back and grabbed her hand. She squeezed mine tight. One of the faster bikes flashed by and the lead goblin got ahead of us. The rest split to make room for him.

"Go, go!" Nina yelled.

"I can't go any faster!" Rebecca answered, aiming for the gap that had opened.

The biker ahead of us revved his engine again, reached into his saddlebag and threw something out in front of us. The front left tire blew, sending us careening back onto the road and across into the other lane. The van rolled to a stop.

I took a deep breath. This was up to me now. I unhooked my seatbelt. "Everyone stay put." I slid the door open and hopped out, slamming it behind me. The rest of the gang rumbled to a stop and got off their bikes. Their faces swam back and forth, each looking like a human for a moment, then back to the misshapen features of the goblins. Was that what they looked like to humans? Just normal biker dudes?

"Trish, get back in the van!" Nina yelled across Rebecca, out her open window. "We'll lock the doors and wait for the trooper!"

That so wasn't going to work. But at least she was trying to take care of me. I blew a breath out, pulled another one in, concentrating. This would be my first fight by myself, if, or when, it escalated to that. And the stakes for this one were so much higher.

Suddenly Jaden was beside me. "Get back in," I hissed. "If your mom leaves she'll have no idea if you're in there or not. Do you really want to hitchhike to Fort Wayne when no one can see you?"

"Not going anywhere."

"But you can't even help."

"I sure can. They're fae." I nearly started crying right then and there. Even if Jaden didn't know how to do anything, he could at least watch my back.

A door opened and closed on the other side of the van. Nina scooted around the front and joined us. "Get back in the van, we'll keep them locked out until help gets here." As if she hadn't already said that.

"Not going to work." I really, really wished it would though. "You should get in. Dan will kill me if something happens to you."

"No way." Great. Nina had that determined look on her face. "Maybe we can talk with them, find out why they're doing this." Jaden and I exchanged looks. Did goblins even talk? I had no idea.

"Don't get your hopes up," I said.

The goblins were close now, too close. They acted like a typical biker gang, out popped the knives and chains. No guns though, that was good. I stood a much better chance against knives.

Jaden held his hands up. "It's fine. I'll surrender."

"No," I hissed again. I had to be the one to turn him in. If Starren caught wind of the fact that not only had I known where he was, but I'd helped him get out of the city, I wouldn't have to worry about getting sent to Faerie. I'd be dead. Permanently. Why had I agreed to this? "Not happening."

"It's worth a try. I don't know what else to do. We don't stand a chance against them," Nina said.

"What?" Oh, the talking thing. She hadn't heard Jaden and she thought I was answering her question. "No talking. It's not going to help." I reached behind and pulled my sword from its invisible sheath, its light glittering in the sun.

The goblins hooted and started laughing. Nina stared at me like I'd grown another head. "Ah, Trish? Where did that come from?"

"Talk later." I took an experimental swing at a goblin that had come a little too close. It swung out of the way easily, its friends laughing even harder. They were short, shorter than me, but so wide. They had to be strong. And the smell they gave off had to be one of their natural weapons, otherwise there was no reason for such a foul stench.

Beside me, Jaden pulled a sword from his pocket.

Thankfully I knew about that from Wade. Wade. We could really use him around right now. Who would have guessed I'd ever want to see his face again? They had popped up at the gas station, maybe they would here too. Right. Like they'd be here when I actually wanted them to be.

Someone tapped on the window behind us. I glanced back in time to see Lucy slide the door open and hand Nina a tire iron, then slam the door closed and lock it. If they got close enough for her to use that, the whole van load was in trouble and Jaden and I were dead.

"Get them," the lead goblin growled.

Four of them lunged at me, the others hanging back. I swung, slicing off a chunk of the first creature's long bristly hair. Jaden moved in at my shoulder and we blocked them as they came at us. With a feint to the left, I drove forward and rammed my sword through the chest of one of them.

The thing shrieked and then dissolved, sending the rest of its gang into shouts of rage. I gagged at the stench it left behind, doing my best not to breathe.

"What are these things?" Nina shouted. I ignored her. Explaining that wasn't at the top of my priority list right now.

Something banged on the other side of the van. Where had the rest of the goblins gone? Shoot. "Jaden quick, the other door!" He took off around the other side, leaving me four goblins to deal with. Four. Not too bad. Definitely better than one troll, right? The goblin in back scooted to his bike and unstrapped a bow. Okay, maybe not better.

"We need the boy alive," one of them reminded the one with the bow.

It grunted.

"I know. That's why I shooting the girl."

He pulled the string back, letting an arrow fly our way. I knocked it down with my sword, then slashed at one of the goblins as it went for Nina. She took a swing at it with the tire iron and made contact with its hand, causing it to let out a screech.

Hollering started on the other side of the van. One of them must have gone down. Or Jaden had. The goblin with the bow let another arrow fly. Something crashed on top the van, and then a goblin landed on me sending me to the ground. Nina was on it instantly, slamming it with her makeshift weapon. She must have gotten in a good blow because the thing dissolved.

I looked up just in time to see an arrow leave the head goblin's bow headed straight for Nina. No time to counter it. I slammed into Nina, knocking her to the ground. Searing pain ripped through my abdomen and I fell to the ground face first, blood soaking everything in sight.

"Trish!" Nina dropped down and rolled me to my side. She dropped her iron and pushed on the wound, no doubt trying to stop the bleeding by applying pressure.

"Now we get them both," the goblin said. He dropped his bow and pulled a wicked curved blade out of a sheath at his belt.

I tried to push myself up, but I was losing too much blood, making me feel like I was trying to swim through jello. Every movement ponderous. The sounds from the other side of the van had stopped. They must have gotten Jaden. This was it. I would wake up in a few hours somewhere in Faerie and Jaden would be gone. Maybe they would leave Rebecca and the girls alone. Probably not.

And Nina… after she'd taken out one of them, what would they do to her? Tears squeezed out of my eyes. I wiped at them. No, nothing could happen to her. I wouldn't let it. I wiggled around, trying to get up, but a tsunami of dizziness hit me, laying me flat back on the ground.

The goblins moved forward. Nina grabbed my sword in her bloody hand and stood above me. She really was amazing. I panted, struggling to force myself to my knees. Why had I put Nina in danger to save myself? I was such an idiot. I should have just told her what was going on. Surely she wouldn't have turned me over to some chop shop to be researched, right? Better than telling her, I should have said no when Starren offered me the deal in the first place. Just let the Council take me, to protect my family. But no. I was too stupid. Too selfish.

Then Jaden ran from behind the van and moved between us and the remaining three goblins. I'd have hugged him right there if I hadn't been flat on the ground and he wasn't fighting for our lives.

Metal flashed in the sun and one of the goblins evaporated. The two left snarled and moved into defensive positions.

"What just happened?" Nina asked quietly. She crouched down beside me again, but kept both hands tightly gripping my sword.

"Help's here."

Jaden went at the goblins, anger in his every movement. He was defending his family, fueling whatever skills he had with a sword and making them twice as effective. And he must have had some serious skill. Apparently goblins weren't the best of fighters, their strength was in numbers. It only took Jaden a moment to feint left then come back and drive his sword through the first goblin. The other one screeched, making me groan because I couldn't cover my ears and hold pressure at the same time.

I closed my eyes as soon as the last one blew away. The pain was getting better, but we had to get this arrow out. I was healing around it and it was going to hurt like heck to push it through.

Nina stood and knocked on the window. A door opened, but I wasn't with it enough to tell which one.

"Call 911, get an ambulance here," Nina said. She sounded totally freaked out. This was starting to get to her.

"No, don't," I mumbled.

"What?" She dropped down beside me and reapplied pressure, though the wound was barely bleeding now.

"I don't need an ambulance. Just help me get it out."

"No, you never want to take an impaled object out of a person except in a hospital setting." Her voice was shaking. Leave it to her to know that.

"Rebecca," I called, admittedly a little weakly. "Come help."

"What can I do?" Jaden asked.

I bit my lip, trying not to cry. "Hold my hand."

"Okay," Nina dropped my sword and gripped my left hand. Jaden moved over and grabbed my right, hovering over me like he actually cared for some reason. He shouldn't let himself. I was turning him in no matter what. I blew out a breath. Where was the fainting when I needed it? That's how my body usually dealt with severe injuries. Fall over, wake up healed. I liked that way much better.

Little black dots swam across my vision. I blinked, trying to clear them.

Rebecca pretty much fell out of the van to help. "What's your power Trisha?"

"Snap off the tip," I panted. "Hurry."

She pulled my shirt up, ripping the cloth around the shaft to expose the wound. Though it was hard to see through the already crusting blood, the wound was just as it had felt. All around the arrow was nearly healed.

Nina bent over the wound and rubbed a bit of the blood away, never letting go of my hand. She stood. "What's wrong with you people?" She yelled. "She needs an ambulance!" She dropped my hand and scrambled for the van.

"Rebecca," I said. It was all I could get out. She hit the remote lock and the van gave a pathetic little honk.

Nina jerked on the door but it wouldn't open. "Unlock this." Nina's voice was getting high. "Now. I need my phone."

"No, Trisha needs your help," Rebecca said.

Nina jerked on the door again and Jaime's little face appeared in the window. Her eyes widened at the sight before Lucy's hand forced her head down again.

"Nina, please," I practically begged. I never begged. Is this what family did to a person?

She gave up on the van, came over and wrapped her arms around my shoulders tipping me forward. I could feel her ragged breathing against my back. Rebecca snapped the head of the arrow off the shaft without warning. I shrieked and fell back into Nina.

Nina leaned me back down against her, holding me hard. "Are you sure about this? There's a lot going on here I don't understand, but that doesn't really make me want to do this."

I nodded, gripping her calf for a little contact. She didn't look convinced.

"Ready?" Rebecca asked.

I nodded again, not able to speak, grateful she'd stopped asking questions and was just holding me.

"Keep her down," Rebecca told Nina. Gripping the feathered shaft with both hands, she threw all her weight into pulling and it popped free, releasing another gush of blood. I wailed, unable to hold it in. Jaden's grip on my hand slipped because of the blood, but he adjusted and tightened his hold. I barely felt the extra pressure as pain rippled through my body.

Rebecca tossed the shaft to the ground and covered the wound with both hands.

Nina gave me a squeeze and moved a sweaty strand of hair out of my face. "Remind me why we aren't calling an ambulance?" she forced through gritted teeth, moving to take over pressure for Rebecca.

"She knows what she's doing," Rebecca said, moving back. At least one adult trusted me.

I closed my eyes for a moment, letting the healing happen. I held my breath as the inside layers fused. Jaden squeezed my hand and I opened my eyes long enough to give him a brief smile. Finally the last piece of skin knit into place. "Okay, you can let go now," I forced out. She didn't. I opened my eyes a crack. "Nina, please, let go." I dropped Jaden's hand and picked up hers, weakly pushing them off my abdomen.

"Looks good," Jaden said, leaning over and staring at my abdomen.

"Stop looking." I glared at him. He lifted his hands and backed off.

Nina took the torn piece of my shirt and used the cleanest piece of it to wipe at my stomach. "It's gone. Where did it go?"

"It's healed, let's get out of here."

"Healed?" Her voice was going even higher. "Just like that?"

"Yep." I tried to sit up and lights flashed.

"Whoa, slow down," Jaden said. "Even a superhealing body needs a bit of time to replace all that blood volume. You're going to have to take it easy for a few minutes."

"I know how this works," I snapped. "Just get back in the van."

Years of trying to hide something like this made a person uncomfortable with the fact that it was out in the open. Now that the pain was finally subsiding, I could fully appreciate the mess I was about to find myself in.

"No use getting in until we change the tire," Jaden said.

"You're sure you're okay, Trisha?" Rebecca asked, squeezing me on the shoulder. That must have been where Jaden got the gesture. I nodded and she stood, dusting herself off and wiping at a spot of blood on her shirt. "I'm going to check on the girls."

Nina pulled me into a tight hug. "Don't you ever scare me like that again. You saved my life, but I'm serious, never again." Her glare was enough to make me flinch. Which was worse, the arrow or this? I didn't answer her order, not wanting to bind myself to some unbreakable agreement by accident. She didn't seem to notice, just continued. "What is going on? What happened to make you heal like that?"

I closed my eyes and gulped, nauseous.

"Are you okay?" Nina asked, hovering. "It is healed, right, all the way?"

"It's healed," I gritted out. "I'm just a little tired now."

She bent over and checked my abdomen again, then felt my forehead like maybe I had a fever. Moms.

"We are talking about this, as soon as we get safe."

"Deal." I tried to smile at her, but everything still felt so wrong inside. Even though I'd healed, my body was still protesting being impaled by a foreign object.

Nina sat back but kept one arm around my shoulder. I sighed and leaned into her, exhausted. "We can't stay," I managed to get out, closing my eyes, just for a second. "Something else will come. And the Trooper is on his way."

I opened my eyes just in time to see Nina's flash of horror as she glanced at my clothes and then back at my face. "That could be bad." She banged on the side of the van. "Rebecca, do you have a spare for this? We need to get out of here."

"Yes, in the back."

Nina stood, practically having to peel me off her. I tried to sit up straighter, but I was so tired. That arrow must have hit some vital stuff. She leaned over and gingerly picked up the tire iron from where she'd dropped it. Apparently satisfied there wasn't anything left over from the goblin she'd killed, she gripped it tighter and started for the back of the van.

"You stay here. I got it. You might be able to use a sword and take an arrow, but I at least know how to change a tire."

I obeyed. I scooted back against the van and leaned on it so I didn't have to lay in the half frozen dirt by the road. It was cold! I just hadn't noticed until now. After talking to the girls for a minute, Rebecca came back around the van and helped Nina pull the spare out.

"That was pretty amazing," Jaden's voice made my eyes pop open. He moved over and sat down beside me. "You have quite the reflexes."

"It has something to do with the healing." I closed my eyes again.

"Impressive no matter what the reason. You must really love your mom to do that for her."

"Foster mom," I automatically corrected.

"That just makes it an even bigger deal. There's more to you than I thought."

I squinted at him. "No, there's not. Just wait until I turn you in, then you'll know exactly what I am."

He cocked an eyebrow at me. "We'll see."

Now what was that supposed to mean? I sighed and closed my eyes again. It didn't matter right now. We just sat there for a moment, listening to Nina grunt as she tried to get the stuff around to change the flat. The thought crossed my mind that I really should go help her, but the woozy feeling that about knocked me over every time I moved changed my mind.

"Do you hear something?" Jaden asked after a minute. Now that he mentioned it, yeah, I did. Sirens. Or maybe a siren.

Lights flashed in the distance. "Someone's coming," I called to whoever was listening.

"Shoot, probably the State Patrol." Nina dropped the tire she'd been trying to wrestle out of position, jogged over and grabbed my arm. "Get changed, quick, before they get here." She frantically started kicking at the blood splatter on the ground. Fast thinker. Kind of made me wonder how she'd gotten so good at covering things up.

But she was right. I needed to get moving. I groaned. I didn't want to do anything quick. She left me and a second later my suitcase hit the asphalt. She tossed a hoodie at me, dug around for a moment before coming up with a pair of jeans. She hurried over and tugged at my t-shirt. I glared at Jaden, who looked away, then let Nina help me pull the old shirt over my head and get the new one on. I could have left the t-shirt under the hoodie, but that was just plain disgusting.

She looked down at herself. She had almost as much of my blood on her as I'd had. After grabbing my suitcase she went around back for a second, then showed up wearing a sweatshirt, her coat gone. Kind of cold for that, but it was less suspicious than blood everywhere. Ha, what wasn't? She came over to help me finish getting changed.

The cruiser idled up beside the van and a huge man squeezed out from behind the wheel just as we finished getting me changed. "Is everyone okay?" He looked around at the motorcycles littering the highway. "What happened to the bikers?"

"They're all gone, thanks for the help," Nina snapped.

"Where did they go? Their bikes are here."

"A van picked them up," Lucy said when no one else answered. I hadn't seen her get out of our van. She was pale. Shoot, even with Rebecca checking on them I'd kind of forgotten about her and Jaime. How was Jaime taking this whole thing?

The trooper flipped open a notepad. "Description?"

"Big and white?"

"Did you get a plate number?"

"Um, no, it just happened so fast."

The trooper looked around again. "I'm going to go call this in, you're sure you're all okay? There's a squad on the way, I called it in when I pulled up. It's at least ten minutes out."

Nina looked at me and jerked her head toward something. Oh, my sword, sticking out from under the van. Rebecca backed up to it and gave it a small kick on the hilt. I winced, hoping it didn't get scratched or something. That was probably the only sword I was ever going to get.

"We're all fine, an ambulance won't be necessary. We just need to get this tire changed and we'll be on our way," Rebecca said.

"Would you like to try to start it, ma'am? That way I know if you need a truck to haul you in? It's pretty beat up, I'd just like to know that it's still running."

Rebecca leaned down like she was going to help me move. I shook my head no. The trooper might find that suspicious. I did have a clean shirt on, but there was a lot of dried blood under that shirt. I pushed off the van and stood. Not too bad. The world was a little loopy, but manageable.

"What's wrong with her?" the trooper asked Nina. "She looks like she's about to faint."

"Just overwhelmed, I guess."

I moved away from the van and leaned against a big rock.

Rebecca turned the key and the van started, but it sounded bad. After a second, it smelled even worse than it sounded.

"Let me get a truck out here to start hauling these bikes away and I'll get that tire changed for you." He left for his car.

"I don't want to wait for him to get back, let's get this thing changed," Rebecca said. "Something else could catch up with us. I want to get to Fort Wayne as soon as possible." She headed around the van to get stuff out of the trunk.

Jaden moved along behind her, her unseen protector. He was a good son. And a good brother. He seemed like a good guy in general.

"You okay?" Nina asked, breaking me away from that thought.

I nodded and bent down, pulling my sword out from under the van and sheathing it. I'd have to clean it later, without the chance of some cop seeing it.

"You scared me, kid." Nina put her arm around my shoulders. Nausea filled my stomach that had nothing to do with the physical part of taking the arrow. I had to lean against the boulder behind me when the world started to spin. She didn't think I was a monster. I hadn't realized until that moment how worried I'd been that she would. She loved me anyway. I was almost relieved enough to cry right there in front of her. Almost.

She shook me. "I was serious though, never again, understood?" She paused for a second. I didn't answer. "I'm not going to ask you to tell me what's going on right now with the chance the trooper will come over, but you better be ready to spill when we get alone." She gave me that look and I knew for a fact that there was no getting out of this one.

And really, there was no reason to hold out now. She already knew the what, now she just needed to know the why.

"What are the chances of something else like this popping up before we make it to Fort Wayne? And why is Rebecca so sure they'll be safe there?"

I was about to answer when the trooper walked our way.

He went to the back of the van and took the spare from Rebecca, who was puffing a little trying to pull it out of the trunk.

"While I change this, let's go over what happened again," the guy said, dropping the tire next to the van and pulling off his gloves.

I groaned. Talk about a long day. And the guy should have been a little more honest about this talk. He grilled us all long after he was done with the tire.

I expected Rebecca to want me to go say something, but Nina steered me away, patting her abdomen. No doubt they didn't want me around the trooper.

Jaden followed me to the other side of the van. I guess he thought it was better to be with the only person he could communicate with than to be with the moms. The pain of the wound was finally gone, but I needed to eat. Like, now.

I could hear some of what was going on with the trooper. Nina, trying to tell the story without the weird stuff. I had to hand it to her, she was pretty good at avoiding the truth when she wanted to be. Who would have thought. She should have been fae.

I closed my eyes and leaned back against the van. The world

spun a little. My stomach was starting to grind into itself. It wasn't as bad as when I'd woke up in the woods, but it was pretty bad. If I didn't get something to eat soon, I was going to be sick.

"Is something wrong?" Jaden asked. He'd been quiet until now, no doubt worried about me answering him out loud and making the trooper think I was crazy. I tried to shake my head no, but couldn't. Okay, that must be a lie.

"Are you okay, Trish?" Nina asked me quietly, scaring me. When had she come over here? I was too out of it, it wasn't safe. And what, did I have the fact that I wasn't feeling well plastered all over my face?

I managed a nod. "Just hungry."

Nina's eyes went wide. "That's why you eat so much. I thought it was just because you're a teenager."

"Yep, that's why. And things like today make it a lot worse."

"I can see that. Rebecca is almost finished up. I'll go find out where the closest place to eat is."

Managing a small nod, I closed my eyes again and slid down to lean against the van.

It seemed like forever before she was back. "The closest place is ten minutes. Can you wait that long?"

"Sure." I tried to smile. Even Nina couldn't whip food out of nothing.

"It's okay," Jaden said. "I'm sure the girls have something in the van. They can't go anywhere without a snack." He actually sounded concerned. I frowned. Why did he care?

We'd just met yesterday. And I'd made it abundantly clear what I planned to do to him. He'd be better off if I died.

"You know, I might have something…" Nina opened the van door and grabbed her purse. After digging around for a moment, she pulled out a roll of mints. She gave me an apologetic look. "Sorry, this is as good as it gets."

"Thanks. Better than nothing." I popped two in my mouth and sucked hard. There was a little jolt like my body was anticipating the calories, then nothing when it figured it out. I smiled at Nina and nodded, trying to make her feel better. She smiled back, looking relieved.

Jaden grabbed my hand and gave it a squeeze. Startled, I almost pulled it away, then thought better of it. He probably needed some physical contact. It had to be hard to be able to see your family but not touch them. I looked over at Nina, who of course had no idea Jaden was even there. She must have felt my stare, because she glanced my way, gave me a strained smile, and patted me on the shoulder.

The trooper came around the van, notebook in hand. "I just need to make sure all your contact information is correct in case we need to get a hold of you about what happened today. Then you can head on out. I don't think you should probably be driving tonight, after all that excitement. Maybe you can find a hotel."

Nina made a noncommittal noise and gave him her cell number and our home address.

He nodded as it wrote it down. "Sorry you had to go through this. I promise you it isn't normal in this neck of the woods. Good luck on the rest of your trip." He looked us over again and then headed for his patrol car.

Yes, now we could get out of here. Nina, Rebecca, and I piled into the van, Nina in the driver's seat. Jaime hurtled herself at Rebecca, sobbing. Poor kid. Lucy looked freaked out too, but apparently didn't want to talk in front of Nina and me, because she stayed quiet. That was just fine.

After a moment of consoling, Rebecca asked me to switch her seats, so I moved up front with Nina and she moved in back to sit with Jaime. I checked that Jaden was in the car and we were off.

It's amazing how agonizingly slow ten minutes can take to go by. Finally there started to be some small businesses, and then a Wendy's. Beautiful, wonderful, Wendy's.

We piled out of the van, Jaden still not talking. Why was he being so quiet? He might be a ghost, but he didn't have to act like one.

"Nina?" I asked. They were taking too long with the girls.

"Wait one second, I'll go with you."

I waited a second. "Nina. Please."

"Rebecca, you got this?" Nina asked.

"Yes, go."

Nina threaded her arm through mine and we started toward the place that was about to save my life. My stomach roared with impatience. We powerwalked across the driveway. The smell of hot food hit me in the gut, making me even more ravenous. I wouldn't have thought that was possible a second ago.

We walked in and got hit by a blast of heat. Some unhappy girl a little older than me slouched behind the counter. "What can I make for you today?" she asked.

"Five burgers and a salad please," Nina said.

I kicked her. She looked at me. "What? I ordered you two."

"Two isn't going to cut it," I whispered.

"Make that seven burgers."

An eternity after Nina paid, the girl behind the counter handed me the bag of burgers. I had one out in a second, half of it gone the next.

Nina looked worried for a second, then laughed. "It's been a long day," she told the girl.

The girl raised an eyebrow but didn't say anything, just handed Nina her salad.

"Thanks," Nina told her and we headed out.

The first burger was history before we even made it off the concrete. I was working on the second by the time we reached everyone else. Nina passed out the food.

I moved over to stand by Jaden. He gave me a small smile. "Feeling better?"

"Yes, just needed to eat." I proved my statement by taking another big bite, holding the hamburger in one hand and digging the next one out with the other.

"You got something there." Jaden reached forward and wiped a thumb across the side of my mouth. Okay, awkward. But nice. Awkward and nice. And so cliché. Why had he done that?

"Hit the bathroom people, and we're out of here. I want to find a hotel before dark," Rebecca said. Ten minutes later, we were on our way.

One good thing about Rebecca being in the back, it meant Nina and Rebecca weren't talking. I wanted to be the one to have that whole discussion with Nina, whenever we could do it with just the two of us.

Nina kept looking over at me, like she was checking on me, but she still didn't seemed too freaked out. Or disgusted. Or whatever other bad emotion I'd assumed she'd have if she ever found out I wasn't normal.

Half-way. We had to be at least half-way. Maybe tomorrow I'd be turning Jaden over and heading home with Nina. If I could figure out a way to find Starren. Maybe the three of us would head to D.C. and I'd take him to the Hall. That should work. It wouldn't be hard to sneak him onto a plane.

"Trish, do the kids and Rebecca know what's going on?"

Oh boy, the talk was coming much sooner than I'd expected. I tried not answering, but Nina seemed to be on to that. She just waited, taking her eyes off the road once in a while to stare at me.

Fine. "Yes, they know."

"Good. Then it doesn't matter if we talk with them in the van."

Well yeah, it kind of did to me, but she deserved to know what was going on and I didn't think there would be anymore stalling. I slumped forward. "I guess not. What do you want to know?"

"So… what exactly was that back at the accident?" she asked after a moment of silence. "Everything that happened blew my mind for a bit, but once I got thinking about it I realized you know a lot more than you've been telling me."

"Why haven't you called Dan? I thought you'd call him right away and he'd show up by now."

"Don't change the subject. Spill. Now."

I sighed. I'd known this talk was coming, but I still hadn't figured out an easy way to explain things. Might as well just let her have it. "There is another world, called Faerie. People from there are called fae. I guess I'm one of those people, even though I don't remember ever being there. We have different abilities, mine is healing."

She looked almost sick for a second, making me tear up. No, those weren't tears. I blinked a bunch of times to make sure.

"You're really careful about this, right? How many people know? Do you know what could happen? They could take you away, for good."

"Yeah, I know." It wasn't me that was freaking her out, it was the thought of me being taken away? Was I reading this right? "I live with you and you didn't know until today."

"True. Let's keep it that way. Continue."

A shiver ran through me. She wasn't the only one that didn't want other people to know. "I didn't want to risk your life, that's why I didn't want you to come. It's not like I'm really risking anything. And you were right, back home. It was Wade that made me disappear for those couple days. He killed me."

"What!" she yelled, the van swerving and making the passengers in the back yelp. She got it under control, but her face was still white. Really white.

"Shh!" I said. I widened my eyes and jerked my chin toward the back. I still didn't really want them to know what was up.

Nina reached down and turned the radio on, switching the speakers to the back. Smart lady. The Martans seemed to be pretty busy with each other, but still.

"Obviously it didn't work out like he expected. Apparently I still heal after my heart stops. I'm sure he wouldn't have left without checking that."

"Why would he do that?" she hissed, thankfully this time at a much lower volume. "Dan and I didn't like him for you, but we would never have guessed he would do that or you'd have been locked in the house."

I shrugged. That was another long discussion. It would make her worry, and possibly make her call Dan. She had taken this whole thing pretty well, considering, but would he do the same?

Nina stared me straight in the face, like she had no idea what to say to that. She had to know I was telling the truth, she'd seen me heal. "But you're okay now? Totally healed? How did he hurt you?"

She looked like she was about to start frisking me looking for injuries.

"I'm fine, don't worry about it." She didn't look too sure. "Seriously, it was healed when you picked me up in the woods."

"Did it have something to do with why we are helping Rebecca and the girls?"

I scratched my head. "Yes, kind of I guess."

"Who's after them, for real?"

"We don't even know." I leaned against the cool window, staring down at the asphalt below. "I thought it was the Council, the rulers of Faerie, but I can't come up with a reason they would want to hurt them. I'm not even sure if they care about them, or if they just want Jaden. He's Jaime and Lucy's brother." They wanted Jaden, sure, but how would killing his family help with that? If they were going to use his family against him, they would have been trying to capture them. The goblin knew I'd pop up in Faerie, but he should have also known the rest of the group were human and would just die. I groaned. This was getting so confusing.

Nina reached over and grabbed my hand, her other hand firmly gripping the wheel. "This all sounds crazy. Why did they want Jaden? And where is he?"

Well that was a tough one. "Because they were worried about his ability. Jaden died. An accident of some kind." I kept it vague. She didn't seem to notice. She had plenty of other stuff to process.

"And they're fine with yours? You aren't in any trouble with them, right?"

"I've got it covered." I hoped. If Jaden kept up his side of the bargain. Where were Cray, Starren, and Wade right now? Hopefully Cray was good. And Starren was okay. She was a little bull headed, but now that she wasn't right here about to kill me I could wish her well. How had the battle against the gorgeous dude gone? She was strong. She could take care of herself, she was fine. She had to be. I couldn't care less about Wade. That was the story I was sticking to, anyway.

Her eyes narrowed. "Did Wade have something to do with the Council?" Wow, she was way too smart.

"Maybe."

"Did they send him after you? I thought you were fine with the Council."

"I am now. Don't worry about it."

She tapped me on the nose with her finger. "Like I've stopped worrying since the day you disappeared. You're going to have to start trusting me. How many of these fae are there?" She paused. "Are Rebecca and the girls fae?"

Trust definitely wasn't in my nature, but even with as much as it scared me, I was starting to trust Nina. Like trust her for real. And at this point it wasn't even about trust. It was that I just wanted to put all this behind me, never have to think about it again. And I never, ever wanted her to know what I had to do to buy my freedom. She hadn't met Jaden, but I knew she wouldn't approve of what I'd be doing to him as soon as we reached Fort Wayne. "I don't know how many fae there are. I've never been that involved with them. No, Rebecca is human and the girls are half."

"Anything else you want to tell me?" She checked the rearview mirror, staring at the Martan family for a moment.

So many things I should tell her. I looked up, catching her kind eyes and I wanted to, just for a second. But I wasn't ready yet. Might not ever be. I trusted her. I didn't even have to ask myself that anymore. But I also didn't want to dredge up all those old feelings. Of being inadequate. Of not belonging. I belonged somewhere now, and I wasn't ever going back to not having that again. Even in my memories. "No."

She squinted at me for a second, like she was trying to decide if I was being honest or not, but didn't ask anything else. After a moment she reached forward and turned the radio off.

"What's so special about Fort Wayne?" Nina asked Rebecca, looking in the rearview mirror again. "Why do you think you'll be safe there?"

Rebecca shrugged. "We're just hoping Trish's friend is right."

"Trish's friend?" Nina looked back at me. Okay, so she had a reason to question that. It wasn't like I'd ever brought anyone home from school.

"Another fae. He should know," I said.

Rebecca didn't seem surprised I was talking about fae in front of Nina. She could probably hear our entire conversation from the back, even with the radio up.

"And you trust this friend?" Nina asked. "Enough to not be worried?" She sounded worried. That was kind of her default right now, which made me feel bad.

"He can't lie," I said. "He might be wrong by accident, but he isn't the kind that gets things wrong." Scratch that. He'd gotten the wrong fae twice before we'd caught up with Jaden. Hopefully this wasn't a wild goose chase. Oh well, we'd had to get them away and Fort Wayne was as good a place as any.

"Why can't he lie?"

Shoot. That was not something I really wanted her to know about.

"No fae can lie," Rebecca answered for me. "It's really convenient for the rest of us."

"I'll keep that in mind," Nina said. "Might come in handy." She winked at me. It came across strained, like she was trying too hard. But at least she was trying. Wait a second, now she knew I couldn't lie to her. Crap. "Where did you meet this fae?"

"Are you going to tell her? Tell her what you were doing with them?" Jaden finally spoke, and now I wished he'd keep his mouth shut.

I glared at him but didn't answer. It wasn't like I was going to be taking him away from his family. They couldn't even see him. "He needed my help with something, that's how we met." Keep it vague. Vague wasn't lying.

"And how did you meet the Martans?" Nina asked.

Rebecca glanced at me as if to say she would defer to whatever I said. At least I hoped that was what that look meant. "A friend introduced us." Kind of.

"How, when they were in Chicago?" All of the sudden Nina's face went blank. "Wait a second. You called me from a Chicago area code yesterday." She turned and gave me the strongest stare I'd ever seen anyone use.

Someone needed to turn on the air. It was getting really hot in here. I tugged at my shirt sleeve, trying not to let her catch my eyes with her death glare.

Her gaze swung to Rebecca. Rebecca nodded in sympathy. Shoot. I was dead.

"Trisha?" Oh, so it was Trisha now. I really was in trouble. I looked to the back seat for support. Jaden raised an eyebrow but didn't say anything. Jaime was sleeping, of course. Lucy screwed up her face into an expression that was as close to sympathy as I'd seen there, but didn't have any advice either.

"Yes?" I stalled, scrambling internally. At this point I totally didn't care if she knew about everything except for Jaden. I would be perfectly happy telling her all I knew about the fae. Everything but that.

She didn't say anything, just raised an eyebrow. Ouch. "Okay, yes, I was there yesterday. I was just trying to help."

Nina looked from me to Rebecca and back to me. "How did you get there? How did you get back?"

"A friend helped." Say as little as possible. That was my only plan here. Anything could lead to me being forced to admit why I'd come, and after that, what I was about to do. She may not hate me for being fae, something I could still hardly believe, but turning over an innocent man? No, she wouldn't go for that.

"You sure have a lot more friends than you've ever mentioned to me." Nina looked like she just wanted to close her eyes and forget everything, but she was still driving. "Next time something like this comes up, talk to me first."

I nodded. Thankfully she let it drop after that, but I knew I'd have more explaining to do later. She was just being thoughtful and not chewing me in front of the Martans.

Rebecca and Nina mostly ignored us for the next hour, Nina asking questions and Rebecca answering from the back, only turning to me when Rebecca didn't know the answer to something. That wasn't often, and sometimes I didn't have an answer either. She actually knew some stuff about my kind I didn't. Her husband must have trusted her completely to tell a human all these things.

And he must have been a strange fae. So far the rest of them I'd met hadn't been too keen on humans. Was that why the Council was so against him? Because he'd revealed the secret to a human? And why were they chasing his family? Lucy had snorted and laughed the first few minutes, then put her earbuds in and ignored the conversation. Jaime was still blissfully napping against her mom. I envied her.

Jaden was staring outside in the middle set of seats.

"You okay?" I asked him quietly.

He looked at me for a second, then back out the window. "I guess."

He didn't look like it. Did I really want to get into that? I sighed. "What's wrong? We're almost done with what you wanted. Your family will be safe."

"Yes, but after tomorrow, when you turn me over, I'll never see them again. They'll take me back to Faerie. If I'm lucky they'll return me to the school. If not, I don't know."

I crushed the guilt. Dan and Nina, Dan and Nina. This was for them. Or for me, but so I could stay with them, which was kind of for them, right? Not selfish at all.

Thinking of my family. "Is the school really that bad?"

"It's not terrible, there's just no freedom. No going outside, the elemental kids would escape. The shifters would go down the drains of the showers, so only baths. They keep us all under lock and key."

Okay, yuck. That didn't sound nice. But it didn't matter. "I'm sorry, Jaden. I have to do what's best for my family."

He nodded. "I know. Family is all we really have."

His statement was a sucker punch. I'd never thought of it like that before, but he was right. Why else would I be fighting so hard for my little thrown together family? Somehow it had become everything to me. And here I was taking him away from his.

But he couldn't even interact with them. It was fine. It had to be fine.

"I'll always worry about them, Trish, even if they are in Sanctuary."

"Hush up, you worry too much. They have no idea where we're going. No one but Cray could find us, and he's on our side."

"You don't think there are others with his ability out there?"

I guess I'd never really thought of that. There were probably other healers out there too, healers who would understand me. Interesting. And Starren and Wade had found us at that gas station.

Nope, not thinking about it. Dan and Nina, Dan and Nina.

Forty something miles. Piece of cake after the last two days. We got gas and seats got rearranged again, Rebecca driving and Nina taking shotgun. The half hour went by quickly. Rebecca and Nina let out a cheer as we passed the city limits sign.

I felt something weird go through me, or out of me, as soon as we crossed into the city. For the first time in my life I felt a nagging pain in my knee. It was really strange, that injury had healed itself months ago. I turned to ask Jaden if he'd felt anything weird and caught sight of Lucy's face. She looked a mixture of horrified and absolutely ecstatic. It was really strange. I turned to see what she was looking at and all I saw was Jaden. "What?" I asked.

Lucy reached her hand out slowly, so slowly it was trembling. She paused for a second, then laid her hand on top of Jaden's.

"Luce?" Jaden said.

The van careened off the side of the road onto the berm and screeched to a stop. "Jaden?" Rebecca said from the front.

"Jade, Jade, Jade!" Jaime yelled. "I told them you were around."

I caught a glimpse of Nina's face. She looked freaked, like maybe this was too much for her. If I'd known this was going to happen I would have warned them all. Cray was dead the next time I saw him.

"This is *the* Jaden?" Nina asked. "The one that died?" She gave me a look that said we were going to be having another discussion soon.

Everyone was too busy to answer her. Rebecca flung off her seat belt, jumped through the opening between the front seats and grabbed Jaden in a bear hug that enveloped Lucy and Jaime as well.

They could see him here. That was so amazing. Oh no, no it wasn't. I started to hyperventilate. No, no. This changed things.

Now what was I going to do? How could I convince him to leave his family and go back to Faerie with Starren, even if he had promised? And how could I drag him away from his family now, even if he still planned on holding up his end of the bargain? No, this couldn't happen. This wasn't the plan.

I took a deep breath, glad everyone was so focused on Jaden that they didn't notice my reaction. It didn't change anything. It couldn't.

"I don't think we should just sit here by the road," I said after a minute of reunion going on in the back. "Fae abilities don't work here, and we're supposed to be safe, but we're just trusting Cray's word."

"Who's Cray?" Nina asked.

"The friend that told Trish where we'd be safe," Jaden said.

"He's the one that needed help?" Nina asked. "Are there fae living around home and that's how you know him?"

"He was on my squad." Truth, but too much truth?

"Squad?" Nina asked. She did not look happy. I better not lose her and Dan by acting fae and covering stuff up when I didn't even know why I was doing it. It would be stupid to mess things up with them when I was going to ruin Jaden's life to get to stay with them. Honesty. Hard habit to form. "What squad are you talking about?"

"The one tracking me down," Jaden said.

"What? Tracking you down? And you brought him to the house?" Rebecca asked Jaden.

"He'd already been at the house with Trish," Jaden said. "I figured it'd be better if I got him to help us than to let him chase us."

"Why were they chasing you?" Rebecca asked Jaden, her face wet. Shoot, I'd thought it was only my mom crying that bothered me.

"How long were you in Chicago? You were supposed to be in school. And you never told me how you got there in the first place," Nina said. Shoot. Nailed again.

"Portals. Fae have portals," Jaden answered for me.

"Like zap you back and forth portals?" Nina looked from me to Jaden back to me. "Why didn't you use them today?"

"I got kicked off the team I was on because I was secretly helping Jaden," I said.

"What? Are they after you now too?" Her voice went to a pitch I'd never heard from her before. But it would be scary, not knowing anything about the fae and wondering if they were after you.

"Oh, no. They don't know I was helping Jaden," I said, trying to ease her fear a little. "I was just so unhelpful they got rid of me."

She sighed, looking slightly relieved. Slightly. "How does this team affect us?"

"It doesn't." At least I hoped it didn't. I didn't want her knowing what kind of person I was, that I would give Jaden back to the fae. Hopefully she would never see that side of me. Though Jaden's transfer had just gotten a lot more complicated. Was the airport inside city limits? Someone might notice if he got on the plane and didn't get off, even if he was hiding in the bathroom when he turned invisible again.

"Let's find a hotel then. Rebecca, would you like me to drive?"

"Yes, if you would." Rebecca snuggled in closer to her kids. It would have been forever if we had to wait on her.

"What's going on with this team?" Nina moved over and buckled her seatbelt without looking, her eyes following my every movement like she could find out the truth by staring at me. I buckled my seatbelt too. It was the first time I'd really cared about wearing it, but I felt a little weird right now. More tired than normal. A little achy. "The team, Trisha," Nina reminded me.

Shoot, sooner rather than later. I didn't want to hide things from her anymore. Family told each other stuff, right? "Fae born on Earth are supposed to go back to Faerie to be trained. I never did, and they caught up with me. They said I could get let off the hook if I helped them with some stuff."

We rolled back out onto the highway and cruised back up to speed, hardly able to hear each other with the din going on in the back. "Faerie? What kind of place is that? Anything like all the bedtime stories? It's a rough place if it is."

"I've never been. But this is what my mom was hiding me from, and if she didn't want me going back, I don't think I want to."

Hopefully the reason she left me at Waterton Heights. But I would probably never know.

"What happened to your mom?"

"I don't know. She dropped me off to keep me safe."

Nina cocked her head and thought for a second. "And your dad?"

"Never met him."

She kept checking me, like she thought her questions were going to make me cry or something. Like I would cry in here with all these people. "What did these fae have you doing for them?"

And here was where I had to be careful. "Hunting fae that sneak over into the human world. They're usually not very nice creatures."

"So not all of them look like people?"

"No."

"Were you in danger?" That worried look, now I felt bad. "Are they dangerous? These other fae?"

"Not really to me." I shrugged. "Not many things are dangerous to me."

"I guess that's true." She looked relieved. I guess an insta-healing kid would make any parent happy.

"How long have you been working for them?"

"Not long. Just since Wade." I shifted in my seat, trying to take some pressure off my left thigh. When had it started hurting?

"Since you disappeared for a few days."

I shrugged, not really knowing how to answer that. She didn't seem to expect an answer anyway.

"Any chance we could not tell Dan about this?"

She gave me the look.

I sighed. "Worth a try."

Nina cruised along just under the speed limit. Wise, we didn't really need to get picked up right now. Not with the party going on in the back. And the van still looked like a wreck, even though it was running, so a cop would probably be more inclined to pull us over anyway. "How long will you have to work for them before you're free?" Nina was looking at me, worry creasing her forehead. I didn't deserve that worry, not with what I planned to do.

I glanced over my shoulder at the family getting noisier and noisier behind us. This discussion sucked. "Not long."

WE GOT INTO TOWN. Fast food places and a couple hotels flashed by. This seemed like a decent enough city. Several shopping centers and a random car parts store later, Nina finally picked a hotel that she thought 'looked safe but affordable.' At least we got two rooms, one per family, which meant I got my own bed. It was six o'clock before we were all settled in. Nina kept hugging me and I didn't have the heart to make her stop. I really wanted to be in the shower. This dried blood was getting itchy.

Nina and I gave the Martans some time with Jaden, which gave me a chance to get that shower, then went over and crashed in their room. Nina ordered pizza while Rebecca re-checked the address for the dialysis place.

Jaime slept in Jaden's lap until the pizza finally arrived. She hadn't left him for even a second. She was doing a lot of sleeping. Hopefully stress didn't make the weird fae disease she had worse.

Lucy passed out pieces of pizza. Jaden tore into his, smearing sauce all over his face, then sending a grin my way. "Real food." That was the first time I'd ever seen him really smile. Sure, he'd smiled when his family could finally see him, but more of a teary smile. This was all guy grin. And it made my heart pitter patter. Stupid heart.

"Who's going to eat this last piece?" Rebecca held up the last box. "Trisha?"

I groaned. "No." Normally I would have no problem, but I could hardly move and I'd only eaten half of what I normally did.

"She already ate most of the large meat lovers," Nina said, laughing.

"I'm going to head down to the lobby and get a paper." Rebecca said. "It should have available apartments in the area. Maybe we can start looking tomorrow."

Lucy flicked on the TV and switched channels until she passed America's Funniest Home Videos.

"Wait, Lucy, please, can we watch that?" Jaime asked when she passed it by. Her words came out all slurred. I guess she wasn't as asleep as I thought she was. Or maybe the magic of AFV had brought her back from Dreamland.

Lucy sighed but switched the channel back. It went to commercial break a minute later. A knock on the door came before the show was back from commercials. We all froze.

Another knock.

Jaden lifted Jaime off his lap, stood and moved toward the door. He reached for his sword that was leaning on the wall and peeked out the window through the curtain. He sighed and reached for the door handle.

"Sorry," Rebecca said, pushing her way in. "Forgot my key."

I told my muscles to let go, but they wouldn't listen.

Obviously we needed some kind of signal so no one got their head chopped off when they wanted back in the room. We were all going to be tense for a while.

"I'm going to call Dan," Nina said and headed for the door.

Not good. She might try to get us to head home before I had a chance to find a way to get Jaden to Starren. I watched him out of the corner of my eye. Every few minutes Jaime would reach over and pat his knee.

The show came on and Jaime started giggling as some guy fell off a roof. Idiot. I bet he wished he had my ability about the time he hit the ground, or at least five seconds after.

"There are quite a few places in here," Rebecca said, tapping the paper with the junky pen the hotel had left on the end table. "I hope that's a good sign, not an indication that no one wants to live in this city. Not that we can ever leave now. We'll be fine, now that we're a whole family again." She smiled in Jaden's direction even though she was talking to me. Her smile faltered. "Mostly whole."

I stood and headed for the door. This was not working out.

Jaden was the enemy now. I had to think of him that way or I was never going to be able to give him to Starren. All that pizza sat heavy in my stomach. That was why I was feeling sick right now, it had to be. Jaden had promised to let me turn him over, I just needed to get back to D.C., talk to Cumat and have him get a hold of Starren. This whole mess would be done. I could get back to not playing basketball with the girls. Maybe they would still let me hang out with them even if I didn't play. I could pretend I was really bad at it, that first day just beginner's luck.

The door to my room was propped open by the deadbolt on the inside of the door. I walked in and Nina was sitting there on the phone. She was listening to what someone was saying. Probably still Dan. Yuck, like I wanted to listen to them. I figured she'd be done by now. It was all either going to be a re-hash of yesterday and all that happened or lovey-doveyness. Which was worse?

"I'll call you tomorrow. Yes, I think we'll probably head home then. Okay, love you too."

Water suddenly sounded good. I walked over to the sink and waited for Nina to say something. She didn't. Okay, the suspense was killing me, had she told him about me? "So. What did you tell Dan?"

Nina flopped back on the bed and stared at the ceiling. "That we are helping a family move to Fort Wayne and we'll be home tomorrow. I left out all the weird stuff, and the scary stuff. We can explain that when we get back."

"So the only thing you told him about was the boring car ride?"

"And the flat tire. There's nothing he can do to help us now, we're already here. If he heard about what's been going on, he'd be here in a couple hours. Probably grab one of his friends that can fly and leave before we were off the phone. I don't want him to bother with that now that everything is under control. We'll help Rebecca and the kids find a place tomorrow, then we're headed home."

"Sounds good." Mostly. Except for what I had to do once we made it home.

She stood, grabbed her pajamas off the bed and moved over to me. "We're going to have quite the discussion though, someday,

when you're ready. You haven't answered half the questions I have."
She tapped me on the nose again, like I was some little kid. I glared,
but I kind of liked it.

She turned to head to the shower.

"Nina." I stopped her.

She turned. "Yeah?"

I grabbed her hand and pulled her into a quick hug. "Thanks
for putting up with me."

She hugged me back, tight, then laughed. "You think you're the
first difficult child I've raised?"

I pulled back, seriously confused. She had other kids? "What?"

"Your aunt Wren." She smiled. "You should have seen her when
she was your age. You're an angel compared to her." She squeezed
my arm and stepped into the motel room.

I leaned back against the rail. Nina had raised Aunt Wren? With
all the crazy stuff going on with my own family, I'd never thought to
ask her about hers. I'd met Dan's parents once, when they were
visiting from Florida, but hadn't even noticed Nina's were never
mentioned. Was she an orphan too?

No wonder she knew how to deal with me. When this was over, I
was going to ask her about them. Where they were, what had
happened. But one thing at a time.

Nina had said she had lots of questions for later. Hah.
Compared to the amount of questions I needed answered, her list
couldn't hold a candle.

Chapter 14

A knock on the door nearly sent me flying out of bed. I pulled my sword, then looked at the clock. 6:30. Even if the person on the other side of the door was someone from our group, I was going to kill him or her. Nina groaned on her bed. Obviously she agreed.

I kept my sword out, flung the sheets off and stalked over to the door. A peek through the window revealed Jaden, looking way too happy for this early in the morning.

I took a deep breath, willing my body to relax, and leaned my sword back against the wall. He deserved to stand there a minute, for waking me up. I stretched and everything popped, making me groan. If I was feeling like that, Nina must have been feeling it a hundred times worse. To say the beds we'd tried to sleep in weren't the most comfortable was a massive understatement. But it hadn't been the bed that had kept me up all night. Stupid conscience.

The knocking started up again. Nina moved past me, flicked off the lock and opened the door. Of course she could just pop out of bed. "What's up? Everything okay?"

Jaden nodded at her, then looked at me. "I was wondering if you were interested in going down to the workout room with me for a bit."

Workout room. Was that code for he needed to talk?

"Aren't you tired from yesterday?" Nina asked. As soon as she said that, the day hit me like a ton of bricks. Wow, I hadn't even been this tired when I woke up after being dead for a while.

"A little," Jaden answered. "But restless. Would it be okay? Just for a half an hour or so?" Why did he have to look so nice standing there? He was at least a foot taller than Nina, and so… nope. Not going there.

"How sure are we it's safe?" Nina asked. Could she stop asking that? I'd answered her fifteen times. And I'd proven that I could take care of myself.

"I'll be with her the whole time," Jaden said.

Nina lifted an eyebrow. I guess him being with me didn't mean a ton to her, since she didn't know him. But compared to Wade, he was already a winner.

"Don't be gone long."

I barely caught it, I was already out the door. What was I so grumpy about? I'd gotten everything I wanted, even better than I'd hoped. Jaden fell into step beside me, his hands in his pockets. That was why. Like it or not, I was going to miss him. That revelation clammed me up. Now I didn't know what to say to the guy. And he wasn't being real talkative either.

The elevator door dinged and we stepped on, riding it down to the basement. Thankfully the sad little workout room was empty, otherwise one of us wouldn't be able to do anything considering the fact that there were only two machines. And that would have been awkward.

I hopped on the treadmill and Jaden went for the bike. "Kind of weird, thinking that after today we might not see each other again," I finally said, the silence being more awkward than small talk. Maybe it wouldn't have been a bad thing if there had been someone else already working out.

"Oh, we will." Jaden just kept pedaling.

"How can you be so sure?"

"I'm sure."

That was helpful, thank you, Jaden, for making me feel better. A minute later he stopped and looked straight at me. "We'll see each other again because I'm going to make sure we do. You're an unusual girl, Trisha Penchant, and I'd like to get to know you better, outside of emergency circumstances. Someday I'll find a way back here."

My face heated up. I looked away from him, praying he hadn't noticed. I had way too much stuff to try to figure out right now, I didn't need to add one more complication. Plus, maybe he was just saying that to make me feel guilty. Trying to convince me not to turn him in. Yeah, I was going to go with that. I slowed down on the machine a bit. Why was this making me tired?

"You might have to come here to visit though, after I get back. Unless I leave the city and sneak on a plane somewhere else, people might get excited if I disappear into thin air, literally."

I rolled my eyes. Why did guys always have the dumbest jokes? "Good luck getting Dan and Nina to say yes to that." Which was a relief, right? It didn't really matter anyway. I was going to turn him in. And even if he was trying to be optimistic about it, we both knew he wouldn't be coming back. The Council was not very forgiving, and it wouldn't be happy about him disobeying them. They would not be training someone who obviously didn't bow to their authority. But what did that mean? What would they do to him?

He was smiling at me, even though I was about to ruin his life. But it didn't matter. I was turning him in. Wasn't I? I had to. Didn't I? What would happen to him? I looked into his intense brown eyes and nearly melted.

"I bet Nina would come with you. To visit, I mean. She seems to be getting along with my mom really well." He kept going with the make believe that we both knew would never happen. But he was right. She probably would, if something weird happened and he did make it back. Awkward. There was a whole lot of awkward in the last few minutes. "Trish…" Jaden's voice trailed off.

"Hmm?" This was the first time he'd ever not come right out and said something.

"What do you think about staying here? In Sanctuary?"

I raised an eyebrow. "I hadn't thought about it at all. I have Dan and Nina."

"Nina seems like a great person, but you'd be much safer here. And around other fae. I think you should at least consider it. Mom would let you stay with them. I already talked to her."

"I think you're forgetting about our deal. I'll be perfectly safe as soon as I turn you in."

Jaden's face dropped and he got quiet. We moved in silence for a minute.

"No. I didn't forget. You never really told me what your deal covered. I'm glad things will be better for you. Really. But this time with my family has just been so amazing. I guess I… never mind. I'll do whatever you ask. You're the only reason my family got here alive."

Manipulating me. That's what he was doing. I'd held up my end, he was going to hold up his. I glanced at him for second, my heart pattering at the sight of him staring off into space. I was going to. I had to. I reached forward and hit the power button, letting the belt coast to a stop before stepping off. "You know I don't want to, right?" It was stupid to let him know how I was feeling, but it poured out without me having a second to consider the consequences.

He nodded and gave me a small smile. "I know. And I'm sure the fact that you are has something to do with Nina. I know how the Council works."

I couldn't look at him after that. He was just going to honor our agreement without even trying to find a loophole? I couldn't do this. Hang out with him like I wasn't going to destroy his life sometime in the next few days. "The others are probably ready for breakfast."

Jaden didn't say anything, just slid off the bike and escorted me to my room. I turned around to face him, but there was nothing to say so I slipped the card into the lock. He waited until I was inside, then just as I was closing the door walked away. I put on the chain and slid down the door to sit with my back resting against it, face planting in my hands. How had this become so difficult?

NINA HAD BEEN in the shower when I got back, then went back to bed. She got a twenty minute nap before someone else knocked on the door. Nina groaned and rolled over. "Your turn."

The peephole showed Rebecca on the other side. She waved even though she couldn't have seen me looking.

The lock clicking open sent Nina into renewed groaning. "Hey," Rebecca said, her cheerfulness making me almost grind my teeth. "I wanted to give you time to get breakfast before we leave. I want to go ahead and stop at the dialysis center so everything is ready to go tomorrow, and then apartment shop. Are you or Nina interested in any of that?"

"Sure, we'll go along," Nina muttered from the bed. "There aren't any flights out until tomorrow anyway, I checked while you were downstairs, Trish. Just give me twenty minutes to get dressed."

"Okay," I got out. Why was I so tired? I should be back to normal after all that pizza and sleep. I could barely understand what she was saying.

"See you in a few. I'm going to take the kids down to eat."

Nina rolled over and practically fell out of bed. I beat her to the sink and started brushing my teeth. I brushed a little too vigorously and spit out blood. Kinda weird when it didn't fix itself. I played with the little piece of gum with my tongue. Okay, more than kinda. Wait a minute. That's what all my problems were. No fae powers in Sanctuary. I couldn't super heal. Shoot. I took a deep breath, let it out.

It was fine. There was nothing to worry about here. I didn't need any healing abilities. Besides, we were leaving tomorrow. It didn't matter. But I did not like this human feeling tired stuff. That would take some getting used to. Or at least it would if I was going to stay. But I was probably never coming here again after this was all over. The Martans would kill me if I showed my face anyway, once they found out I turned over Jaden.

It took us ten minutes to get around enough to head downstairs, which I thought was pretty good, considering. The Martans had a table for us. I followed Nina through the line and grabbed anything that caught my interest, namely oatmeal and yogurt, even though I wasn't really that hungry. Nina sat next to Rebecca and I pulled up a wobbly chair beside her.

Rebecca tossed a newspaper on the table and opened it. "I have these numbered in what order I think we should go see them."

Nina took a bite of her apple and leaned in. "We're never going to get through these in a day. We can hit the most likely ones today, and we'll have a little time to help you tomorrow before our flight leaves at four."

It was a long day. I soon discovered that I would, by far, prefer hunting monsters to apartment hunting. Nothing we went to was quite right. I mostly couldn't blame Rebecca, the stuff in her price range wasn't in the safest parts of town.

It didn't help my mood any that they were planning where Jaden was going to sleep, where he'd park his car when they eventually got him one. That wasn't going to happen, but I couldn't tell them to stop wasting their time without telling them why. I could already see the betrayal on Rebecca and Jaime's faces. Lucy would probably just beat me up.

We got back to the hotel late, changed and fell into bed.

Yay, a repeat the next day.

Breakfast Monday morning was much more subdued.

"How many do we have left to look at today?" Nina asked Rebecca. She was starting to look tired.

"Just five. Hopefully one of these are the one."

No kidding. I dropped my head on the table. I never wanted to do this type of shopping again.

"It's important that you get the one that's best for you guys. How long does dialysis take?"

"Five hours, give or take," Rebecca answered.

"I was thinking we could get Jaime set up and Trisha and I could stay with her while the rest of you go apartment shopping," Nina said. "Do they allow that with minors? That way you can take your time, maybe something will pop up that wasn't even in the paper."

"Our old place did. Are you sure it's safe enough for us to split up?"

"We'll be fine," Jaden broke in. "We need out of this hotel and into a normal life as soon as possible. Cray said we were safe here. I believe him. No one would dare do anything in Sanctuary, even if they had their powers."

Rebecca and Nina shared a mom look.

"You don't have your powers here?" Nina asked me.

I shrugged.

"Why didn't you tell me?"

"I didn't know that was something I needed to bring up."

She looked grumpy for a second. "Well for future reference, yes, that's something you need to bring up. What if you got hurt because I didn't know I needed to worry?"

I rolled my eyes at her. "Worrying is going to keep me from getting hurt?" She crossed her arms in front of her chest and raised an eyebrow, but didn't say anything. I turned to Rebecca. "So are you going to let us stay or what?"

"If you're sure that's okay?" She looked at me, to Jaden and back to me.

"Yes!" we both said, me a little more empathically.

"Jaime? How do you feel about this?"

Jaime looked up from her blueberry oatmeal. "It's fine. I'm used to it."

A flash of something went across Rebecca's face. Hurt maybe. "Okay then, sounds like a plan. Let's hurry up and get this over with."

We finished up eating without much talking. I hadn't heard Lucy say a word all morning. She just sat there with her earbuds in. But she was looking a little happier than normal, which didn't take much. Once everyone finished, we packed into the beat up minivan and headed to the dialysis center. Rebecca pulled up and took a front row parking spot.

"Give us ten minutes." Rebecca's seat belt clicked free. "It will take at least that long to finish the paperwork. Then you can come in and sit with her. Ready, Jaime?"

Jaime nodded and hopped out of the van, dragging her panda with her. I watched a couple vans pull up and unload old people while we waited. That must have been why the parking lot was so empty. Everyone got dropped off. How boring for Jaime. Most of the people here were fifty years or more older than her.

The ten minutes dragged by. Lucy still wasn't saying anything, just looking at Jaden every minute. She glanced at Jaden, then fiddled with her iPod. She probably didn't want to let him out of her sight, even after spending all day with him yesterday. I couldn't blame her. I'd be the same if I ever found my mom. At least she hadn't called me crazy since Jaden popped up. Progress. He was staring out the window and Nina was sitting there texting. What a boring group. Too bad my phone didn't regenerate too. Not that I had anyone to text, but I could be playing Monster Busters.

"Ready?" Nina asked after the ten minutes were up.

Jaden slid his door open and jumped out, followed quickly by Lucy. I slid out my side.

By the time we got in, Jaime was already plugged into a machine, her blood flowing out one tube and back in through another in her arm. Yuck, needles were still scary, even if they couldn't really do anything to me. At least I'd never have to worry about dialysis with my condition. I'd probably look young til I fell over dead.

Jaden kicked me.

"What?" I hissed. That kick stung. It still stung. How long did stuff like that take to not hurt?

Jaden nodded toward his mom, who was talking. To me, apparently.

"You're okay with staying, Trisha? I would definitely feel better if you were here," Rebecca was saying. "You have your..." she made vague slashing moves at the air.

"Oh. It's fine," I answered. Definitely better than apartment shopping, especially since I wouldn't be living in said apartment. "And yes, I have that." Thankfully the invisible sheath still worked here.

"Lucy, are you staying with these three or going with us?" Rebecca asked.

"Are you kidding? I'm going with you. If we have to live in this place at least I can make sure I get a nice room."

Rebecca rolled her eyes. She walked over and gave Jaime a hug, "You're sure you don't mind staying with her?" Rebecca asked Nina for the tenth time.

"Yes, I'm sure. We'll be fine, won't we Jaime? Especially with Trish here to keep us company."

Jaime nodded, a shy smile on her face.

"Don't worry, Mom," Jaden said. "They'll be fine."

"Go find yourself an awesome place to live," I threw in, trying to get the ball rolling. The sooner we got away from this family, the better. They were making my plan very hard to imagine carrying out.

"Be back as soon as we do," Rebecca said, kissed Jaime on the head and then left for the van, Lucy trailing after her.

"Lucy's really not that bad," Jaden said, rubbing the back of his neck. "She just likes to pretend to be."

Nina gave him a smile. "She probably feels safer that way." She shooed him away. "Go on, we'll be fine here."

"See ya, Squirt," Jaden said to Jaime, then headed off after the other two women in his life. Time for the fun to begin. For both of us. He probably was as excited about apartment shopping as I was about sitting here all day. Especially when he knew he'd never be living here.

I settled into a chair beside Jaime and grabbed a magazine off the table between us.

We spent hours playing Go Fish with Jaime and watching kid shows on TV. The bell above the door rang. I looked up from the TV screen, more out of boredom than anything else. Just another old person.

Jaime told a knock knock joke and I laughed even though it wasn't funny at all, just because she was so cute. She smiled at me and my heart did a little flip-flop. How come I didn't have a little sister like this? Maybe Dan and Nina would consider it, if Dan didn't kill me when we got home.

Finally my stomach started to growl. Nina laughed.

"Ah, I might need to ask the nurse about the closest place to eat," I said.

"You're still hungry even without…" she dropped her voice to a whisper. "You know."

"Yeah, I guess. Aren't you hungry?" I was still a teenager, even if I wasn't special at the moment.

"What do you think?" Nina asked, turning to look at Jaime. "Should we let this beast go find something for us to devour?"

Jaime giggled. "Yes, but she has to hurry back. Dora is on in a little bit."

"Can't miss Dora." I stood and stretched. This whole not healing thing made it really uncomfortable to sit this long.

Yuck, I was going to be so happy to leave this town. Being normal should feel nice, but I wasn't liking it as much as I'd have thought.

Nina bent down and pulled her purse out. She dug around and came up with a twenty. "You know what I like. Just grab me something."

"You got it." I winked at Jaime. "I'll try to be back in time for Dora."

The receptionist at the front desk gave me directions for a couple places. I settled on Arby's because I was getting pretty tired of pizza and burgers. Who would have thought that was possible? Not me, not living with Nina and eating all that healthy junk.

The walk went fast even though I was puffing in the cold. Who'd turned down the temperature out here? Or was that just a side effect of the no abilities thing? I ate one roast beef on the way back. Nina would never need to know. Just as the thought finished, I caught sight of Nina running out of the clinic door, her expression nearly sick. I instinctively touched the sword hanging in its invisible sheath on my back for reassurance as I dropped the bag with the rest of the food and ran.

"What? What's wrong?" I grabbed her shoulder, keeping myself up.

"It's Jaime." She strangled a sob. "She's gone."

"Gone?" I yelled. "What do you mean, gone?"

"I ran to the bathroom and when I came back she was gone. The nurses didn't see anything. One of them is on the phone with the police now."

"She didn't just wander off?" The ridiculousness of the question hit me as it was coming out of my mouth. She knew what was going on, she was a kid, but she was smart. She wouldn't go anywhere. And she was plugged into a machine for Pete's sake.

Nina, heaved in another breath and held out a crumpled note.

IF YOU WANT the kid back,
  come and get her.

THERE WAS AN ADDRESS BELOW. "STARREN," I ground out.

What was wrong with her? Fae weren't allowed to attack fae in Sanctuary. She was going against the Council she supposedly was chasing Jaden for in the first place. "Nina, I need your phone."

Nina fished it out of her pocket without saying anything. I punched in the address rather forcefully. It took forever for the webpage to refresh, but then there it was. Where Jaime would be. Right outside the boundary of Sanctuary. Two miles, since we were on the edge of town.

I wadded up the note and stuffed it back in Nina's hand.

"I called Rebecca," Nina said. "They're at least twenty-five minutes out, and that's if traffic is good. We need to have a plan ready when they get here."

"I'm going now." I started following the phone on the map. Two miles, ten minutes a mile, I'd be getting there before the others even made it here. Nina caught up with me. "Why? Can't you wait on them? Please?"

"No." All I could see was Jaime's face, white with fear. No way I was waiting around to see if Rebecca could remember how to get back here when she was upset, to see if traffic was good, if they didn't get stopped by a cop meeting them at the clinic who wanted the whole story. Nope, just me against Starren and Wade. Outside of Sanctuary. Bring it on.

"I'm going with you," Nina said, upping the pace even more.

I grabbed her hand and pulled her to a stop. "Rebecca is going to need you. And," I pointed to a non-existent line on the map on her phone screen, "once I get to here, you aren't going to be able to keep up with me. I'm going to have my abilities back, and you would just be something for me to worry about."

"You think I'd stay here to help console some lady I met a couple days ago while my daughter is in danger? Think again. And whether I can keep up with you or not is irrelevant. I'm going."

"Suit yourself." I started off at a jog.

Nina caught up right away, her long legs keeping her right beside me with quite a bit less effort. Okay, hopefully the boundary was even closer than I'd thought.

"I need my phone," Nina said after a minute. She didn't even sound winded. Did she jog while I was at school? Kind of sad that I didn't even know. That would change when we got home, I'd know everything. If I survived this meetup.

I took another quick look at the map and passed it over.

She called someone. Rebecca. No answer, so she left a voicemail with detailed instructions on where we were going and how Rebecca and Lucy were to stay clear, but it was okay if Jaden wanted to show up. Just in case. There must be really bad service around here, or Rebecca was already talking with someone else, because if my kid was missing, I'd be glued to my phone.

After ending the call, Nina handed me the phone. We jogged on in silence, breath puffing in the cool air. We stuck close to whatever highway it was we'd come in on. My legs were starting to burn in an uncomfortable new sensation.

Was this what people meant when they talked about runners fatigue? We finally made it the first mile, and I knew the instant we stepped over the line. The lungs that I'd thought were about to burst filled with new air, the stich in my side dissolved and my legs were ready to take on that next mile without any problem.

Unfortunately for Nina, the same thing obviously didn't happen to her. If I'd had the time, I would have been seriously impressed at how well she was doing. For an old lady. Older lady. Whatever.

"I'm going on Nina, don't get yourself in any trouble." Nina slowed a little, obviously upset. I didn't look at her, couldn't look her in the eye. I just pushed forward, charging on toward Jaime. Starren wouldn't hurt her, would she? She was just a little kid, just bait. No way Starren would hurt her. Wade? Much as I hated the guy, I couldn't see him hurting her either. It was fine. I was going to find them, sneak in and grab her, and that would be it.

The little map had showed a small road just off the highway. I hiked along for a minute. It was mostly fields. Dead, empty, winter fields. That didn't seem like a good sign. There was only one mailbox along this road, and it was a pretty pathetic one. It hung off the post sideways by one bent and rusted screw. Obviously no one had been getting mail here for a while.

It wasn't a driveway leading up to the mailbox, it was a lane. Or at least it had been. Weeds grew along the packed dirt trail. It wound through the trees and out of sight around a bend covered in brush. I slipped into the shrubbery beside the lane and moved on at a good clip, trying to keep as quiet as I could. Right now I really wished it was summer and not fall, more leaves for cover and less on the ground, crunching.

I did my best not to make any noise, but I spent most of the trip down the lane stopping dead still and wincing.

Definite city girl. Finally the long lane ended at an old rundown farmhouse. Had someone actually lived in that? Why else would there be a mailbox? If they were inside, hopefully I'd be able to see them through the huge picture window in front.

No sign of activity. I couldn't see Starren actually stepping foot in that place. I crept around the edge of the slight clearing, trying to get a better look. No luck. I stopped and looked up into the branches above me. How hard could it be, really? Little kids did it. I looked around for a low hanging limb, found one I thought looked okay and grabbed on.

This was easy, no problem. I let out a satisfied huff of air and reached for the next branch, clamping onto the first one with my legs until I had a tight enough grip with my hands. After clambering up on this branch, which was thick enough to actually stand on, I looked around for another. Nothing. Not even close. I wrapped an arm and one leg around the trunk of the tree and leaned toward another branch.

Just out of reach. The bark of the tree bit into my hand as I leaned out even farther, nearing the point of no return.

Come on, this had to work. I started to tear up. No, no, couldn't do that, not right now. Jaime needed me. Then the branch I'd been working so hard to reach slowly moved toward me, the tree popping a little. I froze.

The branch stretched closer and stiffened within easy grabbing distance. "Thanks?" I whispered. The tree didn't answer. I shoved down the trickle of fear attempting to make its way through my body. Between the fact that I was about to have a confrontation with Starren and Wade and the fact that the trees were helping me, this was getting to be a bit much.

I wiggled up the trunk, its limbs hovering close by like it thought I was going to fall. Very polite to an intruder. I was just going to have to trust it really did want to help. I settled into a good spot and looked down at the old farmstead, patting the tree in thanks. It shivered like a happy puppy. So weird. Time to think about that later.

Movement below. There was that dirty, double crossing, no good ex-boyfriend of mine coming around the corner. He looked down the lane and then went back behind the house.

"Now the question is if Jaime and Starren are back there too. And if there are reinforcements," I said under my breath.

A whisper went through what was left of the fall leaves, sweeping out from my tree and spreading through the trees around me. It flowed in a ripple around the clearing and came back to the tree I was in, stopping there. A twig reached out and tapped me on the shoulder three times. I wrapped my arm around the trunk and tried not to hyperventilate. This strange nature stuff had been happening on and off, but nothing this extreme. I didn't need another thing to worry about right now.

The twig reached out and tapped me again, and again it was three times. Either there were three people over there or this twig was messing with me.

"I need to get over there," I whispered. The trees around me rustled, then with a pop the large limb I was braced on reached over and intertwined with a branch from the next tree over, creating a bridge. I took a deep breath and moved across, as much because I didn't want to offend these things as anything else. "Thank you," I whispered to the first tree, then again when I got to the trunk of the other one, just to make sure it didn't feel left out.

It took seven limb bridges, but I finally made it to the other side of the house. Jaime was sitting there, an uncustomary pout on her face. I guess she was entitled. Wade was pacing, and Starren was just standing there with her eyes closed. Okay, I'd found them, now what? I settled back against the tree to watch for a minute. It wasn't ten seconds later that a small branch tapped me on the shoulder.

I nearly fell out of the tree. How long was it going to take for me to get used to that?

"What?" I asked, annoyed. The branch pointed to the corner of the house. Movement. Jaden walked around with his hands up. What was that idiot doing? Didn't he know Starren couldn't be trusted? "Why couldn't you have warned me sooner?" I hissed at the tree. The branch pulled back, looking slightly wilted.

How had he gotten here so fast? Never underestimate a worried mother's driving I guess. I waved at him, trying to catch his attention without drawing Starren's. He either didn't notice or was pretending not to. He had to know I was around here somewhere. It was too late for me to do anything. Wade caught sight of him and nudged Starren. She whirled in his direction, jerking Jaime over next to her.

"I know it's really me you want, let's just get this over with," Jaden said.

"That's true. Get over here." Starren tugged Jaime closer.

"Who are you talking to?" Jaime asked, so quietly I could barely hear her. Shoot. She couldn't see him.

Jaden raised his hands higher above his head. "No need for that. Just let her go. I'm here, just like you wanted." Wonderful. Now I was going to have two Martans to save instead of one. Aww man, and I was going to, wasn't I? If I didn't turn Jaden over myself, it literally did me no good to have him taken. Now what?

"Jaden?" Jaime asked. "Are you there?"

Jaden looked sick for a second, then his expression hardened. "So you kidnapped my little sister." Jaden's voice was dangerously calm now. I hadn't seen him lose his temper before, but I got the feeling that if he did, it was going to be a sight to behold. And this was the most likely scenario for that to happen that I could think of. I leaned a little out on the limb I was on, trying to come up with some plan. Nada.

"I'm sorry," Starren's voice was cold, like she didn't mean it. But knowing her, there was no way she'd say it if she didn't. "I don't have a choice, I can't explain it and you wouldn't understand why, but this is beyond my control."

"Well you're right about one thing, I don't understand," Jaden said. "She's just a kid." Jaden looked over toward Wade. "What about you? How do you feel about taking kids from their families?"

He crossed his arms in front of his big chest, a muscle twitching in his jaw. But he didn't answer. So much for him being a good guy that had followed the wrong orders like he'd been trying to get me to believe.

"Fae don't have families," Starren answered for him. "You know that."

Jaden ignored her. "And how does the Council feel about you breaking one of the most ancient laws?"

"Ha," Starren snarled. "You aren't getting us on that." She gave Jaime a little shake. "Sanctuary doesn't extend to humans."

"But she isn't just a human. She's half fae."

Starren instantly paled. More worried than I'd ever seen her. She'd stayed so calm with the trolls, so focused with the hyran. It was almost scary to see her look like that.

"She's your step-mothers child," Starren whispered.

"Yes, but also my father's."

"Where's Trisha?" Wade broke in after a second with Starren not answering.

"I don't know," Jaden answered.

Wade looked around. I shrunk against the tree trunk, feeling exposed with most of the leaves gone, but his gaze stayed ground level. "I don't like this, Starren."

Wait. Here was my chance. I was supposed to be turning Jaden over anyway. This was the perfect moment, if I could convince Starren it had been the plan all along. Even if they didn't believe me and wouldn't accept this as payment for my dues to the Council, at least I could get Jaime out of there. I scrambled down the tree and burst into the clearing.

"I'm here."

Wade's sword whipped my direction, but Starren just coolly kept her grip on Jaime.

"Trish!" Jaime yelled. "She's here to save me," she informed Starren, who glared at her.

"I got him here. My part of the bargain is fulfilled."

Jaden wouldn't look at me.

"You got him here?" Starren was looking at me like I was crazy. "You helped him escape."

"I was keeping track of him, making sure I'd be able to turn him over. I didn't have any way of getting a hold of you, it's not like you have a cellphone. He's here, isn't he? I fulfilled my part of the bargain." They had to believe me. Had to.

"Trisha?" Jaime asked, her little voice sending nausea through my stomach like a freight train. I avoided her eyes, and Jaden's too for good measure. This was all working out like it was supposed to. Like we had agreed. He had said this was fine. But Jaime wasn't supposed to be involved. The best I could do for them would be to get her back to Rebecca.

Rebecca. She was going to hate me.

"Sorry, Trisha," Wade said when Starren didn't answer. She still looked slightly shell-shocked that she'd broken fae law, "but your offer was rescinded."

"What?" They couldn't do that, could they? Fae weren't able to break deals, it was in their blood.

"You didn't stay with the team, therefore you lost anything that would have come with that. We're taking you in too."

"You and what army?" I snarled. They weren't taking me without a fight, and with Jaden helping it would be a rough one.

"Calm down, Trisha. Faerie is a nice place," Wade said. "You'll like it there once you have a chance to settle in. You'll be watched for a few years after you go through the training process, but it will go by fast. You'll be considered for a permanent spot on our team, if you do well. Things are so much better there than here in the human world. Beyond your imagination. And I'll be there. We always talked about leaving your fosters behind and starting a life together, here's our chance."

I glared at him for a second to tell him he wasn't helping. And him being there really wasn't incentive. There was nothing in Faerie for me. And how much of me would still be me after I got through their training? "You know I tried," I said to Starren.

"Trish could still help us, Star," Wade said. "I'm sure she has a good reason for being here, probably just keeping an eye on the family until we got here." His thought process was lame and we all knew it, but I almost appreciated the fact that he'd tried.

"I tried with the Council, I really did," Starren actually sounded sad. "But they wouldn't accept what I said. They want her almost as much as they want Jaden." She left it unsaid, but no doubt the Council had been waiting for this the whole time. They had wanted me to help while they needed me and then fail, so they could swoop in and force me to Faerie. Typical.

Great. I'd given them two Martans and myself. I was losing ground here. Time to stall so I could think. Or so Jaden could think. So someone could think. I asked the first question that popped into my head. "Where's Cray? Doesn't he have enough guts to face us?"

"I didn't tell him where we were going," Starren answered. "Don't you have any consideration for others and the trouble you can get them in? You think I couldn't figure out what happened back in Chicago? He helped you. And if the Council found out there would be serious consequences. I won't put him in that position. Now come with us and this," she gave Jaime a little shake, "can go back to its family."

"Jaime," Jaden hissed. "Her name is Jaime."

"Yeah, whatever, just get over here."

"No," I said. "Let her go first." Starren could easily have something else up her sleeve. No way I was letting her get away with Jaime. Even if that meant turning myself over. I'd find a way back from Faerie. Eventually. Hopefully Nina and Dan weren't dead from old age by then.

"Give me your word you won't resist and I'll let your sister go," Starren said.

"Got a plan?" Jaden whispered through clenched teeth.

Why did everyone always assume I'd have a plan?

"No," I whispered back, not having the heart to come up with a good retort. "Your power couldn't warn us about this back before we hit Sanctuary?" I asked.

Jaden shrugged. "I can't control it yet."

Starren put the blade of her sword against Jaime's neck, not drawing blood but definitely leaving an imprint. "Hurry up and decide already."

"Come on, you got us, let the kid go," I said. "She'll be out of the way and you'll have one less thing to worry about."

Starren jerked her head in my direction and Wade lifted his sword and took a step forward.

I took a step back. "You got us, you got us, no need to get violent."

"Hands in the air," Wade said.

My stupid pride didn't let me respond right away and Starren tilted her sword just a tiny bit, drawing a little blood and causing the poor kid to whimper. Starren was so dead. If Jaden didn't whack her, I would. This was not okay, no matter what she had going on that made her do this.

"Alright, alright. I won't fight back," Jaden said.

I groaned. He was fae, couldn't he have thought up something better to say to give himself a loophole?

More distracting was in order since neither of us had come up with anything yet. "How did you find us?"

Starren laughed. "Good old-fashioned detective work. I asked myself where you'd be going, and Sanctuary was the only place that made sense. Once I had that worked out, all I had to do was call the dialysis centers in town." She put her fingers up to her ear, mimicking a phone. "Oh yes, I forgot my daughter's appointment time, when should we be there?" she said in a voice much higher than her natural one. She put her hand down and leaned toward me, expression changing to menacing. "It wasn't that hard. The mom left a little too much behind. We found paperwork and Wade knew what dialysis was. That it needs to happen quite often. I would have expected better from you."

"Well I would have expected better from you too. Snatching someone out of Sanctuary? I don't think the Council is going to be very happy." I was bluffing. I really had no idea what the Council would think.

"An attack would draw too much attention in Sanctuary, so we just needed a way to get you out of the city limits. This was the easiest way I could come up with. They will forgive me not knowing the child is a half breed." Starren looked done talking. "Let's get moving." Starren shoved Jaime forward and waved Jaden toward her with the tip of her sword. I started to drop my hands, but her eyes went to slits and I popped both hands back up in the air. Think. Think.

"Jaime, head on out kid," I said as we inched forward. "Just follow the lane for a bit and you'll find your mom."

Jaime turned around and looked Starren in the face. "Why are you doing this to us?" she asked quietly. Even Starren softened a little at the kid's question.

"I don't have a choice. I have to follow orders."

"Please don't take my brother. Not again. Whoever told you to do this is mean."

"True enough, but that doesn't change anything."

"Why do you want to hurt us?" Jaime asked.

I took advantage of the distraction Jaime was creating and lowered my hands. Starren didn't seem to notice. I glanced at Wade. He lifted an eyebrow but didn't say anything. Was that a go ahead? He didn't look like he was liking any of this situation either.

I stroked the sword in its invisible sheath hanging on my back. I'd wait until Jaime was a safe distance away, then things would get messy. Hopefully in a way that was good for me and Jaden. I took a deep breath, the enormity of the situation hitting me. There was no going back from something like this. Not showing up for training could be held against my mom, but not me since I didn't know any better. Straight up attacking an agent of the Council? That was a big no no. Were Dan and Nina worth going against the Council? Yes. They were my family now. Would I even be able to go home with Nina? Figure that out later.

"Let the kid go. You have to hold up your end of things."

Wade came forward and roughly pulled Jaden's hands behind his back and tied them together, then came over and gently took mine. I glared at him and he looked absolutely apologetic, but tied them too. As soon as he nodded toward Starren, she shoved Jaime a few steps up the lane.

"Get out of here, kid."

"No," Jaime sent eye daggers in Starren's direction. "Not without Trish. And my brother, if he's here."

"Just go, kiddo," I said. "Jaden wants you to."

"But I'm scared," Jaime whispered.

I jerked at the ropes, testing them. Pretty tight. I started wiggling my hands. "I know. But it's better like this. Your mom is waiting, go on now."

Jaime ran forward and hugged me, stuck her tongue out at Starren and charged down the lane. "I'm going to tell my mommy on you!"

"I guess she has a little of Lucy in her," Jaden said with a sigh.

"Let's get this over with," Starren said.

I rubbed against the ropes, burning my wrists over and over and stopping for a second to let them re-heal. Starren walked us toward the old house. Was there really a portal here? That was the only reason I could figure out why she would want us in there. I continued tugging at the ropes until finally they loosened. We were just getting to the house when my right hand slipped free. If it was two against two I would like our odds after seeing Jaden fight. But he was going to be less than useless. This was all on my own.

Without giving anyone the time to notice, I reached back and jerked my sword from its sheath, cutting Jaden's ropes in one quick swipe. I was getting good at this. I twirled away from Wade and went into a defensive position. Jaden maneuvered behind me.

"That's it, Starren, just let us go."

"No." She lunged at me, barely giving me time to get my sword in front of hers to stop the blade from driving straight through me. The ring of metal and whatever my sword was made of reverberated through the small clearing. Starren drew her blade back and glared at me, murder on her face. She took another swing. I blocked, ducking out of the way.

She came straight after me, blows raining down with wicked speed, me barely having the time to block them even with my quicker reflexes. She slashed her sword through the air and jumped forward, slamming me with her body and knocking me back away from her. The distance gave me a second to close my eyes and allow all the training with my mother to come flooding back.

Out of the corner of my eye I got a glimpse of Jaden. He was just standing there. Right at this moment, I hated everything that being fae meant. He'd made a deal. He couldn't go back on it. A whistle sounded in the air and I barely got my blade up in time to block a swing toward my neck. Multi-colored sparks sprayed around us. I blocked and jumped around an old well. Starren followed me. Wade started around the other side.

I blocked another thrust. Starren jumped forward and slammed her shoulder into my gut, flying me through the air and right through the big picture window in the front of the farmhouse.

It was almost surreal, flying through the air, glass shards exploding around me. I hit the wood floor inside and my whole body howled. I stumbled to my feet, groaning, just as Starren jumped through the window frame.

My right thigh pulsed, something warm running down into my tennis shoe. Shoot, was that blood? I glanced down and sure enough, I was bleeding all over, tiny cuts everywhere from the glass. I gritted my teeth as my body pushed little shards of glass through my skin, sending them tinkling to the floor of whatever room this was.

My movement was sluggish for a moment as my body struggled to heal so many things at once, giving Starren a chance to circle closer. This was not going to end well if things continued in the direction in which they were moving. I lifted my sword, nearly letting out a groan at how much it weighed right now.

This was where all the bad guys taunted the good guys in the movies, but Starren was strangely silent, a ferocious level of concentration on her face. The front door banged open and there was Wade. I almost ran to him. I'd take him over Starren any day, but she circled between us, moving me back into a corner.

Think, think, think. More thinking in the last week than in the rest of my life put together. I hated thinking.

Something crackled under my feet and I looked down to see a bunch of leaves. The old farmhouse must have a hole in it somewhere. Wait. Leaves.

Wade had worked his way over to my left, Starren to my right. I swung the tip of my sword back and forth, first facing one, then the other. Time to get back to nature.

I shrieked, throwing Wade off guard and charged him, trying to knock him over. I just bounced off. He caught me as I fell, arms clamped like iron around my body. I thrashed around trying to get free, but he didn't budge. I grabbed the last piece of glass working its way out of my skin and jabbed it into Wade's arm. He let out a howl and dropped me, giving me the chance to get past him and jump back out the shattered window.

A glance showed Jaden, standing in the exact place I'd left him.

Stupid fae blood. I ran to him and started dragging him toward the woods. He was stiff, but he was able to move with me jerking on him.

Starren and Wade were on our heels, not a surprise considering how slow we were going. Starren was right on my tail, so I turned back to face her. She slid to a stop, waiting for Wade to move around behind me.

"This is it. Just let us take you in, please Trisha," Wade said. "I'll make sure you're happy in Faerie, I promise."

"Not likely," I snarled. "Get them," I ordered.

Starren and Wade looked confused for a second, trying to figure out what I meant. Nothing happened.

Seriously? This was not the plan. *Help us!* I begged internally.

"Please?" I said out loud. Still nothing.

Starren's eyes narrowed in my direction and Jaden was looking at me like I was crazy. So much for that plan.

That slight distraction only stopped Starren for a minute before coming at me again. I blocked, then a strange rustling went through the trees. We all froze, looking up in unison.

The trees around us creaked and groaned into life, branches snaking toward us. Wade whacked a branch off with his sword, causing the stump to writhe away in seeming agony before being instantly replaced by another.

A pile of kindling formed around Starren as she whacked at anything that moved. I pushed Jaden toward the lane. We made it a few feet before the sounds of fighting stopped.

"Trisha," Wade groaned out. I gave Jaden another shove and spun around. Both Wade and Starren were wrapped in branches, twisting tighter and tighter.

"Go on," I told Jaden.

"No."

I rolled my eyes and jogged back to Wade. "Okay, that's good, you can stop now," I told the trees. The branches slowed, but didn't stop their sluggish creep, tightening their grip around their victims. I hesitated for a second, then reached forward and stroked one of the branches. "Really, you can stop. Thank you."

This time the branch listened. It made me shiver a little.

What was going on? What if the trees decided to listen to Starren instead of me? I had no idea why they were helping me. The groaning, popping and rustling stopped as the trees settled in. The only sound left was Wade panting, hard.

"What's wrong with you?" I asked.

"Can't…breathe…" he barely got out.

"Oh!" Now here was an interesting situation, as George Bailey would say. Nina made us watch It's a Wonderful Life at least once a year. Yes, a girl didn't find herself in this situation very often. Having this much control over a murderous ex-boyfriend. His face was starting to mottle. I sighed. "Fine. Please loosen up a bit," I asked the tree. "But not enough for them to get away." I didn't know how specific I needed to be with a tree, but I figured more instruction was better than not enough.

The branches grudgingly gave them both a little breathing room. Wade gulped air. Starren just stared at me.

"What are you?" she asked.

Um, good question. Obviously this wasn't normal or they would have used it against me. "Wouldn't you like to know," I said, even though I was in the same boat.

She snarled at me but didn't have a comeback.

"Now tell Jaden he can go."

"No." She glared.

I glared back.

"I will tell that branch to squeeze as much as it wants to. But only if you don't tell Jaden he can go," I threatened. "Otherwise I could just have it take care of you, and he would be free anyway." Maybe I should. Maybe it would be better if they couldn't interact with the human world.

Starren groaned and slumped forward, the tree branch dipping under her weight before bringing her back up. "Jaden, you are free from your word."

"Thank you," I said. I stared at them a moment, considering. Wade knew. I could tell by looking at him that he knew what I was thinking. Being crushed to death would be a horrible way to go, even if they did wake up fine in Faerie. I couldn't do that to them.

"Who was that guy? Back at the gas station?" I asked.

Wade visibly slumped in relief. "A bounty hunter. The Council decided to start sending extra fae to help with the situation."

I tipped my head, confused. "Then why were you fighting?"

Wade didn't answer.

I glared at Starren and the trees seemed to know what I was feeling, because the branch began to tighten.

"Stop, stop!" she huffed out. "Vilan is known for getting results. How he goes about it isn't always pretty."

She didn't elaborate, but I knew what she meant, even without her saying it. They had protected us. I didn't know why, and somehow I didn't think I'd get an answer for that question. But it didn't really matter at this point.

"Thank you," I said. I actually meant it, no matter what their motives had been. I turned and started up the lane.

"Wait!" Starren yelled. I paused. "Who are your parents?"

Right to the point. Typical Starren. I glanced back over my shoulder. "I don't know. Why?"

She slumped without answering. But she'd finally just come out and asked. All the hinting before this was so obvious now. Was that the real reason I'd been 'asked' to join the team? It didn't matter anymore, and I wanted out of here.

"Hey!" Wade yelled when I started to leave. "You aren't going to just leave us here, are you? How did you get them to do this? Tell them to let us go!"

"I'm sure you'll figure something out," I yelled back over my shoulder.

"You better never leave Sanctuary," Starren yelled after us. "I'll be waiting. The second you do, you're done!" The gravity of what had just happened hit me. Never leave Sanctuary. No Dan, more importantly, no Nina.

Starren kept yelling threats at us. I ignored her and stopped at the next tree. "Hey, let them go after we're out of here, 'k? You know, a while after we're out of here." The tree shivered in response and I took that as a yes.

I made it to Jaden and drug him after me.

"What was that?" he asked.

I shrugged. "It isn't normal?"

He looked at me like I was crazy. "Ah, no. Commune with animals, yes, and sometimes they'll help us out. Plants grow a little better if there are fae nearby. Nature just obeying in general? No."

I shrugged again. No use letting him know that I was slightly freaked out too. "Where are the moms?"

"I told them to take off when Jaime got back, but they're the moms, I doubt they did."

We followed the lane back and were most of the way to the road when a tree crackled in the underbrush and tossed something out in front of us. Whatever it was jumped up and charged at us. My sword was instantly pointed in that direction and up to face the human like figure heading our way. I was getting good at this.

"No, no, don't do anything!" A frantic voice yelled as the figure slid to a stop.

I squinted, but whoever it was had been rooting around in the dirt too long, apparently. He was covered head to toe. "Cray?"

"Yes, now can I come over there?" He sounded like he was about to cry.

"Sure." I pointed the tip of my sword down. Cray ran over and practically stuck his body to mine as he frantically pulled leaves from his hair.

"What is that thing doing?" he finally asked.

"The tree?" I put the tip of my sword to the ground and leaned on it.

"They like Trish," Jaden added.

Cray looked at me in the same way he'd been looking at the woods a moment ago. Shoot. Out of everyone here I'd have thought he would know what was going on. Speaking of him being here. "What are you doing out here, Cray?"

He shook out his jacket and twigs fell to the ground. "I followed Starren and Wade in case you guys needed help."

I just stared at him for a moment. He had to be telling the truth, but I couldn't figure out why he would help us. Without the ability to lie, he had to be on our side, but it didn't really make much sense.

"Are you sure that's why?" Jaden asked.

Cray got kind of pale. "Yes?"

"And it had nothing to do with the fact that Starren knows you helped us in Chicago and now you need somewhere to crash?"

"Crash?" Cray blinked several times, looking like he was trying to process. "That means somewhere to live in human, correct?"

Well that pretty much covered why he was here, but why had he helped us in the first place? Not really fair to ask, I guess. Everyone was entitled to their secrets, as long as it didn't affect me.

Now what? I didn't even know what was going to happen to me, let alone him too. But we couldn't stand here, who knew how long until the trees got bored and let the dream team go. I sighed. Yet another complication. "Okay, come on."

Cray's face visibly brightened. "Thanks." We left for the van, everyone quiet. Jaden was watching me, which made me really uncomfortable, and Cray stumbled along swatting at bugs. It was him Jaden should be watching. I liked Cray just fine, but I had a suspicious mind.

The trip back along the dirt road was much shorter than weaving back and forth through the trees trying to be quiet like on my way in. I was still studying Cray when the trees gave way to sky. I took a second to sheath my sword. No reason for the moms to see it out.

"Trish!" I was pulled from my thoughts to see Jaime bailing out of the minivan ahead and charging my way. I expected her to hit Jaden, but remembered she couldn't see him just as she launched herself at me. I caught her and she wrapped her arms around me, nearly squeezing me to death.

"What's this?" I asked.

"Thank you for standing between that scary girl and Jaden." Shame washed through me at her innocent statement. The plan had been to turn him in. I would have if the Council hadn't changed things with Starren. I looked over at Jaden, but he wouldn't meet my eyes. Rebecca, Nina and Lucy piled out of the van and surrounded me too, almost enough to make me claustrophobic. Cray hung back behind.

"Are they gone?" Rebecca asked, gripping onto Jaime like she was never letting go.

"Yep, they're gone. For good." There was no way they would risk going against the Council again by breaking Sanctuary. We would be fine, as soon as we were back in the city limits.

She put out an arm and pulled me into a hug too. Kind of awkward with the three of us, but who was I to tell her no after what she'd just been through?

"I was so worried, those bad people were mad at you," Jaime said. I squished her close, letting out a huge sigh and breathing in her kid smell. She wiggled out of my arms and launched herself at Rebecca.

"Trish is so awesome Mom, you should see her fighting with a sword. She took care of us."

Rebecca turned to look at me. I just rubbed the back of my neck with one hand. "How do you know about that? I told you to run."

Jaime looked down at the ground. "I watched from the trees for a couple minutes, until I got scared."

I closed my eyes. That could have turned out so badly. If I had been able to convince Starren I had brought Jaden there to turn him in…

"What's he doing here?" My eyes popped back open at Rebecca's question. She was gesturing toward Cray.

"He came to help," I answered. He had come to help, even if he didn't get to.

"Who is he?" Nina asked. Oh yeah, she wouldn't know.

"A friend. He helped us in Chicago the day before you and I got there," I said.

Nina walked toward Cray and stuck her hand out. "I'm Nina. Thanks for your help."

Cray got wide-eyed but stuck his hand out to meet hers.

"Is Jaden here? Is he okay?" Rebecca asked, interrupting my eavesdropping.

"Yes and yes."

Rebecca's shoulders slumped in relief. "And you're sure they're taken care of?"

"Yes."

"Why am I not convinced of that?" Nina interjected. "I seem to have heard it before."

"For real this time. Starren and Wade got taken care of. And I don't think anyone else is going to go rogue and come into Sanctuary. The Council does NOT like being disobeyed."

And I really didn't think they would attempt anything close to Sanctuary again. When the Council found out they'd done this they were going to have enough to deal with. I felt almost a twinge. Was that sympathy? Nah, it couldn't be, could it? Being around a family wasn't good for me. I was developing too many feelings. But what would happen to Starren now? She hadn't known Jaime was part fae and hadn't meant to break the law, but that wouldn't matter to the Council. Oh well, she could take care of herself. There was nothing I could do.

Rebecca grinned, a huge happy, relieved, full out grin. Good to see. "How did they get taken care of?" The grin fell off her face. She looked at Jaime. "You didn't have to…"

"Ah, no. But it's a long story," I answered, nodding toward Jaime as if to say I didn't want to go into it in front of her. Rebecca nodded. Jaden looked at me for the first time. I shook my head no. I wasn't going to tell them what had really happened. Not a single reason I could think of to let them know how my freak factor had just doubled.

"That sword had better be done being used," Nina was saying beside me. She pulled me in for a one armed hug and held me there. I wiggled, trying to get free but she just held me tighter. "Now that you have your son and I have my daughter, we'd better get out of here," Nina told Rebecca.

Her daughter? I leaned into the hug a little bit. Maybe hugs weren't all bad. And this might be the last one I got. I swiped my arm over my eyes, telling myself the misting there was because of the weather. Of course it was. I didn't need Nina and Dan. I didn't need anyone. I was really good at surviving on my own. Starren knew where I lived in D.C. Even if I didn't stay in Sanctuary, I couldn't go back with Nina. They were just going to have to take in some other mouthy foster kid.

The pain in my chest grew until I couldn't even look at her.

Rebecca, Jaden, Lucy and Jaime headed for the car together. Nina stayed back to walk with me. Cray trailed behind. He really was going to have to get over being scared of humans if he wanted to stay with me. It was kind of annoying.

"So…" I tried to come up with something to break the awkward silence.

"So…" she copied me. "Don't you ever do that again. I know you're some kind of superwoman, but you're still my daughter and I'll kill you myself if you run off like that even one more time. I was about to come in after you."

"No!" Just the thought was terrifying. What might have happened to her if she had? Just another hostage. Or worse, if they didn't have any use for her. Would Wade have been able to kill her? She was only a human to him, I couldn't see him caring at all. Or what if she'd seen all that tree stuff?

How much weird could she handle and still love me?

"What was I supposed to do if you didn't come out? I waited because I figured I'd be less than no help, probably get in the way, but I was about to try anyway."

The thought sent a shiver through me. Starren would have used her just like she'd used Jaime.

"I didn't want you to get hurt," I admitted out loud. "And I couldn't leave Jaime out there."

Nina pulled me in, tightening the hug that still had not ended. "I know. But knowing that didn't help me any when I was waiting back here with the doors locked and the van in drive."

We all climbed into said van, Rebecca checking with me to make sure Jaden was on board. The ride back to the hotel was quiet. Jaime conked out after about two minutes, no doubt physically and emotionally exhausted. Lucy kept giving me these strange looks, but she hadn't had anything to say to me yet. She was eying

Cray too, but I couldn't tell if she thought he was weird or thought he was hot.

We had to stop for a whole bunch of hugging and a little crying when we crossed the line into Sanctuary and Jaden popped into view. It wasn't as bad as the first time, but still made me uncomfortable. That's when Lucy started talking, bothering Jaden about everything before the moms had to get his side of what had happened. He followed my lead and didn't bring up the help we'd gotten from the foliage.

It seemed like an eternity before we finally pulled up in front of the little rundown motel.

Everyone surrounded me on the way up, keeping my bloody clothes from curious eyes. Poor Nina was going to go broke if I kept ruining clothes at this rate. A pang hit me. Or she would, if I was still going to live with her. Jaden was carrying Jaime, who hadn't even stirred as he pulled her out of her seat. Poor kid, between dialysis and getting kidnapped, she had to be whipped. At some point I was going to have to hear her story too. Nausea flooded my stomach. I'd have plenty of time. I could visit them whenever I wanted, now that I couldn't leave the city either.

We escorted the Martans to their room. "We'll be back," Nina told Rebecca. "As soon as Trish gets changed."

Cray looked about to panic, gaze flicking to the Martans and then to me. I waved him after Nina and me. I'd probably have to share a bed with Nina tonight. Ugh.

I groaned in sheer joy when I caught sight of the shower. I had dirt, bark, and blood all over me. "I'm taking a shower," I said over my shoulder as I bolted for the bathroom.

"But, Trisha, I…" Cray started to say, but I slammed the door in his face. Now was a good a time as any for him to start adjusting to being around humans. Hopefully he didn't blurt anything out to Nina that I didn't want her to know.

I took my time under the water, savoring the heat even though the spray sputtered every once in a while. Forcing myself not to think about the whole left behind thing and the fact that Cray and Nina were together in the room was tough, but I did it, just for those few moments of relaxation. I got dressed and moved out of the bathroom to stare at myself in the mirror there. What now?

"Feeling better?" Nina clicked off the TV.

"Much." I brushed at the massive tangle that was supposed to be my hair.

"Hot water fixes a lot of things. Cray said he needed some quiet time and left. I didn't know what to do so I let him go." He was such a chicken. There was an awkward pause.

Neither of us really knew what to say after that.

"Did they find an apartment?" I asked after a bit. Stupid hair. I jerked on the brush, ripping a little out and almost yelping. Nina patted the bed beside her and I moved over.

She held out her hand for the brush and I gave it to her. This would never happen under normal circumstances, but right now I needed every mother/daughter type moment possible. I was going to be alone again. Very soon. No way they were going to get me to try another family. Not when I already had one, just in a different city.

"Yes, apparently they did find one. That's how we got there so fast, actually, they were already on their way back when I called Rebecca. The place isn't in an area I would want to live in, but I think it's better than where they lived in Chicago. I changed our tickets while you were in the shower, we can catch one in the morning for D.C. The flight isn't too bad, like three and a half hours or so."

I didn't answer her. Couldn't bring myself to answer her. How could I tell her that I wouldn't be going with her? That after all that she'd done for me in the last few days, I was just going to skip out, let her take all the heat from social services for a missing kid? But what choice did I have?

"We'll get you home, then I'm not letting you out of my sight for a while. These attacks are over, right? For real?"

Well, no time like the present. I turned and she stopped brushing, looking at me quizzically.

"I can't go back with you."

Confusion spread over Nina's face. "What?"

"I can't go back with you. If I leave Sanctuary, they'll be after me again. It wouldn't be safe for Dan or for you. I'm staying here." At least until she was gone. Then maybe I would take my chances out in the world, I'd see later. It all depended on what this city had to offer.

Nina grabbed my hand but didn't say anything. She looked like she was processing. I pulled my hand free and took the brush from her, going at the snarls with renewed gusto. I'd done all this crap to keep the one thing that was important to me, and in the end I'd lost it anyway. Life was awful sometimes.

"I told Rebecca we'd be over," Nina said after a few seconds.

"I don't really feel like it, thanks." Not with Jaden giving me those sad looks because he knew what I'd given up. And Jaime and Rebecca treating me like a hero, which made me feel even more guilty. The first person I'd be okay with seeing from that room would be Lucy, how weird was that?

"Yeah, me either. I'll shoot her a text and order us some food. Do you know what Cray would want?"

I shrugged. I had no idea.

"Is he in trouble now too, since he helped you?"

"Yeah."

"So he's stuck in Fort Wayne."

"Yeah." Where were these questions going?

"How well do you know him?"

That was a good question, actually. How well did I know him? Not well at all. I didn't even know what food to order him. But I had to trust him. He'd given up a lot to help us, though I still didn't know why. "He was part of the team with Starren, Wade and me, but he defected the same time I did when we found out Jaden wasn't evil like we'd been told."

"So he has nowhere to go?"

I looked at her. She looked upset. Of course she was upset. It would have been worse if she hadn't been. "He has nowhere." She went quiet after that, and I was grateful. I slipped off the bed and went back to the mirror, ripping at the few tangles I had left in my hair. It was going to be a long night.

Chapter 15

Dragging myself out of bed in the morning was not fun. Not fun at all. Was this how normal people felt every day? Stupid Sanctuary. Nina's side of the bed was empty. What time was it anyway? I squinted with sleep blurry vision toward the clock. 8:30. There was a lump in Cray's bed. I made my way to the bathroom, changed and looked at my toothbrush for a second. That counted, right?

"Trisha?" I turned to see Cray half sitting up in bed. His longish hair was a mess, sticking up all over the place and his glasses were still sitting on the end table so he was squinting.

"Yeah?"

He grabbed his glasses and finished sitting up, moving his legs to sit Indian style, a term he probably wouldn't understand.

"What's the plan?"

What was the plan? Spend time with Nina today, obviously, but what after that? I couldn't get an apartment. I couldn't turn invisible here. Or could I? I gave it a try.

Nothing. Apparently there was nothing magical about my sheath, the scales just acted like a chameleon because my sword was invisible, but no matter how hard I tried I couldn't be.

"No plan yet, Cray. I'll let you know when there is one." I headed for the door, not wanting to stay in here and talk about this right now. I wasn't going to cry in front of Cray. No way. He was here because of me. I was going to figure this out for the both of us.

Not knowing if to be sad that Nina wasn't here to hang out with when we wouldn't be seeing much, if any, of each other after today or happy that we weren't doing sappy together time was a pain. I liked my emotions all sorted out, thank you very much.

She wasn't on the landing when I walked out, so I moved down to the Martans room. I knocked and after a couple tries, Lucy opened it.

"Whaddya want?"

"I'm looking for Nina." I shifted my weight, trying to see behind her. Jaden was sitting on the bed. He looked at me and gave me a small smile, like he wasn't quite sure how I was feeling about him since he had gotten his fairy tale happy ending and I hadn't.

Lucy moved in front of me. She didn't look very happy.

Had Jaden told them what had went down back at the farmhouse? Hard to tell, Lucy never looked happy.

"She isn't here," Lucy said. And she made it obvious I wasn't welcome to be there either. What was her problem? I'd proved many times over that I wanted to help. Too early in the morning to worry about that.

"Thanks," I muttered and started for the stairs. I nearly ran into Rebecca, holding hands with Jaime. "Morning," I mumbled. "Have you seen Nina?"

"Not since she came for the van keys this morning."

"Van keys?" What was she doing? Surely she hadn't left for the airport without even saying goodbye. I squinted at Rebecca, trying to remember if Nina's stuff was still in our room when I'd left, but the sleep haze was just too strong and I couldn't.

"Are you hungry?" Jaime held out a banana. "I was going to bring this to you."

I reached out and took it from her even though I really wasn't hungry. The one nice thing about Sanctuary. "Thanks, kid."

She scowled at me. "Don't call me that anymore, now we're friends."

Leave it to her to get me to smile. "True. Thanks, Friend."

She grinned. We stood there in silence for a moment. I guess none of us really knew each other, so without people attacking us we didn't have anything to say. Jaime gave me a little wave as her mom tugged her up the stairs carrying all kinds of food toward their room. They were probably going to have breakfast together as a family. I looked at my sad little banana. I might as well get used to meals alone.

I walked back to the room. I could see if Nina's stuff was still there, maybe call her from the hotel phone. I grabbed the handle and pushed, but of course it didn't move. Uh oh. I patted myself down, looking for my keycard. Nothing. I banged on the door. No answer. I hit it again. Cray had either fallen back asleep or left after I did. Perfect. I groaned, turned my back and slid down the door to sit on the icky carpet. No way I was going to sit over with the Martans.

Getting slightly hungry, I peeled the still very green banana and took a small bite. Gross, but better than nothing. I finished the stupid thing and threw the peel on the floor, leaned my head back against the door and closed my eyes.

This was my life now. Scrounging for food and sleeping against doors. Might as well get used to it.

Footsteps. I didn't open my eyes. I didn't care right now. Someone paused, then slid down the wall to have a seat next to me.

I cracked an eyelid. Just enough to see a pair of guys tennis shoes. Too big to be Cray. We sat there in silence for a while. I sure didn't know what to say, and he must not have either. I pretended he wasn't there. How did you talk to someone you'd tried to turn over to their enemies to save yourself? He didn't seem to be holding it against me, but I sure still felt awkward about the whole situation. Besides, what did we have to talk about?

After a while he let out a sigh and stood. "Thank you. For saving Jaime. If I can ever do anything for you… Anything. Ask." And that was it. He left.

I pulled my knees up and buried my face in my sweats. Tears leaked. I wiped them away with an angry swipe, but they just kept coming. That was so totally not cool of him to do that.

"Trisha? Honey, you okay?"

I squinted up through the tears. There was Nina, concern written all over her face. I hadn't even heard her come up.

She sat a bag of groceries and what looked like some clothes on the floor and knelt down. "What's wrong? Are the Martans okay? Did something happen?"

I reburied my face, slightly embarrassed that she'd seen my tears. "They're fine," I got out.

"Can we move this into the room then?" she asked. "This floor doesn't look very clean. You might be able to get sick now that you don't heal." I heaved out a sigh and opened my eyes. She had stood and was holding out her hand. I grabbed it and let her pull me up, helping her with the bags.

We moved into the room and she pulled a couple of things out of the bag, sitting them on the counter. "Morning, Cray," she said toward the bed.

He gave a little wave but didn't push the covers down enough to show his face. He'd been in here the whole time. Jerk.

"Wanna tell me what's wrong?" Nina asked.

"I'm tired." So true. So tired.

She moved over and pushed me into a chair, then sat on the bed. "Wanna tell me what's really wrong?"

I looked away from her. At anything but her. I didn't really want to do this with Cray in the room. But I couldn't lie. "Guess I'm just going to miss you. And Dan. A little, you know?"

"Trisha." Nina grabbed my face in both hands, forcing me to meet her eyes. "You aren't going to miss us."

How could she even say that? Yeah, I hadn't been the best of kids for sure, but that didn't mean I wouldn't miss them. Did she really think I didn't care about her at all? I was so bad at this stuff.

Nina let go of my face and reached behind her, grabbing some brochures that she waved in the air. "Check these out. Which one is your favorite?"

I reached forward slowly and took them from her.

Apartments. Housing divisions. A realtor.

"I found one today that we can move into until we get a house. Dan is flying out tomorrow. I told him some of what happened, that we needed to keep you somewhere safe and he said he'd be out to make sure that we're okay. He doesn't know about us moving yet, but when he hears this story he'll be on board. His flight…"

She lost me there. I wasn't even listening now. She was out looking at places this morning. Dan was flying in tomorrow, would probably be leaving his job. For me. We were going to be a family. A real family, that cared about each other, that took care of each other. They were leaving their place in D.C. The place they loved.

"Wait, Nina," I interrupted whatever she was saying. "Are you sure? You love D.C. You have so many friends there. What are you going to do here?" I swallowed a lump in my throat. "Think about this before you do anything," I forced out. That was as close to telling her that I thought she was making a mistake as I could get. Her whole life was in D.C. She'd grown up there. Her friends, her church, her gym, her everything.

She looked at me like she thought I was crazy. "I have. You're here, we're here. It's that simple."

I couldn't help it then. I burst into tears. And I didn't even care that she was there to see them. Nina held me until I was done. So many unanswered questions about my parents, about my abilities. But it was fine. I would probably end up living here forever anyway, never getting answers.

"Just so you know, I couldn't explain all this to Dan over the phone," Nina said. "I didn't want to take any chances on being overheard, so he knows we got into some trouble but has no idea about any of the weird stuff." I sat up and wiped at my face. "You do realize you're in for an interrogation once he finds out what's been going on."

Ugh. Yes. But that was part of being in a family.

There was a rustle from the other bed. I'd almost forgotten that Cray was back there. He had popped his head out from under the blankets and was blinking at us.

"What about Cray?" I asked Nina.

She sighed, then gave him a little smile. "Mind answering a few questions?

He looked at me and then back at her. "No?"

"He can't lie, right?" Nina asked. Ugh. I had hoped she'd forgotten about that.

"Right," I answered.

"Do you mean me, Trisha, or any of the Martans any harm?" Nina asked Cray.

He shifted in the bed, then answered. "No."

"Will you always be loyal to our family?"

Cray paled a little. Nina didn't really know what she was asking there. For fae, always was a really long time. And there were no breaking promises for fae. I watched him intently, trying to read what he was thinking by his face.

He sat up and moved to the edge of the bed, looking Nina right in the face. "Yes. I will be loyal to our family."

He'd said our. That was really fast and kind of strange.

Nina stared him down for a moment, then looked satisfied. "We'll see how it goes. Dan always wanted a son. If Trish trusts you, I trust you. You helped her, you're part of the family."

I still wasn't sure about the trust part, but it was my fault he was here. I'd asked him to help. Cray sat up straighter and smiled, a real, true, smile that I couldn't remember ever seeing on his face before.

"Thank you."

Well apparently I was going to have to learn more about Cray if we were going to be living in the same house. That wasn't a bad thing. I'd keep an eye on him, but he probably didn't have anywhere else to go, so just from a selfish standpoint he would want to keep the Inza's happy. But I was not going to think of him as a brother, too weird.

So many things had gone wrong, and yet here we were, with the most important thing gone right. How had I gotten so lucky? Whatever higher power there was, I was thanking them right now, and would be for a very long time. Even an hour ago I wouldn't have believed that this could end up so right. I slung an arm around

Nina's shoulders and pulled her in for another hug. Even I hadn't gotten enough of them this time.

Things were going to be confusing for a while. A new city, new brother-ish figure, no abilities. So many questions about my parents and why Starren wanted to know about them so bad. But that was okay. Nina caught my eye and smiled. I smiled back. It was okay as long as I had my family.

Links and Such

I really hope you enjoyed getting to know Trish and company in book one! Ready for book two? Trish and her friends get into all kinds of new trouble.

After everything Trish has done to get to Sanctuary, nothing on earth could get her to leave. Or so she thought.

But when Wade shows up with news that Starren's life is in danger, her conscience refuses to let her sit idly by. Even if that means abandoning her everything she's worked so hard to earn. Luckily, those who love her won't let her go alone.

Faerie is a vicious and dangerous place where humans are hated, which is a problem since Dan and Nina were too stubborn to let her leave them behind. Here, nothing is ever as it seems.

As trouble escalates and the mission becomes deadly, can Trish draw enough power from her abilities to save her team and herself, or was this mission doomed to fail from the start?

Follow me on Facebook and Twitter for updates on new stories!

https://www.facebook.com/cassiegreutman/

https://twitter.com/writeranrider89

Or join my newsletter for a free short story about Trish first coming to live with Dan and Nina:

https://dl.bookfunnel.com/pq98nn1jof

About the Author

Growing up, it was impossible to catch Cassie Greutman without a book in her hand, even at the most inappropriate times. Since then with the rise of ebooks, it's only gotten worse. With her full-time job of caring for over thirty horses, some of that has changed to audiobooks, but you can bet there is always some type of story rattling around in her brain. She has always loved stories in any format, whether that is a movie, video game, or book form, and hopes to tell stories that catch a person's imagination and interest like so many have done for her.

A finalist in the Cinematic Book Competition with Screencraft out of over 1200 entries, and five star ratings with Reader's Favorite, who do reviews for most of the large publishing houses, Cassie has been throwing all of the extra time she has into improving her craft and bringing her writing to best it can possibly be. When she isn't stuck in a book, of course.